Wedding Favors

ANNE TENINO

A BLUEWATER BAY STORY

RIPTIDE
PUBLISHING

Riptide Publishing
PO Box 6652
Hillsborough, NJ 08844
www.riptidepublishing.com

Wedding Favors
Copyright © 2015 by Anne Tenino

Cover art: L.C. Chase, lcchase.com/design.htm
Editors: Sarah Frantz Lyons, Delphine Dryden
Layout: L.C. Chase, lcchase.com/design.htm

ISBN: 978-1-62649-293-6

First edition
April, 2015

Also available in ebook:
ISBN: 978-1-62649-292-9

Wedding Favors

ANNE TENINO

This one's for all the loggers I've known. Sorry I dissed you so much when I was younger.

TABLE OF CONTENTS

CHAPTER ONE

S *o. Much. Stuff.*
Lucas shook his head, surveying his friend Corbin's garage, close to horrified by the amount he'd packed into it. He'd always thought of himself as a guy who left a small footprint on life, but apparently he'd been a bigger consumer than he'd realized. It hadn't seemed like so much when it was still at his old studio, but now, after cramming it all in what had seemed like ample space? The buckets of glaze and the mess of tools and the furniture . . . the number of just *things* was overwhelming.

Even in the back of Corbin's truck it hadn't looked like this much stuff—though they'd had to bring it over here in two loads, so that might have tipped Lucas off if he'd been thinking. But he'd been in a fog of urgency this morning, needing to get the goods and get out without running into his ex. Besides, Corbin had said he could only get away from the office for a couple of hours.

Lucas shouldn't have insisted they get it today, probably. It wasn't as if he'd been dying to get his hands on his stuff to actually *use* it. He'd felt compelled to move it, though, because he couldn't handle one more phone call from Drew insisting he could come by anytime. "It's as much yours as mine." *Dick.* As if he didn't know that? Drew couldn't have annoyed Lucas more if he'd pissed on all of it.

So. Now it was here, after languishing for more than three months at the house Lucas used to share with his partner. Well, technically, it had been languishing in his former studio.

Lucas stepped toward his kick wheel, still under a tarp held on with bungee cords. He hadn't touched the thing since before he'd left Los Angeles for an artist's residency in Missoula last August, long before he'd ended things with Drew in November. He hadn't produced any work at all since returning from Montana in mid-October, and pretty damn soon he had to—in December he was supposed to show at the gallery store of the Museum of Contemporary Craft. That gave him only nine months to come up with a large body of work.

The thought of the looming deadline made his heart seize for a moment. Fortunately, his phone—tucked into the shirt pocket over said heart—rang, shocking the organ back to its normal rhythm and preventing him from dwelling more. Yanking the cell out of his pocket, he glanced at the name. *Audrey*.

About fucking time. "I haven't heard from you in *forever*," he said in greeting, and if that wasn't revealing of his mental state . . . It had only been a week since they'd spoken. In college they sometimes went a month between conversations, and two weeks wasn't unusual even now. What could he say? If he couldn't expose his vulnerability to his best friend, then what the hell did he keep her around for?

"I know," she sighed. "I've just been . . ." She sucked in a breath with such force it whistled in his ear. "I'm getting married."

"You're—" Lucas wasn't used to having to untangle Audrey's words like this. They normally communicated so well. All the important stuff, at least. Well, he'd thought they were communicating important stuff, mostly about his breakup and Drew's infidelity and his state of mind, but apparently he was the only one who'd been sharing. He yanked the phone away and stared at it, while birds chirped happily in the sunshine outside this cramped, dark space, oblivious to his confusion. He brought it back to his ear, knuckles digging into his cheek. "Wait, you're *what*?"

"Getting married." The timidity in her voice was a bit reassuring. A sign she cared enough to be worried about his reaction to her blindsiding him.

"Married," he repeated. He leaned forward, as if it would help express his bafflement. "*Married*?" That was just— "I didn't even know you were *dating* anyone. Why wouldn't I know that? Oh my *God*." The full implication hit him—worse than her keeping a significant life event secret from him—and he straightened up again. "You've been seeing a *local*. You're *engaged* to one." No wonder she hadn't told him. Since she'd moved back to their mutual cesspit of adolescent angst—i.e., the redneck town in Washington where they'd grown up—this exact fear had been lurking in the back of his mind, and occasionally it leaked into the front and then out of his mouth when they talked.

"He belongs to one of the pioneering families of the area," she said, a totally justified twinge of shame in her tone.

Worse than he could've imagined. "I *told* you no good could come of returning to Bluewater Bay. We were gonna get out of that town and never go back!" If she tied herself to some hick into that incestuous backwater, she'd *never* leave.

"I know," she verbally cringed. "It's just . . . It's your brother."

"My—" Seriously, he couldn't breathe. She'd knocked the literal wind out of him from a thousand miles away. Or maybe it was figurative wind. "*Zach*?" *Obviously*. He only had the one.

"Yes," she said in the most pathetic voice he'd heard from her, ever. "I've been seeing him about six months now."

"You only moved back there seven months ago!" His fingernails dug into his palm as he screwed his eyes shut, trying to make this all disappear.

"I didn't mean to?"

Not disappearing. "I cannot believe you didn't even tell me you were seeing him, now you're *marrying* him?" Lucas swung around, staring out into Corbin's backyard, thinking about going out there to pace. It might help his agitation, because he couldn't take it *all* out on Audrey. It wasn't as bad as it could have been. Zach wasn't violent, stupid, inbred, or on meth, which were all viable options in that part of the world. The guy definitely had flaws, though. "He's a thirty-two-year-old man who lives with his *parents*."

"Because your mother asked him to move back in and help when your dad was injured, which you totally know."

"Yeah, but Dad's fine now." According to Mom, at least. She claimed early retirement was the best thing that had happened to his father since the microbrewery opened in town.

"Well, he's staying there until the wedding to save up for the house we're going to buy in the next couple of years."

"Oh, is that the wedding you didn't tell me—*your best friend*—about?"

"You haven't always had a great history with your brother." The tentativeness in her voice was drying up—she'd given him all the time to register complaints that she would. "I didn't need you being all bitchy and pessimistic."

"Don't *say* that."

She huffed. "You can totally be bitchy."

As he was demonstrating. "Yeah, but 'pessimistic'? If you were worried about that, it means you had hopes for the relationship from the *beginning*."

"Well . . . duh."

"So, if you had hopes, why didn't you tell me about them?" Even knowing he would have been resentful listening to her wax on about her glowing love life while his domestic situation was in the shitter didn't mean he was okay with her excluding him. "I would've listened." To at least half of it. Probably that much. Enough to give her his perspective. "Normally, you'd want my opinion, even a bitchy one, but since you didn't, that means you were serious from the get-go. Like, you've wanted him to get down on bended knee since your first—"

"He did, actually, you know. Kneel. In the middle of the Resort at Juan de Fuca's dining room. He even had the waiter bring the ring on a tray and present it to me with a flourish." There her voice went, going all gushy and soft.

"Oh my God, I don't want to know." His *brother*. Being sentimental and adoring and probably gazing at her like a Disney prince who'd found his cartoon princess, except straighter. *Blech.* He covered his eyes, trying to stop the mental image from forming. *Too late.*

"I'm sorry." And she was, he could hear it. "It's true, I did have hopes and I didn't tell you . . . exactly. I mean, remember our sophomore year when we didn't go home for Thanksgiving and got drunk in San Francisco instead, and I told you—"

"You said you'd *kinda* had a crush on Zach. Past tense. When you were in high school. Not that you wanted him as your husband, *now*." Why hadn't she told him how much she actually liked Zach? Running his fingers through his hair, he explained that away as the answer occurred to him. "You didn't tell me how much you liked him then because it made you feel too vulnerable." If it had meant that much, even ten years ago . . . this really was happening.

"Exactly."

"You're really that into him?" How could he begrudge her getting her secret wish? Well, other than because she'd been keeping it secret from *him*.

"Yes." Audrey sighed. Not a sad sigh, more a settling one. Like she'd successfully cleared a hurdle. Telling her closest friend something she knew might upset him.

"I can't believe you're getting married." *Nice.* A hint of wistful nostalgia had wormed its way in where it wasn't invited.

"Me either. It's so . . . amazing."

"It is," he admitted, giving in completely to the part of him that wanted what was best for her. He wandered over to a stack of dried clay in bags and leaned against them. "Sorry. I really am glad that you're happy." He hadn't been very supportive so far, and he'd been trying to be better about that. Ever since Drew told him he wasn't responsive enough. "You *are* happy, right?"

"I really am." A wash of certainty flowed through the phone with her words. "This is so right, Zach and me."

Okay, fine. He believed. Possibly even approved. "I guess if someone arranged a redneck lineup and made me pick one out for you, he'd probably be my first choice."

"Thanks." Her voice would dehumidify Puget Sound. "We'll work on your enthusiasm."

And probably not get very far. "So, I suppose this means I have to be the best man?" Wasn't it tradition for the groom's brother to do that?

"Noooo," she said. "Not the best man . . ."

Zach didn't want him? That hurt a little, to his surprise. Enough to make his free hand fly up to touch his chest. "What *are* you going to have me do?" Whatever she wasn't saying couldn't be worse than being rejected by his brother. Sort of rejected. "Just tell me."

They'd probably made up some bullshit position for him, afraid he'd get pissed otherwise. *Wise move.*

"I want you to be my man of honor."

"What's that?" Although he had an inkling, and he was pretty sure it wasn't bullshit.

"Like the maid of honor, except, you know, you aren't a maid."

"Well, that's true." In spite of his mood, he cracked a smile. "I could be your man of honor."

"Thank you." She may have tried to hide her sigh of relief, but he caught it. Was he really so difficult to deal with?

"I'm flattered." White-lie time, but she *was* his best friend. "Am I going to get to wear a tux?" Would he look good in one? Didn't everyone?

"You don't have to. There aren't any rules about what a man of honor should wear—whatever you want, within reason."

"Of course I'll wear a tux, what else would I wear, a dress?"

"Weeeell . . ." she teased.

He snorted, holding his palm up to the empty air in front of him. "No. It's fine if that's what you're into, but *I'm* not."

She giggled, and it was good. Gave him a bit of a warm feeling inside. Then she told him all about the deep-red silk charmeuse she'd chosen to make her dress out of. "It's a perfect match for the ring Zach bought me—it's the most beautiful ruby in an antique setting, you won't believe—"

"My brother bought you a ruby?" That seemed incredibly insightful of Zach. Lucas would have pegged him for a big-box diamond store guy. "Did you tell him to?"

"*Nooo*. I had no idea he was going to ask me to marry him so soon. He picked it out all on his own." Her voice fairly preened.

Maybe Audrey and Zach *were* meant to be, if his brother knew her well enough to get exactly what she'd probably choose herself.

"You're really doing this." It slipped out alongside a wistful breath. "And I'm going to be your man of honor."

"Believe it, Lu. You will be." Then, like the good friend she was, she took their conversation from too close to the bone back to a level he could handle. "You *have* to be my—let's just call it 'MOH,' okay—you have to be my MOH, because you promised you would."

"When?" How? He hadn't even known she was getting married.

"Do you not remember that conversation in high school? I offered you groomsmen in return."

Oh, wait, maybe he *had* promised something like that . . . "Uhhhh." Squinting, he could almost see Audrey sitting in the booth across from him at their hangout, going on about nebulous future weddings. In his defense, it *had* been over twelve years ago.

"You don't remember it at all, do you?"

He did, mostly, but he played along. "Well, vaguely . . ."

"Rest assured, you said you would."

"I so rest. Let's go back to you offering me groomsmen." *That* he could recall clearly, her telling him the maid of honor always slept with one of the dudes in the wedding party, so she'd hook him up too. "Are any of them into guys?" And how hot were they? Hot enough to interest his quasi-inert libido?

"Gabe Savage is the best man."

Oh no. "No, he's *not*."

"He is." He could imagine her nonexpression, the one she'd have if she'd told him that in person. Tightened mouth but everything else slack and blank.

Yeah, he wasn't going to let that slide like she was hoping. "That's supposed to be an incentive? I have a *history* with him, which you know all about because I told you when it happened." The morning after Gabe had taken Lucas home, acted like he was into him, and given him his first handjob, then left, dropping the *I have feelings for you* act. It wasn't so much that Gabe had used him, it was that Gabe was the kind of guy who thought he'd had to manipulate his way into Lucas's pants. Seriously, he wouldn't have been that hard to get, even back when he was clueless about sex. "He *played* me."

"He was just a stupid kid twelve years ago, he's a pretty nice guy now."

"He's great at making people think that," Lucas snarked.

"I like him."

"He's not trying to seduce *you*."

"C'mon. Imagine him in a tux."

While compelling, it didn't cancel out his past with the guy. He *hated* being lied to like that. "I'll be your MOH, but I'm not sleeping with the best man." Snippy, but under the circumstances she'd have to accept it.

"No one's gonna make you," she said with a bit of a grumble. "Okay, how soon can you get up here?"

"What?" She almost sounded like she expected him tomorrow. "When's the wedding?"

"A month and a half. May twenty-third."

"You're *pregnant*?"

"See, it's things like this that make it so obvious you're gay." She totally avoided the question. "People in actual danger of getting pregnant? They know that no one really gets married anymore simply because they're knocked up."

Does not compute. His confused thinking process did the robot. "So you *are* pregnant?"

She snorted. "Not likely."

Now he believed. "Okay, but a *month*?"

"Month and a half."

He let his silence do the speaking.

"I know," she sighed. "It's soon, but it's either May or not until next winter. Zach's too low on the totem pole to get fire season off."

"There aren't any wildfires on the Olympic Peninsula." He could count on one hand how many he remembered hearing about, and he didn't need fingers to do it.

"But he works for the *Washington* Department of Natural Resources, not the Olympic Peninsula. He could get sent anywhere, and Eastern Washington has fire season into November."

"So have a Christmas wedding."

"No," she barked, then softened drastically—what he'd call whining if her voice hadn't gone so airy. "I want to be married to him now, Lu. I want to know he really is mine."

To puke or to melt? That was the question. He settled for muttering grudgingly and kicking the concrete floor with the toe of his shoe. "Fine. I understand."

"That's why I need you up here as soon as possible, sweetie." Ah, the wheedling had begun. "I need your help planning it."

"What do you mean, you want me to plan your wedding? What makes you think I'd be any good at it?" *If she says it's because I'm gay, I swear to God, I'm going to—*

"I said *help* plan, and I'm asking you as a *professional artist.* Helloooo."

God bless her for calling me an artist. A lump of gratitude formed in his throat, which he had to clear out before he could talk. "Well, I'm trying to be."

Few seconds of silence. "You thought I was going to say it's because you're gay, didn't you?"

"Uhhh, yeah."

"Please. I've known way too many gay guys to believe you all get some kind of decorating gene. And what do you mean, 'trying to be'?"

He swallowed. "Well, I mean, I haven't really been producing any—"

"Lucaaaaas . . ." Drawing out his name like that meant only one thing: she was putting on her teacher hat and going to school him.

"Audrey, c'mon, don't—"

"You're a famous artist who actually manages to support himself on his work—"

"I'm not *really* famous." Only craft people knew who he was.

"—How is that *not* 'producing anything'?"

"I'm talking about how it *feels*, now. Since . . . you know." Since dumping Drew and losing the income from Drew's gallery. Since returning to Los Angeles and discovering his life wasn't as ideal as he'd thought.

"I get that, but think of all the people who'd love to be in your shoes."

"I like being well-known for what I do. I *do*. It's just . . ." His partner had spent years telling him he wasn't good enough to make it in a *real* fine arts discipline.

"It's that fucking dick you were hooked up with." She'd never liked Drew, not even in the beginning, back when Lucas had liked him enough for both of them.

"It was a little more than hooking up. We own the house together, and all my sales went through his gallery, so untangling all that stuff is like getting divorced. We even have a lawyer. Let me take the opportunity to encourage you to sign a pre-nup."

"Oh, Lu, I'm sorry. I didn't mean to make light of it."

He shrugged, even though she couldn't see it. "'S'okay." It was, too; all of it was ground they'd been over. He'd whined about it numerous times while she, apparently, had been falling for his brother. No wonder she hadn't told him, he was probably a total buzzkill.

"That's all the more reason for you to come up here, to get away from Drew and that whole scene." She meant the fine arts scene, or Rarified Elitists on Parade, as they referred to the uber-hip gallery hoppers in their less sober and more giggly moments. "You don't have a reason to stay there anymore."

"I have *friends*." He scowled at the form of a male torso that had partially exploded in the kiln. It was missing all of its left thigh and most of the groin. Emasculated sculptures were generally a failure. *Sensing a theme.* He, too, felt like something essential was missing, he recognized that—it was the reason he'd lived in the one-room loft over Corbin's garage for months with no amenities but a hot pot. "So what if my relationship ended? Rub it in, why don't you?"

"I'm not rubbing it in; I'm just pointing out that there's no reason you *have* to be in LA. You can work up here just as easily. Seattle if not Bluewater Bay."

"I can't afford Seattle. And my studio is here." Surrounding him. Didn't matter that it wasn't actually functional at the moment; he didn't feel inspired anyway.

"Last time we talked you told me you were moving your stuff out of it. Are you still staying in Corbin's 'guest apartment'?"

She was going in the most obvious direction, and there was nothing he could do to stop it. So he propped the phone to his ear with his shoulder, crossed his arms over his chest, and slouched, but kept the sullenness out of his voice. "Yes." *Most* of the sullenness.

"You're storing everything there, now? In his garage?"

"Yeah," he muttered. "So?"

"I've *seen* Corbin's guest loft, he had it built when I still lived in LA—"

He snorted because of course he knew that, he didn't need to be told *all* the obvious things in the world.

"And I *know* how much you had packed into your studio. There's no way you have room to work. You don't even have a kiln, do you?"

"Where would I set up a kiln here? Where would I even set one up *there*?" He couldn't work up the spirit to argue for staying in Los Angeles, but he wasn't ready to give in and agree to leave, either.

"Well, you can keep some of your stuff over my store, and probably rent studio space in an industrial building or something. Bluewater Bay *has* to be about ten times cheaper than LA."

"Prices haven't been driven up by that movie they've been filming there?" Apparently there was some kind of Twilight-esque hype going on with some books centered around the town. He tried to remember the details, but all he could come up with was that it had been going on a couple of years, and the place had "really changed for the better" according to his mother, brother, father, and every dog in town.

"It's a television series," she corrected. "*Wolf's Landing*—I can't believe you don't watch it—but no, they haven't gone up *that* much. Just enough to save the town from financial ruin and make my opening a dress shop here viable."

Cheaper *would* be good, and Audrey had really been successful with her store, Tiffany's Breakfast. *This could be the shock to the system I need.* Or not . . . "I don't know. Maybe I shouldn't leave until the 'divorce' is final."

"Would it ruin your claim on the property if you left?"

No. He'd made sure before he'd moved his stuff out of the house, then again before moving the studio. "Not really."

"Come up here, then. I need my best friend by my side for support. That's what the man of honor *does*."

She presented a compelling argument. God, was he really considering this? Los Angeles might be sunny much of the time, but he'd felt like a gray cloud had settled over him months ago, before he and Drew ended things. Things had been bad since he'd returned from his residency in Montana.

Audrey knew him well, jumping on his hesitation to object again. "Oh, just come up here and help me with my fucking wedding."

"Well, when you put it like that . . ." He huffed theatrically. "I guess I will." Immediately, his gloom began to lift, for the first time since he'd come back to California. He just couldn't believe it was because he'd decided to return to a place he'd been so desperate to escape twelve years before.

"Yay!" she cackled. "So you can be here by next Friday, right? The engagement party your parents are hosting is that night."

Next *Friday*?

Gabe was looking forward to spending the evening in bed right up until around the time Seth was in the shower. That's when Zach texted him. Shucking his jeans—he was planning to join Seth in that shower, after all—he glanced down at his phone on the nightstand and read the message.

Audrey talked Lucas into coming home for the wedding.

That stopped him cold, fingers frozen on his waistband for a second while his gut and heart clenched up expectantly. Then he brushed away that spark of longing like flicking dandruff off his shoulder, the same way he had for the last decade plus—it was only some conditioned reaction that'd started in high school—and snatched up the phone. Gripping his tongue between his teeth, he typed out a response, trying to hit the right damn tiny letters the first time. *I'd fucking hope so since his brother is marrying his best friend and he's the man of honor.* Hadn't that been what Audrey had called him?

It only took seconds for Zach to respond. *He promised her he'd be here in time for the engagement party.*

The spark in his chest that he'd been ignoring flared up, consuming a little too much of the available oxygen. He'd known Lucas would come up for the wedding sooner or later, but the reality of being face-to-face with the guy in less than two days made some things he'd probably been avoiding thinking about crystal clear.

He and Lucas Wilder had unfinished business, and this might finally be his chance to settle things between them.

Zach texted more, grabbing his attention again. *She says he's living over some friend's garage and he's "rootless." Told him to come up here until the ceremony, and he is. Guess things are pretty bad.*

If he's moving home? Gotta be. Lucas had always believed he didn't fit in around here. Far as Gabe was concerned, Lucas had fit just fine, but it wasn't about what he'd thought, was it? Lucas'd figured he stuck out like a sore thumb, and staying in Bluewater Bay would have chafed and rubbed him raw in places Gabe couldn't imagine.

God knew the place had chafed *him* some over the years before and after Lucas left. Still, though, it was his home.

Back when Gabe had found out for sure Lucas was going off to school, he just hadn't been able to let the guy leave without a taste of him. So he had it—one taste, a quick jerk, and Gabe walked away.

Then, for the next few months while Lucas was still around, Gabe had stayed as far away as he could. Nothing had happened between them other than that one night. Yet Gabe never forgot him. It wasn't so much that he'd been pining after the guy for twelve years, only that he measured every other guy against him—although he was pretty sure it wasn't really *Lucas* he was measuring everyone against, because he'd barely known the kid, not as a lover, at least. It was the *idea* of him that Gabe had kept using as a yardstick. His ideal vision of what they could have had together.

Working out the *why* hadn't worked out the problem, though. But hooking up a few times now just might clean up that old baggage. This'd be the first time Lucas would be around for an extended amount of time since escaping Bluewater Bay.

The phone in Gabe's hand dinged at him, reminding him he was having a chat with his best friend.

You and Seth work on those last few acres today?

Zach's question startled him. Because, shit . . . *Seth.* He'd had the guy up to help out as a second sawyer. And now the dude was taking a shower, expecting they'd hook up, just like usual.

Gabe's feelings for Seth were best described as *I wouldn't kick him out of bed for eating crackers.* As far as he could tell, Seth's sentiments toward him ran along the same vein. It worked out—they were friends, they hooked up when one of them was horny and not getting it anyplace else (usually Seth—dude had a real big appetite for sex), and they sometimes picked up a third for some extra fun. About the perfect setup.

Am I interrupting something? Zach added a sly winky face after that.

Nope. Gabe texted right quick, because he really didn't need Zach thinking what he was thinking, or saying anything to Audrey about it. God knew who she'd tell. *Nothing to interrupt.* Except for Seth's shower, which, come to think of it, he didn't hear running anymore.

You telling me he isn't still there?

He's here. Cleaning up. Gabe winced as soon as he hit Send.

Heh. Slut.

Then he's going home.

The bathroom door opened behind Gabe, and Seth's voice floated out on a cloud of humidity. "Thought you were gonna join me."

Gotta go. TTYL. He muted the phone before tossing it onto the mattress and turning to face Seth. Then he found himself saying, "You're a pretty damn good time, but I think we need to cool it for a bit."

Seth screwed up his brows and shook his head. "What the hell?"

Yeah, what the hell? Flopping onto the bed next to his phone, Gabe settled against the headboard like he was as relaxed as could be. "Just, you know, we been seeing a lot of each other, maybe it's time to take a break."

"Huh." Now Seth was nodding, walking over to the chair where he'd thrown his pack. Silently, he started digging through it, and the whole time he had a twisted smile on his face. Or maybe it was a sneer. "So, you don't think we should hook up anymore?" he finally asked after taking out some clothes.

"Pretty much that's what I'm saying." He thought it had been clear, if a little out of left field.

"It's not like we were dating or anything. This is just, you know, a convenient arrangement." With a flick of his wrist, Seth lost the towel. "Not much to end." As he stepped into a pair of briefs, his eyes flashed under his lashes—checking to see if Gabe was watching him.

Which he was, but that suddenly seemed kind of rude since he was no longer going to partake. He sat up, getting out of bed and finally stripping off his dirty jeans, angling away from Seth. "Guess I'm ready to rearrange things." He pulled on the semiclean pair of sweats he'd found by stepping on them, tucking his junk away before turning back to the guy. "Thought it would be polite to let you know."

"Thanks." Seth's voice bit at Gabe's guilt. "It's 'cause Lucas is coming back, isn't it? You want him." The guy yanked up his jeans and buttoned them, then crossed his arms over his chest and planted his legs wide.

Shit, he already knew about that? *Small-town gossips.* Apparently they were a real thing. "Lucas who?" That probably wasn't going to fly.

Seth didn't even need words to express his scorn, he just flared his nostrils and quirked his brows.

Bending over to search for a shirt allowed Gabe to hide on the other side of the mattress for a few seconds. The whole time he was looking for it, Seth was silent. Probably waiting until Gabe came out from under cover, then he'd blast him with some kind of crap about waiting twelve years for Lucas Wilder to remember his existence. That kind of misinterpretation was enough to make a man want to crawl under the bed and refuse to budge. But then he found a damn shirt, which meant he had to straighten up or admit cowardice.

Seth let him have it. "You always were weird about sleeping with more than one guy at a time." Now he was all derision and shit. He flicked a negligent hand toward Gabe and started dressing again.

"I never cared if you fucked around with other guys." He sometimes even thought it was hot.

"Yeah, but you'd care if Lucas did, wouldn't you?"

That wouldn't be hot. Gabe paid close attention to his shirt, careful to do it up right. 'Cause he left the house and wandered around misbuttoned all the time. *Not.*

"What I meant was, you're weird about guys you're romantically involved with messing around."

"Who said shit about romantic involvement?"

That twisted smile-sneer reappeared as Seth threw his shaving kit into his bag. "No one needs to, man. All they have to do is say his name and watch you try not to react."

"You're delusional." Gabe made a scoffing noise to back up his lie.

"Whatever." Seth rolled his eyes and slung his pack over his shoulder.

For some reason, he couldn't just let him leave after that. "See you at the engagement party?" he called after Seth.

Glancing back, Seth tipped his chin. "Yeah." As he walked out of the room he added, "Been nice doing ya."

A moment later, he banged out the front door and down the staircase.

Well, that *could've* gone worse . . . "Sorry," Gabe muttered to the air once he'd heard Seth's motor turn over down in the parking strip, and his wheels crunch on gravel.

Shaking his head at himself, Gabe found shoes and left his apartment. He had to feed May, June, and July their dinner of grain and hay. He'd have his own up at the main house—featuring things other than hay—with Momma and Gramma.

As he crossed the winter pasture between the stable and the house, the mist was starting to rise. It had been a sunny day, and the ground was soaked from a winter's worth of rain. They'd have fog tonight. Tomorrow looked to be clear again, which would burn it off, but not before Gabe's favorite kind of dawn, where he could watch the mist clinging to the valleys that cut through the Olympic foothills.

To the east, a wall of cloud already blocked his limited view of Bluewater Bay. Normally he'd see a few of the taller buildings downtown. The ones over three stories. So, like, a half dozen of them.

It was contrary that from the here, the town looked the same as it had his whole life, but the closer he got to it, the more he saw the changes those Hollywood people had made. Maybe, if those changes had been made twelve years before, Lucas Wilder would never have left.

Not likely. He'd never felt a connection to this land like Gabe had, or even like Zach. The Wilder family had been here just as long as the Savages, but it'd been obvious Lucas didn't care. He never seemed to miss it. In the few times the guy had been home (and Gabe had found an excuse to swing by his parents' house for ten or fifteen minutes), Lucas's discomfort and jumpiness had been right up front for everyone to see.

For him, it was the opposite. He loved this farm. Even now, when it was about to enter a long dry spell, so to speak. If he stood in the field between Momma and Gramma's house and his place too long, invisible roots would grow out the bottom of his feet and hold him there. He could sense himself sinking into that soil his ancestors had first claimed over a hundred years before.

Meanwhile, rootlessness seemed to be working out for Lucas. They were total opposites, and he had no idea in creation why he couldn't get over the guy. After twelve years, he damn well should've. It was time he tried his plan B and finally worked Lucas out of his system.

Might've made a better plan A.

CHAPTER TWO

*G*abe's mood had gone to hell by the day of the engagement party, along with the weather.

He shouldn't have kicked Seth out. Getting off a few times would have eased his muscle tension. 'Course, doing that with his own hand had done some good, but it didn't stop the stress from creeping back as he walked through the misting rain out to the work site, leading the team. July kept balking at little things like leaves on the ground, but Gabe wasn't stupid. The damn gelding just didn't want to be out here on such a cold, clammy day. July wanted to get back to the stables, his cozy blanket, and a few flakes of hay.

Well, tough, because they had to skid the rest of the trees he and Seth had harvested out to the landing so they could be loaded up and hauled off.

And there was partial blame for his mood—the damn mill was supposed to pick up yesterday, but there were only so many knuckleboom log trucks in the world, and theirs had all been tied up. So he had to get it done today, in a big-ass hurry, then get ready for the party. It'd be his first official duty as best man. Far as he could tell, though, he didn't actually have to do anything except show up, preferably after showering off the dirt and dressing up kinda nice.

Well, maybe really nice, because you never knew who he was gonna bump into there. Like the man of honor.

Which was the other reason for his shitty outlook. Since he was being honest with himself about having unfinished business with Lucas, some part of him had decided to dump a whole load of doubts, chief of which was: what if he was the only one of the two of them who cared to remember that night? The last time Lucas had visited,

Gabe had made a bit of an effort to talk to the guy, but he'd gotten brushed off. The Wilder family had been going through some rough shit, though, with Carl being injured, so Gabe had chalked it up to bad timing. But it could've been that, for Lucas, Gabe was just some inconsequential thing in his past.

Didn't matter how much his brain turned that around or which angle he looked at it from, he just couldn't know the truth of it. Worse, it was worrisome how much time he'd spent the last couple of days thinking about it. Better not to think much at all. Work was a great distraction for not thinking much.

The horses settled into their jobs once they began, leaning into the harness every time he hitched them up to the next log. June had been doing it a long time—over twenty years—so she was calmer about it. In another few years he'd have to retire her and send her out to pasture like her mother, May. July was June's foal, and he had some piss and vinegar in him. Gabe could just imagine what the black gelding would be like if he'd left him intact. So much for inseminating her with that purebred Shire—Gabe had been looking for cooperative spirit, not teenage angst or whatever the equine equivalent was—but that'd been a hell of a fine-looking stallion, at least in the vet's stud catalog, and the price had been right.

About midmorning, he unhitched the team. He could section this next lot and then eat what he'd packed for lunch before putting the horses back to work. First, though, he needed to refuel the saw.

He'd just finished and was about to replace his earplugs when his mother's voice asked from behind him, "You got a plan for what's gonna happen once you're done with this parcel?"

Gabe didn't turn toward her, or even flinch, although it'd come out of nowhere. What, she'd started practicing stealth as she came through the forest? She knew better than to walk up unannounced on a guy working dangerous equipment. "You *know* I got a plan." He yanked on his glove with a little too much force, and the leather seam at the tip of the index finger slipped under his nail, pressing it up to the point of discomfort.

"Don't you snap at me, Gabriel Sutton Savage."

"Sorry, Ma." She didn't want him to snap, she shouldn't be poking at his sore spot. What the hell with her starting this conversation now, outta the blue? Woman hadn't even said *hello*. Couldn't she have brought it up over breakfast?

No. Because Gramma had been there, and they had a tacit agreement not to worry her.

Still could've picked a better time. Grabbing up his chainsaw from the log he'd set it on, he prepared to fire it up and end this impromptu family meeting. He didn't need to go over it again. Since the age of seventeen, he'd known this time would come: the last day he'd cut any trees for a few years. Even skidding with the horse team—a notoriously slow logging method—he'd run out of harvestable parcels. A timber operation that covered three hundred twenty acres like Savage Tree Farm was only sustainable over the long term if logged selectively. Every year, Gabe cut about a quarter of the next mature section. The stand that was supposed to be mature this coming year, well . . . fifteen years ago, Gabe had convinced himself to clear-cut it and a couple of other parcels besides, instead of letting his mom and Gramma go into debt paying his grandfather's medical bills.

In the present, he still had some work left to do before he ran slap-bang into the reality he'd created back when he was young and inexperienced. 'Course, the regret was unavoidable. He should've gone into debt; they'd owed nothing on the farm, and he could've paid a loan off by now. Then he wouldn't be staring down the barrel of no logging for the next few years. It was either that or clear-cut the whole damn thing, then sell it off to one of the big timber companies around here.

That'd never happen, not as long as he drew breath.

"I don't mean a plan for how we're gonna get through this; we've settled that." Momma's hand landed on his shoulder, and this time he did flinch. But then he relaxed at the touch, releasing the pull cord and letting the saw dangle next to his thigh. When she squeezed, he bowed his head, suddenly ashamed of being a dick to his ma.

"Sorry," he repeated, but meant it this time.

"I'm talking about what *you're* gonna do."

He turned to face her again, trying to avoid her obvious trajectory. "What I always do in the off-season. Hire out the team for other stuff and take it easy."

Half her mouth quirked up, but the other side pulled down into a semifrown. She glanced around, like she was inspecting the still-standing trees around them. "This ain't your regular off-season, Gabe. It's gonna last a fair bit."

"I know." Dammit, he'd snapped again, but she didn't correct him, just let him correct himself. "I'm the one who made this mess, and I'm not likely to forget that."

"I'm not talking about that anymore. We've done it to death, and I supported the decision at the time." Hugging her arms around herself as if she were cold, she gazed off into the stand of firs. "You made this farm your responsibility when you were still just a kid, and this is the first chance you've had in all those years to do something *you* want to do. So, I'm asking if there's anything you want that you never had time for before."

Lucas Wilder's face flitted through his mind, but that wasn't much of a life goal, now was it? *Shrug it off.* "I like working, Ma. This place has kept me going." It got him through Grampa's lingering death and gave him something to work toward that was bigger than himself.

She sighed. "You're so much like your grandfather."

No, he wasn't. He clenched his teeth on the objection, though, because she'd heard it all before. "I'll figure something," he said instead.

"Once you don't have a job needing to get done every day, you'll go stir-crazy."

Probably. "I'll try not to lay that on your doorstep, then."

"I'm not telling you not to be ornery or angry, Gabe. I'm telling you, if you need anything from me, let me know, including having someone around to bitch at."

"S'pose it's a good thing you don't expect me to be all accepting 'bout this." A smile cracked his irritation like ice on a pond. 'Course, it froze back up again. "Don't worry, Momma. Something'll come up."

Speaking of being like ancestors, she firmed her chin just the way his grandma did. "I'm also telling you to stop blaming yourself."

Aw, hell. "Guess I'll have to work on that too."

Mostly, though, he put it out of his head once she left, because he'd already worn a rut in his mind thinking *that* over, and it hadn't gotten him anywhere either.

A few hours later he was finally back at his place, and July finally had his damn blanket and grain. Gabe started undressing as soon as he hit the door of his apartment, beginning with peeling his baseball cap off his sweaty brow and tossing it on the table. As he was unzipping his hickory shirt, the damn cell phone rang in his pocket. He didn't plan on answering, but he glanced at the name in passing and it was Laura Larson. Well, that'd be Laura Haakinson, now that she'd married. He hadn't called her, and he couldn't think of any reason why the vet'd be calling him, so he answered.

"Hey, Gabe," she began after the preliminaries. "I got a three-year-old you might want to take a look at. Turns out he's from that mare you had out of June about ten years back."

That was weird. Generally, if someone wanted to sell something, they, you know, advertised. Far as he knew, the local veterinarian didn't usually shill livestock. "I'm not really in the market for another gelding right now." Last thing he needed was to spend money on frivolities, plus he barely had enough grain for his own horses until the winter crop came in.

"He's a stallion, actually."

"Then I'm *really* not in the market—"

"He's free. Do you remember that 'urban farmer' type you sold a mare to near Port Angeles?"

Did he ever. One of those kids who grew up in the city, then hit their twenties, bought a pair of work boots, grew a handlebar mustache, and invested Daddy's money in starting up a Community Supported Agriculture–type farm. This guy had gone one further and decided he needed a horse to work the land. "Hell yes, Joshua Warburton. What's he done to my mare?" Didn't matter that the dude had bought her fair and square, not if he was fouling her up.

She sighed, but it ended on a laugh. "He's got a neighbor of about the same type, and *that* guy's stallion broke through the fence when Agatha was in heat—"

"He's calling her *Agatha*?" He was pretty sure he'd named that one Dahlia—family tradition was to name the fillies they were planning on selling after flowers—but he'd also had a few mares out of June over the years and maybe remembered wrong. He'd only sold one to a hipster farmer near Port Angeles, though. The guy'd had to take teamster lessons from him for a month afterward, to make sure he could actually work the horse. He'd paid for them, but even that healthy chunk of change hadn't been worth the aggravation of listening to some natural-born urban dweller trying to get all "down-home."

"Yeah, that's what she's called. Anyway, she foaled about three years ago, and this is the result."

"Should teach those idiots how to build a fence," he muttered to himself.

Laura chuckled in his ear.

"So he didn't have him cut, huh?"

Now she was sighing. "Against the advice of his vet."

"Which'd be you."

"Which would be me," she agreed. "Anyway, Joshua's finally thrown in the towel and admitted he isn't up to training a work horse."

"I'm not taking on some beast that someone ruined, Laura," Gabe warned.

"He had help," she assured him immediately. "He got some 'horse whisperer' type to come out as soon as the colt was born and they did a decent job of imprinting. Since then, he's done all right, but Blackie is pretty spirited—"

"If you tell me his name's Black Beauty—"

"Black*berry*. Although God knows why, because he's not black. He's also a mutt—the father is an American Saddlebred who's pretty fine looking and apparently places nationally in dressage, but I'm not his vet so I don't know much else."

Could be worse. June was a (nearly) purebred Friesian, and he'd usually had her inseminated with Friesian stud, so it was really only two bloodlines . . . He took a second to chew on it. "You say he's free?"

"Joshua claims that you're the only person around who can handle Blackie, and the guy says he just wants the horse in a good home. Can't convince him to put it up for sale."

He *could* provide a good home. He'd been around horses since birth. "Tell you what, if I take him? First thing you'll be doing is gelding him."

"You should see him first, Gabe. He's beautiful. Not saying I won't emasculate him if you want—"

"I wish you wouldn't use that word."

"Most of my male clients do." *She* clearly enjoyed, it, judging by her tone. "So are you interested or not? No one can train a workhorse like you."

"Flatterer," he muttered.

She laughed. "Whatever works."

Well, shit. "I guess I can take a look at him." Laura wouldn't steer him wrong, but that didn't mean she had it right either. If the stallion did work out . . . Well, a trained workhorse could go for five grand or more. In the end, he promised to call Joshua and arrange a meeting.

Once off the phone, he finished stripping, but his mind was preoccupied by what the hell he'd just agreed to— *Only gonna look.* All through his shower, he was figuring how he'd feed another equine mouth, and whether taking on a new horse was worth what he'd get out of it in the end. It kept him from letting his mind wander over to revisit what he'd been thinking about all day: Lucas Wilder.

In that respect, he was kinda grateful to that hipster. Guy still needed to learn how to build a damned fence.

"Remember," Audrey was yet again warning her teenaged employee. "After you set the alarm code, you only have about thirty seconds to get out."

Lucas was pretty sure only he caught the girl's slight eye roll.

"And Maisie?" Audrey asked sharply, hands on her hips, waiting until the shopgirl trained her full attention on her. "Do *not* bring your boyfriend in here and let him hang out, *or* try to leave early. I'll know."

"I wouldn't!" Maisie protested, but she couldn't quite meet Audrey's gaze.

Following Audrey upstairs to her apartment a minute later, Lucas offered to stay. "I mean, if you don't trust her to close up shop, I could skip the engagement party—"

"*That's* a record." Audrey stopped on the landing and whirled on him. "I've been waiting for you to find a way out of this party all day. It took you until—" She checked her watch. "Three thirty to actually try, though. You're really maturing. Of course, you only arrived in town at noon."

He scowled but didn't give up. "It just seemed you weren't totally comfortable with leaving your store in the hands of—"

"She'll do fine. Maisie just needs to be reminded of the rules, but she's a good kid at heart." Audrey waved off the subject and turned toward her apartment, so he obediently followed. The stairs opened onto a small square, with doors on the other three sides. The apartment was directly opposite the landing from them, and to the left was the only bathroom up here—old buildings had such random layouts. To the right was Audrey's design space, where she'd set up a bed for him. "I can work in my apartment just as easily," she'd told him right after giving him the tour and letting him dump his stuff. He'd only taken what was absolutely necessary *and* that he could fit into his car. The rest he left in one of those mobile storage units at Corbin's—he didn't know where he was going to settle after he escaped Bluewater Bay again, so there was no use in dragging all his stuff up here, right? It was only for a month or so, then he'd find someplace to live and work, lock himself in his studio, and not come out until he had enough decent work for his show next winter.

Truth was, he *was* a little jealous of Audrey. He hadn't quite confessed to her yet, but he was more in favor of her opening up shop here now that he'd seen it. She owned the property, thanks to an inheritance from her grandmother, and he was starting to think it had been a good investment. The building was beautiful, both inside and out. Sheltered in the lee of Sandy Bluff, it had unusually large windows for a location so near the Strait of Juan de Fuca and its weather.

Earlier, looking for the store, he'd driven past twice before seeing the name painted on the window. *Tiffany's Breakfast* was written in a large, forties-style script traced with gilt, and underneath it was the more simplified tagline, *Fashions vintage and new. Audrey Kilpatrick, designer*. It reminded him of an old-fashioned bank, with rough-hewn stone colonnades between the plate glass on the main floor. The brick facade was painted barn red, with darker burgundy trim boards.

He didn't even remember it from when he'd lived in Bluewater Bay. Had he noticed so little then, or had it changed so much? In spite of knowing he wasn't the world's most attentive person, he was pretty sure it was the latter. The downtown was thriving—completely unlike the last time he'd visited, more than two years ago—and offered the occasional glimpse of a famous person. Used to that from Los Angeles, he found he couldn't care less.

As soon as he'd unpacked his car that afternoon, Audrey had dragged him to lunch at Annette's, and the patrons had reminded him so much of the film types in Los Angeles (there were even the ubiquitous loud-talking producer sort) that he'd sometimes forgotten where they were. At least, until someone he'd grown up around walked in. Those people all did a double take when they spotted him. Most had waved, or said hello and one or two raised an eyebrow. A few people chatted, and twice he'd relied on Audrey's adroitly dropped hints to remember names.

Without fail, everyone who dragged them into conversation would ask at some point, "Now, how's your mother?" and each time he nearly said, "You probably know better than me." But that would be rude, because in this part of the world, asking after one's mother was the height of good manners. God, this place was still so *provincial*. Well, parts of it. The parts that hadn't gone Hollywood.

"—*listening* to me?" Audrey's voice clanged around inside his ear, yanking him back into the present moment.

"Ummm . . ." No point in lying, she knew him too well. He shrugged. "I was thinking." And staring sightlessly at the flowers she'd arranged on the high, narrow island separating the kitchen area from the living area. The space was more loft than apartment, really. "What did this building used to be again?"

She harrumphed but answered. "It was built to be the hardware store. They must have kept the tack up here. The electrician I hired found a couple of bits and cheekpieces behind one wall when he was rewiring the place. Now stop getting all self-involved and help me get ready for my party."

"Fine. But I want it noted that I find the duties of the MOH onerous." He made an overly prim face for her, but then ruined it by smiling when she did.

"Duly noted. You want the bathroom first?"

"You're the bride." He waved a negligent hand toward the landing. "Pretty sure they get to shower before attendants." He needed to spend a few minutes up here anyway, checking out the other changes in his hometown from this new vantage point. Watching the bustle of

Bluewater Bay through her huge panes of wavy glass, he could see how people could come to a place like this and find it quaint or charming.

Of course, anyone who'd grown up here could never view it that way.

The party started at five thirty, and Lucas and Audrey were about fifteen minutes late. Pretty good, considering their track record.

"Are you nervous about seeing Gabe again?" Audrey asked over the staccato tap of her heels as they walked down the hall toward the cafeteria.

"Yeah," he answered absently. Who had an engagement party in an elementary school? "Why is this happening here, again?"

Audrey's arched brow was in her tone, he didn't need to look at her. "Because: your mother."

"Oh yeah." Mom was a lunch lady. "She's making the food?"

"No, she just got permission to hold it here. I *told* you this, Lucas." She didn't sound annoyed so much as tired. Probably of his only listening to half of the things that came out of her mouth.

"I know. Sorry." He really was too wrapped up in himself, lately. More so than normal. He needed to make an effort here. One's best friend didn't get married every day, or—hopefully—more than once.

"So," she said, in the manner of someone who was about to bring up a subject only she took delight in discussing, "you *are* nervous about seeing him."

Lucas halted, then turned to her when she did the same. *Who?* They'd been talking about . . . "Gabe? You mean him? Why would I be? I've seen him since *that* happened." Oh shit, he'd just admitted it, though, hadn't he? Holding up a hand—even though she was just looking at him smirkily and not actually about to say anything—he added, "I just said yes because that's what I usually do when I'm not actually paying attention."

"I know." Audrey sounded more amused than annoyed. "It's just that pretending nothing happened for twelve years gets awkward. This is the first time you're really going to have to interact with him."

Lucas faux-gasped and clutched his chest. "You never said I had to *interact*." He walked on toward the cafeteria, and a second later Audrey's feet tapped along behind him, moving faster until she caught up and looped her arm through his, which he took as a sign that she didn't intend to push the topic.

"Ha. Ha." She didn't give up, not that he'd really expected her to. Instead she jogged her elbow into his side.

"It's not like it's all on me. We were taking turns avoiding each other."

"This is official, though. You're the MOH, and he's the best man. It's sort of like he's your date."

"He's *not* my date to the wedding." *Mental note: get a date for the wedding.* "Don't worry, I'll be very civil."

"That's what I'm worried about," she muttered.

To say that he and Gabe had been avoiding each other the last twelve years wasn't entirely true. Gabe had definitely avoided him after that night, until Lucas left for college. In the years after that, Lucas had only glimpsed the guy in passing, until his last few visits home, when Gabe kept dropping by his parents' house, trying to make conversation.

From that point, the avoidance was all on him. They'd done a one-eighty from those few months after he and Gabe had . . . done what they did. *Handjob*, a tiny voice squeaked from some hidden corner of his mind, then slipped back into the shadows. His brain always tripped up on the specific details of being with Gabe, but the sense memories—*those* were crystal clear. Every once in a while, in the middle of sex with later partners, the slide of a lube-slicked hand against his skin would take him back to that moment, and he'd be consumed with it again, just like then. Dizzy and exhilarated and hazy with lust. It had been a great first experience. It was what had happened afterward that had soured it for him. Gabe had admitted to playing Lucas, then avoided him like the plague. It had hurt in surprising ways that had nothing to do with sex. Well, not much.

He'd been *so* naive.

"I happen to know," Audrey said very close to his ear, chin digging into his shoulder, "that Gabe is nervous about seeing you too."

This time he didn't halt so much as jerk to a stop, and only partly because she'd startled him. "What? Wait, are you, like, trying to get us *together*?"

"Not at all." Her drawn out, soothing tone was all fake. "I'm just saying that you aren't the only one."

No matter how much he squinted at her, she didn't back down. "You sounded like it for a second there," he finally grumbled, shuffling his feet into walking. She fell in beside him. "Just so you know," he added, "I'm *not* buying his lines again."

"What if he just wants to hook up?"

He chewed on that for a few yards of elementary school linoleum. "No. He burned that bridge." Once a player, twice shy, and who cared about mixing metaphors?

"Wow, you're really nursing that hurt, aren't you?"

He tilted his nose up and kept his focus on what was in front of him. "What can I say, I'm a grudge holder." It wasn't a label he'd ever given himself before, but he'd embrace it now.

"You're as worked up about this as you were when you found out Drew was cheating on you."

Subject change, sweet. "He wasn't *cheating*, exactly." He finally looked over at her, just as she yanked him to a stop with a hand on his arm.

"Oh, honey." She performed the head bobble that indicated she was about to slap him in the face with some reality. "Don't even. You guys may have had an open relationship, but you had rules, and he was breaking them."

True. He shrugged, because what else could he say?

Planting her hands on her hips, along with that silly little clutch purse, Audrey started in again. "You just shrug when I bring up a years-long relationship that ended badly four months ago, but when I mention Gabe Savage *maybe* playing you twelve years ago, you get snarly."

"Hate it when you point out insightful shit like that." He shoved his hands into his pockets and brought his shoulders up around his ears. "It's just, he was my first—I mean, you know, not *that* kind of first—"

"I know."

"And he sort of . . ."

"Hurt you."

Swallow. "I guess." He nodded as acceptance sunk in. He'd been hung up too long on the events of one night with a guy he had no real contact with after, when it shouldn't matter at all. It *should* be one of those things he only recalled in nostalgic moments, sitting around with friends and talking about guys they'd been with. It *should* be a story he told with a smile teasing the corners of his mouth, but as far as he could remember, he'd never told it to anyone, not casually.

Audrey's expression softened, and she slipped her arm through the crook of his elbow, nudging him along until they were on their way again. "Maybe this is your chance to put all that behind you."

"Maybe so."

As they drew closer to the party, and the sounds of conversation and laughter began to filter out to them, Lucas got increasingly nervous. By the time he followed Audrey through the door, he couldn't swear his fingers wouldn't tremble if someone wanted to shake hands.

Someone like Gabe.

The first people he saw as he walked into the room were his parents, though. It shouldn't have surprised him that they were here—they were *hosting* the thing—but it did, making him gape a second until his mother yanked him toward her. "Lucas!"

"Hi, Mom," he managed, wrapping his arms around her and squeezing tightly for a second. Then she let go, and his father dragged him into a hug, and surprise turned to shock. He stood there mute and frozen, trying to recall if this had ever happened before. *No.* And he'd have laid all his money and the left half of his brain on it *never* happening. This person *embracing* him was the same one who'd nearly gotten violent when Lucas came out to him?

"It's been too damn long, you," Dad said, oblivious to Lucas's confusion and adding a couple of hearty slaps on his back. Affectionate hitting, not the abusive kind. Not that his father had ever actually struck him, but Lucas had been scared a couple of times.

"Uhhh . . . yeah?" Cautiously, he lifted his own hand and patted his father's arm. The world didn't end, but the hugging finally did, with an unprecedented amount of hair ruffling and shoulder squeezing.

Then there was beaming as his father inspected him from his feet to his hairline.

"You're looking mighty healthy, boy. Damn, it's good to see you."

"You too," Lucas said on autopilot, but then he really *saw* his father and realized the man had his hair in a ponytail.

A *ponytail*. And wearing a *suit*. A light-colored one he couldn't be sure wasn't *linen*.

"Join the receiving line," his mother urged, nudging him along a corridor of people. In a daze, he still managed to greet Mr. and Mrs. Kilpatrick—across from his parents—before ending up next to Audrey. He wanted to hiss urgent questions about his parents into her ear, but she was too preoccupied, standing arm in arm with her fiancé, beaming.

"Hey, Zach." He nodded past her at his brother. He'd missed saying anything before, too caught up in Audrey's parents and his mental fog.

"Good to see you, man." Zach grinned, then reached around his bride-to-be and squeezed the nape of Lucas's neck with real affection.

That he understood—he and his brother might not have always gotten along well as kids, but the last few years they'd communicated more. Lucas would almost say he understood his brother. Unlike his father.

Leaning behind Audrey and keeping his voice down, he asked, "What is up with Dad's hair?"

"Later," Zach said quickly. "We'll talk." Then he turned away to greet someone new.

It was now occurring to Lucas that it had been a while since he'd seen his family, and it might have been a good idea to meet with them for the first time someplace more private.

"Hey."

When Lucas turned toward the gruff voice on his right and found Gabriel Savage there, for a split second, everything contracted. As if life had removed the past twelve years and simply put an apostrophe in its place. The guy seemed so *familiar*.

After a second or two of Lucas staring at him, trying to figure out what was happening, Gabe asked, "How've you been doing?"

"Fine." Lucas half smiled, strangely disassociated.

Then Gabe turned to see who was making their way down this apparent receiving line, and the reddish scruff and the very square angle of his jaw was absolutely beautiful for one split second: a perfectly described line of the kind Lucas was always trying to capture in sculpture.

He came back to earth with a *thump* just before he lost all touch with reality and traced the curve of Gabe's Adam's apple with his fingers.

Dammit. The guy looked good. Like, three extra *o*'s good. *Goooood.* And still a ginger, as if that could change. Had he grown more chest hair? *I don't need to know.* It was so unfair how those khaki pants hugged his ass and that his shoulders were so broad under that blue-striped dress shirt. What was it they used to say? *He cleans up purty.*

Oh no. Not even one full day in this town and it was all coming back to him.

"Lucas," Audrey said loudly in his ear, with that special bite to her tone that told him he'd been zoning out when he should have been listening. "*Of course* you remember Mrs. Larson."

"Of course," he repeated, and took the papery, wrinkled hand of one of Bluewater Bay's oldest and most honored citizens. Not that he could recall why she was so important. Maybe extreme age? She looked like she was rounding on a century. "That's a very becoming hat." It was one of those molded straw ones, dyed a strange shade of blueish green. A fake bird was perched to take flight from it, just below the crown.

She beamed. "Why thank you! I've had it for *ages*." He'd thought they were done, but she kept peering at him, all the lines that wreathed her face wrinkling in expectation as she cocked her head just so.

Lucas scrambled for something else. "How are your grandchildren?" She had a ton, didn't she?

"Doing just fine. I believe you were in the same class as my youngest grandson, Seth." She did something with her lashes that—in someone else—he'd think was flirty. "I'm sure he'd love to reconnect with such a handsome young man as yourself." Then she pursed her lips coquettishly.

Oh my God. Old Mrs. Larson, who was ninety-nine if she was a day, was trying to play *matchmaker*. Just like his best friend. "Is it something in the water?" he asked.

She blinked, without the fluttery this time. "I'm sorry, sometimes I don't hear as well as I used to—try my left side." Clutching her hat, she stood on tiptoe, angling until her ear was right in front of Lucas's mouth.

"Mrs. Larson." Audrey saved him. Her voice had just the right touch of socially acceptable laughter, along with the necessary volume. "Lucas is just being silly. I'm sure he'd love to see your grandson again." Baring her teeth at him, Audrey laid a hand on his arm, then squeezed until her nails dug in.

No, I wouldn't. But he smiled stupidly and nodded and agreed with whatever she said.

"I don't want to hook up with Seth Larson," he hissed in her hair once she'd disentangled them from Mrs. Larson. "Was she *seriously* suggesting—"

"She's been doing it with her other grandkids since they were in diapers," Audrey murmured through the side of her very social smile. "At least she's an equal-opportunity marriage broker. Now hush, because here comes the grandson himself."

He got out about half a groan before she stomped on his foot. If only she'd done it a little harder, he might have been able to hobble off in pain before he actually had to speak to Seth Larson.

"Hey there, Lucas. Long time no see."

Objectively, Seth was pretty good-looking. Not *gooooood*, but definitely attractive enough that—if it were someone else—Lucas would have been interested in a little flirting. But subjectively, he had issues with this guy. Seth been out in high school (albeit not by choice) and had always been trying to get chummy with him, totally ignoring all of Lucas's very clear "no trespassing" social cues. *Pushy prick.*

Not to mention he was blond and had a jaw-skimming beard and a neat little mustache, exactly like Drew.

"Hello, Seth." Lucas bared his teeth. "Nice to see you," he lied for good measure.

"I bet." Or at least that's what Lucas thought he heard, but the guy said it too low to be sure, and then he moved on.

To Gabe.

And oddly, even though his voice wasn't any stronger than before, as he leaned into Gabe's body and said, "I left my toothbrush at your place last week," in his ear, Lucas heard it loud and clear.

He didn't hear Gabe's response, though, because he turned toward Audrey and enthusiastically greeted whoever she was talking to. If those two were fuck buddies, he wasn't making it any business of his. Instead, he threw himself into his duties.

It was exhausting. He'd hit his limit of stilted social interaction long before they'd greeted everyone, and soon was relying mostly on Audrey pinching the back of his arm and repeating names he couldn't remember. But finally the end was in sight.

The last person into the room was Kitty, Audrey's older sister. Scowling and slouching her way down the gauntlet, he got the impression she wasn't totally happy. Maybe it was her makeup. It almost looked as if she'd penciled in evil-villain brows, the kind that flew up on the ends. Or not. He couldn't quite put his finger on it. When she reached him, Kitty narrowed her eyes, tossed her hair behind one shoulder and pointed her nose in the air. "Hello, *Lucas.*"

What was with the emphasis on his name? "Hey, Kitty. How're you doing?"

"About as well as can be expected . . ." She flicked him with an up-and-down look. "Under the circumstances."

"Oh." Had he offended her without realizing it? He nodded and fervently hoped he could feel his way through whatever was going on. "Great."

"And how are *you*?" She threw in that angry chin slant she and Audrey shared.

"Um, fine?"

"You should be, since you got the plum assignment."

What? It couldn't be avoided—he turned to Audrey for help, but she was facing off against her sister and ignoring him. The rest of their greeting committee was breaking up around them, wandering off, but he couldn't escape until Kitty had moved on. Audrey would kill him if he tried.

"Well," Kitty announced, straightening. "There's my *husband.* I should be by his side."

"What did I do?" Lucas asked as soon as she'd stomped out of earshot.

"Nothing," Audrey snapped. "She's just sulking."

"About not being in the receiving line?" He would have given up his place for a spot at the bar.

Audrey huffed, still squinting after her sister, but that was all the answer he got.

Which meant he had to figure this out on his own. What had she said? *Plum assignment.* Uh-oh. "How does Kitty feel about me being your MOH?"

She shrugged. "I don't know." But her lips tightened into a hard line of determination.

"You haven't told her?"

"Oh, I told her," she said airily, in direct contrast with how she'd flexed that muscle below her ear. "I emailed her about it. Then I trashed her reply without even opening it."

"Weren't you *her* maid of honor?" He remembered multiple conversations about the dress Kitty had forced Audrey to wear. "And doesn't that mean she's supposed to be yours?" He wasn't totally clear on wedding etiquette, but he was pretty sure that was some rule or other.

"Personally? I don't care. It's *my* wedding, and you're my man of honor." She sliced her hand through the air. "That's all there is to it."

"Okay." Lucas made the universal gesture of acquiescence, showing her his palms. "That's fine."

"It's *our* life. Mine and Zach's. It should be the way I want, and I'm not here to make anyone happy except myself and my fiancé."

"Fine," he said again. "Um, but does this mean she's mad at me too?"

Finally Audrey stopped glaring at Kitty and turned to him with a grimace. "I guess it does. Sorry."

"It's *fine.*" His mantra. Shoving his hands into the pockets of his slacks, he tried to smile reassuringly at her.

Crossing her arms over her chest, Audrey squinted in her sister's direction again. "I don't know why she's upset. She gets to be a bridesmaid, just not my main attendant."

"She's a bridesmaid?" Should he have asked about this earlier? "Are there other bridesmaids?"

"Do you remember Becca Paulson?"

"Of course." They'd hung out with her all the time in high school. He wasn't *that* forgetful. Of course, he hadn't seen her since.

"She's Becca Lundgren, now. Anyway, she's the other bridesmaid."

"I didn't know you kept in contact with her."

Glancing swiftly around the room, Audrey leaned closer to him. "Honestly, I didn't, really. But she looked me up when I moved back. I *like* her," she added defensively. "And sometimes she helps me out with the store."

Ahhh. "Who are the other groomsmen?"

"Mike Saito and Jeff Blevins."

"Oh." He nodded knowingly.

"You have no idea who they are, do you?"

Nodding morphed into head shaking. "No."

"You need a minute alone, don't you?" Patting his arm—right where she'd been pinching him, which kind of muted the kindness of the gesture—she nodded at her own question. "Go ahead. We're going to be here awhile, you should probably pace yourself."

"No, I'm good. Really." He bared his teeth maniacally.

"Just go," she ordered, pointing toward the door to the school playground.

God forbid he should defy a direct order when it was in his best interest to follow it.

CHAPTER THREE

*G*abe didn't know exactly what he would say to Lucas, but he followed him out of the cafeteria anyway. Well, he waited a minute or so first, before straightening up from his fake slouch at the bar. He had to get this initial conversation over with, or he'd psych himself out too much. Convince himself he was in love or some stupid shit.

As he started to meander toward the door Lucas had gone through, Zach caught his eye and gave him a knowing nod. Then shared a significant look with Audrey.

"Shut up," Gabe muttered as he paused in front of them. He was about sick of the way those two were around each other, communicating like they shared a brain. Zach was so in love with Audrey he'd scream it to the world given a chance, which was kind of sweet, but that didn't mean Gabe had to admit it. "Just 'cause you two are biting the bullet, you think everyone wants to?"

"No one suggested any such thing," Audrey said smugly.

He thought about arguing it, but he'd likely come out on the losing end of that even if he was right. Woman had a quick tongue.

Outside it was still drizzling, and nearly dark. It wasn't that late, but with a cloud ceiling this low, sunset came a lot earlier than it should've for mid-April. It took a bit of huddling under the roof overhang, checking out the shadows, before he saw anyone move in the covered play court. An extra thick column shifted, revealing it was really the silhouette of a man leaning against a regular-sized post. A shortish man with wide shoulders and a slender body that hadn't changed much since high school. Lucas had muscled up a bit. No one could call the guy stringy, but no one would call him bulky, either.

Far as Gabe was concerned, *sleek* fit him as well now as it had twelve years before. The silhouette shifted again—Lucas hunching up, like he might be cold.

Should be—the fool came out here without a coat.

Gabe snuck up on him. Not on purpose, more like he was about ten feet away before he realized he'd been stalking Lucas like prey, staying upwind and not making a sound. When he cleared his throat, Lucas flinched and twisted to face him, all in one fluid movement.

"What are you doing out here?" he asked. Gabe could only just make out his startled expression in the near-dark, and for a moment it was exactly like seeing him that night in Lucas's room all those years ago. Right after Gabe had kissed him the first time, and just before the second one.

He was smart enough to know that kissing him now probably wouldn't smooth over this years-long awkwardness, but his body wasn't: it was responding to the sense memory. *Say something.* He forced out words, barely hearing them over the pounding in his eardrums. "Just came to see if you needed company." *Hell.* Shutting his eyes a second helped him reset. "Or, you know, want to talk." Yeah, he'd built this up too much. He should've made a bigger effort in the last decade to normalize relations between them, then every word he said now wouldn't seem so freaking loaded.

"Really," Lucas said flatly, then he leaned against the post again, crossing his arms over his chest and steadily regarding Gabe.

"Um." He couldn't help but chuckle just a bit at his behavior—he was acting like a kid with his first crush. Which was pretty much what Lucas had been to him. Recognizing that sobered him up fast. How the hell was he supposed to handle this now? *Gotta be up front.* Just launch in. "Okay, I know things've been weird between us since, well, since you left, and we've kind of avoided each other—"

"Listen, if you're just looking for a hookup?" Lucas half snorted, a gentle puff out his nose. "Give me the courtesy of coming out and saying it this time."

This time? Something wasn't adding up here. "What if I'm not just looking for a hookup?" *Shouldn't'a said that.* "I mean, say I'm just looking for a friend?" Oh, yeah, *that* sounded better. *Shit.*

Lucas sniffed, and angled his body away.

This was going sideways in a hella hurry. "Where'd that come from anyway?" The guy was acting like Gabe had tricked him into their last encounter.

Lucas didn't answer, not exactly. "I should thank you, I guess. For teaching me the first time out of the gate that for some guys it's easier to lie than admit they just want sex."

What the fuck?

Lucas's teeth flashed lighter in the dark for a second, sneering. "What I don't get about guys like you is that you thought you *had* to pretend you had feelings for me."

"You think I was *playing* you?" Well there was a scenario he hadn't thought up. Sure, he'd thought maybe Lucas would be pissed he had avoided him after that, but not that the guy would think he'd manipulated him.

"Oh, I don't know, Gabe." Lucas swung his head around, chin jutting forward. "Let's review the facts: you picked me up on the side of the road one night after finding out I was gay, acted all concerned about me, took me home to a house you *knew* was deserted, then came into my room when I was undressing and kissed me before offering to jerk me off."

"Okay, yeah, that all happened." It just hadn't seemed so, well . . . exploitative, not before Lucas said it with a tone so sour a tang of lemons hung in the air. "But none of that means I was lying to you about what I wanted." He'd said it straight out—*your dick, my hand. Stroke you until you come*—first time he'd ever been so direct, and he'd never forget the words. They made him flinch every time he remembered them, even while they got him hot.

"Then." Lucas straightened up, tightening his body so much a halo of tension quivered around him. "*Then*, when it was all over and you got off, you said, 'Thanks for a good time.' It was, like, Players 101."

"You're leaving out some mighty pertinent details." Like all the shit that had led up to that farewell. He'd been pissed by then, at both of them, but mostly himself for not being able to let the guy go without touching him first.

"Oh?" Lucas's tone went syrupy. "Such as when my parents came home and you pretended we'd just been talking?"

Well that was just unfair. "What the hell was I supposed to do, Lu? Tell them what we'd been doing? I was protecting you as much as me."

"Yeah, you *were* protecting you, because you aren't gay, are you? You just have an 'appreciation of the male form.'"

Damn, the shame from having that repeated back to him bled away some of his growing anger. "Why do you only remember the shit I wish I hadn't said?"

"It'd be easier on you if I didn't, wouldn't it? But it's all crystal clear." Lucas tapped his temple with his finger, derision easy to read in the set of his mouth.

"You ain't got half of it right," Gabe returned softly. Lucas was showing him more emotion than he had since he was a teenager, when he'd blushed and stammered every time Gabe walked into the room. That's how Gabe had known Lucas would let him kiss him that night, and hell if *that* didn't sound manipulative. *Maybe* I'm *remembering this wrong.*

"I *get*—" Lucas marched right up to match his toes to Gabe's, sending Gabe's pulse on a little trot around the yard "—that I'm supposed to pretend it wasn't a big deal because I'm a guy, but you know what? It *was* a big deal. You *used* me. I was eighteen, and naive, and I didn't know what was what. I don't care what your opinion of me is, now, though."

The hell he didn't. "You sure about that? Think you doth protest too much." Up close like this, he still looked so good, even when his pale-blue eyes went icy like they probably were this moment, if Gabe could've made them out in the dark. Lucas's face had always matched his body, some features strong and prominent, and others sleek and slender. It made it so easy to read his emotions.

Lucas went on as if he'd never heard a word. "You and Seth and whoever else you're fucking can laugh behind my back all you want, but for the next month, during the run-up to my brother and Audrey's wedding? I expect you to act like a decent guy. The kind who—"

"I'm not fucking Seth."

Finally Lucas faltered, mouth gaping a moment before he asked, "You aren't? What was that about the toothbrush?"

He'd known Seth had done that on purpose, he'd just hoped Lucas hadn't heard it. "It was him being a jerk." He'd like to leave it at that, but as had so recently been proven to him, small-town gossips were good at getting the word out. "We *used* to hook up, when it was convenient."

"As if I care," Lucas snapped, then backed up, eyeing Gabe as if *he*'d been the one to bring up Seth. "What I'm saying is, I'm not falling for your act again."

"It wasn't an act." Damn, he could feel the pulse throbbing in his temple. "You wanna know what it was? It was you. When you were sixteen, one day I came by the house to find you in the kitchen, licking peanut butter off a spoon." Twining his tongue around it and then sucking it into his mouth, letting it glide back out reluctantly, covered in saliva and desire.

For a split second Lucas's eyes went wild, like a startled colt, but then he narrowed them again and set his jaw. "What are you *talking* about?"

"You weren't wearing much." Gabe took the liberty of not really answering his question this time, and of stepping closer, until every breath Lucas took was caressing his ear, or so he could imagine. "Just a pair of gym shorts. The waistband of your underwear was creeping up your back, peeking at me like it was sending out an invitation." Or a white flag of surrender. Those shorts had been as shapeless as a Catholic schoolgirl's skirt, but Gabe had just been able to make out the rounded muscles of Lucas's ass pushing against the fabric. The bumps and dips of his spine disappeared under the elastic, like stepping stones leading to a secret hideaway. "And I knew right then."

Swallowing, Lucas lifted his chin before croaking in an almost normal tone, "Knew what?"

"Why you'd been so skittish around me. Barely able to talk, and never meeting my eyes. You *wanted* me." Heat trickled through him as Lucas's lips parted on a gasp, and he was as sure now as he'd been then. "You know how I figured that out?"

"I wasn't that into you," Lucas whispered.

Lie. "*I* wanted *you* that much. I almost copped a feel that second."

"Why didn't you?"

"I coulda done it, Lu. Reached right out and burrowed my fingers between your legs, tested the strength of your cheek with my thumb."

A high-pitched, nearly silent gasp was Lucas's only response.

"But I didn't because I respected you."

Screwing his mouth up into a look of disgust, Lucas yanked himself right out of the spell of lust Gabe had been wrapping them both in.

"*Respect*? What, you didn't want to sully me?"

Mistake. Or not the right word. Something. Gabe tried to get on program with the mood change, but his blood was still thrumming through his extremities, prepping them for imminent intimacy.

"But two years later it was okay?" Lucas threw out a questioning arm before pacing a couple of steps away to show Gabe his back. "You're doing it again, aren't you?"

"No." He'd totally lost control of this, and he'd been so fucking close to making Lucas understand. "I'm telling you—you know when you said I pretended I had feelings for you?" Shit, was he really going to admit this? He sort of had to if he was going to salvage anything. "I *did*. When I found out you were leaving..."

"Shut up." Lucas's tone dripped with disbelief, and so did his expression when he turned around. "You wanted in my pants, Gabe."

Well, yeah. But not only. "It was more than that."

"You *told* me you just pretended to be into me to get some."

"No, *you* said that, and I just didn't say otherwise." Leave it to Lucas to miss the subtle shit.

A small, questioning line formed over his nose, but his lips tightened up. "Same thing."

"Hell no, it ain't!"

Suddenly his expression cleared, and Lucas pointed his finger at Gabe, nearly shouting, "You told me being with you would bring me nothing but pain."

"*Staying here* would get you nothing but pain. Those are the exact words." Near as he could remember, but damn sure he remembered it better than Lucas. "If you'd stayed here—for any reason—you'd never stop regretting it, and whatever that thing was that kept you from leaving? You'd grow to hate it." If things had been different, Gabe wouldn't have let go of him. "You were dying to get the hell out of this town, and I wasn't gonna be the thing that kept you here a minute longer."

Jerking his chin carelessly, Lucas sneered. "You couldn't have kept me here."

Verbal jab to the ribs. "Well excuse the hell out of me for thinking I might. Sounded like I maybe could when I asked you back then."

"I never said that," Lucas shot back, but the question mark grew in his brow again.

"That's right." He could see his agreement threw Lucas off, as those wrinkles of doubt spread across his forehead. "You never answered the question at all, did you?"

"You wouldn't stay here just for me, would you?" He'd asked it intending to dissuade the guy from even thinking about it, but he'd be lying if his heart hadn't been praying for Lucas to say yes. If he had, though, then Gabe would have been forced to *make* him go. Although that was damn close to what had happened in the end, at least as he recalled it.

For a second they teetered there, on the edge of lining up the recollections of their mutual past. Hand-tinted images that didn't reveal the whole picture on their own, but could make it leap into bright life if combined. Lucas was open to it—it was in the way he stood with his arms slack by his sides and the way his eyes widened as he stared at Gabe.

But then he shook his head and straightened up his spine, holding himself rigid and his nose aloft. Not as certain as before, but definitely resistant. "I'm not listening to this anymore. When we're with Zach and Audrey, we pretend things are cool, but otherwise? Leave me alone. Can you do that? Be civil to me?"

"Hell yes." He could be a lot more than civil, given the opportunity.

Lucas nodded firmly, then stalked off, passing out into the drizzle without flinching, the set of his shoulders stiff as he yanked open the cafeteria door and marched through it into the light and noise.

Gabe couldn't do much but watch. He knew when to let someone strategically retreat. This battle wasn't lost yet, though, because Lucas remembered that night in full Technicolor, just like he did.

Just, they hadn't quite reconciled those memories, but it'd happen. Then Gabe could move on.

Lucas drank too much at the engagement party. He pretended it was because he was with people he hadn't seen in forever, like Audrey's other bridesmaid, and other friends from high school who were still living in Bluewater Bay.

In reality, he'd tied one on to forget about Gabe Savage. He woke up Saturday morning with a headache and a bad taste in his mouth, but it had all been in vain—he could still remember the night before.

Fucking Gabe. With his sincere face and his lying tongue and his twisted history of them. The worst part was that Lucas had been falling for it, exactly like he'd sworn not to, because: peanut butter.

He'd loved peanut butter. Still did, but Drew had trained him out of eating it from the jar. Lucas's arguments about them sharing bodily fluids anyway, and pointing out they'd never offer *guests* PB&Js were swept aside. Too weak to stand against Drew's disgusted faces and comments about Lucas's total lack of decorum. Shame was a great motivator for breaking bad habits.

Apparently, though, Gabe had liked it when Lucas ate peanut butter. Had been turned on by it. Or maybe by his sartorial choices when indulging, he wasn't clear, but still. If Lucas were to, theoretically, eat peanut butter out of Gabe's jar . . .

Don't go there.

Yeah, bad idea.

Good thing Gabe had said that thing about respect. *Respect.* Such a perfect example of the kind of parochial, conservative, good ol' boy mentality he'd been fleeing when he left this town. Had the guy seriously thought he'd respond positively to that? It offended him on so many levels—including his sexist bullshit-o-meter, and he wasn't even a girl—especially since, two years later, Gabe had clearly *stopped* respecting him. That was what had kept him from believing it when Gabe made that comment, *"When I found out you were leaving . . ."* Trailing off suggestively was such a dead giveaway. He'd known he couldn't come up with the right words, so he'd hoped Lucas would for him. Manipulative bastard.

If he lay here all day, he'd be rerunning that scene the whole time. Especially that part about peanut butter.

Maybe Audrey had some? That got him out of bed in spite of the headache, because for some reason he was sure if he could lick some of the gooey stuff off a spoon, it'd cure his hangover. No use clinging to the condition if it couldn't block out what had happened.

Throwing on a pair of sweats over his briefs seemed like the polite thing to do. And the bare wood floor of Audrey's studio was cold on his naked toes, so he needed socks. The whole room held a chill—wasn't it heated? He'd never asked. Making a mental note to do that, he pulled a hoodie on over his T-shirt on his way across the landing to the main apartment, in search of magical elixir of nut.

Heh. *Magical elixir of nut.* He'd have to tell Audrey that one. She'd appreciate it.

But as soon as he opened the door, the sight of his nearly naked brother standing in front of those huge windows blinded him.

"Ahhhh!" Clutching at his eyes, he stumbled, hitting his shoulder on the sharp edge of the doorjamb.

"Hey, Lu," Zach greeted him. "Surprised you, huh?"

"Oh my God, put something *on*."

The bastard chuckled. "You've seen me in boxers a million times. Shit, you've seen me in less. We grew up together in a one-bathroom house."

"This is *different*," Lucas insisted, separating his fingers just enough to see his way to the kitchen area. Far as he could tell, Zach wasn't doing anything about his indecency. "This is postcoital near-nudity."

"What makes you so sure of that? We make too much noise?" Bastard had a smile in his voice.

Apparently, Audrey had already had some magical elixir of nut. He'd liked that phrase so much better when it referred to peanut butter, not penis butter.

Gag.

"Oh, be nice." Audrey's footsteps behind him almost tricked Lucas into turning to face her, but when she added, "And go put some clothes on," he knew it still wasn't safe to look.

Zach's chuckle drifted to Lucas's ears, but so did his footsteps as the guy headed behind the row of bookcases that separated Audrey's bed from the rest of the apartment.

"Is he gone?" Lucas asked quietly. A new thought occurred to him. "Are *you* decent?"

"She's a fair bit better than decent," Zach called. "She's *fine*, and don't you forget it."

"Audrey."

"Yes." She appeared in front of him, wearing a purple velvet bathrobe that, of course, looked beautiful on her, clinging to her curves. His brother must eat that up.

"I really think we'd all be happier if you had a place with real walls."

"No." She smirked at him. "I'm pretty sure only your happiness depends on walls. Just be grateful I put you in my studio instead of the living area."

He shuddered. Then he probably *would* have heard them last night. "Does he stay over a lot?"

"Mostly just weekends." She patted his arm before turning toward the wall of cupboards. They were new, faced with a plain blond wood, in total contrast to the industrial-slash-Old-West feel of the rest of the place. "I have cold cereal or oatmeal. If you want more, you have to make it yourself."

Lucas snorted, because he'd been a victim of her cooking and he wasn't stupid enough to repeat that experience. "Do you have peanut butter? I won't eat it out of the jar, swear," he said quickly when she whipped her head around and narrowed her eyes.

"In the tall cupboard, other side of the fridge." She pulled out a bowl and spoon while she was speaking, pushing them along the counter his way.

The narrow island was the only place to sit and eat, unless he wanted to flop onto her couch. She'd kill him if he got anything on it, though, and he didn't want to clean peanut butter out of the upholstery, so he pulled a stool out from underneath and settled in.

"What are your plans for today?" Audrey sat next to him, placing her bowl of cereal in front of her.

Swallowing a lump of peanut butter was more difficult than he remembered. Sighing, Audrey got up and got him a glass of water. He had to drink half of it before he could answer her. "I told Mom I'd visit them. After that?" He shrugged. "I don't know."

"Zach and I are hanging around here today, working on wedding stuff. You could come to dinner with us later if you wanted."

There certainly wasn't anything else to do. God, a month plus in this town might kill him. "Okay."

His parents' house was exactly where it had always been, and looked exactly the same, but if Lucas hadn't already seen his father the previous night, he wouldn't have believed he was in the right place. Even so, he had to confirm it again by glancing around the neighborhood. To the southwest he could see the spire of St. Gommar's, and behind him he could just see the corner of old Mrs. Larson's house.

In front of where he'd parked, though, was the anomaly—his father, wearing a tie-dyed shirt and a rolled-up bandana to hold his hair back. He stood at a potting bench, planting small seedlings into black baskets. As far as Lucas knew, his dad had never grown anything in his life, and he wouldn't be caught dead in a shirt like that.

But it was definitely his father who, when he saw Lucas, beamed and started toward the car. "Hey, son!"

This man couldn't be more of a polar opposite to the last time Lucas had come home. More than two years ago, right after Dad had broken his back in a logging incident. It had been a horrible trip— Mom was stressed out, his father was in a hospital bed in the living room and as ornery as all hell, and everyone was depressed. Since his dad had been an employee of a logging company and not a contractor, workers' comp paid his bills and even gave him disability benefits, but Lucas couldn't miss the strain of finances. When he left, he'd tried to give his mother a thousand dollars, but she'd fled the room, sobbing, and refused to come out of the bedroom until just before Zach took him to the airport.

Apparently, things had gotten better. Maybe he should have figured that, since Mom had assured him many times since that his father was doing well. Great, even, especially after he found a pain medication that really worked for him.

God knew what *that* drug cocktail must be like.

Lucas's ruminations ended when his door flew open and his father pulled him out of the car. Once he was standing, his dad clapped a palm on the back of Lucas's neck and used it to urge him away from the vehicle and toward the house. "C'mon inside and see your mother. She's been on pins and needles, waiting on you." When he was a kid, if Dad led him anywhere like this, it would've ended in misery, but *this* grip was totally different. More of an affectionate cupping than a digging in of the fingers.

What the hell had happened since his last trip home?

What had happened in the last few years was his father had started smoking weed.

And growing it, apparently. Hydroponically. In Lucas's former bedroom. In fact, he now also grew it for *other* people who needed it. That was a more recent thing. "Once them lawmakers pulled their bunched-up panties outta the cracks of their asses and realized it ain't that big a deal," Dad explained, then guffawed.

Mom chortled right along with him.

"Isn't the change in your father *amazing*?" she whispered across the kitchen table to Lucas when Dad went into the pantry for a second to fetch some tea. "He's like a changed man since he healed up."

Tea. Lucas's *father* was making him a nice cuppa. If he saw anything that looked even remotely like dried fungi going into that pot, he was going to have to run for it. Blinking at his mother's beaming, expectant face, he worked up an answer. "It's sure something."

She hunched closer toward him, eyes crinkling up at the corners. "He's been real excited for you to come home and see." Her happiness dimmed a few seconds while she said, "You know, since your last trip, he was so . . ."

"I know." He dropped his voice lower to match hers. "Mom, how long has Dad been . . . drinking tea?"

"Oh, 'bout a year'n'a half, now." Resting her chin in her hand, she gazed toward the door Dad had disappeared through with a lingering smile on her face. "Green tea helps keep the inflammation from flaring up in his back."

"But you said he was healed."

"Lucas," she chided, slapping his arm playfully. "I told you this a dozen times. He's got some lingering pain and he will have for the rest of his life. It's a small price to pay."

A cold shiver crawled down Lucas's spine, just like every time it occurred to him that his father could have been paralyzed. Maybe a quadriplegic. Until Dad's accident, he hadn't even been aware someone could break their back and not injure their spinal cord. "It is," he agreed. "So that's what the pot is for? Pain?"

"I'd prefer you to call it 'cannabis,'" Dad said, emerging from the pantry and showing the first traces of the sometimes surly father Lucas remembered. Then he loosened up again. "Keeps the haters off-balance. You can disrespect a slang term, but you can't knock a scientific name, now, can ya?"

"I guess not." The tea kettle began to shrill, and his father rushed over to the stove while his mother got up to help, rubbing the small of Dad's back a second as she set three mismatched mugs next to him.

They looked so . . . happy.

"To answer your question, yeah, I take the cannabis for pain." Dad was speaking loudly, head canted just enough to bring his cheek into profile and for Lucas to see his mouth moving, but his attention was clearly on pouring steaming water over the tea bags Mom had put in each cup. "Tell you what, son, it made a world of difference once I got off them narcotics. I just couldn't take that shit anymore." Dropping a quick kiss on Mom's cheek as he handed her a drink, he grabbed the other two off the counter and came to the table. He hooked the back leg of his chair with his ankle to pull it out, and for a split second Lucas's mind whirled. That move was so totally his father. One of those small idiosyncrasies of body language that one never thought about until every other single thing about a person had changed.

"What's with the hair?" he asked absently, still caught up in watching his father settle into his seat, looking for other similarities to the former guy.

"What's wrong with my hair?" Dad's fingers gripped his mug handle tighter, and his lower lip poked out just slightly.

More of the old man showing through. Which might explain why Lucas let some of his own teenage brattiness out. "Just because you smoke pot now doesn't mean you had to go hippie. You know that, right?"

His dad didn't let things escalate, though. Instead he scoffed, waving his hand dismissively. "'Course I know that. I ain't 'gone hippie.' Lotsa guys grow their hair long nowadays, son. Get with the twenty-first century."

"Do lots of guys wear tie-dye too?" He'd only ever seen the bohemians wear it in southern California—although that was about every third person—and he'd never expected to see anyone wear it *here*.

Just like he'd never expected an honest-to-God embrace from his father.

"Well," Dad admitted, looking down at it. "It's a *mite* bit hippie. I like the colors. Sometimes they kinda dance for me." He shrugged, then eyed the mug he'd set in front of Lucas. "You gonna drink that tea or yap until it gets cold?"

Lucas lifted and sipped. It kept him from saying anything else.

"Now, are you all settled in at Audrey's?" Mom didn't let him answer. "I'm so sorry you can't stay here, Lu, but since your father is growing marijuana—"

"Cannabis," Dad corrected.

"—in your old room—"

"It's fine, really." It was more than fine, it was a relief. His head might explode if he found out about *all* the changes to his dad at once. He needed to preserve some of the mystery a while longer, for his sanity's sake.

Mom carried the conversation until they'd all finished the tea. Her eyes went shiny as she waxed on about Audrey, and her cute dress shop, and her sense of style, and how pleased in general she was to be getting such a wonderful daughter-in-law.

"And a looker, to boot," Dad added, then grinned when Mom slapped him playfully on the shoulder.

Seriously. Alternate universe.

"Well." Dad added a guttural stop to the word in that characteristic way of aging hicks, shoving his chair back from the table at the same time. "Gotta get back to it. Cannabis seedlings don't repot themselves, y'know." He stood, smiling down at Lucas. "I'll say it again, son. It's damned fine to see you."

"You too, Dad." An exhalation of relief escaped with the words, but the torture wasn't actually over. He'd been duped into thinking the only threat was from his father.

As soon as Dad's feet had clattered down the side porch steps, his mother started in. "S'pose you expected Gabriel Savage to be your brother's best man."

"Yeah." Her tone and the way she kept glancing at him, then looking away, tripped all of his internal alarms. She was fishing for something. "I mean, since Audrey claimed me as her man of honor, Gabe's the obvious choice." He'd been Zach's best friend since before Lucas could remember.

Tilting her head, Mom smiled. "I think he's always been a little bit sweet on you."

What? Inarticulate noises escaped him, but other than slamming his hands down on the table, he didn't manage to communicate much of anything.

"Last few times you visited, he came up with reasons to drop by. And he always asks me about you, if I run into him."

"You *know* he's gay?"

"Zach told me years ago." She clucked her tongue at him. "But before that, I sometimes wondered—you remember when you found out you got into that college, he dropped by here to congratulate you one night?"

Prickles of memory sluiced down his body, tingling through his skin from his head to toes. *That night.* He couldn't escape it. "He did," Lucas croaked. "Stop by."

"Such a nice boy," his mother mused.

He snorted. If she knew what kind of congratulations had really gone down in his bedroom all those years ago . . .

"Well, a man could do worse than Gabe Savage."

Oh my God, she was angling for a son-in-law to go along with her daughter-in-law. It *had* to be something in the water. "*Mom!*" Would she accept silver salt and pepper cellars instead?

"What?" Her hand fluttered to her breastbone in the perfect parody of innocence.

"Are you— It sounds like you want me to *date* Gabe."

She frowned thoughtfully, as if pondering the idea for the first time. "He *is* a very nice boy. And handsome. Good income too, plus he's got that farm—"

"I just got *out* of a relationship, if you'll recall. Remember Drew?"

Sitting up poker straight, she responded, "Drew was a perfect gentleman." She fiddled with her tea mug. "Very polite."

Polite. What compliment would she bestow next, *adequate*?

But she was right. The one time Drew had visited Lucas's family in Bluewater Bay, he'd been icily courteous the whole time, and had spoken very slowly, as if the natives might not understand this *furriner* otherwise. Lucas had hoped (although not really believed) that he was the only one who saw through that frigid civility.

That had been a more painful trip home than his last one. Lucas had swung between anger at his partner and embarrassment over his family the whole time. Now, shame gut-punched him. He should have kicked that bastard out of his parents' house the first time the guy had wrinkled up his nose and claimed to not be hungry rather than eat something as colloquial as pan-fried morels. They were fifty bucks a pound in Los Angeles, but he couldn't bring himself to eat the ones Lucas's father had gathered for free at a jobsite?

No wonder no one liked Drew. The bigger question was why Lucas had. Maybe he should have paid more attention to his family . . . although, right now, his mother was trying to get him to date another guy who'd done him wrong. Except, even if she knew about that night in high school, she'd still see Gabe as a definite step up. It was in the rest of his universe—outside of Bluewater Bay—that dating a logger with his own tree farm would be slumming.

It was like being shrunk down and inserted inside a snow globe and looking out at the big, wide world one used to inhabit. A distorted perspective; as wonky as the view from that world into this one.

Mom changed the subject again, probably because she knew him well enough to sense his confusion and discomfort. Hours later, when he finally said good-bye to his folks, the discordance between the parts of his life was still lurking in the pit of his stomach.

CHAPTER FOUR

Flat Earth pizzeria hadn't been around when Lucas was in high school. They'd had a Pietro's, where everyone went after sporting events and ate some of the worst food created by humans. In his experience, Bluewater Bay didn't do Italian well. He'd been skeptical when Audrey and Zach had dragged him to this restaurant, but he was pleasantly surprised. The crust was thin and the sauce was redolent of tomato, rather than relying on lots of other flavorings.

Zach and Audrey weren't as interesting as the food. Well, not to him—their interest in each other was nearly palpable. An unexpected longing tugged at his heart, laced with pride. It made no sense that he was proud of them for falling in love, but telling himself that didn't stop him from swelling with it every time Zach nuzzled the side of Audrey's head, or Audrey kissed his temple.

Well, for a little while. Then it got nauseating.

"Gotta take a leak," Zach announced after one particularly sickening display.

What a suave guy.

Audrey thought so, judging by the way she smiled at him as he stood. "We'll be fine here, sweetie."

Uh . . . yeah. What could possibly happen in the few minutes it took him to pee? Audrey could meet someone she liked better?

"So now that you're getting married, are you going to learn to cook?" he asked as soon as his brother was out of earshot.

She shrugged. "Zach can cook."

True. Their mother had made them help her so much, even he knew how to cook the basics.

She clasped her hands in front of her on the table and leaned over them, face brightening. "Guess what I'm getting him as a wedding gift?"

"You give a present to the guy you're marrying?"

"Of *course*. He'll give me one. I can't wait to see what it is."

"Okay, so what's your gift to him?"

"I'm having your mother write down all her recipes, then I'm having it bound in hardcover."

"How . . . thoughtful." Would Zach like that? He couldn't tell—Audrey seemed to have a better understanding of his own brother than he did.

"I know, right?" She wiggled her fingers at him in a hushing motion, just as Zach got back to the table. He settled into the booth next to Audrey, scooting until he was right up against her and could put an arm around her shoulders. Lucas couldn't say whose sigh was more contented—his brother's or the vinyl cushion under the guy's butt.

"You know, honey." Predictably, Audrey snuggled up under his arm and turned toward him. "Lucas and I were just talking about something that reminded me we need to come up with little gifts for everyone close to us. Wedding favors."

"Oh. Yes. I agree." Zach nodded stiltedly, in keeping with his stiff tone. He sounded like he was reading lines from a script. "We certainly do. Lucas, I'd sure appreciate it if you would help us out with that."

Instead of responding to him, Lucas cut out the middleman and went straight to the boss. "You know I haven't been feeling inspired," he told Audrey. "And why are you coaching him in manipulating me?"

"I wasn't coached!"

"I just thought if you knew he wants to give people some of your work also—as well as me, I mean—you'd be heartened. Motivated to produce something."

Making a face at her, he turned back to Zach. "Do you even *like* my work?"

"Hell yes." Zach goggled at him. "'Course I do."

"No, not just because you're my brother and you think you have to like it. I mean really, do you *like* it?" He didn't do realism so much, and bronzes of lifelike cougars and leaping elk seemed to be the style of choice for the redneck set. Plus he'd made a lot of male nudes.

"Well I don't like the naked men so much." Zach grimaced. "But that stuff you do with the shaped lines? It seems like it moves, like, I could catch it undulating out of the corner of my eye. Petrified wind, or something." Blushing, he glanced at his fiancée. "Least, that's the way I see it."

Amazing. Lucas sat stunned, staring at his brother. He *got* it, completely.

"That's a perfect description," Audrey was saying, beaming at Zach.

"It is," Lucas echoed when he regained speech. Along with that ability came a tickle of something he hadn't felt in a while, not since he'd left Montana. Interest in making something.

It was *only* a tickle, though. "You really think your friends would want my work?"

They both looked at him like he was crazy. "Well, yeah," his brother scoffed. "Even if they don't appreciate your style. You're famous."

Okay, not the most flattering way to put it, but honest. *Ish.* "I'm not famous, though. Only to people who're into fine crafts."

"What the hell is 'fine craft'?" Zach twisted his lips up in confusion. "'Z'at anything like fine art?"

"It's the same thing," Audrey answered.

"Kind of," Lucas said at the same time, then explained. "It's a term used to describe artwork that isn't traditionally considered 'fine.' Crafts are things that aren't only aesthetically pleasing, but have a function as well."

"Whad'ya mean?"

"Well, like, a painting doesn't have a function."

"Yes it does, it sits on the wall and looks pretty."

Lucas sighed. "Okay. The function of a painting is to be the best painting it can. But the function of a piece of pottery is to look good but also do a more practical job, like hold liquid."

"Hell if that doesn't sound like a distinction a bunch of elitists came up with." Zach adjusted his shoulders until the set of them read *disdain*.

If Lucas didn't know better, he'd assume that was what Audrey had told his brother to say, but judging from the way he'd said it in a natural voice (as opposed to earlier) and how she placed her hand on his cheek, pulling Zach around for a quick kiss, murmuring something in Zach's ear that made him blush and grin—

God they were *disgusting* together.

Anyway, that had to be Zach's actual opinion. Which might just mean Lucas had been selling his brother short. He ignored the icky feeling in his stomach that thought created—he could dwell on it later—and explored that small itch of interest some more. Maybe he *could* make some stuff. "Just little things," he said aloud.

"That would be fine," Audrey gushed, disentangling herself from Zach to lean over the table. "Token gifts, nothing more. Maybe two dozen? You'd have total artistic freedom, Lu. You could do *anything*."

Freedom. The tickle of interest bloomed into a something more: a full-on *caress*. Was that what had been missing from his work? That he'd been making stuff he knew would sell rather than what he'd really been excited about? "I don't have my kiln here." Not a real objection, because there had to be a way around that.

"Can't you build a kiln? You called me when you were in Missoula a half-dozen times raving on about the wood-fired kilns your fellow artist-in-residence was building."

Damian had done a whole series of hand-built, wood-fired kilns, and every time Lucas watched the flames kindle on a new one, he'd felt the excitement kindle in his chest. They were the complete opposite of the gas-fired downdraft kiln Lucas had left in California.

He wanted to do that. Fuck the multi-thousand dollar kiln he'd had designed. That had been Drew's idea. *"To keep your work consistent."*

Like changing the channel on a television, Lucas's brain tuned out whatever else Audrey was saying and started flashing images and snippets of sense memories across his internal viewing screen. All moving too fast to be described, giving him ideas and plans that he couldn't put into words, not yet, but then it cleared and resolved and—"I can do it." The ends of his fingers tingled and thrummed with excitement he hadn't felt in *months*. A consuming desire to try something just to see how it turned out. He could *totally* experiment with this, because he didn't have a gallery owner/partner telling him what would sell best, or a client demanding something made to bizarre and impossible specifications. Did he? "You said I could do *anything*?"

She snorted. "Anything that will start you working again."

Zach cleared his throat. "Uh, just no penises."

"No penises." Holding his hand up as if he was taking an oath, he promised, because it didn't matter what he made, as long as he did it his way. He grinned, nearly laughing with the happiness of it all. "I'll start practicing my fig leaves. Oh." His excitement came to a screeching, terrifying halt. "Where would I build it? I'd need an outdoor space I can pretty much destroy, and access to lots of firewood—"

"I already know a place," Audrey assured him. "Don't worry." She was nearly bouncing in her seat, eyes alight with the same exhilaration Lucas was feeling.

"Okay." He nodded, catching his breath. "Okay, so when can I see it?"

She glanced at Zach, who nodded slightly. "Tomorrow."

"Awesome." Now that he was motivated to work? He didn't want to waste any time.

Unfortunately, it wasn't that easy. After they got back to the apartment from dinner, he retreated to his room and let Audrey and Zach have alone time (hoping alone time wouldn't be overly loud). It wasn't out of courtesy so much as out of wanting his own space. He had a creative process he'd honed through trial and error over the years—mostly error—and it began with him sinking into the zone. To do that, he needed to shut everyone out and let himself get totally wrapped up in his own mind.

It wasn't hard. Being totally self-absorbed was pretty much his natural inclination anyway, and he itched to get started making *something*. All he wanted was to get his hands dirty again. Shape things with them.

He was so caught up in his head that he was sitting on a stool at Audrey's worktable before he realized all he could do tonight was doodle in his sketchbook. Not only did he not have any of the supplies he'd left at Corbin's, he didn't have a studio yet. He *needed* a studio, with clay and sculpting tools and worktables—at this stage of the creative process, he didn't have any images for drawing, just a feeling of what he might like to make. Only working with the medium would do.

He scribbled all over a couple dozen blank pages and surfed the internet for an hour before, exhausted with frustration, he gave up and went to bed.

Sleep failed him, though. His brain kept insisting he remember what Zach had said at dinner, about his work being petrified wind. God, he'd totally been misreading his brother, assuming Zach had horrible taste and wouldn't be able to understand Lucas's conceptual work. Sold him short.

Possibly he'd done the same thing with his father, only remembering the parts of the man he'd disliked or been afraid of. Parts he couldn't seem to find much trace of, now.

Those doubts led him to wonder if he'd misread other people, like Gabe.

He said he'd had feelings for me.

Maybe, when Gabe said he'd had too much "respect" for Lucas, he hadn't meant it in some condescending, patriarchal way. Maybe he'd meant something more like . . . "cared about."

And all those years ago when Gabe had asked him if he was thinking about staying in town? For a split second, Lucas had considered it if it meant he could hook up with Gabe again. His hormones had been going haywire from his first non-solo orgasm, and he was eighteen; stupid, gonad-prompted decisions were expected, at least until he'd calmed down. He wouldn't have actually *done* it, though.

Except, it was possible that Lucas's expression had told Gabe he *would* stay for him. Based on what the guy had said at the engagement party, Gabe had known that they'd eventually break up badly because Lucas wasn't emotionally capable of staying.

Assuming a real relationship had been on the table.

Still, Gabe could have been less of a dick about the way he'd told him that.

Maybe. If what Lucas recalled was what Gabe had actually said. Although he *was* certain the guy had admitted to manipulating him.

Well, pretty certain.

Thinking about all of that while trying not to kept him awake well past twelve.

What kept him up after that was Zach and Audrey having sex. With his pillow wrapped over his ears, he couldn't hear them unless he tried. Unfortunately, some warped part of his brain went into hyperfunctional mode and he couldn't *stop* listening for the small creaks and giggles and moans.

Hours later, delirious from the trauma and lack of sleep, he decided he had to be manufacturing some of the noises in his own head. It was either that or his brother could last an inhumanly long time.

Fuck this. Crawling out from under the blankets (and his pillow), he found his earbuds, plugged them into his phone, and fired up that white noise app he'd once downloaded and never used. He usually tried to avoid the static in his own head, but this one time he embraced the blissful oblivion of it and fell asleep.

Hay sold for a hell of a lot of money in the southwest nowadays—they kept flirting with droughts in that region—so Gabe planned to seed the north pasture with trefoil. Things kept getting in the way of his plans, though. Not just the mill putting him off until Friday, but on Saturday, Momma and Gramma had decided to rearrange the living room, and God knew they needed his help for that.

Sunday was supposed to be clear until near noon, perfect for farm work. He was planning on using the ancient tractor rather than the team. Figuring they'd not be doing much for an extended period, he'd worked the horses plenty this week, even harnessing May up for an afternoon. She'd been eager to get started, but exhausted by the time he'd led her into her stall that evening, with July snorting and whinnying next door. Stupid kid didn't want to work, but then got himself in a dither when someone else took his place.

Yep, that morning, bright and early—well, a little after eight, so not so early—he was all set to finally get started . . . except he made the mistake of checking his email first. There was one from Laura Haakinson, giving him Joshua Warburton's email address, home number, and cell phone, "just in case you don't have it yet."

Clearly, his vet wasn't going to let him forget about that stallion.

Cursing to himself, he called the hipsterman farmer. Best to get it over with. "Hey there, Joshua," he said when the guy answered. He slipped into his most countrified drawl. "Doc tells me you got yourself in a bit of situation."

"Well, don't you know it," Joshua replied, unsuccessfully mimicking Gabe's speech and cadence. "It's this damn foal—"

"Laura said he was a three-year-old."

"Uh." Joshua's fake accent bled away. "At what age isn't he a foal anymore?"

Gabe worked to keep his smile out of his voice. "On about a year. He's a colt right up until he's four or so." He shouldn't mess with the guy, it wasn't nice.

Just a lotta fun. He toned down his colloquialisms, but kept the drawl while asking Joshua questions about the horse. Guy was being cagey about it, though. "Let me get this straight: he's halterbroke"—damn well better be at three years—"and you already have him ground driving?"

"I thought I was up to training him, really, but—"

"You're about one step from getting him to pull a load, why the hell you wanna up and give him away?" It made no sense.

"He stopped," Joshua announced, like it explained everything.

When it was clear that was all the explanation he was going to get, Gabe asked, "Stopped what, exactly?"

"He stopped doing *anything*. Sometimes I have to chase him around the corral for an hour just to get his halter on."

Corral. Dude thought this was the Old West. Stifling his sigh, Gabe used his most patient tone. "Are you disciplining him?" They'd spent a fair amount of time on that when Joshua was taking lessons. The guy had no problem *asking* a horse to work, but he sucked at telling them when the situation required it.

"I tried, it's just he's so *friendly*. Like a huge dog who wants to play all the time," he whined.

Gabe wasn't a big proponent of striking a horse until all other avenues had been exhausted, but this was Joshua, who needed to level up on sternness. "Did you try using the encouragement stick?"

"Gabe." His tone suddenly went firm, showing just how stern he could be. "He needs someone who isn't afraid to be his boss and I'm just—" He took a deep breath. "I'm just not that guy. I've thought about this a lot, and you're the best man for Blackie. I'm barely keeping up on my regular farm chores, I don't have time for training him."

And I do? Well, yeah, he did. "All right, I'll come take a look at him, but I'm not making any promises about taking him off your hands."

Joshua's grateful thanks were still echoing in Gabe's ears when he finally hung up. He'd agreed to come this afternoon, so he'd have to move quick to get that field seeded in time. He'd just let the horses out into the pasture and was headed toward the machine shed to start the tractor when he heard the high whine of a car engine. The house, outbuildings, and pasture were on a bit of a plateau, but most of the farm was hilly. Anyone coming here had to make it up a hell of a slope or two. They were definitely headed this way—Savage Tree Farm was the end of that particular road. Probably a friend of Momma or Gramma—all of his friends owned trucks, and the motor on the vehicle was struggling too much to be a pickup. Since the women were still at church, he waited to see who it was.

A little white sedan appeared at the peak of the driveway. It looked familiar, but he couldn't place it. Where the road forked, the car turned toward the outbuildings and him, not toward the main house. Zach and Audrey, that was who it was. And someone in the backseat—had to be Lucas.

Ducking his chin, Gabe grinned to himself for a quick second, then schooled his expression. Lucas had pretty much shut him down, but Gabe knew it was just a matter of time before he got a chance to practice being civil to the guy. He hadn't thought it'd be this soon, though.

As they parked, he stepped out of the shed, remembering that Zach had hidden a little—well, kinda big, actually—surprise in there, and he wouldn't thank Gabe if his bride saw it before the wedding.

"What's going on?" he asked, holding open the passenger-side door for Audrey as she got out.

She smiled but didn't answer until Zach had come around to stand with them.

Lucas crossed his arms over his chest in the backseat and didn't budge.

"Remember on Friday night when I mentioned Lucas will need some place to work on his sculpture?"

"Uh, yeah." At the engagement party, after his run-in with the guy, Gabe had gone back inside and propped up a wall for a while, until Audrey came and stood next to him, surveying the room just like he was and explaining out of the corner of her mouth that his farm was perfect for her plan. There'd been talk of how to persuade Lucas that setting up here was a good idea. "I remember. Doesn't look like he's too into it, though." Bending over, Gabe gave Lucas a grin and a wiggly-fingered wave.

Lucas's eyes paled to their most aloof, icy blue before he cranked his head so far the other way he all but screwed it off his neck.

Gabe couldn't help it, he chuckled. If the dude wanted to convince him of his indifference, he was doing a piss-poor job.

"At least we got him *up* here," she said quietly. "Maybe you could, I don't know, show him around."

Zach shifted his weight and cleared his throat. "Yeah. Show him around."

"You're so whipped," Gabe told him conversationally.

"Yep, I am." The idiot smiled. "C'mon man, if you give him a tour of the place—"

"Didn't you say you even had studio space? With a sink and everything?" Audrey clasped her hands in front of herself fervently, like she was praying. "That'd *really* convince him."

"Why the hell are you two trying so hard to force me on him?" He shoved his fists into his jeans pockets, to keep from mimicking Lucas's pose. He'd known these two had a matchmaking bent blinding their judgment, but couldn't they see they were doing more harm than good?

"We aren't," Audrey insisted. "It really is about his work, and this really is the perfect place."

This was getting annoying. Yeah, he had a bit of a crush on Lucas still, but he wasn't gonna let the guy hang around, reminding him over and over that *he* had no use for Gabe. "There are other perfect places, I guarantee you."

"But it'll take time." Zach took Audrey's hand, gazing at her. "And she has her heart set on him making wedding favors. If we have to help him find another place to work—"

"'Cause you know he won't do it himself." Audrey rolled her eyes.

"Why not?" He was an adult. Not that he looked much like one, brooding in the back of Mommy and Daddy's car. "If he wants to do some artwork, he'll figure it out."

"That's just it, he hasn't wanted to for months. When I asked him to make stuff for us, he got excited about it for the first time in forever. That hasn't happened since he and his partner broke up." Audrey leaned forward. "He's been in a slump. It's an artist thing."

"I know what a slump is. Is this 'partner' the dude that cheated on him?" She'd mentioned something about that once.

Audrey nodded, but seemed content to let him mull it over now that she'd said her piece.

He wandered over to some tall grasses a few feet away and picked one with a long stem. Thinking was easier if he had a stalk to chew on. Also, from here he could see Lucas without having to stoop.

His chin was still set and his arms were still folded up high on his pecs, while he stared haughtily out the window. *Brat.* Made Gabe wonder why he even had a soft spot left for the guy. Probably because he had lips made for sulking. And sucking. *Hell.* He sighed, about to tell Audrey and Zach he couldn't imagine Lucas agreeing to this when something caught his attention.

Actually, something caught Lucas's attention—the muscles around his eyes tightened while the ones in his jaw loosened, and he jerked forward slightly, intent on something in the horse pasture.

Gabe followed Lucas's line of sight to see what had him so fascinated, and . . . it was May. Taking a dump.

Nah, that can't be it. A car door creaked open, but Gabe didn't turn toward it. He was too busy trying to figure out what he was missing.

"Shhhh!" Audrey hissed, which seemed unnecessary since no one was speaking. She'd clutched Zach's arm excitedly, and they both watched Lucas walk toward the steel panel fence as if he was in a trance. By then May was done and had moved on, cropping grass as she went, but Lucas was staring at the steaming pile of horse shit.

Then he said something. Not quite loud enough to hear from the driveway.

"What?" Audrey turned to Gabe. "What did he say?"

He shrugged. "Hell if I know." Better find out, though. Spitting out his grass stem, he made his way over to stand next to the guy, not so close he was threatening Lucas's virtue, but close enough that he could make out some of the finer hairs on the nape of his neck. "Find something interesting?"

"This place is perfect," Lucas murmured. "I can totally work here."

"Great." He guessed.

Lucas turned, glazed-over eyes slowly focusing on him, changing until they went a little bluer, but not frosty like earlier.

Okay, yeah, he did get a little jolt of pleasure over thinking Lucas would be hanging around, perverse as that was. It wasn't like *he* had anything to do with the decision. Apparently, that was all May. And her feces.

Never thought of horse manure as a motivator, but whatever worked.

He should have seen this one coming. Except by the time he woke up that morning, he'd been excited about getting to work again. A duller, more weary kind of excitement, but enough to distract him from noticing how Audrey and Zach were so careful about what bits of information to give him as they got in the car. He hadn't even thought about why they *all* needed to go, especially since it meant leaving before nine because Audrey had to be back by eleven.

Obviously, she'd had to come along in case he needed *handling*.

Nothing alarmed him, though, not until they reached that last fork in West Twin River Road, where bearing left would *only* lead to Savage Tree Farm. They'd reached the point of no return, and he'd realized where they were headed. "I'm not okay with this," he'd announced, but had been ignored.

All his bad mood from the middle of the night had come crashing back down, then. "I have no intention of getting out of the car, not without an apology from both of you."

Audrey had sighed. Zach's knuckles went white as he gripped the steering wheel with more force.

Fine. He'd sat there waiting them out, knowing full well he was behaving immaturely, brooding in the backseat. But dammit, they'd *misled* him.

Then that mare had lifted her tail, and as she dumped her load of manure in the pasture, memories had dumped into Lucas's mind. Things he'd seen and wanted to try. A whole plan formed in seconds, as obvious as horse manure but much better smelling. *Burnished blackware.*

To make that, he'd need livestock manure, or a reasonable substitute, but who needed a substitute when he could have as much as he wanted by walking around Gabe's pasture and picking it up?

Mental note: get rubber gloves.

With a pit kiln and the right kind of clay, he could explore something wholly new to him.

He'd agreed to work there before he even realized he'd said anything.

"Great," Gabe replied, resting his elbows on the fencing pipe, and simultaneously bringing Lucas back to the land of other people's existence.

Was it too late to back out? One of the horses he was watching suddenly kicked its heels up, then danced around in a trot. Frisking. Like he was just so happy to live at this paradise, with the dramatic view of the Olympic Mountains and the emerald trees and the picturesque farmhouse. *Dammit.* He wanted to be here too, even if it came with a frustrating, sexy redneck. "I'll need a lot of firewood."

"Got plenty," Gabe returned.

"I'll pay you for it, of course."

The guy just dipped his chin, but otherwise didn't respond. It was annoying.

"Tell him about the studio space." Audrey's voice came from right behind him, and Lucas nearly jumped.

"I'll do you one better and show it to him," Gabe said. Still watching the horses a second longer—the hyper one had gone back to grazing placidly—he readjusted his ball cap. "You ready?" He turned and caught Lucas's gaze.

The amusement was plain to see in his muddy-blue eyes. He was gloating about Lucas giving in, wasn't he? *Dick.*

"Um, is it going to take long?" Audrey asked, her gaze flickering between the two of them a little too intently. "I have a couple of customers to meet with at eleven."

Zach placed his hand on the small of her back, beaming. "Tell Gabe who."

"Well, you can't say anything. I mean, I want to respect my clients' privacy, but . . . it's Anna Maxwell, the executive producer of *Wolf's Landing.* I have a woman who's part of the production staff, Fjóla, who's been buying from me for a while, and she's bringing Ms. Maxwell in this morning. It's just to look, though. No guarantees or anything."

"She'll love your stuff." Lucas waved a negligent hand. "Make sure you show her that soft-knot shirt."

"Of course. It's my signature piece this season."

"That's cool." Gabe nodded at her, his sly smirk growing into a friendlier expression. "This'll only take a few minutes."

As Lucas trailed behind Gabe through the long grass, not checking out his ass in those jeans at all, Audrey caught up with him. Zach seemed to be going to look in the outbuilding Gabe had been standing in front of when they drove up.

He couldn't stay mad at her. "Online last night, I found a place in Sequim that might have enough supplies for me to do a few tests." He'd have to call and make sure they had a red-bodied clay, and terra sigillata, although he could probably get by without it for a while. *Because I have horseshit.*

"Are you going to have Corbin send up your stuff, then?" She looped her arm through his as they walked.

"Now that I have a place to work. Probably. Anyway, the website says the store's open until six tonight, so I'll head over this afternoon."

"You can ride with me." Gabe had stopped right in front of the main barn. "I gotta head over there too. Meeting a guy at five on the other side of Port Angeles."

"No, it's fine," Lucas responded quickly. "I'll just drive myself." The last time he'd ridden in a truck alone with Gabe, well . . .

Gabe didn't push it, but that hint of a smirk reappeared.

Whatever. Just because he'd promised to be civil didn't mean he had to be chummy. Instead he showed great interest in the building in front of him. In fact, he'd always loved the Savages' barn—it was huge, with vertical wood siding so weathered it looked like it had been treated with creosote except for where the boards overlapped and the thinnest slice of reddish tan peeked through. It didn't have the traditional roof shape, but was built in more of a horse-barn style—a two-story central structure with single-story additions running down both of the long sides.

Opening a door in the southeast corner, Gabe announced, "This is it."

Almost ceremoniously, Audrey dropped his arm. "I'll wait out here."

Sure, send him into the lion's den alone, with the lion. She ignored his frown, of course.

Fine. He followed Gabe inside, totally unsurprised to find that—like everything else about this place—it was perfect. Mostly empty, with workbenches built into three of the walls and cupboards on the fourth. For an outbuilding it had large windows that let in tons of natural light, and a sink next to a second door that must lead into the barn proper. Most of the center of the room was clear, just waiting for him to fill it up with his stuff.

Sighing in resignation, Lucas admitted, "It'll do."

"It was Grandpa Savage's office. His eyes went bad the last couple of years, so we put in bigger windows. You probably need that, huh?"

"Yeah, it's good. It's really good." So good he felt like kicking something. "Thank you for your hospitality. For letting me work here," he added stiffly.

"Don't sound too happy about that." Gabe stood with his hands jammed in his pockets, more serious now. Like he really didn't know if it measured up. He shouldn't even care what Lucas thought, not after the way he'd been acting since they arrived.

Oh, God, he had to apologize. "I'm sorry I was such a dick earlier."

"Well." Gabe glanced around, then met Lucas's gaze. Blue eyes shot with mossy-brown streaks really shouldn't look so good with dark-red hair. "On that note, if you expect me to be civil to you, I don't think it's unfair for me to expect the same in return."

Lucas half smiled, somewhere between amused at himself and ashamed. "You're right."

"Guess I wouldn't ever want it said I was inhospitable to a guest." He was less serious now, and stood straighter. God, he did actually care what Lucas thought, didn't he?

Lucas did the thing he'd do with anyone else—placed his hand on Gabe's arm and sincerely apologized this time. He *knew* he often got too self-involved, which ended up hurting or offending people. Except this time, he didn't manage more than, "I'm sorry," because Gabe's arm was warm and vital under the soft knit of his T-shirt. Alive in a way that spoke to something in Lucas's body and *dammit* why was he still attracted to this guy? Shouldn't what had happened twelve years before have killed off his appeal? *But he's being so nice to me, now.*

And it *was* twelve years ago. And Lucas *may* have been remembering it wrong.

As soon as he realized he'd been holding on to Gabe too long and studying his face too intently, Lucas jerked away, pretending to inspect the room, but in reality imagining a force field between his body and the large, burly one next to his. It didn't work—he could still sense energy running between them, as if together they completed a circuit.

"I'll be out in the machine shed if you need anything," Gabe said after a second, then he retreated, taking his heat with him.

The weatherman was wrong. It started raining before Gabe could get going on the trefoil. Planting a crop in the Pacific Northwest during the spring was dicey for just this reason. A tractor driven on muddy ground would compact the dirt so much that nothing could grow. He should've seeded last fall, right before the wet-season started, then he wouldn't have to—again—postpone planting the hay.

Well, hell. Nothing better to do than stand in the bay door of the shed, watching it pour. The rain shrouded the hills so they almost looked like one of those Chinese landscape paintings on a scroll.

Did Lucas paint? Back in high school, he used to do a lot of drawings, Gabe was pretty sure. Aw, fuck, there he went thinking about the guy again. After the scene this morning, he was pretty sure that, while they might come to friendly terms someday, he could pretty much forget about finishing any "business" with him, which was for the best. Then his attraction to Lucas could die on the vine. One more overripe, shriveling grape of lust.

Prolly better find something to do and stop moping.

Maybe he could call Joshua Warburton and move up their appointment.

Like always seemed to happen, as soon as he thought about dialing someone up, his phone rang. Never seemed to fail. Pulling the cell out of his pocket, he checked the number, but didn't recognize it. Could be Joshua on another line. "'Lo," he answered.

"Hi."

His moping ended at the sound of Lucas's voice, and he could swear the rain let up a little. "Hey there."

"Um, my car won't start."

"Did you try turning the key?"

"Ha. Funny."

"Well, are you asking me to come look at it?" He could, he supposed, although horse mechanics were more his department than the vehicular kind. Cars were Zach's thing.

"It's an electric-gas hybrid, everything's computerized. It's probably something that'll cost me five hundred just to have Holly's Haus of Imports look at it sideways."

"Ah." Gabe grinned to himself, waiting Lucas out, sure where this was going now.

"So, um, I was wondering . . ."

"Were you?"

He sighed. "Is the offer to give me a ride to Sequim still open? Please?"

"I suppose I could be talked into that." He looked at his watch, figuring timing and fighting off his growing hopeful expectation. *Just 'cause he needs a ride doesn't mean he wants a ride.* "We'd have to go there first. Can you be ready in twenty minutes?"

"I'm pretty much ready now." Lucas's voice had gotten lighter, maybe a little breathy. "I'll be waiting for you in Audrey's shop."

"Sounds good."

Well, now, there was something to do. He jogged to the barn and grabbed his parka. He'd go ahead and haul the horse trailer. Might as well prepare for all eventualities.

In town, the rain was letting up, or maybe it was just coming down harder at the farm. It was barely a sprinkle when Gabe pulled up across from Audrey's shop. He got lucky—there were two adjacent parking spots, so he could fit. Lucas appeared before he could shut off the motor, running across the street and around the front of his truck.

"Whew," he said as soon as he'd pulled open the passenger door. "I lived in Southern California too long. This almost seems like real rain."

"You got a tan, though. Fair trade-off." He meant it as a joke, of course, but the way Lucas climbed into his seat and buckled his belt was a little too stiff and a little too silent.

Apparently, Gabe had to pretend he didn't notice any of the physical changes in the guy. But he did. *Hair not as dark, muscles lean and sleek, no longer on the stringy side . . .* He could sit here the next ten minutes and catalog them. *Now, there's a shitty idea.*

"What's with the trailer?" Lucas was arranging a messenger bag on the floor, but it didn't look so much like avoidance. More like it was necessary or he wouldn't have any legroom.

"I'm going to see a man about a horse," Gabe answered, putting the transmission in gear.

This time, Lucas laughed. "Seriously? You have three already."

"Well, Laura Haakinson—you remember her? Used to be Laura Larson, Seth's cousin. Anyway, she became a veterinarian, and she's got the care of most of the livestock around these parts. She found this stallion she thinks I need, and I don't think she's going to leave me alone about it until I at least take a look." He turned left onto Main, just barely making it past some fancy Jaguar parked too damn far from the curb. Those Hollywood types didn't understand the first thing about etiquette in a small town. Like not blocking the street in case someone came through with a long load. "Place sure has changed since you lived here."

"It's crazy. Every time I walk around town or go out to eat, I see something I never thought I'd see here. Like Levi Pritchard walking down the street holding hands with that other guy. He's an actor, too, but I can never remember their names."

"Mmm, Carter Samuels. He's the hot one." Gabe leered at the road because they were going around the S curves on the east end of town and he had to keep his eyes on it.

"No." Lucas snorted. "Levi Pritchard is the hot one."

"It's prolly a toss-up."

"Never thought this would happen."

"What?" Taking a quick glance, he found Lucas looking at him, face very serious. "The town changing like this?"

"That, but more I never thought I'd be talking about hot guys with you."

Shit. "You know, Lu," Gabe began in his most conversational tone. "I think if we're gonna put the past behind us, we should maybe stop bringing it up."

He kept his focus solely on the highway for the next few silent seconds. They passed the urgent care clinic, and the tires were really humming on the wet pavement before Lucas said, "You're right. Except . . ."

Please, not one more thing he can blame me for. "Yeah?"

"You can still fill me in on all the dirt that's happened in the last twelve years. I mean, the gossip Mom wouldn't know."

Phew. "I can do that." Just telling him who all had married and divorced and slept with someone else's spouse would keep them in conversation until they hit Port Angeles.

CHAPTER FIVE

"*Who's that?*"

Gabe had been feeling guilty about dragging Lucas along with him to look at this horse, but after driving the guy all the way to Sequim and halfway back, not to mention waiting an hour and a half while Lucas bought up half an art supply store? He didn't feel the tiniest bit bad anymore. "That, my friend, is a hipsterman farmer."

"Oh, duh." Lucas's face was all screwed up as he peered out the windshield at Joshua Warburton, who was standing in the middle of his driveway and waving happily. "I guess hipsters have reached full cultural saturation, huh?"

"I don't know about them being cultured," Gabe muttered as he pulled the pickup to a stop. Joshua's wide straw hat brim came jogging up to the driver's side window, followed by his mustache, with his face bringing up the rear. He looked like he was dressed up to play Amish farmer for tour groups. His black blazer appeared two sizes too small, and the suspenders peeking out from underneath were the real deal—leather tabs and buttons rather than clips.

"Why would he wear white socks with black pants?" Lucas asked quietly.

"I think that's the least of his sins."

"Hey, Gabe," Joshua cried as he yanked the door open. "Glad you're here, man. Who's your friend?" He leaned across Gabe's lap, sticking out his hand for Lucas to take. "I'm Joshua Warburton, but you can call me Warburton."

This guy was so straight he didn't even realize how suggestive hovering over Gabe's groin was. Which was fortunate, because if it were a real offer, he would've had to turn it down, no regrets. Sharing a quick, amused look with his "friend," he answered, "This is Lucas Wilder. Just moved back to Bluewater Bay after some years in the big city." He slipped into his twangiest accent without even thinking about it. Joshua just provoked it out of him.

"I'm only here temporarily," Lucas said as they shook. "I came home for my best friend's wedding."

Oh, yeah. Couldn't forget that, could he?

"We don't have a lotta daylight left to burn," Gabe said too brusquely, but he *did* want his lap back sometime soon.

"Oh." Withdrawing from the cab of the truck, Joshua frowned. "You guys can't come inside and sit a spell? My wife made a pie."

"Sorry. Had to pick up some supplies." He hiked a thumb at the bed of the pickup before getting out of the truck. "Lucas'll want to get 'em put away right quick." 'Cause clay went bad so fast and all.

Lucas heard that as he rounded the front of the vehicle, and started to object. "Really, it's not that big—"

"A load. I know, you didn't get everything you want, sorry 'bout that." He clapped a hand on Joshua's shoulder, letting go as soon as possible. "Now, let's go see this stallion of yours."

As Joshua led them toward the red-and-white-painted barn, Lucas rolled his eyes.

Gabe shrugged and grimaced.

Lucas smirked back at him, then called to Joshua. "What kind of pie did your wife make, Warburton?"

Little shit. He might just eat a slice if Lucas would joke around with him some more, though.

"Mincemeat. It's an old family recipe. Well, someone's family. She found it on the internet?"

"Oh." Lucas made a gagging face as soon as Joshua wasn't looking over his shoulder at them anymore.

A whinny drew their attention to the horse in the barn's side lot, and a quick check confirmed it was a stallion, so that must be the one he was here to see. He was a pinto, with a large splash of black on his breast and another on his rump. Smaller spots dotted his belly and brisket, as if he'd kicked up some mud onto his white coat.

Gabe whistled because, seriously, that was a fine-looking beast.

"Wow," Lucas said softly. As they got closer, a jagged stripe down the stallion's back became visible, along with the splotches of color in his mane and tail. Even the feathers on his mostly white legs had some color.

The big reveal came as they reached the white-washed fence (how the hell much time and money did Joshua spend keeping the damn things clean? *City slicker*), the horse cantered over, mane and tail high and quirked.

"He's blue roan," he said in surprise, forgetting his twang.

"That's what Dr. Haakinson calls him," Joshua agreed.

Not a true one, but his markings were definitely black sprinkled with white hairs.

Well, hell. Laura had been right, the stallion was worth coming to check out. He was happy. Playful. Cantering in a ring around the paddock, he passed them once, then when he flew by again, he nipped off Joshua's hat without missing a beat.

"Hey!"

Gabe chuckled. Horse had good taste. Great taste, in fact—he halted midcorral and dropped the hat, planting one pale hoof directly on the crown, then took off again.

Must not like the Amish.

"See?" Joshua whined. "This is why I have to get rid of him—he's out of control."

Gabe bit his tongue on saying, *It's really about you.*

"He's just got spirit." Lucas was kinder than he would have been. Inhaling audibly, he added, "He's *beautiful*, though, which makes up for a lot."

"Sure does," he said just loud enough for Lucas to hear. The three of them were leaning on the fence, watching the horse do his thing. A playful stallion could be a real damn handful. If he took the beast, he'd be making an appointment on the way home with Laura.

Although how many blue pinto Friesians were there in the world? *Prolly not many.* A horse like this one would make some mighty fine-looking babies

"What's his name?"

"Blackberry," Joshua answered Lucas. "I call him Blackie."

"Why in tarnation did you name him that?" Gabe flinched inwardly even as he spoke, because who *ever* said tarnation? No one outside of a movie. Joshua didn't give him any funny looks, but Lucas sent him some serious side-eye.

"When he comes around again, look at the biggest spot on his flank." Just as Blackie took his turn along the far side, Joshua pointed. "There. It's shaped like a berry."

It was. "Wish I could unsee that," he muttered, and was rewarded with an amused grunt from Lucas. Even with the damn name, he wanted to take that horse on looks alone. Not enough of a reason, though. He needed more information. "Well, the day ain't getting any younger." Putting his boot on the bottom rail, he started climbing into the paddock. "Let's see how we get along up close and personal like."

If Lucas had been the one who'd gone into the paddock, he would have immediately jumped back over the fence, because Blackie came right for Gabe, eyes wild and doing a great impression of an enraged stallion. Gabe simply stood calmly, and at the last second Blackie shied and danced back a foot or two before halting.

Thank God he'd stopped before Lucas's heart had. Snorting softly, Blackie tentatively stretched out his neck, sniffing the hand Gabe offered up. Then he took a slow step forward, and another, letting Gabe stroke his nose. Nickering, he came even closer, until Gabe could scratch under his mane—something he had to reach up to do because the stallion was taller than the man by at least a foot. At the head, but that wasn't where they measured horses, was it? It was the withers.

The knowledge that Gabe was supposedly a very adept horse trainer had lurked in the back of Lucas's mind, but he'd never seen him in action before. When they were kids and teens, he'd rarely visited the Savage place, not unless Zach dragged him along. He didn't know an experienced wrangler from the standard Saturday night club boy in chaps, but watching Gabe with Blackie now, it was so clear that he *understood* that horse. Within five minutes, he had a halter on the stallion, and had clipped a lead rope under his chin.

"He's never that cooperative for me," Joshua whispered, and Lucas flinched. He'd been so caught up in the silent communication happening between man and beast he'd forgotten anyone else was around.

As if he'd heard the man, Blackie chose that moment to try to escape, tossing his head to dislodge the grip Gabe had under his chin. Well, attempting to dislodge it, but unsuccessfully. He danced back, pulling Gabe along, but clearly working for every inch of ground he gained. Lucas gasped when Blackie suddenly changed tactics and tried to rush forward, but Gabe planted a shoulder in the horse's chest and shoved him back.

And so ended the great equine rebellion. After that, Blackie resembled a meek lamb more than a stallion, following Gabe around the paddock, stopping the instant Gabe did, and even backing for him at some signal Lucas didn't catch.

"His ground manners are pretty good, once he knows you aren't gonna play," Gabe called over as he draped the lead rope across the stallion's neck and then let go of it, retreating a few steps. Blackie stood still, all his quivering attention focused on the human in front of him. After a few seconds, Gabe went back to him, murmuring and patting his neck. Muscles flickered under his hand, and Lucas felt what Blackie did as Gabe caressed him. Because he'd been there, hadn't he? Been gentled by that same stroke when he was scared and uncertain but desperately wanting to be touched.

Don't think about that now. If any more blood left his head, he'd have to breathe into a paper bag. Tearing his eyes from Gabe's fingers, he asked the guy next to him the first thing that came into his mind. "So, why Warburton instead of Joshua?"

Slouching, Warburton rested his chin on the top rail of the fence, next to his hand. "Joshua was the most popular boys' name in the US the year I was born."

"It's a nice name." It could certainly have been worse.

"I just wish my parents had chosen something . . ." He made a circular, searching gesture in the air with his fingers. "More unusual."

Oooooh. Thank God he had lots of experience soothing angsty hipsters. "I'm sure if they'd known how important being obscure would become for our generation, they would have."

Warburton blinked at him, then smiled. "That's nice of you to say."

"I'd like to put him under a harness," Gabe called then, and Warburton rushed off to the barn. "This won't take much longer, Lu. Sorry."

"It's fine." It was cool to see. More than cool. "I like watching you work." *Dammit.* Somehow, the "with him" got left off, even though that's what he'd *meant* to say. He could feel himself flushing, so he hid. Ducking his head and pretending interest in something on the ground near his feet.

Right then, Warburton showed up in the paddock with a mess of leather straps and hardware, so Lucas never had to hear what response Gabe would make to that, or even see his sly smirk. The guy already knew people found him appealing—exhibit A was twisting himself up in tack in an effort to help Gabe right this second—Lucas didn't need to feed his ego any more.

Instead he fed his own fascination. He didn't try to make any more conversation with Warburton once the guy joined him at the spectator's rail again, he simply got lost in the flow of horse and man working together. Blackie responded so readily to Gabe, even once he had blinders on and couldn't see him standing behind him, holding onto the long reins. The exercise seemed to be the precursor to pulling a plow or carriage. As Gabe followed him around, clucking and saying the odd word or two, Blackie would go faster, or slow down. Once he stopped and turned. They worked together smoothly, with only a few glitches that Lucas could recognize. Gabe clearly knew what he was doing, and had no doubts in his abilities.

That kind of confidence was sexy. Ridiculous as it was, Gabe's competence created a faint tightness in Lucas's abdomen. The first stage in his personal cycle of lust.

Thank God the show soon seemed to be over. Gabe was taking the harness off Blackie, murmuring to the horse and patting him once he was free. Then he came walking over to them, something in his stride almost menacing, and stood directly across from Warburton, squinting at him. "You're a darn fool, Joshua."

"Warburton," Lucas corrected, then realized he should shut up and stay out of this.

"Why?" The guy goggled.

"For giving him away." Gabe seemed oblivious to the horse trotting up behind him. "He's got a *yes* attitude, good conformation, his gaits are beautiful, the whole package. Didn't you say his sire is registered?"

Warburton nodded, then swallowed.

"And I know his dam is. You could prolly get a grand for him, easy, just on speculation about what kind of foals he'll throw, but you're just going to give him to me?" Gabe didn't even flinch when Blackie loomed over his shoulder, sniffing at their confrontation, but he did pat the curious head next to his ear.

Up close, the stallion was even more breathtaking. Lucas had never noticed the underlying structure of a horse's skull before, not quite like this, but the long arches of bone that described his nose were prominent under his skin, one on each side of his face. Nearly symmetrical, with tiny differences most people wouldn't see unless they were studying him this closely. A gray splotch curved up over the left side of his muzzle, in counterpoint to the bone arch, while most of the rest of his head was white. *Opposite in color but mirrored in line.* Possibly most amazing of all were his eyes—dark as expected, but with a light ring around the edges.

"—well, hell." For some reason, it was Gabe's mutter that pulled Lucas out of his haze rather than whatever argument they'd been having before. He watched as the guy scratched his head under the ball cap, then readjusted it a couple of times, folding the brim crosswise in his fist as he did it. "Guess I gotta take him, then," he finally said. He pierced Warburton with another narrow look as he added, "But if he comes out some kinda champion and I put him up for stud at a thousand bucks a whack, you're gonna hear from me."

Well, that was not threatening.

Warburton reached across the fence, grinning and nearly bouncing with happiness. "Deal. Shake on it."

Sitting in the cab of Gabe's pickup while the other two guys were loading the stallion into the trailer, Lucas was safe from any more inconvenient desires. For the time being. It was tempting to go out and watch them work, because it didn't sound like it was going well. There was the occasional raised voice, and more than once what sounded like a horse hoof hitting the side of the trailer.

He resisted temptation, though. Bluewater Bay was just west of the Olympic rain shadow, meaning they hadn't had to go very far east this morning before the weather had cleared. That meant right at the moment, he had early evening sun to drowse in as he checked out the contents of Gabe's dashboard. The guy was obviously a collector; one of those people who picked up every fascinating rock or piece of rusted antique tool. Had he always been like that? Lucas didn't know, but finding beauty in everyday things was a personality yardstick for him. Everyone he'd ever known who did so had always measured up.

Musing about that and idly surveying Gabe's collection, a bright bit of ribbon snagged his attention. At first he thought it was attached to some kind of seedpod Gabe had found fascinating, but as he peered at it, it resolved into an old flower. A faded and desiccated carnation that he couldn't stop staring at. Like it held some special meaning he couldn't put his finger on. Squinting harder, he leaned forward to get a better look.

The sound of the driver's side door opening startled the curiosity right out of him.

"Hey." Gabe looked good, with all the extra *o*'s. A rough, sexy, working man. His ball cap was in his hand, and his hair was messed up like he'd been running his fingers through it. His grin was huge, and his eyes were sparkling. The smudges of dirt on one cheek and his chin completed the picture.

Oh. My. God. I have to stop this. Lucas stretched and yawned before saying, "Hey," back. Meanwhile, Gabe was doing something in the space behind his seat.

"You want some water?" He pulled out a couple of small bottles and tossed one to Lucas. After twisting off the cap and chugging most of it down, he made that satisfied sigh people did and then finally climbed into the cab.

"So, Blackie's all loaded?"

"Yep." Laying his arm along the back of the bench seat—faint warmth and the ghost scent of horse and outdoors radiating off of it—he simply looked at Lucas. "He's never been in a trailer before. Finally got to see some of that feistiness Joshua was whining on about, but we got the stallion settled. Tell you what, though: I'm not keeping that stupid name. Gotta think of a new one for him."

Lucas nodded, gazing back at Gabe, not sure what the guy was expecting from him. "New name. Check." His brown-blue eyes looked so intense with the color that being outside all afternoon had brought to his cheeks. "So, um, Warburton has quite the straight-man crush on you."

Snorting, Gabe finally turned his attention to putting his key in the ignition. "Warburton." He chuckled.

"You were messing with him, weren't you? Talking like a huge redneck on purpose." While he used a lot of the local lingo, he didn't usually say stuff like "tarnation," as far as Lucas knew.

Of course, *no one* said that. Although Warburton was probably about to start.

"Well," Gabe began, dropping a wink his way as he started up the truck. "Urban folk have expectations about us hillbillies, and there's nothing I like better than to fulfill those expectations. Makes me feel like I'm doing the world a real service." The transmission clunked into gear as Gabe prepared to back up. Alternating between his side mirror and Lucas's, he fluidly worked the steering wheel, while Lucas was caught in a surreal state of awe, watching him.

He was so skilled at it. Moving the truck and trailer into a reverse turn slowly enough to get it right, but fast enough to reveal his expertise. Not too fast—not with the recklessness of someone showing off. *Drew would have done that.* Gabe didn't need to show off, because he knew what he was doing, and he knew he was doing it right.

Then Gabe halted the pickup, and his strong fingers wrapped around the gear shifter, just the tip peeking through his tight fist and the tension in Lucas's gut swooped lower, settling just behind his balls. Stage two of his personal cycle of lust. Well, three, actually.

Oh God. He was getting hard from watching a guy *back up a trailer*. So wrong.

But man, what he wouldn't give to be that gear shift knob right now, as Gabe tugged on it firmly, slipping it into drive without the slightest uncertainty.

"What's up, Lu? You got a funny look on your face."

Yes. Probably he did. "Uh, nothing, just thinking." And the expression was now probably offset by a lovely shade of red. Tearing his eyes away, he focused out the passenger-side window as Gabe started forward, pulling onto the road.

A few miles down the highway, once he'd fought off the new wave of lust, what Gabe had said earlier about intentionally acting like a big hick came back to haunt him. When his father had met Drew, Dad had seemed so painfully backwater. More redneck than Lucas recalled him being before. At the time, he'd chalked it up to changes in his own perspective, and how far he'd come from this tiny town.

It hadn't been that *he'd* become more cultured by comparison. No, it was his father's subtle mocking of Drew. And possibly of him too.

Which he'd totally deserved. "I'm an idiot."

"Wouldn't say you're an idiot," Gabe responded to his self-talking. "Just you aren't always the most observant guy in the world."

That hammered the nail right on the head. *Time for a little escapism.* "Do you care if I nap on the way back? I didn't get a lot of sleep last night."

"Fine with me. I texted your brother, and he'll pick you up at the farm."

Lucas bunched up his coat to use as a pillow, trapping the ball of fabric under his head. "That's cool." He'd have to unload and put away his supplies, anyway. Which reminded him. "Next time you want to use me as an excuse to avoid mincemeat pie, warn me first." He had to say the last part through a yawn, but he was confident Gabe understood it, based on the way the guy laughed.

Gabe had thought he and Lucas had gotten over some kind of hurdle today, but the pervading silence of their return trip made him wonder. Lucas had been awake since Bayview Ridge Cemetery, but didn't say a word all the way through town, or out to Gabe's place on the other side. He just rested his head against his window and watched the droplets of water form and then stream along with the speed of the vehicle. Or maybe he was watching the lights of town go by; Gabe didn't know and wouldn't ask. Something about Lucas felt melancholy almost, and his jaw had that slackness it got when he was lost in his own head.

When the pickup's headlights fell on the weathered side of the barn, Lucas stirred more, stretching and groaning.

"We're back," Gabe announced unnecessarily, to have something to say.

"I see that. Um, you need any help with Blackie?"

He was about to say no when the exterior yard lights came on, all but blinding him. A man's silhouette came out of the barn toward them. "That'll be Zach."

Lucas was shading his eyes, blinking, but Gabe could make out the confusion wrinkling up his brow. "He's been here waiting for us?"

"Someone had to feed the horses since I wasn't gonna make it back in time." It was near eight, and they expected dinner by six. Truth was, Momma could've done it just fine, but he'd had a whole other reason for calling Zach—other than just fetching Lucas. "He can help me get that stallion. You worry about your own stuff."

"Okay." Lucas rested his fingers on the door handle. "Um, thank you. For taking me to Sequim. It was pretty far outta your way, so if you want me to pay for gas—"

"I don't need you to do that."

Solemnly, Lucas nodded. "I was going to say you should bill my clients." Indicating his approaching brother with his head, he grinned. "That's one of 'em right there." He was climbing out of the pickup before Gabe could chuckle.

"Hey." Zach rapped on the driver's side window. "You gonna get out?"

"Quit your bitching," Gabe responded automatically, opening his own door.

Bringing a horse to a new home at night wasn't ideal, but at least they didn't have to introduce him to the others for a bit. Once they were in the barn July did a lot of whinnying, though, and Gabe had to keep a very tight grip on the stallion where the lead rope met his halter in order to keep him from bolting. Or challenging the gelding. That'd be the next test—he'd gotten along fine with his dam at Joshua's, but how would this horse do with new ones? Contrary to what he'd said or thought, Gabe hadn't called Laura on the way back, though. He'd see how the stallion mixed in with rest of them before he made a decision about getting him gelded.

Zach led the way down the aisle along the stables. "I got the stall on the end ready for him, like you asked. Next to June."

"Yeah, that's better than next to May. She's getting curmudgeonly in her old age." She was just as likely to kick him as to ignore him.

Once they had the stallion in his box and as settled as possible, he and Zach stood outside, watching over the half wall as he paced around and sniffed at things. There were a couple of flakes of hay, but he hadn't calmed enough for that.

"He's sure a looker," Zach said softly.

"You won't believe his trot. It's a thing of beauty. He's gonna make a hell of a picture pulling that carriage, if you get it restored in time."

Zach didn't even try to deny he'd been avoiding the job. "Funny how when it was June I was gonna be driving, I wasn't feeling real motivated, but now that I see this guy, I just might come up here tomorrow evening."

"Good. I'm sick of that thing taking up space in my shed." Zach had bought it over three months ago, full of ideas about proposing to Audrey during a ride along the streets of Bluewater Bay, but he'd dropped the ball. Or maybe he'd jumped the gun. Guy'd been eager to pin his woman down. The plan now was that Zach would finish it in time for the wedding, and then he'd drive his new bride from the Resort at Juan de Fuca's chapel to the reception hall, with a couple of extra loops around the grounds, since the chapel was about ten feet from their destination.

"I could take it down to Mom and Dad's, I guess—"

"I'm not serious. It's better up here, anyway. She's less likely to see it."

Zach turned to him. "You didn't tell Lu about it, did you?"

"Nope. I can keep a secret."

"So, you gonna have him gelded?"

"Lucas? No. Probably not getting this guy cut, either." He rested his arms on the stall wall, and the stallion nuzzled at them a second or two before moving on.

"No jokes about my brother's manhood," Zach said.

Good idea, because it was no joke. He kept that to himself, though.

CHAPTER SIX

*G*abe's plan to work Lucas out of his system had been unsuccessful so far. In fact, he figured he'd worked more of the guy into his system, if his inability to stop thinking about him was any indication. By Wednesday morning, when Lucas showed up in a teeny-tiny gray car after arriving in Audrey's white sedan Monday and Tuesday, Gabe was about sick of being largely ignored. So once Lucas was in the studio, he stopped by, going in through the doorway that connected his grandpa's former office with the barn. "Hey."

Lucas jerked his chin up, eyes already hazy and unfocused. Or maybe more focused on whatever was going on his head. "Hey."

Casually leaning his shoulder against the jamb, Gabe tried to get the ball rolling. "So, Holly's got your car figured out, then."

"Uh-huh." Lucas nodded, blinking. "Um, it was some kind of sensor in the engine. Or somewhere." Then he bent over that big mass of clay in front of him again.

"Good to hear."

"Thanks," Lucas mumbled.

That had been Gabe's cue to retreat and try again sometime when Lucas wasn't totally self-absorbed. Far as he could see, that was never, though. At least not those few days.

Fortunately, Zach showed up at the farm every evening that week to work on his carriage, so Gabe got to hang out with *someone* willing to talk to him.

"You gonna re-cover the seats with leather?" He took a sip from his beer, leaning against the wall of the machine shed and watching the guy work that night. Always nice to laze around while someone else did their chores.

"Of course." Zach snorted, reminding him of an indignant horse. "Only the best for my woman."

"Wouldn't want her dainty butt to suffer the touch of vinyl."

Picking up his own beer, Zach gulped some down, then scowled at him before bending to his job again. He'd finished the sides with a palm sander, but he had to smooth out the trim details by hand. It was a delicate job, and he'd been doing it for two days now. A testament to how much the guy wanted to get this perfect. It was kinda sweet.

"So, how're things going with my brother?"

Hell if that wasn't payback for mocking the dude's dedication to Audrey. Exhaling heavily through his nose, Gabe figured he might as well come clean. "Pretty sure he doesn't hate me." Lucas'd been doing a good job of avoiding him this week, though, in spite of coming up every day to spend time in that studio.

"Tell me something I don't know," Zach scoffed. "I'm pretty sure he *likes* you."

Coulda fooled him. Shoving off the wall, he wandered over to the workbench and picked up a crescent wrench for no particular reason. "Why the hell are you asking me about this?" Sure, they talked about their love lives when things became too obvious to ignore—like with Audrey—but this was different, wasn't it?

"Not like I don't know what happened between you two."

"Lemme guess," Gabe gave up his idle tool inspection and turned around to find Zach smirking at him. "Lucas told Audrey, and she told you. I'd already figured that one out."

"Oh yeah?" Zach was full-on grinning. "Now how's that?"

"The way you two were trying to make a love connection? I'd have to be brain dead to miss it."

"Just checking for signs of life." Zach chuckled and returned to his sanding while Gabe wandered back to his habitual holding-up-the-wall spot.

He couldn't claim he liked having Audrey and Zach know his business. Them focusing on what might happen between him and Lucas made it into a bigger deal than it should be. Plus, it'd make failure a bit harder to take. "What if we don't end up together? You gonna kick my ass for taking advantage of your little brother when he was young and innocent?"

"Well." Zach stood up, rubbing his lower back and then arching like he was stretching the muscles. "I'm thinking that you've had enough payback for 'taking advantage' of him." Straightening, he raised his brows at Gabe. "And if anything happens in the future? You're the party most likely to get hurt."

Gabe's snort didn't come out as derisively as he'd have liked. "Shit," he muttered. "Is it that obvious?"

"That you're into him for more than sex? It is to me. But I've known you a long time. I know you better than I know him. That kid." He shook his head. "Always been a bit of a mystery."

"He's not so hard to figure out. Long as you realize he's mostly living in his own world."

"Yeah, but what the hell goes on in there? That's what I don't get."

Gabe shrugged. Neither did he, not totally, but figuring Lucas out was a lot like training a horse. He had to read all the nonverbal cues and understand the basic nature of the beast, then they'd get along fine. He had that basic nature down—had since high school—and he was working on the nonverbal stuff, next step was to establish a bond of trust. Which was where he'd fucked up all these years, by staying away and letting misunderstandings erode any connection they'd had.

Not that he wanted to train Lucas, exactly.

"Think I'm done for tonight," Zach announced while wiping down his work with a soft cloth. "Actually, I'm done with all the sanding. I'll start varnishing her next time I'm up."

"You gonna be here tomorrow night?"

"Nope." He smiled, but Gabe had the feeling it wasn't for his benefit. "Audrey's taking the evening off, and we're having a date night."

"You're a besotted fool." Nice to see the guy getting what he'd always longed for, though.

Zach pointed at him, wearing a faux-serious frown. "And don't you forget it." Dropping his finger, he added as he walked out, "Wouldn't hurt you to indulge in a little besotment."

He couldn't argue, but it wasn't like it was all his choice. He followed Zach through the door, turning off the lights as he left.

Since it looked like Zach really was gonna get that carriage done in time, Gabe supposed he'd better have that stallion trained to pull it.

During a break in the rain Thursday afternoon, he stood at the pasture gate, watching Blackie alternately eating and running along the fence like a greyhound. Placid to hyper in point five seconds. Introducing the horse to the rest of his herd had gone all right; only May had any real issues with him. Young stallions tended toward the playful—and often the aggressive, but not this one so far—and his natural curiosity led him to try to engage with the old mare more than once. He got chased and nipped at for his trouble. Least she hadn't kicked him.

June tolerated the stallion's antics much like a grandmother would, which made sense because she was that, and July pretty much just followed Blackie's lead. Maybe that had been the gelding's problem all along: he only needed a friend his own age.

Blackie. He still had to come up with a better name.

It was tempting to just call him August and be done, but there was a family tradition to uphold—this horse wasn't born on the farm, although he was a direct descendant of January, Great Grandpa Savage's original Friesian mare. He really should fit both those qualifications, though. On the other hand, would anyone care after Gabe? He'd probably never have a son or daughter to pass the farm on to anyway.

"What are you doing?" Lucas called from over by the barn. When Gabe checked, the guy was heading toward him. First time Lucas had sought him out since they'd climbed out of the truck Sunday night. As he came closer, Gabe thought he could detect signs that Lucas was back in the land of the nonartistic humans, or whatever. For one thing, he wasn't drifting along in Gabe's general direction but walking with purpose toward him. He must have finished that big clay sculpture he'd been working on.

"So, what are you doing?" Lucas repeated, stopping next to him and placing his hands on his hips. He was a little out of breath. Guy should exercise more. Although his bare arms were surprisingly well-defined. 'Course, he played with mud all day, so he had to use them a lot.

"Thinking about names for that stallion."

"What do you have on the list so far?"

"Not much." He shrugged. "Horses that roan color are sometimes called 'Blue.'" Naming horses wasn't really his department. He suspected that was a family trait, considering the way they generally went about it.

Lucas made a face. "That's *so* original."

Well he had a point there. "Better'n 'Blackberry,' or 'Blackie.'"

"'Black and Blue'?" He had a little bit of dried orangey clay caked in the short hairs next to his ear. It made him look so young. And cute.

"That's no good—it'd just end up being shortened to 'Black' or 'Blue.'" Then they'd be back where they started.

"Bruise," Lucas said, as if talking to himself, brow knotting up as he gazed at the stallion lollygagging around. Then everything changed—his brow unknotted and his eyes went wide, as if he'd just made the most amazing discovery in the world. "Bruce!"

Gabe's blood raced and his pulse hammered. He *ached* to get that kind of excited pleasure from Lucas in response to something he did. To have Lucas turn toward him just like this—planting his hand on Gabe, not the damn fence rail—because it was *him*.

Not because the guy'd given a stupid horse a stupid name.

"Uh." Gabe had to clear his throat. "Guess that'd do."

All over again, Lucas's face screwed up as he gazed back at the stallion. "Or Hulk? Like, Bruce Banner is the Hulk? That's kinda . . . Sometimes my mind goes weird places."

Well, hell. That tinge of embarrassment on Lucas's cheek made Gabe's mind go weird places. *Cool your jets.* "Bruce is good. I can register him as Savage the Bruce, 'cause they like that long-ass fancy name shit."

"Why are you registering him at all?"

"I do it with any horse I might breed. It makes their foals more valuable."

Lucas's lips quivered like he was suppressing a smile. "I thought you were going to have him fixed."

"Gelded. Yeah, so did I, but . . ." He gestured toward the horse because that was the best explanation he could give. "Then I saw him. Can't believe he was an accident."

Lucas laughed. "You make it sound like his parents had to get married." The blue of his irises didn't warm up when he got happy, exactly, more like they thawed from glacial to Pacific Ocean.

Gabe smiled with him, but mostly because of his eyes. "Far as I know, pretty much no one *has* to get married anymore. They tend to go on and have the kid regardless. Not that I've been paying much attention."

"Me neither, but Audrey's been schooling me." Pushing away from the fence, Lucas hugged himself, rubbing his bare arms.

Need any help with that?

"Well, it's nice to know you don't have any harmful intentions toward Bruce's testicles."

I got some intentions toward yours, though. Goddammit, he needed to stop egging himself on.

Lucas tilted his head up, frowning at the gray sky. "It's still so cold for the end of April."

"You've been living in California too long. This is about normal." He stifled the urge to offer his coat. He had a sweatshirt on underneath it, he'd survive. But that seemed a little too intimate, and he didn't want to startle the guy and make him flee when they were getting along.

"I wonder if it's going to rain again," Lucas mused, still squinting at the clouds, before dropping his chin and focusing on Gabe again. "Oh, um, so tomorrow? I'm planning on doing a prefiring. It's cool if I use the wood in that shed where I dug the kiln?"

Wasn't much of a shed, just four posts holding up a tin roof. "That's why I put it there."

Lucas nodded, kicking at the ground. Lingering, like he had more to say. If so, he needed to get it said, because his lips were turning blue, and Gabe didn't know how much longer he could avoid offering to warm them up for the guy. "What's prefiring?"

"It's where I light a fire in the bottom of the pit and let it smolder all day to make sure the ground is dry enough to get a really hot temperature later. I'll also use the heat to burn off any residual moisture in the test sculpture I made. So, to get it going, I mean, it's kinda wet—"

"What do you need?"

"Some really pitchy wood?" Lucas bit his lip. "If you don't have any—"

"I'll haul some up there tonight." He had enough firewood to last through next winter. Momma and Gramma used a lot, but he hardly did. He'd had a furnace put in the barn a few years ago for his place. It heated the studio now too.

"Thanks." Lucas sighed, tense shoulders relaxing. What, he thought Gabe would refuse? "I was thinking about doing an overnight prefiring, but Audrey wants me to look at flowers for the wedding."

"Zach told me they had 'date night' tonight."

"Well, that's his date, I guess, because Audrey expects him to be there too."

"You're playing third wheel?" He could offer to be a fourth, but there was no earthly reason he needed to help with their floral arrangements.

"I guess." Lucas shrugged, then shivered, shimmying his shoulders.

"Let's go inside, get you warmed up." Gabe started toward the barn, but Lucas didn't follow.

"I have a coat in the car, and I need to go anyway." Lifting his hand, he gave an awkward half wave. "Um, so, see you tomorrow? I'm going to get an early start. I should be here by nine or so."

Nine was early? Gabe rubbed his chin to hide a quick smile. "All right." He nodded toward the newly christened Bruce. "I got a guy coming to take a look at him 'bout ten thirty."

"You're not selling him, are you?"

"No, I'm looking for horses to breed him to. This guy has Friesian and Friesian-cross broodmares, and I'm thinking we might work out a deal." All he'd had to do was send Earl a short video of Bruce—well, he'd been Blackie then—and he'd gotten a one-sentence email in reply the same day. *I'll be there Friday to take a gander at him.*

"You don't waste any time, huh?" The sideways glance Lucas sent him was strangely flirty, but then he dropped his gaze. Was that some kind of double entendre, or was Gabe thinking too wishfully?

He didn't know how to answer it if that was the case, so he replied to the question as if anyone had asked it. "Well, if Bruce wants to hang on to those testicles, he's gotta start proving their worth."

Lucas pressed his lips together, meeting Gabe's eyes, and he *knew* they were both thinking along the same lines, coming up with a myriad of responses: *If I had a dime for every guy who told me that*, or *Do you say that to all the boys?* and even the classic *That's what she said.*

I'd like to hold on to your *testicles.*

That last one might be just him. "Get a move on, or you'll catch cold."

Hunching his shoulders more, Lucas shivered again. "Okay, see ya." Then he hurried to his little gray car.

Watching him drive off, Gabe tried to parse out what had happened, there. He got vibes off the guy that told him Lucas would be open to more contact, but they were so faint he couldn't be sure it wasn't just how Lucas was, now. And, truth be told, Gabe intended to make damn sure Lucas wanted it to happen before he touched the guy. If they got together again, he wasn't interested in repeating the mistakes he'd made last time around.

Gabe made him nervous. A lot like the nerves Lucas'd had around him in high school, but for different reasons. As he got to the fork in the road that signaled he'd truly left Savage Tree Farm, a tightness in his chest eased, and he took his first deep breath since he'd suggested the name Bruce for that horse. The way Gabe had looked at him right after that had pierced through all Lucas's social walls and made him feel naked. It was uncomfortable, like every other time he suspected someone saw his dorky, socially maladapted, hidden self. As if he'd left the fly of his soul unzipped, and his tighty-whities were exposed.

It took him a while to realize that while the thought of all his flaws hanging out in front of Gabe unsettled him, it was also kind of hot. *That* was new, and he was pretty sure it was in this case only. Only half paying attention to the sharp curves of West Twin River Road, Lucas tried to pinpoint why the sense of being emotionally exposed to Gabe made his abdomen tighten with lust. He couldn't nail it down, but the more he thought about it, the hornier he got, until by the time he was on the highway and driving past the Bluewater Bay city limits sign, he was close to squirming.

It was embarrassing, even if no one could see. To make things worse, his embarrassment fed his lust, which fed the embarrassment. He was trapped in a desire feedback loop.

When he parked in front of Audrey's store, he was half-hard. Thank God he could take the exterior entrance to the apartment stairs and avoid her until she closed up shop. Getting out of the car escalated his excitement, though. A breeze was blowing off the strait, penetrating his jeans and briefs. The contrast between the wind and the heated blood filling his dick made him even stiffer.

There was only one thing to do. After letting himself into the foyer, he took the steps two at a time, unzipping on the way up, humiliatingly needy. He'd shoved his hand into his underwear and grabbed his dick before he was all the way through the door to his room. Slamming it shut behind him, he leaned against it and stroked himself, squeezing his eyes shut. Either trying to dispel the image of a knowingly smirking Gabe watching him, or trying to encourage it.

"You need it that bad, huh?" imaginary Gabe taunted, sending a final jolt of desire down through Lucas's core to his nuts, grasping them tight and wringing the cum out of him.

Afterwards, panting and sagging against the door while wiping his hand off on his shirt, he couldn't decide what was with the shame kink. He had his share of proclivities, but that had never been one. Did it have something to do with turning thirty? But that had happened months ago.

Was it a onetime thing, or would he want Gabe to make him grovel?

I draw the line at asking him to pee on me. Fortunately that thought wasn't even remotely appealing. When he and Gabe *did* get together, he'd just have to—

Oh.

Forgone conclusion. The only question in his mind about hooking up with Gabe was *how soon?*

Well, that cleared up one thing: if he wasn't positive Gabe wanted him as much as he wanted Gabe? Nothing about that fantasy he'd just had would have been hot.

A half hour later he was all cleaned up and presentable when Audrey came upstairs to fetch him for the flower viewing or whatever.

"C'mon." She flapped her hand in a *hurry up* motion as he left his room. "Your brother is meeting us there."

He shoved his arm into his leather jacket. "If Zach is going, why do I have to be there?"

"Two reasons." Which she counted off on her fingers. "First, you're the MOH, so you have to be at all things where a decision has to be made—"

He *did*?

"And second, I want someone who'll actually offer me a valuable opinion."

That stopped him just as he was taking the first step, but Audrey poked him in the back so he had to keep moving.

"I love your brother, but he's at a stage in our relationship where I can't do anything wrong," she explained as she followed him down. "Well, and he doesn't really give a damn about flowers. He'll just agree with whatever I say."

"Gotcha." From what he'd seen, his brother was overjoyed to be her yes-man at every opportunity.

Zach's behavior at the florists didn't change Lucas's opinion. One would think he'd just won a salmon derby or bagged a six-point buck with the way he beamed and rocked back on his heels, his thumbs hooked in the belt loops of his uniform pants. But he wasn't watching his prey take the prize, he was watching his bride-to-be debate color schemes and flower types.

For the first time, it occurred to Lucas that his brother might have been in love with Audrey far longer than six months. After all, Audrey had admitted to having a secret crush on Zach in high school, so the reverse could have been true. Even though Zach was a dick to her half the time back then.

"Lucas, what do you think of these narcissus?" Audrey demanded his attention before he could follow that train of thought any further.

"I think they'll clash with your dress." The ruby charmeuse would look horrible with such a stark white. It even clashed with her engagement ring. Oh, huh, he did have opinions about this process.

Some interminable time later, she'd settled on "antique cream" peonies for herself and her bridesmaids and various combinations of other flowers for specific purposes Lucas couldn't remember.

On the way back to her apartment, they picked up a pizza for dinner. By the time they were sitting at her island eating, he was totally over flowers. The thought of his upcoming MOH duties filled him with dread. "So what other appointments do you need me to go to with you before the wedding?"

She waved a negligent hand. "I'll write you a list with dates and times."

Oh, *that* did not bode well. *It's your best friend's—and brother's—wedding. Suck it up.* "I'll set alarms on my phone for each of them." Otherwise he'd never remember.

Audrey shot him a grateful smile as she chewed and swallowed. "There's one thing I think you might want to hand off to someone else, because it requires planning ahead." Squinting, she sized him up and down, at least as much as she could from her barstool. "The bachelorette party."

"Oh my *God.*" The hand he slapped over his mouth was too late to stop his horrified exclamation. Plus his fingers were greasy from the cheese.

Zach—sitting on Audrey's other side—snorted, but didn't otherwise offer an opinion.

"Yeah." Audrey pursed her lips. "I thought you might have that reaction. That's why I think you should let Kitty organize it."

Lucas was nodding before she finished. "Perfect. Your sister can do it. That's just fine by— *Ooooh.*" He pointed at her as the obvious hit him. "That will help make up for her not being the maid of honor, won't it?"

A smug brow tilt from her was confirmation enough.

"You're kind of an evil genius, you know that?" She awed him; he'd certainly never be able to manipulate anyone so deftly.

Preening, Audrey patted her hair, then helped herself to another slice.

After dinner, Lucas took the dirty dishes over to the sink while Audrey and Zach wandered to the door, arms around each other, murmuring. He averted his eyes because he didn't want to see their mushy good-bye scene. It didn't last long—he heard the latch click shut while he was still loading the first plate into the dishwasher.

It was as he was loading the last of the silverware that he heard it open again.

Then the murmurs started up all over.

Whirling around, he was just in time to see Zach disappearing into Audrey's boudoir with an overnight bag.

"Uhhhh . . ."

"Hmm?" Smiling softly to herself, Audrey was straightening up odds and ends lying around, which she did every night before going to bed.

"So, Zach's staying?"

She nodded, then snapped off the lamp on the end table. The dimness didn't seem to affect the shiny excitement in her eyes.

Oh, no. "Didn't you say he only stayed over on weekends?" He'd thought he had another day to buy the earplugs he kept forgetting to stop for.

She planted one hand on her hip. "I said *mostly* on weekends." Well, he'd managed to dampen her obvious joy a little. Not exactly a moment worthy of patting himself on the back.

But still. "Have you guys ever considered trying that abstinence-before-marriage thing? I hear it makes the wedding night really . . ."

Audrey narrowed her eyes at him. "We'll do our best to keep it down," she snapped, then she turned and marched behind her bookshelf/room divider.

Staring after her, Lucas tried to reassure himself. It *was* reasonable. They *were* all mature adults who understood that people in love did this . . . kind of thing. *He* certainly would expect his own fiancé to stay over in his own apartment whenever they wanted (if he actually had a fiancé). *I can handle this.* If they didn't make any noise, simply knowing what they were doing wouldn't be enough to freak him out, right?

Was that the sound of tongues slurping?

"Zach?" he called, cringing. He had to interrupt now, because very soon it would be way too late. "Do you have a sleeping bag I can borrow?"

A moment later, Zach replied, panting around his words. "Yeah, whatever. Go away."

"I concur," Audrey called, similarly breathless. "Leave."

Their voices were like nails on a chalkboard, but he couldn't escape quite yet. "Where would I find it?"

"Mom and Dad's garage, in the back, top shelf." At least, it sounded like *top shelf*, but that part was garbled, like his mouth had found something better to do.

Shudder. Lucas fled the scene.

Sneaking into his parents' garage was at the upper limit of Lucas's "stealth" abilities. He didn't have many to begin with, because he wasn't in the habit of burgling camping equipment (or anything else), but the situation demanded it. He couldn't simply knock on his parents' door and ask for the sleeping bag for the same reason he couldn't ask to crash on their couch: he'd have to explain why he wasn't staying at Audrey's. Seriously, he just didn't have the cojones to tell them he couldn't listen to Zach and Audrey making wild monkey love, even if his dad was high for the entirety of the conversation.

So instead, he parked on the street a few houses from theirs and walked as casually as possible down his parents' driveway. Ten feet from the garage, light burst forth like an illumination bomb, and Lucas's heart jumped back into the darkness behind him, taking his body with it.

Crouched next to the fence, palm over his chest to keep his rapid pulse from giving him away, he steeled himself for Dad to come charging out with his 12-gauge.

It took a good minute before he realized his parents must have invested in one of those motion sensor lights. Fortunately, there was an entrance on the house side of the garage, away from any dangerous fixtures primed to reveal him. He crept around the back of the building to get to it. When he opened the door, he was prepared for the screech of hinges, and kept the noise to a bare squeal by carefully turning the knob and inching it ajar.

Finding the sleeping bag was shockingly easy after that—it was the only thing on the top shelf in the back—although he did stub his toe on his father's planting bench, plus he had to pretend he couldn't hear the scrabbling of mice. He decided not to push his luck and look for an air mattress also.

Breaking and entering was surprisingly nerve-racking, considering he was (in essence) only borrowing stuff from his parents. His heart rate didn't return to normal until after he'd started his car (thank God for silent electrics) and driven all the way to the edge of town.

Where he turned left onto West Twin River Road.

He could see only one totally legitimate excuse for why he might need to sleep someplace other than Audrey's. He was going up to Gabe's place and lighting the prefire in the pit kiln now. If he fed it all night between naps, then he'd be able to do the main firing in the morning.

It *wasn't* a booty call. Did one bring one's own sleeping bag for a booty call? *I think not.*

His nervous system didn't buy that, though. It knew one didn't beat off to the thought of a guy in the afternoon, then show up that night at said guy's house without expecting a little something-something. He'd felt shaky since stealing the sleeping bag, but by the time he pulled up to the Savages' barn, his fingers were trembling. At least, when he wasn't white-knuckling the steering wheel.

Oh thank God, the lights in the second story were still on. For some reason knowing Gabe was still up was such a relief, Lucas slumped with it, bowing his spine and heaving out some tension with a huge breath. Closing his eyes, he gave himself a few moments. Then a few more.

Tap tap tap.

"Jesus!" If he weren't still wearing his seat belt, he would have hit his head on the roof.

"Sorry." Gabe's voice filtered through the closed driver's side window. "Didn't mean to scare you."

Unpeeling his hand from the steering wheel, Lucas found the latch and opened the door while Gabe backed off to give him room. "It's okay. I'm just kinda tense." One leg still in the car and one on the gravel drive, he waited for Gabe to ask the obvious question, marshaling his explanation for being here, now.

"I was about to call you," Gabe said instead, lifting his arm to reveal he was holding his phone.

"You were?" Like sometimes happened, Lucas's mind went staticky, trying to tune in to the response that he hadn't expected. *Booty call?* it offered.

"Yeah, your storage pod thing arrived about ten minutes ago." With the yard light behind him, Gabe's expression was unreadable, but the tilt of his head seemed amused. "Didn't you pass the truck on your way up?"

"Uhhh." He squinted, trying to see into his memory. Nothing. "I was sort of spacing off, I guess." Moving as if he were sore, he placed his other foot on the ground and then stood. "My pod." Corbin had gotten that taken care of pretty fast. "Isn't it late for a delivery?"

"Yeah, driver had some trouble finding the place."

Well, that wasn't surprising. "Where is it?"

Gabe stepped back, turning until Lucas could see the arch of his brow as he swept his hand out and pointed at the big white cube that had been perfectly visible the entire time.

"Man," Lucas groaned. "I'm not really— It's just, I had to leave Audrey's so I wouldn't overhear them going at it, and then I broke into my parents' garage to steal Zach's sleeping bag, and I thought—"

Gabe's warm palm squeezing his shoulder stopped Lucas's babbling in its tracks. "It's cool. I wouldn't wanna listen to them either."

"Aren't you wondering why I'm here?"

"Sure." Gabe faced Lucas and shoved his hands into his pockets. He stood only a few feet away, which was enough to start the tension swirling in Lucas's abdomen.

Or maybe it was the dorky way he'd forced the issue of his reason for coming. "I'm going to prefire the kiln tonight instead of in the morning."

Gabe's head bobbed to the side, as if agreeing and considering in the same motion. "Okay."

He should have just said *booty call.* Then they'd be kissing and pawing at each other instead of awkwardly standing there, staring.

"Lu?" Gabe asked softly, and Lucas's breath caught for a second.

"Yeah?" His body stretched toward Gabe, his muscles and bones lengthening and leaning in his direction.

"You gonna check the stuff in that storage thingy?"

Oh. "Um, yeah." He swallowed back his anticipation, pausing a few seconds before heading toward the cube. Behind him, the fading crunch of shoes on gravel told him Gabe was leaving.

Dammit. Not at all what he'd wanted.

Maybe I should just tell him what I do want.

Maybe. Sighing, Lucas sorted through the keys on his ring until he found the one that opened the storage unit.

CHAPTER SEVEN

*A*fter Lucas left that afternoon, Gabe had spent a couple of hours getting to know Bruce a little better. Now that he was in a new place, the stallion had become shy, refusing to come to Gabe of his own volition. He'd prick up his ears and watch Gabe with an unwavering focus whenever he got near. He'd even allow Gabe to approach, letting him take hold of his halter, but if Gabe simply stood there and waited for Bruce to make a move, the horse would eventually snort and whirl around to gallop off.

So that afternoon Gabe had tried a new tack and fetched some old apples from Momma's pantry, holding them out over the fence. May, June, and July trotted right up, but Bruce hung back, pacing frenetically from one side of the small herd to the other, before finally nosing July out of the way to get a treat and a pat from Gabe.

Success.

It had made him think of Lucas. Pretty much everything had since the guy had come back to town, but this time his thoughts were more above the belt than below. Normally, Gabe pursued any guy he was into, just like he'd been the instigator that night all those years ago. This time—and he was more and more certain there would be a this time—he wanted Lucas to invite his touch. He wanted some extra confirmation that he was welcome.

The simple idea was enough to heat him up a little, and preoccupy him all through stabling and feeding the horses, then dinner with Momma and Gramma.

Most of his thoughts on the subject were of the X-rated variety. That had been disconcerting, especially when Gramma asked if he thought that new stud was going to work out.

"I sure the hell hope so, but I don't know how interested he really is." Scooping more mashed potatoes onto his fork, he'd already put the food into his mouth before he realized they were both frowning at him.

He swallowed hastily. "In pulling that carriage. Don't know if he'll take to it."

"I thought you were gonna breed him," Gramma said.

Gabe choked on his own saliva, then had to wash it down with water. "Yep," he croaked. "Gonna breed him." He hated that word when applied to guys, but man, saying it out loud sent a bolt of sensation down his spine.

"Well." She pointed her spoon at him. "That's right smart, 'cause he's sure a beaut."

"He is that," Gabe mumbled into his napkin.

He might have covered his mistake to Gramma's satisfaction, but Momma didn't stop squinting at him suspiciously until he'd taken his dishes to the sink and rinsed them.

Having a big semitruck come barreling up the driveway had gotten him out of the house before she could corner him and start asking questions.

After the storage guy had left, when he'd seen another vehicle driving up to the barn, he'd known it was Lucas before he could make out more than the headlights. And when the guy opened his door, the faint vibes of interest he'd picked up this afternoon were so strong they'd about knocked him flat.

'Course, that could have been his own desire rebounding on him. Then Lucas had gazed at him, lips slightly parted and eyes going to soft-focus, but not zoning out on him—zoning in.

That was when Gabe decided that, even though he wouldn't make a move before hearing Lucas admit to wanting him, he'd help the situation along as much as possible. Give the guy as many opportunities as he could until Lucas finally did beg to be touched. By him.

Beg. He snorted at his wishful self, grabbed the things he'd need for the night, and headed out to bait the trap he was laying.

He made it to the shed before Lucas did, which was perfect. If he was already in situ when the guy showed up, it made his sleeping here more of an inevitability. And he was all for Lucas thinking of them getting together as inevitable, so anything he could do to reinforce that impression, he'd make happen. Lighting the camp lantern he'd brought, he then laid out his sleeping bag on the upwind side of the pit kiln. As he finished, Lucas walked into the circle of light, blinking at him.

"Oh." He was carrying about as much as a human possibly could, hugging a huge cardboard box to his middle with one hand, and holding a mess of tools in the other. One of them was a very long pair of tongs, which he had balanced on his shoulder with his bedroll hanging off the back end. "Hi?"

"Hey." Gabe stood and peeked into the carton to see those pieces of whatever Lucas had been making all week resting inside.

"So, you're gonna stay out here too?"

"Thought I'd better keep you company. Scare away the bears." He smiled and carefully lifted the box from Lucas's hold, setting it down next to his bag.

"Think the only bear I'm in danger from is you," Lucas mumbled.

You got that right.

As Lucas walked around to the opposite side of the pit and put the rest of his stuff down, his movements were a little jerky, and the color in his face seemed high. Gabe didn't know how to interpret those details. Did it mean he'd totally misread the guy and Lucas didn't want him around? Or did it mean he'd gotten it right and Lucas was nervous?

Whichever, it didn't much matter. Either way, Gabe would find out, and that's why he'd come up here—to find out exactly what Lucas wanted from him. With him.

For now he sat back on his haunches, attempting to seem as nonthreatening as possible. "What can I do to help?"

Yanking his head up, Lucas peered at him, wide-eyed. "Um, lay the kindling in the pit? I mean, lay the pitchy wood down in a way that allows air to—"

"'S'okay." Gabe winked, to take any sting off his words. "I can build a fire."

He had a few different methods for that, depending on what needed burning.

Gabe really knew how to light his fire.

Of course, Lucas had expected no less—the guy was the quintessential country boy. He could probably skin a deer with his teeth at the same time. Skills Lucas hadn't come close to learning while growing up in this town.

But Gabe's interest in what he was doing kept him from feeling inadequate. He'd been crouched next to the pit—on the nonsmoky side—since he'd laid out the kindling so perfectly an hour or so ago, watching Lucas's every move.

It made him feel a bit . . . on display. It was a dynamic he'd never expected to find anything other than uncomfortable, but in this case, he didn't completely hate the attention. It made him shy, sure, but also tingly at the same time.

Right now, Gabe was waiting for Lucas to explain why he was lowering the greenware onto the shelf surround he'd left halfway down the wall of the pit when he'd dug it.

"To make sure they're all fully dry before I fire them." He paused, tongs still gripping the precariously balanced leg piece he'd been placing. "Now that the flames have died down, it should be warm enough to drive off any residual moisture in the clay—" there, it would be stable enough, but not touching anything else. He let go of it and drew the tongs out, careful not to handle them too far down "—but not so hot it'll make the pieces explode."

Nodding, Gabe bent his head to the fire again, and Lucas felt the loss of connection between them like a death. A minor death—maybe a pet finch, or a mouse: something small, but not unnoteworthy. A tiny—

"C'mere." Gabe beckoned as he shifted to sitting, resting his back against the stack of firewood. "You got everything organized, and the fire's nearly all coals, so let's just wait a bit. 'Sides, you're standing in the smoke."

It was true, although it had died down so that there was very little wafting out. Enough to occasionally sting his eyes, though.

He had no reason to stay here, and lots of reasons to go sit next to Gabe. Dragging the tongs behind him, he made his way around and then dropped down next to him. Close enough to sense that heightened awareness two attracted bodies created, but not close enough to smell him. "It only needs to be fed enough to keep it burning cleanly," he babbled, nodding at the kiln. "Like, perfect for marshmallows." It was nearly there now—popping and crackling actively still, but almost to that point where the fire would seem to be sleeping, if not for the intense heat and light. The hibernating dragon stage. A strangely romantic one.

"Mmm." Gabe nodded. His hands were clasped over his kneecaps, fingers digging in and hanging tight. Was he tense, sitting that way? Did he want to be doing something else, like holding Lucas close and tight?

I beat off thinking about you when I got home, nearly percolated out of him, offering Gabe the ultimate opportunity. That was what he needed, wasn't it? If Lucas just put himself far enough out there, Gabe would take him up on the offer. "You don't have to stay. Not if you don't want to."

Almost as bad as admitting to masturbating.

Gabe clenched his teeth, or did something else that made his whole jaw flex. "Are you saying you want me to leave?"

"No." His heart *thunked* heavily. "I'd like it if you kept me company."

Swinging his head around, Gabe met his gaze, then his eyes fell to Lucas's mouth for a few taut seconds. Lucas leaned closer, tilting his chin, so very, very ready to be touched by Gabe. It would be different than their last first kiss—Lucas wouldn't be immobile from shock. He parted his lips and waited for Gabe to close the distance between them.

"I'll stay, then," Gabe said, completely ignoring Lucas's assumptions and hopes. Worse, he turned back to the fire. "So. Did your ex send you that storage pod?"

Scrambling to catch up to the sudden mood and subject change, he answered, "No, my friend Corbin did. I'd been staying at his place for the last few months since Drew and I broke up." Wait, did this have something to do with why Gabe hadn't made a move? "I don't really talk to him. My ex." He didn't really want to talk *about* him, either, at least not now. Leaning forward, he poked at the fire with the tongs.

"Why's that?" Obviously, Gabe *did* want to talk about him.

"Um." Lucas tried to deflect. "How do you know about him?"

"Well, word gets around in a place as small as Bluewater Bay."

"I remember." Like about one possibly being gay, which had pretty much ruled his social interactions in high school. "So what's the gossip?"

"Word is he cheated on you and you walked out." In Lucas's peripheral vision, Gabe's tensed fingers eased, and his legs shifted, like he'd rested his full weight on his back, where maybe before he'd been holding himself a bit rigid.

The guy *was* nervous. Or had been. Why wasn't he now?

"Sort of." Grimacing, Lucas traced a design in the dirt between his feet, the unwieldy tongs nearly overbalancing into the pit kiln before he yanked them back and tossed them over by the side of the shed, nearly out of the cocoon of light and warmth. "It wasn't cheating, exactly."

"Mmm." Gabe's chin dipped in his peripheral vision. "What exactly was it?"

He'd never felt so stupid in his life. Or gullible. "It was him breaking some rules. We had an open relationship?" Glancing over, he looked for signs of confusion—for all he knew, open relationships hadn't reached this part of the world, yet.

"I couldn't do that. Let my guy sleep with someone else." Gabe met his gaze levelly. "Not if I was serious enough about someone to live with him."

Lucas swallowed, consciously holding himself back from going in for another attempted kiss, even though they were within such an intimate distance, and most of his onboard systems were signaling it was a *go*. *That's what you thought last time. Focus on the conversation.* "Hooking up outside of our, um, partnership was supposed to be casual only."

A dry smile flickered across Gabe's face. "I take it, at least one time, it wasn't."

"Last fall, I went to Missoula to do an artist's residency for three months, and that whole time Drew was having *uncasual* sex with another guy." A younger, blond guy, who worked out at a gym and painted abstracted landscapes. A guy who didn't *craft*, like Lucas did.

"Now, that had to suck." For a split second, Gabe leaned toward him, pressing his shoulder against Lucas's sympathetically. Then he straightened up, facing front again.

If only it had *sucked.* "To tell you the truth," Lucas confessed. "I was kind of relieved when I found out I had a reason to break it off with Drew." Saying it out loud made him woozy, and he had to pull up his legs and hang his head between his knees for a second or two.

"Sounds like you already had a reason for leaving." Gabe's hand landed on his back a second, comforting and sizzling at the same time, but then it slid off.

He couldn't focus on that touch, because now he was lost in the shame of what he'd let happen. It was so hard to explain, and Lucas's quick shrug wasn't enough of an answer, not anymore. Taking a deep breath, he straightened up, trying to decide what to say, since this would be the first time he'd talked about it. Admitted to the reality of it. "When I got off the plane from Missoula, he was there to meet me, standing right outside security, and seeing him . . ." He shook his head. "It was like getting sacked by a linebacker. He *looked* different."

"He changed that much while you were gone, huh?"

"No." Lucas hugged his shins, letting his spine slump again. "He was exactly the same. Same square-framed glasses, same sandy hair cropped close to his head, same tiny goatee. I even recognized the jeans he was wearing. He spent hours before I left agonizing over the hem length. Not too long, but just short enough to show a little bit of sock when he wore his loafers."

Gabe groaned. "A hipster."

Resting his chin on his kneecap, Lucas nodded. It had been something underneath that outward shell that was completely different from the man he'd first fallen for. As if he were an alien being inhabiting a human, subtly shifting his host's physiology to suit his needs. At least, at first Lucas thought it was Drew who'd changed, but later he began to wonder if it was him, or possibly both of them together. "It was like he didn't fit me anymore."

"I hear you," Gabe murmured.

"So when he told me about the other guy, I left. It was the perfect excuse, you know?" He needed to see Gabe's expression, maybe to gauge how messed up he was by how disgusted the guy looked.

He was frowning, but thoughtfully. "I guess sometimes we don't see the reality of a thing until we leave it, then come back."

"I took the easy way out," he said, just in case Gabe didn't understand. "Because at some point in the last few years, I'd fallen out of love with him, and I was too self-involved to even notice."

Gabe's frown softened, and even curled into a small smile. "You sure know how to beat yourself up, but good."

Blinking repeatedly didn't help that make any more sense.

Sighing, Gabe shifted, turning his body more toward Lucas's, resting just his left shoulder on the woodpile, now. "Lots of people get stuck in relationship ruts, Lu. Then one day they wake up for some reason. Happens all the time."

"Has it ever happened to you?" Why should the thought of Gabe being in a relationship he knew nothing about bother him?

"Not really. But I've been on the listening end of it happening to someone else a time or two."

Oh, so no big breakups in his past? Or breakups for a different reason? He wished he had the balls to ask, or even knew why he was scared to. Staring at the coals again, he got lost in thought, and the next thing he knew, Gabe's huge hand was stroking his back again. In small, soothing circles, like his mother used to do when saying good-night to him.

Then Gabe's fingers dipped lower, to the waistband of his jeans, in a very nonmaternal way. Lucas squeezed his eyes shut and froze, waiting to see what Gabe would do. *Go further. Go further.*

Once again Gabe pulled away. The rustle of clothes next to him told Lucas that Gabe was moving a lot. Then standing up.

"I'm gonna go to the little boy's tree one more time, then hit the sack."

Shit. "Okay," Lucas croaked, then cleared his throat and finally opened his eyes. "I'll load some wood on, then go to sleep too."

What the hell did he have to do to get Gabe to *really* touch him?

CHAPTER EIGHT

*T*oo bad he'd laid his sleeping bag out on the other side of the kiln from Gabe. He should have moved it right next to his while Gabe was answering the call of nature, but he'd been too uncertain about exactly what was happening between them. It seemed, most of the time, as if Gabe wanted him, but he was holding back. Waiting for something from Lucas, presumably, but Lucas couldn't understand what.

So instead, he only moved his bag close enough to Gabe's to be upwind from the drift of smoke that the fire was still putting out. About a third of the pit circumference lay between them. Gabe had returned just as Lucas was crawling into his bed, still wearing his jeans and hoodie since he'd have to keep getting up, at least if he was going to stoke the fire.

"G'night," was all Gabe had said before turning out the camp lantern and settling in. Once he was covered up, though, he'd whipped his shirt off over his head, but it wasn't any kind of signal as far as Lucas could tell. After that he'd simply curled onto his side, facing Lucas, and closed his eyes.

And now they were both sacked in for the night. The silence wasn't awkward, exactly, more like expectant. On his part only, though, because Gabe appeared to be sleeping. One naked, brawny arm was hugging the outside of his sleeping bag, and he had his hand tucked under his head, biceps bulging alluringly. Lucas couldn't stop studying him. Tracing the shapes that made up the whole man. The mellow light threw his face into relief, like an inky art print that only described the shadows of a person, but somehow captured their true countenance. A duochromatic image, flickering orangey and black.

And then the glimmer of an eye.

Gabe was watching Lucas watch him.

The needle on the awkward meter jumped, but Lucas's lustmeter redlined. He was instantly out of breath and the tightness of desire pervaded his whole body. *What do I do to make this happen?* Licking dry lips, he asked, "Are you gonna make a move on me, or what?"

It took a second before Gabe answered, his voice deeper than normal. "Do you want me to?"

Yes. "I don't *not* want you to. I mean, we're both here, and . . ."

"This isn't like that last time, Lu." Gabe pushed up onto his elbow, revealing some of his red-gold chest hair and one dark nipple. "No misunderstandings— You gotta ask me for it."

Oh God, he wants me to beg. Ungh. "Please," he whispered. "Come over here and get naked with me." Even as he was saying the words, Gabe was crawling out of the sleeping bag. Lucas tried to untangle himself from his, wanting to meet him halfway, but he had to pull in a lungful of air and finish it. Ask for what he really wanted. "Let me suck your dick."

Gabe was on top of him before Lucas managed to free his legs. Wrapping one arm around his waist and nudging him onto his back while his hot breath blew into Lucas's face. "Say that again."

"I want to suck your cock," Lucas repeated. The clinging smell of woodsmoke nearly overpowered Gabe's natural scent, but it was there, and that strange familiarity Lucas had experienced the first time he'd seen the guy last week returned. That sense of the past and present both being *now*. It also primed him, renewing bodily memories of Gabe touching him twelve years before, making desire pump even harder through him.

"Thank God," he whispered to himself, lips almost brushing against Gabe's. *Kissing in three, two, o—*

Gabe drew himself back from Lucas, looking down at him. "Why's that?"

Now that they'd finally gotten to this moment, where Lucas could run his hands all over Gabe's skin and trace the shapes of his muscles and bones, he couldn't make himself do it, not until he got some signal from Gabe that it was really going to happen. "I've been trying to figure out how to get you to touch me all night."

"All you had to do was tell me what you wanted." He still didn't move, not for many seconds. Waiting for more?

"I want . . . to be naked." He bit his lip to kill an embarrassed smile.

"That all?" Gabe's expression was so serious. Demanding. Anticipation seeped through Lucas, right alongside squirming self-consciousness, and for a second he flashed back to this afternoon, when he'd jacked off to thoughts of Gabe being exactly like this.

"I want—" He had to pause for breath. "I want to feel your body against mine. And I want—I want to wrap my fingers around your dick."

Finally Gabe came to him, lowering his head and searching with cold fingers under Lucas's shirt and sweatshirt. "We can make that happen."

Lucas let his own hands fly free, skimming up Gabe's chest, getting tangled in hair. A hard nipple caught at his palm, so he stopped to rub it. "Then I get to suck you," he said, but most of that was muffled by Gabe's mouth.

Gabe's kiss this time was nothing like the one many years before—there was no hesitation on Lucas's part about opening wide for him, and none on Gabe's part about sliding in deep and drawing him out. Wrapped up in the taste of Gabe, and the heft and solidity of his hairy body, Lucas barely noticed taking off his shirt, but he was completely conscious of the texture of Gabe's skin. His back was smooth, while his chest was crinkly with hair and brawny with huge, firm pectoral muscles that Lucas couldn't stop running his hands across.

Then Gabe was pulling him back, gripping Lucas's hair in his fingers. Ending their kiss. Panting and dazed, Lucas waited for whatever came next.

"Just a sec." Gabe pushed up, taking all his body heat with him, and the cold, damp air washed over Lucas's exposed skin. He shuddered and was about to complain, but Gabe was back. Carrying his sleeping bag. "It's cold."

Crouching down, he nudged Lucas over, then stood again. The light from the coals spotlighted his groin and the way the front of his sweats bulged, hugging the package inside. The line of his dick was clear, bowing out and up to the right.

Need to taste that.

Lucas was rising up to his knees, reaching for the waistband, when Gabe bent over.

Oh. "What're you— How did you know these sleeping bags could zip together?"

"Zach and I got the same ones at the same sale." Lying down, Gabe scooted closer as he pulled the zipper up, working his free arm under Lucas's head. He paused momentarily for a quick kiss.

Lucas grabbed Gabe's hair, trying to get him to come back for more, but Gabe resisted as he finished his job. "Please tell me you and *Zach* don't zip these bags together."

"Hell no." Gabe grinned, finally done, focusing on him again. Playful now. "Only person I mated this bag to that one for is you."

"What a sweet thing to say."

Gabe got serious again, watching silently as he peeled off Lucas's jeans, cupping his dick though his briefs. Digging underneath, he gripped it in his fingers, stroking.

"Oh God." Lucas bucked his hips, shoving further inside Gabe's grip, until Gabe let go to shuck his own pants and Lucas worked his underwear the rest of the way off. He was totally focused on Gabe, though, waiting for the big reveal. To see if what he remembered was as good as the real thing.

The real thing sprang out from under the elastic waistband, and it was better, at least from the little he could see in this light. Fatter and veinier, thickest in the middle and tapering to the head, then flaring out again. "You go commando."

So hot. He threw his leg over Gabe's thigh before the guy had his sweats all the way off and pressed against him, seeking out Gabe's cock with his own by feel, until they bumped and rubbed each other. Gabe groaned and wrapped his arms around Lucas, one huge hand palming his ass.

Suddenly his world spun, but it was only Gabe rolling them until he was on top, smothering Lucas in heat and skin and the scent of sex. He *totally* knew how to make something burn. Rocking, he ground their dicks together, skirting that perfect boundary of pleasure and pain. As hot as the fire in the pit, and just as searing. Lucas arched his spine, opening wide and wrapping his legs around Gabe's, dragging the sensitive soles of his feet up Gabe's calves, then gripping Gabe's hips between his thighs, until the friction created between hair and skin scalded his nerve endings.

"I thought," he started, but Gabe kissed him, curling his tongue under Lucas's and then around it before pushing away, propping his upper body with his arms and putting more power into his thrusts. Pulling back farther, dragging his balls against Lucas's.

Things were going blurry. *Probably lack of blood.* Every drop of it was pounding through his groin right now.

"You got something to say?"

Oh, yeah. "I thought I was going to blow you," he panted.

"You wanna stop this?" That taunting note in his voice was *perfect.*

"*No.*" Wrapping his arms around Gabe's shoulders and his legs tighter around Gabe's thighs, he strained to press them closer together, to absorb all of Gabe's weight and heat. "Please don't stop."

"That's what you said last time."

"I remember." He shivered with it. "I mean it in a totally different way. Except the same." *So close.* The base of his dick throbbed with his pulse, and it was starting to beat in his eardrums too. "I thought we weren't supposed to bring up the past anymore."

"Sorry." As if in apology, Gabe changed his rhythm, circling his hips and massaging the most responsive of Lucas's sweet spots, right under the head.

"I think—" Lucas gasped, his toes curling up on themselves. "Think 'm about to—"

"Yeah," Gabe grunted, then his cock jerked and shuddered, and his cum began spilling out onto Lucas's dick and belly. Warm and slippery, and Lucas could swear it was calling to him, demanding his nuts tighten and his muscles seize up and push out his own orgasm. He was still coming when Gabe semicollapsed on top of him, gripping the back of his head and engulfing his mouth, kissing him through the rest of it.

In the quiet afterward, once Gabe had stopped kissing him and moved so that he had an arm around Lucas's abdomen and his head on Lucas's chest, everything glowed. The coals that reflected off the roof of the shed, and Lucas's mood and his genitalia, and even the strands of Gabe's hair he was twirling languidly around his index finger.

He hadn't had sex that good in forever. A lot like their first time: a blur of sensation and desire and a mix of emotions he wasn't sure he understood. It hadn't just been good, it had been epic. Who knew why? Maybe because he'd come full circle—gone from his first lover, through a bunch of others, and was now back to that first guy. Whatever, he hadn't gotten off like that for . . . *twelve years*. Jerking in surprise, he accidentally yanked his hand back, pulling on Gabe's scalp.

"Hey," Gabe mumbled, then lifted his head, blinking sleepily.

"Sorry," Lucas said, cupping Gabe's cheek for a second, then stretching for a quick kiss. "I must have fallen asleep."

Nodding and yawning, Gabe pushed off of him, which was a bit of a relief—he was a big guy—but also a loss. Then he dug down into the depths of the sleeping bags for something. When he'd found it, he started wiping up the cum from their abdomens with it.

Lucas smiled and stretched. "That isn't my shirt, is it?" He hadn't brought another one, but at the moment he didn't really care.

Smirking, Gabe pulled out the impromptu cum rag. "Your briefs." He tossed them over toward the empty cardboard box.

"That's fine." Lucas rolled onto his side in response to Gabe's nudges. "I can go commando too."

Spooning him, Gabe *mmm*ed against the skin of his neck, and it resonated down Lucas's spine. He relaxed into the body heat with a sigh, wrapping their fingers together on his chest.

Gabe kissed his nape, then scraped his whiskery chin across it, making Lucas squirm. "I hope you know this wasn't a one-time thing."

The after-sex glow warmed him again, like slowly dying coals flaring in a breeze. "I know."

In the morning, when Gabe woke up, he was torn between letting Lucas sleep and waking him too. There wasn't time for them to fool around—he was already late for feeding the horses—but he nearly did it anyway out of a need to figure out what was going to happen between them.

That seemed like an awfully damn clingy move. Besides, Lucas had gotten up a couple of times in the night to feed that fire, and probably needed his rest. So instead, Gabe slid out of the bedding, trying not to let in too much freezing air, and got dressed as silently as he could, in spite of his chattering teeth. It wasn't raining at the moment—only lightly sprinkling—but it would be one of those days where the heavens would be pissing on them one way or another for the duration. Least it wasn't windy, only cold and wet.

Before he left, he took one more good look at Lucas, or at least his dark-brown hair, which was the only thing visible outside of the bag. Did the guy have the right clothes for a day like this? If Gabe came back up later, he'd double-check that Lucas didn't need a raincoat or something.

Then he made himself walk down toward the barn, knowing full well there was no *if* about him coming back. Probably as soon as he'd finished his chores.

He didn't have to, though. After he'd fed and watered the horses, brought firewood up to Momma and Gramma at the main house—where they'd forced him to eat a piece of toast and drink some coffee before he could leave—he came back to the barn to find Lucas standing in the doorway between the stables and his studio.

"Hi." Lucas smiled at him, faded-blue eyes soft and brown hair tousled. The picture of relaxed and happy.

Tension he hadn't wanted to acknowledge he was carrying eased out of Gabe's shoulders at the sight, and he headed straight for him, not stopping until he was close enough to reach out and pull Lucas to him. "Hey." He wrapped his arms around the guy's back. God, he was short. His forehead barely came up to Gabe's lips. He grazed his jaw across it, getting Lucas's hair tangled in his whiskers.

Showing no hesitation, Lucas slid his hands up Gabe's chest, then lifted his chin.

That looked like a request for a kiss, so Gabe gave him one, brushing his lips across Lucas's a few times before going deeper. The guy deserved a proper good morning, after all, even if Gabe didn't have the time for an improper one.

Under his fingers, Lucas's cheek was just starting to feel scratchy from lack of shaving, and he tasted like sex and morning breath.

Surprisingly hot combination. Gabe was settling in for a short make-out session when Lucas ended their kiss and pulled back far enough to meet his eyes. "I need to get that kiln up to firing temperature this morning."

"Want any help?" He had a shit-ton to do before Earl got here, but maybe he could fudge some of the details. Bruce didn't have to be one hundred percent groomed, did he?

"I'm fine." Lucas cupped the back of Gabe's neck. "It's not that hard. I just have to bring up the horse manure, everything else is there. Oh, but can I borrow that big rake thing you use to clean the stables?"

"'Course." At least Lucas's preoccupation with May's taking a dump was starting to make sense. "What're you gonna do with the manure?"

"It goes on top of the fire."

Huh.

Dropping his arms, Lucas started stacking his hands to illustrate as he explained. "I put a bunch of the firewood in the bottom on top of the coals, then the metal grate I brought up?"

Gabe nodded, remembering the round steel screen resting against a corner post. It would be just about right to fit across that shelf Lucas had left in the pit.

"Then I put the pots on the grate, arrange more wood around them, but so they won't get crushed, and pile manure on top of it all."

It was probably best to give him the benefit of the doubt and not second-guess that he knew what he was doing. Still. "Gonna have to work pretty damn fast to keep it from blazing up on you while you're stacking it."

Confidently, Lucas nodded before turning to look toward the kiln shed, even though there was a solid barn wall between it and him. He could probably see it just fine in his imagination. "Anyway, once it's all going, I'll throw that extra metal roofing you gave me on top, then return to town." His hands landed on Gabe's biceps, and his attention was back on him for a moment. "You don't care if it burns itself out without me around, right? There's no fire danger on a day like today, and it's mostly going to smolder once I cover it."

"It's fine." Of course the guy had to leave. He'd barely brought any clothes. Gabe had known that, but he tightened his hold on Lucas anyway. "Think Zach'll stay at Audrey's again?"

Lucas nodded, frowning down toward the ground and absentmindedly picking at the fabric of Gabe's coat sleeve. "Probably all weekend."

"You could stay here if you want." His heart lurched. "At my place."

Lucas flashed him a quick glance. "I need to take a shower, and all my stuff is at Audrey's, so . . ."

Gabe's brain scrambled to come up with a way to get him in *his* shower. "I got a spare toothbrush lying around. Not sure where it came from, though."

Lucas pressed his lips together, like he was trying to keep something inside.

What could that be? Gabe watched him struggle to keep a smile from blooming.

"I think that probably came from Seth Larson."

Oh, hell. "I guess you don't wanna use it, then." He wouldn't in Lucas's position, at least, should he be in that position. Not if he wanted himself to come back as much as he wanted Lucas to come back. *You are tying yourself up in knots, dude. Cool off.*

"I have to be here later to take out the fired pieces, but I could plan on staying? Bring some stuff to wear tomorrow?"

And Sunday. He kept that to himself, only nodding. "Why don't you get here in time for dinner, then? I was going to make some elk steak." At least, he was if Lucas was going to be eating it.

Judging by the way the guy's eyes lit up, that appealed to him. "I haven't had good venison in *forever.*" He looked just as excited and pleased as he had when he'd named the stallion.

Well, damn. It wasn't exactly him reacting to Gabe, but they were getting closer to the genuine article.

Inspiration hit Lucas as he was driving away from Gabe's farm. *Peonies.*

The image of Audrey's chosen flower popped up in his brain like a slide, each external petal backlit, and he had it. The germ of the idea for her wedding favors.

He'd never been able to lay his finger on what prompted a brainstorm, but this time he decided to chalk it up to fantastic sex. Because: *wow*.

Thank God Gabe had never left Bluewater Bay. A guy like him would have been snatched up in a hot second. He was a totally macho top (Lucas was pretty sure), *and* a ginger with a beautiful dick.

Plus, of course, that thing about him being a real and actual lumberjack.

At any club in Los Angeles, Lucas would have to beat the queens off with a stick—and possibly a machete. Which he'd totally do because poor Gabe would stand there, bewildered by the attention and helpless with confusion. And be utterly endearing in the process.

Not happening. He'd never take Gabe to a place like that. It would be cruel. Being lusted after for the stereotype he represented would make him feel cheap. Plus, if Gabe ever saw how many guys he could have, and of what caliber, Lucas would never stand a chance. He very, very much wanted to stand a chance with Gabe Savage.

More so than he could comfortably think about.

So. Peonies.

He'd never made sculptural assemblages before, but it was really intriguing, even before pulling the pieces out of the fire. Maybe, if this test went well, for Audrey's wedding he'd make small groupings that could be multiple figurative objects, or just one linked together. He thought it over most of the way back to town, but by the time he'd parked in front of Tiffany's Breakfast, he was fixated on Gabe again.

The man was potent. No wonder Lucas had briefly considered—for about a second—staying in Bluewater Bay all those years ago. Gabe packed a wallop. In fact, his magnetism was so great, it was a wonder Lucas had managed to evade it at all.

"Hey!" *Rap-rap-rap.* Zach, that fucker, was standing beside his window wearing a shit-eating grin.

"Yes?" Lucas hollered though the glass.

"Where were you last night?" Smirking, Zach rocked back on his heels like he had all day, but his car keys were in his hand and he had his uniform on. He must have been on his way to work.

Lucas could probably outlast him. He faked misunderstanding, mouthing *What?* and pointing at his ears until his brother rolled his eyes and crossed the street to his pickup, still smiling to himself.

Asshole. Did Lucas give Zach crap about his sexual escapades with Audrey? *No.*

Pushing away the thought that he just might have given Zach a hard time if Zach hadn't convinced Audrey to marry him (and God knew how that had happened), he got out of the car and let himself into the exterior entrance.

Where Audrey was waiting.

"Oh, hellooooo," she crooned, rising from an overstuffed, art deco chair he'd never seen in this foyer before. "So glad you found your way home."

"Um, it's not that difficult." He'd been finding his way home from Savage Tree Farm for over a week.

"It's not," Audrey agreed, far, far too willingly. "In the evening. But this is the next morning, which means a whole new angle upon which to—"

"Shut up."

That worked long enough for him to bound halfway up the staircase.

"So that's a yes?" she called after him.

"'I have no idea what you're asking me."

"I'm asking"—she hollered as Lucas walked into his room—"if you hooked up!"

Slamming the door didn't seem like an adequate response, but it was all he had. She didn't really expect an answer anyway. She'd already know. Fortunately, it was nearly time for her to open up the store. He was pretty sure she didn't have Maisie helping out today, and she'd never close down the business, even for a few minutes, to come and harass him about getting some. Which meant he had a few hours alone, to sketch out some of his ideas.

If he could keep his mind from daydreaming about Gabe, and what he wanted the guy to do to him when he got back there this evening.

CHAPTER NINE

*B*efore leaving Audrey's, Lucas did something somewhat uncharacteristic: he made a plan. Gabe had said he had to ask for what he wanted, right? Well, he had, and he hadn't gotten it. *That* wasn't going to happen again.

As a result, he drove to the farm in a state of unrelenting excitement, gingerly avoiding potholes and other bumps in the road that might set him off. Maybe he should have waited and put the plug in at the barn studio before going up to Gabe's apartment. A mental picture formed in Lucas's head, of Gabe walking in on him bent over a workbench with his pants and briefs around his knees, pushing a bright-red Butt Bomb up his ass.

Oh God. That had possibilities. *Ungh*. Shimmying his shoulders, he tried to shake off the wave of desire, afraid he'd never make it without creaming his jeans otherwise.

By the time he parked in front of the studio, he was considering the merits of a quick jerk session before knocking on Gabe's door. But that wasn't what he really wanted, either. So instead he grabbed the bag he'd packed and walked right through into the barn, then turned left to climb up those stairs for the first time.

Gabe must have heard him, because he was standing in his open doorway when Lucas reached the landing, wearing a clean white T-shirt and faded denim. His hair was damp and dark red, with nearly imperceptible tracks in it from his comb. Like topographic lines.

Ignoring the sudden, gnawing shyness in his gut, Lucas said, "Hi."

"Hey." Gabe took his hand, pulling him into the apartment and his arms, then cupped the back of Lucas's head, hovering just outside of kissing range, even after Lucas tunneled his fingers into Gabe's hair and went up on tiptoe. "Why are you smiling like that?"

Like a fool? "No reason." Gabe's eyes were so close they were almost blurry as Lucas gazed into them. *Oh, fuck it.* "I'm happy to be here."

"Me too." Finally Gabe's lips landed on his, nudging his mouth open at the same time he was helping him untangle himself from his coat sleeves. They let his jacket fall to the floor, then Gabe's fingers took a leisurely trip down Lucas's spine to the small of his back.

How long before he found out Lucas's secret?

Well aware he was a few steps ahead of Gabe on the arousal ladder, he tried to stifle the small noises that wanted to escape his throat. But Gabe smelled so good—like soap and clean skin and a hint of horse—and his chest was so hard pressing against Lucas's, and his huge hands were gripping and caressing Lucas's butt cheeks . . . it was hopeless. He gasped when Gabe squeezed them together, jostling the plug.

"Don't want—" Gabe started kissing his neck "—dinner first, then?"

"*No.*" Lucas tilted his chin up to give the guy room to work, squirming like a kid who had to pee, rubbing himself against Gabe's body, trying not to actually hump his leg. To distract himself from his own erection, he went searching for Gabe's dick, massaging it through the jeans when he found it. "I wanna eat *you.*" He found the buttons of Gabe's fly, working them with his fingers until Gabe grabbed his hand.

"Let's take this into the bedroom," he said over his shoulder as he led Lucas through his place. Glancing around quickly, Lucas saw a kitchen to the left and a couch to the right, but didn't get much more than that. Judging by how fast Gabe was moving them along, he was as eager as Lucas.

They made it to the edge of his bed before he stopped and spun them around, grabbing the hem of Lucas's T-shirt and yanking it over his head. Lucas did the same in turn, then slid his arms around Gabe's neck and rubbed their naked chests together. Hair caught at and teased his nipples and belly, sending small *zings* of pleasure through him. Then Gabe was kissing him while unzipping his jeans, so Lucas pulled on Gabe's fly, popping all the buttons out of their holes in one go. *Such* a satisfying sound.

Gabe's cock sprang out into his hand. Breaking their kiss to see it, Lucas nearly fell to his knees right then. The room was dark—the lights weren't on yet, and the sun had almost set—but he could get a better look at Gabe's dick now than he'd gotten last night. Grasping it in his fingers, he smoothed his thumb down the length of it, watching the color change under the pressure.

"Mmmmm."

"You have a beautiful dick," Lucas whispered, tracing the flared edge of the crown with his fingertip. "If it was a joint, it'd be the perfect fatty. The one the ganja heads are always striving to roll up and smoke."

Gabe laughed, although he barely had the breath for it. "That a compliment?"

Nodding, Lucas lifted his head long enough to give him a quick kiss, then he returned his attention to exploring Gabe, working further along the shaft, past where it widened, down to the root of it, buried in hair. Gabe's fingers flexed on Lucas's back, pulling him closer until his hand was captured between them, wrapped around Gabe's cock, with his own pressing into his wrist, still trapped by his briefs.

Gabe was working on fixing that. He dug under Lucas's waistband, pushing his pants and underwear down. Lucas toed off his shoes, because they were about to be in the way, then stepped out of his jeans when Gabe let them drop to his ankles. He refused to let go of his prize, though, even when they were pressed together again, tongues deep inside each other's mouths.

He'd nearly forgotten about the plug when Gabe's fingers went searching between his ass cheeks and found the end of it. "What's this?" He pressed against the base of the plug and angled his head again, coming in for another kiss.

"What do you think?"

"I think you want me to fuck you." He tugged on the base until the widest part of the plug was threatening to slip out, making Lucas draw in a quick breath and reach back to grab Gabe's wrist, stopping him.

"I do want you to fuck me. Later. Right now I want to taste your cock." Blowjobs were best given with something in his ass. He almost liked it more than being topped, especially when it was a beautiful dick like Gabe's.

Gabe didn't let go, though. He held Lucas's gaze, and the muscles in his wrist flexed under Lucas's fingers as he twisted the plug, smiling slightly when Lucas gasped. "You sure about that?"

"Almost," he breathed, closing his eyes as Gabe twisted it the other direction, pulling out a bit, stretching Lucas's hole more and increasing the friction against his nerve endings. "Kinda sure."

Gabe's lips brushed against his. "I dunno, I wanna watch my cock slide into your ass pretty damn bad." He thrust his dick through Lucas's fist, dragging the fat head across the center of his palm and leaving a thin trail of moisture.

Ungh. "I really want to suck you." He forced his reluctant eyelids to open, biting his lip to keep another one of those nervous, embarrassed smiles from breaking free at what he was about to offer. "You can fuck my throat." He'd never said anything like that to a sex partner . . . but wow, what an aphrodisiac, especially when Gabe's pupils dilated in reaction, and his nostrils flared.

Then he let go of the plug and freed Lucas's hand from his dick, jaw flexing as he dropped his arms. Letting Lucas have what he'd asked for. Lucas got on his knees, sliding against Gabe's chest as he went, pausing at Gabe's belly button to lick inside it. He let his tongue drag down the happy trail, until his face was burrowing into Gabe's pubes. "You smell so . . ." A deep breath drew the scent of skin and musk inside him.

Gabe's hand landed on Lucas's head. A *go* signal. Lucas wrapped his fingers around Gabe's cock, giving himself another second to anticipate and desire. "I think I've been waiting to taste this for the last twelve years."

"Mmmmmm." Thrusting slightly, Gabe pressed against his lips.

The first delicate lick across the head made Lucas's taste buds wake up and salivate. Meaty and thick and strong—those were the only words he had to describe the flavor. And maybe gamy. Engulfing Gabe's head with his lips, he sucked, confirming it. *Definitely gamy.*

"Yeah," Gabe whispered, widening his stance and canting his hips forward.

Starting small, with only a few inches, and working up, Lucas fell into the Zen of it, getting lost in the slide and slurp and especially the taste. Until he couldn't tell where his tongue ended and his gag reflex began. When Gabe moaned and twisted Lucas's hair in his fingers, yanking his head to just the right angle, Lucas said, "Fuck yes," but of course it came out as *hmmm-hmmm*, since Gabe was in control of things now, thrusting instead of receiving. Nearly at the boundary between mouth and throat. *Perfect.*

When Gabe pushed past that barrier—*so much* like that moment when his sphincter gave way and a cock penetrated him—Lucas nearly came, hands-free, ass clenching around the plug.

Then Gabe pulled out, tightly gripping Lucas's head to keep him from following as he withdrew his cock. Mouth still open, hoping Gabe would fill it again, Lucas looked up in question.

"Turn around?" Everything about Gabe was hard, except for those words. His stare and his facial muscles and his hold on Lucas's hair and especially his dick.

Lucas did what he'd been asked, pivoting on his knees as Gabe let go of him, then grabbed the edge of the mattress to brace himself.

Moments later Gabe was kneeling behind him, pulling the plug out so slowly that Lucas was sure he punctured the sheet with his fingernails. He didn't even think about a condom, not until he heard the crinkle of one being opened. Then Gabe's cock was pushing inside him, pressing past any resistance from rebellious muscles that hadn't gotten the memo: Lucas was dying for this. "Please."

Going deeper, Gabe leaned forward, increasing the pressure and ache. "Please what?" he asked, then tongued Lucas's neck, beginning to rock. A slow rhythm that made Lucas moan and his toes curl.

"Please do exactly that," he gasped out, arching his back and pushing himself further onto Gabe's dick until he got what he most wanted—Gabe's damp skin plastered against his, from his lower back to his thighs.

"You like it deep."

"Yes." More than anything. More than the glide of a cock across his prostate, and more than the burn of stretching around a meaty head and shaft. Although those things were shudder-worthy too. "Mostly," he panted, "I just love to be fucked."

God, the things he admitted to this man. He'd have to be embarrassed later. At the moment he couldn't care less, because Gabe had circled his arm around Lucas's hips and was using the hold to keep him close, and in sync with the tempo he was setting. A short drag out and a swift thrust in. Fucking Lucas steadily until they were both dripping with sweat and Lucas was hanging by his fingertips from the edge of the bed, trembling.

"Please," he repeated, but this time it was half wail.

"Ready?" Gabe grunted as he shoved home again.

Nodding frantically, too out of breath to say anything more, Lucas tried to unclamp one of his hands from the mattress. Before he could, Gabe was fisting his dick, engulfing it in his hand and working it, twisting down while he thrust in.

Lucas came immediately, shooting and moaning and grinding his ass into Gabe's groin. The timing was perfect, because Gabe swelled inside him, then pumped out his own orgasm, his muscles spasming in counterpoint to Lucas's, and so deep inside him it felt like Lucas's own body shuddering and releasing. Coming in stereo.

It took forever for him to catch his breath, hanging his head between his outstretched arms for so long they eventually gave out, and Gabe pulled him back as he collapsed, until they were both lying on the floor, side by side, panting.

First fucks were never like this, at least not for him. There were always negotiations, and uncertain moments, even embarrassing ones. But they hadn't even had to field the "top or bottom" question. *Thank you, deity who watches out for gay men, for this top you have delivered unto me. I'll sprinkle glitter in your name at Pride festivals until my death.*

Aloud he only said, "Wow."

"I'll say." Gabe was smiling and sleepy-eyed when Lucas rolled onto his side to face him. "For a guy who's so afraid to overhear his brother having sex, you're a bit of a deviant."

Oh no. Was this going to be a problem for them? He'd spent years listening to Drew go on about his more "perverse" urges—and that covered a lot more than eating peanut butter from a spoon. God, what had he done? He never revealed any of his kinks this early with a guy, afraid of just this reaction. Gabe might have seemed into it at the time—

Gabe interrupted his internal freak-out by scooting closer, then cupping Lucas's ass and squeezing it. "That was pretty damned hot."

Phew. He owed that fairy a lot more than glitter. He was probably going to have to wear a tutu and wings while throwing free condoms from a parade float.

It had been a hell of a fine day.

By the end of it, Gabe had two new things on his to-do list: write up a stud contract and introduce Bruce to his harem. That second item would probably have to be repeated a few times, but trailering the horse to Arlington or hosting some of Earl's mares here was better than Gabe having to hold a fake vagina for a horny stallion. He wasn't going to make any money off the deal, but it wasn't going to cost him much, and it was a big step toward Bruce earning his keep in future stud fees if his foals out-performed him.

Mostly, though, it had been a good day because of that other fine stud. The one he'd left napping in his bed when he got up to start dinner. The one whose eyes had gone shiny with excitement when he was sucking Gabe's dick.

The one whose arms were wrapping around him from behind right this second, as a matter of fact. And whose lips were pressing against the bare skin on his neck.

Lucas was much more affectionate than Gabe would have guessed. He'd thought he might have to curb his urges to touch Lucas or risk freaking the guy out, but so far it didn't seem like an issue.

"What are you making?" Lucas rested his cheek against Gabe's shoulder blade and laced his fingers together on Gabe's belly. "It smells good."

"Venison."

"Mmmmm, I remember." He tightened his hold for a second, then let go. As Lucas came to stand beside him, leaning his hip on the counter, Gabe leaned over and kissed him, then went back to stirring the gravy.

"I was just about to wake you up. It's almost ready." Once this thickened, it was all done. He'd even made mashed potatoes.

"Should I set the table?" Frowning, Lucas looked around. "Do you have a table? Oh. You already set it."

"Yep. Go find yourself something to drink from the fridge and sit down. Can you grab the salad off the top shelf?" Glancing over his shoulder, he saw Lucas pulling out the bowl. "I'll bring the rest of the food over in a minute."

He should have turned on some music. The extended silence while he finished the gravy and poured it into the pitcher, then got the potatoes and meat out of the oven, was working on his nerves. He hadn't cooked dinner for a guy since he'd been seeing that dude, Tyler, from Port Angeles. That was a few years back, now.

It had been even longer since his stomach had tied itself up in knots like this. He hadn't had a case of jitters this bad since, well, since Lucas had left town.

"Are you all right?" Lucas asked once Gabe had put dinner on the table, then grabbed himself a beer. He stopped in the middle of pulling out his chair and stared at him, trying to decide how to answer.

"Uh." Slowly he sat. It was too late to say *I'm fine, why?* or make up some lame answer. "I guess I'm kinda— This is a little weird, Lu." He set his beer on the table and rested his hands on either side of his plate. "I've known you forever, but . . ."

"You don't really *know* me." Lucas nodded, like it made perfect sense. Maybe he felt the same way.

"Not so much anymore."

"What do you want to find out?"

Everything. "Well, for starters, I want an opinion on the food I slaved over a hot stove to make for you."

Again Lucas's eyes went shiny with excitement, and he picked up his fork, inspecting the platter of steak. Nice to know some of Gabe's non-sex-related skills could make him happy too.

"You made a ton." Lucas selected one of the bigger ones, then reached for the gravy. "Is this mushroom?"

"No better kind for venison." Finally, the butterflies in his stomach had settled enough for Gabe to start eating too. "And I made a lot so we can have the leftovers for breakfast."

Turned out there was a better reaction to be got from Lucas than the shiny eyes. When he put the first bite in his mouth and started chewing, his eyelids fell closed and he moaned.

The same kind of noise he'd made earlier, suckling on Gabe's dick.

He decided to take it as a compliment on both counts. "You haven't had venison since you left here?"

"No." Lucas's eyes popped open. "I mean yes, I've had it. It's just . . ." He bent down, looking at his steak, prodding at it with the tines of his fork. "It's not the same."

Huh.

"I mean, I've had it in England," he went on, still poking at the meat, arranging it on the plate as if about to take up his knife and cut another bite. But he didn't. "And it's close, but not quite." Dipping his head to the side in a way that suggested his eyes rolled along with it, he added, "I've ordered it in really expensive restaurants in Los Angeles, but it's, I don't know, *tamed*. It's all about organic-this and free-range that, but it's not the same. It doesn't taste right. This." The tines of Lucas's fork clinked against Gabe's cheapest—and only—dinnerware as he made his point. "It tastes exactly like it should. Like my childhood."

Well, fuck me. He wanted to drag the guy across the table and tip his chair back until they both fell on the floor and could rub full-length against each other, grinding and tongue-fucking and—

"Sorry." Lucas interrupted Gabe's fantasy.

"Why do you do that?" He threw his napkin on the table, and it landed with an impotent *shush*.

"What?" Lucas gaped at him.

"Why do you say something that's so, I dunno—*accurate*—then apologize for it?"

Mouth snapping shut, Lucas swallowed. "Not everyone . . . gets me."

"*I* get you." He couldn't fucking *stop* getting him. "So give that shit a rest."

Lucas lowered his head and went back to playing with his food, but much more gently, as if his heart wasn't really in it. "Okay."

Dammit. Now he had to try to normalize things after that little outburst. "What's England like?" He wasn't much for travel, but that was one place he'd always thought about seeing. If he could've driven there.

"A lot like here, actually. It rains a ton, and the landscape is similar to Western Washington's." He scrunched up his nose. "At least, the parts without mountains. I was in York for a couple of months a few years ago, and the things they call mountains?" He chuckled and shook his head.

"They have deer, huh?"

"Well, they have *venison*. I have no idea what kind of deer it comes from."

Keep the conversation ball rolling. "You ever think about living someplace besides Los Angeles?"

"Yeah." Spreading what was left of his mashed potatoes out on his plate, he picked up his knife and started drawing designs in it, swirling lines of brown gravy through it, silent for a minute.

Why the hell had he asked that question? It made him conscious of really caring about the answer. Gabe gave up on the salad he'd been eating, appetite gone. "I always believed you were meant for bigger things, you know."

Jerking his head up, Lucas lifted his brows questioningly.

"Bigger than Bluewater Bay, not necessarily better." He smiled, to take any possible sting out of his words. "Far as I can tell, though, you *did* achieve better."

Lucas swallowed. "You know I'm only here because Audrey asked me to come, and I had to get out of there. Los Angeles. I mean, all that stuff I told you about my ex . . ."

"I remember." About realizing he no longer loved the guy, and he'd been fooling himself. No wonder he'd been depressed.

"I didn't tell you everything." Licking his lip, he then sunk his teeth into it before letting go to continue. "Drew and I met because I sold a lot of stuff in his gallery." Lucas sighed and sat back in his chair. "Actually, it's more like a store, but he refuses to see that. He sells really high-end, handmade things, but they're what most people in the art world think of as *craft*. Stuff with a real function. Like my pieces? They were mostly tea sets and other dishes. Decorative ones that I put a lot of thought and work into but not purely art."

"Craft," Gabe repeated, trying to recall an article he'd read on Lucas, when he'd gone out searching for information on the guy after his last visit. It had talked about his sculptural "concepts" a lot. "You do art, though. I've seen it."

"I do." He nodded. "I like doing the conceptual stuff, but I really need the functional stuff to make me feel . . ." He wrinkled up his forehead. "Grounded?"

Did he ever get *that*. "It brings you back to the basics, so you can build on it." It was why Gabe would never leave this land—it was the foundation for the structure of his life. Lucas had that same groove going on, but for him it was in the artwork. The guy had more country boy in him than he realized.

For some reason, Lucas had planted his elbows on the table and hid his head in his hands. Hell, maybe Gabe had that wrong, or Lucas didn't see it the same way. He should've known better than to try to get all philosophical.

Lifting his head, Lucas ran his fingers down his face, pulling at his features. Like he was trying to wipe himself clean. "I was dying to escape this town because I thought no one got me, but now that I'm back . . ." He sighed. "I was so wrong."

I understood you. Gabe stayed silent, though. Whatever he'd felt back then wasn't the issue, was it?

"Anyway." He erupted into movement, adjusting his plate on the table to some new, mysteriously better position. "Drew sold 'fine craft' because he could move enough of it to support himself and the gallery, but he was always looking down his nose at it."

And probably at Lucas, for making it. "Dick." It needed to be said, although Gabe usually tried not to dis anyone's ex. Never seemed to go well.

Lucas didn't react to that, though. Instead, his gaze sharpened, going from soft-focus to penetrating, trained on Gabe's eyes. "You *do* get me, don't you?"

Embarrassed, Gabe croaked, "Guess so."

The tension in Lucas suddenly eased, loosening up a small smile and dropping his shoulders a little, and Gabe's embarrassment bled away as he watched.

"Thank you." Lucas picked his utensils up again, holding his knife ready to cut another bite of meat. Except he didn't. "What did I do to my potatoes?"

Gabe laughed and started in on his dinner again, listening to Lucas explain the difference between art and craft. Apparently, he made sculptures for big shows in galleries, and the "crafty things" for stores like his ex's. "I have this major show coming up in a little over eight months, and I haven't made *anything* for it. Honestly, when I was still in California I couldn't even face dealing with it."

"And now?"

"It's still a huge pain, but I'm positive I can do it. I feel *motivated*."

"Sounds like coming back to town was a good move for you." Made sense to him. Audrey'd said Lucas was rootless, so where better to go if he wanted to fix things?

"Yeah, but it's not a long-term career solution. It's too . . ." He shifted in his seat like he had an itch in his shorts. "Small."

"That's what I'm saying." Gabe smirked at him. "You were meant for bigger things. Does it matter so much where you live?"

"Not really, but if I'm closer to a gallery that's got my stuff in it, I don't have to pay shipping costs to send them stock. Plus it's harder to meet the right people if I'm not in an arts area." He screwed up his forehead. "I loved San Francisco. If I can afford it, I might move there."

By the time they were done eating, Lucas was telling him about Los Angeles.

It sounded like hipster hell.

"Is that all you can find in California? People who are slaves to fads?" He started to clear the table, and Lucas jumped up to help.

"Sunshine." The plates he'd picked up clattered into the sink. "But there aren't any really hairy guys. Well, now there are, because it's popular to have hair again, but I never seemed to hook up with many of them. Drew had a beard and mustache this last year, but he still manscaped everywhere else."

Leaning against the counter, Gabe snagged Lucas as he walked by, loosely circling his arms around the guy. "What the hell is there to recommend the place, then?"

"Nothing like this." Sliding his hands up under Gabe's shirt, he started to comb the hair on his belly with his fingernails. It sent little shivers into Gabe's groin. "I forgot how much I liked body hair on a guy," he murmured. He was working his way down, into the waistband of Gabe's sweats.

"Now how do you just forget something like that?" The small of Lucas's back was so sensitive. Gabe could lightly brush the bare skin there and Lucas's breath would catch and his lips would part.

"I don't know, just . . . a series of guys who weren't hairy. It seemed like it wasn't on the menu." Leaning closer, he kissed along Gabe's jaw, then down his neck.

"You're in luck. Hair is the only thing on the menu at Chez Gabe."

After that, it was a hell of a fine night too.

CHAPTER TEN

*G*abe got up at his usual time Saturday morning to feed the horses, and it took him about two seconds before he knew in his bones a big storm was coming. He had things to do that couldn't be put off, so he wasn't able to go back up to bed with Lucas after his chores were done.

He finished all the training goals he'd set for Bruce by ten, which was a relief, and started mucking out stalls when he saw Lucas was raking out his pit kiln. It was kind of nice that Lucas had his own thing to do, because Gabe usually had a farm task waiting, even these days. The few times he'd had boyfriends stay over in the past, that had always been hard to negotiate. A lot of them didn't understand that he didn't get weekends off.

When Seth and guys like him had stayed over, it hadn't mattered. They were just hookups.

Lucas was something else. Something nebulous, in that gray area between hookup and boyfriend. Even knowing there was no future for them and that the guy would eventually leave town again, Gabe couldn't convince himself that there was anything casual about the sex between them.

By the time he'd finished scooping poop and bringing the horses into the barn to wait out the bad weather, Lucas was back in his studio. Gabe poked his head in to see how his stuff had turned out, and found Lucas in front of one of the workbenches with a conglomeration of black ceramic shapes in front of him that he was putting together like a puzzle. He had that entranced, slack-mouthed expression on his face, and before he placed each piece, he'd fondle it awhile, staring at it, then at whatever he was building, then back at the piece. Keeping silent so as not to startle him, Gabe watched him go through the same ritual three times, until he fitted an oblong shape into a slot on the upper side of the puzzle, and it all resolved into an image.

"Whoa."

Lucas started and whirled at Gabe's voice, and Gabe rushed toward him, afraid the whole sculpture would fall, but it stayed put.

"You scared me." Dropping his shoulders, Lucas slumped, then straightened.

"Sorry, I was trying not to." From this angle, the sculpture looked a little familiar. "Is that Bruce?"

Turning back around, Lucas tilted his head and regarded it for a few seconds. "It does look like him. I didn't really mean for it to be him. It's just a horse."

It didn't look exactly like a horse, but it *did* look like it was about to run off with the wind. It gave the sense of being a playful stallion more than any perfect reproduction of Bruce would have. Yet somehow it was all just a bunch of pieces unless it was assembled. Up close, Gabe could see that some of the sculpture had a subtle sheen to it, and other parts were dull black. It gave the horse even more movement, and defined his shape, especially in the bones of the muzzle. In the oblong head there was a deep indentation that looked like it should be an eye, but it was empty.

Gently, he ran his fingertip along the edge of it, worried still about jostling it too much and having it all collapse. "Are you gonna add something here?"

The sculpture didn't move, even though the weight of the piece was balanced on three skinny legs. The fourth one was curled up just under the breast, obviously frozen midcanter.

"Yeah, I'm trying to figure out what to do about that." Lucas grimaced, picking up a blackened cloth from the bench and twisting it in his hand. "I made a little hollow ball that was supposed to fit inside there, but I can't find it in the ashes. I raked them a bunch of times. This is only a test, though, so I probably won't even finish it."

"That's a *test*?" He gaped at Lucas. "What are you going to do with it?"

Lucas shrugged.

"Can I have it?"

Lucas's wide eyes met his. "If you really want it, but I'll make you a better one later."

"I don't want a better one, I want that one." For lots of reasons he couldn't put into words, or didn't want to. Reasons that had to do with what the two of them had been doing while that sculpture was in the fire pit.

"Okay, um, let me finish cleaning it, then I'll put it together for you upstairs?"

"Sounds good." He stuffed his hands into his pockets, not sure if he was supposed to leave now. Maybe, since Lucas had bent his head to his work again, rubbing at it with that cloth.

As Gabe was about to back off, though, Lucas said, "I saw you with him this morning. When you had him drag that log."

The memory made Gabe grin. "Thought it was going to take me till the storm hit to get him to do that without balking, but all he did was give me a funny look and then get right to it."

"So, what's the purpose of having him do that?"

"Eventually Bruce has to be trained to pull a load, so I start him with dragging a log, just to see how he does." He'd done it perfectly, then, once Gabe had unhitched him, Bruce took off, tossing his head and cantering around, occasionally dancing in place. The playful twin of the beast he'd been when he was doing his job. After a minute or two of that, he'd trotted back to Gabe, looking for treats. "Joshua had it right when he said that horse is kinda like a big dog."

Lucas smiled. "You're so good with him."

"Nah, it's more that he knows what he's doing. Or what I want him to do." It was true—a lot of it had to do with the horse's personality and intelligence.

"How big is this storm supposed to get?" A worried frown creased Lucas's forehead, but he kept rubbing that rag on the sculpture.

"Sounds like a big one." *Aw, hell.* The obvious had just occurred to Gabe. "If you want to get back into town before it gets bad, you better hurry it up."

That distracted Lucas from his job. He whipped his head around and trained his frown on Gabe. "Oh, um. I thought you wanted me to stay tonight too, but I can—"

"I want you to stay. The whole weekend." Fuck not disturbing him too much. Gabe palmed the small of Lucas's back with one hand and curled his other arm around the front of his waist, pulling him closer. Close enough to make out the faint smudges and the fine hairs on his face. He brushed his lips along Lucas's jaw, where a shadow of beard darkened his skin.

Sighing, Lucas reached for Gabe, gripping his belt loops and the back of his neck. "Good."

Damn straight. He still had a lot of the guy in his system to work out. "We better hunker down though, before the weather hits. I'm gonna go upstairs and build a fire."

The electricity was out by early afternoon, and the clouds were so thick there simply wasn't enough daylight for Lucas to keep working in his studio. The sound of the rain beating against the windows helped create a perfect atmosphere for him, and he'd gotten a lot done on figuring out Audrey's wedding favors, at the stage where he was hand-building a basic form, just to make sure the aesthetics worked as well in 3-D as they did in his sketchbook. For the actual bowls, he'd need his potter's wheel, which was still in the storage cube.

Carrying the pieces of the Bruce sculpture in a box, he was on his way up to Gabe's place when the apartment door opened, and Gabe came out. He was shrugging on one of those bright-yellow vinyl jackets every guy who worked outdoors seemed to have. He already wore the matching vinyl pants.

It defied logic that he should seem so virile swaddled in fluorescent plastic.

"Hey, Lu." Gabe pulled a pair of work gloves out of his pocket as he trotted down the stairs, stopping midway to kiss him, then continuing on. "Momma just called and one of the old oak trees near the house dropped a big limb on the shed where they keep the backup generator—"

"You have a backup generator?" he asked Gabe's back as he hit the main floor and then continued across the barn, into the deeper shadows.

"Only up at the main house, and right now they don't have squat. You and I are roughing it, either way," Gabe called back, voice buoyant. "Anyways, I gotta go up there and clear the debris, then see if it's salvageable."

Good lord, did he think going out in weather like this was fun? *Probably*. No wonder he could make rain gear look virile.

"Do you need any help?" That's what he was supposed to offer, right? *Please say no*. Mechanics really weren't his thing. Or being outside in storms. He preferred being inside and cozy with a naked guy.

"Nah, it's fine." Gabe's answer floated out from the darkness, then he appeared in the weak daylight spilling out from the studio door, carrying a gas can in one hand and a chainsaw in the other. "Gotta get the branch off, shouldn't take much, and after that it's just me tinkering. You going to set up that sculpture?"

"Yeah." He lifted the box, indicating that he carried it, even though Gabe already saw. "Then I'm done for the day."

Gabe's eyes flickered up and down his body, and for a brief second Lucas felt naked. Then he felt dirty. Literally—he had clay on his jeans and T-shirt, mostly smeared in long streaks from wiping his fingers on his clothes. "Looks like you need to get out of those clothes."

A leftover electrical charge from twelve years before sparked up between them. Those were the words Gabe had used that night when a rain-soaked Lucas had been standing in the Wilders' kitchen. Then Gabe had come looking for him while Lucas was still getting dressed.

All the negativity he'd hung on those events was gone, though. Now thinking about the past propelled him back down the stairs, meeting Gabe at the foot of them. Reaching up with his free hand, he pulled Gabe's head down toward him and dirty-porn-kissed him, sliding his tongue in and out in the most explicit and inviting way possible, making it last until he was out of breath, then slowly drawing away.

"Well, now." Gabe eased into a smile. "Hope that offer's still on the table when I get back."

"It will be."

"Mmm." Gabe didn't leave. He kept his chest against Lucas's, arms weighed down with the tools he was carrying. "I'll be taking you up on it as soon as possible."

There was nothing like that glint in a man's eye to make a guy feel desirable. "You better."

Gabe couldn't seem to tear his gaze away, staying within inches for a few more seconds before leaning forward again and carefully tracing the shape of Lucas's lips with the tip of his tongue, then engulfing them and pushing inside. He pressed his hips forward until his hardening cock was rubbing Lucas's belly.

Ungh. Lucas yanked back as soon as he could make himself, although not quite able to let go of Gabe's neck. "You gotta go. The sooner you do, the sooner you can come back and get naked with me." Forcing his fingers to uncurl, he unearthed his nails from Gabe's skin.

"I left a bunch of candles for you if you need light. Matches are on the table." Kissing his forehead, Gabe whirled and walked off, like he might need to do it quick or he'd never get it done.

Up in the apartment, Lucas changed into sweats and a long-sleeved T-shirt, then lit every candle Gabe had left, placing them around the living room—so many it looked like a Gothic film set—before hunting for a spot to assemble the horse sculpture.

Just like in Gabe's truck, the bookshelves on either side of the stove were cluttered up with keepsakes. A couple of crude wood carvings someone had done, and things like old corncob pipes and antique tobacco tins. There were even a few flowery, delicate cups and saucers.

Eventually, Lucas found room on a narrow table beside the door. It was flush against the wall, so it was a pretty stable spot. Sorting the parts in the box before taking them out, he slipped into the headspace he'd been in before, down in the studio.

Once he'd finished putting the piece together, he wandered over to the window in the living room, staring out at the mountains, and began to mull over Audrey's wedding favors. Images and words floated around in his head, bumping into each other and sometimes making connections. *I should— Yeah, that would fit like this and . . . rough spot. Could use that.*

Gabe's hand landing on his ass jolted him back to the real world, and he shifted gears from cerebral to carnal in about two point two seconds. He pushed back into the hold just as Gabe's finger was pressing between his cheeks, though his sweats. *Ungh.*

"Hope you kept this warm for me." Gabe's nascent beard tickled Lucas's neck and the words caught at his senses the way Gabe's whiskers did his skin. He smelled like green wood and two-stroke engine fuel and fresh man sweat mixed with rain—all the cues of masculinity that had been programmed into Lucas's primal brain before he was old enough to know better. And yet he'd spent his entire adult life denying he was into that rugged, macho, beer-swilling, Bambi-hunting kind of man.

He didn't want to deny his libido anymore. He wanted to live out every sex-slave-of-the-mountain-man fantasy he'd ever had. If he'd had any; if he hadn't, he should have. *Definitely have them in the future.*

Turning to face Gabe, he didn't give either of them a chance to say anything else before pressing their lips together, then their bodies. Undulating against him and picking up the kisses where they'd left off at the bottom of the stairs. Gabe still had work clothes on, but he'd taken off the rain gear, which made him even nicer to rub against.

"I should take a shower," Gabe said when Lucas slid his cheek along Gabe's jaw, abrading his skin.

"No." He gathered the hem of Gabe's shirt in his fists, pulling up on it. "God, no. I want you sweaty and smelly and coming in my mouth."

"If I stink—"

"You smell *fantastic*." He dropped to his knees to work on the boots, eyeing Gabe's dick slowly plumping up the jeans in front of his face. *Can't touch yet.* Lifting up one pant leg, he found the star of his high school fantasies—gray tube socks with safety orange bands ringing the top. *Fuck it.* He was ripping open Gabe's fly before finishing the thought. "You went commando again." The smell of Gabe's dick floated out before Lucas had it fully revealed. Rich with body musk and the sex they'd had last night— He *adored* that scent. It did things to him: ratcheted up the tension in the pit of his stomach and made his fingers tingle and mouth water.

Impatient, he yanked the jeans down, and Gabe's cock popped out like it was spring-loaded, then bobbed gently right in front of Lucas's face. He wanted to suck it into his mouth, and slide it through his fist, and rub it on his skin all at once, but he was transfixed a few moments by the sight of it in candlelight. Blood-flushed and plump and veiny. Like a sausage dying to be eaten. Ruddy now, it would be an almost angry-looking scarlet once he was fully hard, but the head was a little more purple. His pubic hair was the perfect match for his dick. A textbook example of an analogous color scheme: red-violet, red, red-orange. Although Lucas couldn't swear it would go over well as a classroom model.

"What're you doing?" Gabe asked as he palmed the back of Lucas's head. Not gripping it, simply caressing.

"I'm going to stick this down my throat until I gag on it." He wrapped his hand around the shaft and slid up the length of it.

Fingers flexing on his head, Gabe brought him closer to his dick.

"I still got my pants around my ankles."

"Yes, yes, you do. It's perfect, it makes me feel all . . ." Sucking in a breath through his teeth, Lucas wiggled his shoulders, eyeing Gabe up and down as desire shuddered along his back. Only the parts Lucas needed access to in order to properly service him were exposed. "Subservient." More shivers crawled over his skin when he admitted it.

"Well, then." Gabe's smile grew slowly, and he switched his grip so he was holding Lucas by the hair tightly enough to make his scalp tingle. "Get to it, boy." He positioned the head of his cock at Lucas's lips, pressing forward until he'd made them part for him. Deep in his throat, Lucas *hmm*ed, expressing how much he liked that. Sucking a nice dick was a process that had to be done right so both parties were satisfied, and he was dying to do a thorough job.

Cupping Gabe's balls in his hand, he shoved his left into his own briefs, gripping his dick, working it as Gabe thrust into his mouth, slowly going deeper. Each time he pulled back on Gabe's cock, suctioning like a vacuum cleaner, he pulled his hand up his own dick.

Wrapped in the scent of Gabe's skin and the hint of cum and exertion, he drew it out as long as he could, holding off his own excitement by force of will until Gabe pushed into his throat and shot his load. That was the permission he'd been waiting for, and he didn't stop sucking as he moaned and stroked himself through his own orgasm. Then Gabe flopped down next to him on the living room floor and gathered him into his arms.

Panting, Lucas ran his hand through his hair, then started giggling uncontrollably when he realized he'd just plastered it with cum. Gabe lifted his head, looked at him, and started laughing too. Eventually they quieted again, and Gabe tipped Lucas's chin up for a long kiss. "You're a kinky boy," he whispered.

Instead of alarming him like it had the first time Gabe had brought it up, this time Lucas felt a little smug, and very, very content.

CHAPTER ELEVEN

*G*abe had freckles. He didn't have many on his face, and never had, in spite of the red hair, so when Lucas was returning from the bathroom (after rinsing out his hair) to the nest of blankets they'd made in the living room and saw Gabe sitting up, showing his naked back covered in them, he *oooh*ed in delight.

"What?" Gabe tried to turn around but Lucas had knelt behind him, trapping Gabe's hips between his knees.

"How come I didn't know you had these freckles?" Was it the candlelight that made them so alluring? It had certainly made Gabe's cock delicious.

"Dunno," Gabe muttered. Lucas ran his fingertips lightly over them, certain he could feel the texture change here on Gabe's shoulders, where they were the thickest. He even had them on the back of his neck.

"You get them from the sun?" Like on every man who worked outside, they faded away, blending into his natural skin tone where it wouldn't be exposed to much UV radiation. "How come you don't have any on your face?"

"I wear a ball cap when it's sunny. That feels good." Sounding less sullen, Gabe leaned back into Lucas's body, sighing as Lucas ran his palms down to his chest. Then he went back to tracing designs on his shoulders, still strangely awed by the little marks.

"I can't believe I never noticed these before," he murmured. His fingertips tingled as he touched them.

"Guess you haven't spent a lot of time behind me."

Lucas immediately got the oblique reference, and his pulse sped up. "Are you saying you want me to top you?" He bit his lip, trying to decide how to proceed.

"Not unless you want to." Craning his neck, Gabe met his gaze. "That's not what I meant."

"I don't really . . . like that." He forced himself to maintain eye contact.

Eyebrows rising in what looked like mild interest, Gabe asked, "You never top?"

"Sometimes, but I usually feel like I don't know what I'm doing."

Gabe's sly smile started quirking up one corner of his mouth, a lot like he'd appeared when Lucas was blowing him. "Well you see, the penis is inserted—"

"Not 'don't know what I'm doing.'" He shrugged one shoulder. "Just . . . I never can figure out if the guy I'm with is really into it, or faking, or lying about liking it, or what. It's easier not to. That sounds really selfish, doesn't it? I know it does, but . . ."

When Gabe turned, Lucas backed up and sat on his behind, making room for him. "It's honest. Can't do what you're uncomfortable with, that's no good for either person involved. I'm sure the hell not going to shed any tears if we keep doing things the way we have been."

Thank God.

Gabe cupped Lucas's cheek and pulled him forward for a kiss, then took him with him as he stretched out in their impromptu bed. Lucas half expected a demonstration of the way they'd been doing things to follow, but Gabe seemed content to hold him. They had been having a lot of sex in the last two days. More than Lucas was used to in such a short period, so it was nice. Lying there, listening to the storm howl outside.

"You think you'll get a lot of blowdowns from this?" The rain spattered extra hard against the roof just then, like it was taunting them. Or maybe it was daring them. Lucas squinted up at the ceiling, trying to decide.

The beefy shoulder under his head shifted in a shrug. "After the storm passes, I'll have to go out and check for windfall. That might keep me busy for days, cutting that all up for firewood. Guess I'll be selling the extra."

Which reminded him. Shoving up, he propped himself on his elbow and looked down at Gabe. "Don't you already have a bunch of work to do? I mean, on the farm?" *Wait.* "You haven't been logging the whole time I've been here. Unless I missed it?" It wasn't like he didn't get lost in his own head for hours at a time.

"No, you're right." He pulled Lucas toward him, getting him to lie down again, this time with his head on Gabe's chest. As Gabe spoke, Lucas could feel the words vibrate through him. "Remember when my grampa died?"

"Of course." Now probably wasn't the time to tell him the same day he'd found out Gabe's grandfather had pancreatic cancer was the same day he'd first realized he was in lust with Gabe.

"Yeah, well, you know I was just seventeen."

Lucas nodded when Gabe hesitated.

"Momma helps me run the farm, but Grampa was kinda traditional, and he raised me with the expectation that I would take care of things, you know?"

"Yeah."

"So we started getting these medical bills, and it was so much damned money, more than I'd imagined we'd ever have, and I thought *I* had to come up with the solution."

Now he remembered it, overhearing a conversation between Gabe and Zach back then. "You clear-cut part of the farm to pay the bills."

"Yep." Gabe sighed heavily. "Which means that now I either take trees that are too young to fetch the best price, or I wait a few years and pick up the harvest rotation after we get past this hole in the schedule."

"You feel guilty." Reaching out, he petted Gabe's thick mat of hair, trying to soothe him. "You shouldn't. You did what you thought was best."

"I know that." Gabe chuckled humorlessly. "But it still feels like I failed him somehow."

"Your grandpa?"

"Yeah."

There was nothing Lucas could really say to that, so instead he pressed kisses to Gabe's chest, on all the exposed skin he could find. "So, are you guys going to be all right?" He wasn't sure it was okay to ask, so he tried to phrase it in a way that Gabe could interpret to mean whatever he felt most comfortable talking about. Sure, Lucas could mean "all right" financially, or emotionally, or even not be talking about the farm's future at all.

Gabe told him what he really wanted to know, though. "Yeah, Momma and I have been planning for this, so we'll get through it. It helps that I won't be hiring anyone to help with the farm. We're doing little things to keep the income stream up, like I was gonna plant some hay when there was a break in the rain at the beginning of the month."

"'Was going to'?"

"Didn't get it planted in time, and now it's just too damn late, even if we get another full week of no rain." The muscles under Lucas's hands flickered, like something had passed through them. "We'll be all right, though."

"You should've let me pay for gas." Lucas bit his lip as soon as the words escaped him. *I should've kept my mouth shut.* He'd known too many proud farmers and loggers who'd fallen on hard times to think that was going to go over well.

"Nah." Gabe's voice went throaty, but then he cleared it, and his tone became practical. "See, I set us up for commercial fueling a long time ago, and that means we get a discount, plus I can write off mileage as a business expense, which works out to about another forty percent off—"

As Gabe went into a detailed explanation of income tax law, or something like that, Lucas's mind started to whirl.

"Jeez, I should have you try to figure out my contracts with Drew's gallery," he said when Gabe had finished. "It's not like our lawyer is getting it worked out. He told Drew not to release my back stock until we come to terms about breaking the agreements. That was my only outlet for the smaller pieces I make."

"Relationships always seem to come down to finances in the end, don't they?" Gabe's snorted laugh was only half-amused.

"Seems so." He rested his chin in his palm.

Gabe stroked his fingertips up under the hair on the back of Lucas's neck. "Are *you* gonna be all right?"

His shrug was probably unconvincing, but he didn't care at the moment. "Eventually. I'm living on savings until I find a new gallery, or my next show sells out. If it does. It's one of the reasons being in Bluewater Bay for a while is good—it's cheap."

"It is that," Gabe muttered, thoughtfully gazing at the ceiling.

Lucas gazed at Gabe. There were small lines beside his mouth. A guy in his early thirties would have a few wrinkles—*he* did around his eyes—but the ones bracketing Gabe's lips gave the impression of struggle and determination. Maybe choosing to stay here wasn't the easiest, safest choice for everyone, like he'd always assumed. "You care so much about this farm."

"Hell yes." Tucking his thumb under Lucas's chin, he refocused on him. His eyes were dark in the candlelight, but the strength of his bond to this land was clear in them.

He'll never give this place up. "It's so sad you had to cut all those trees." Lucas kissed the fingers nearest his mouth.

Gabe half smiled. "Sometimes you gotta make sacrifices for the people you love."

Late Sunday morning, back in the bedroom again (although still without electricity), Lucas found himself luxuriating in the simple pleasures of being well-sated, well-fed, and lying next to a truly superior guy. This weekend had been the kind he'd always wanted to have with a boyfriend, but had never really achieved. Probably because he'd been trying for it. Maybe it had to be just like this to work— letting things happen naturally, with no expectation that they were building a relationship. He wasn't worried about where things were going to go, since they both knew where they were going to end up. There was no pressure.

He and Drew had tried to have a similar weekend once. They'd gone up to San Francisco and stayed in a hotel just off Union Square. Their plans to stay in bed all day had never made it past eleven though, and Lucas couldn't recall being this into the sex, anyway. Just the scent of Gabe could make him hard. Of course, he'd always been very responsive to the smell of a man.

In his mind, though, that particular trip with Drew had a special glow around it. A warm, sweet memory that had nothing to do with the sex or even the man. He squinted at the raindrops on the window, trying to bring the exact reason into focus. *Oh.* "My wheel."

"Hmm?" Gabe roused himself from where he'd been napping, and rolled over, pressing against Lucas's back and throwing an arm around his waist. "'Zat?" he mumbled.

Reaching back, Lucas pressed the sensitive center of his palm against Gabe's hip bone and dragged it around the curve, just for the tactile sensation and how it made all the muscles in his lower back tighten up in anticipation of more touch later. "Thinking about my potter's wheel." He'd found it at random that long-ago Drew-weekend, at a flea market they'd stumbled across near Haight-Ashbury. A homemade kick wheel with an old-style tractor seat on it, the kind made of metal and pressed into a butt shape, with holes for ventilation so one's ass didn't get too sweaty. The guy who was selling it claimed an art teacher from Oregon had built a bunch of them in the sixties. Drew had thought he was crazy, but the second Lucas sat on it and spun it up, he'd known he had to have it. It made throwing a pot seem so much more *present* than the electric wheel he'd used.

He couldn't wait to get it out and start using it to make Audrey's wedding favors.

The problem was, it weighed about a half ton. "But I'm going to need it," he said, just as Gabe had started to snore against his neck. He'd have to get at least one more guy up here to help them get it out of the storage unit.

"Wha'?" Gabe pressed his groin against Lucas's backside, trapping his semihard dick between them. "Give you what you need," he mumbled, then rocked against him a couple of times before petering out.

Squirming around, Lucas found Gabe's eyes still closed, and his breath going wheezy again, like he was falling back asleep. But his cock was plump and reddened, if not fully hard. More draping with potential than drooping flaccidly.

"If I make you come, will you do something for me?" he whispered, then kissed Gabe's chin.

"'Course," Gabe slurred, clearly not really conscious. He might never remember agreeing, but that was no reason not to play with his cock.

Grinning, Lucas wormed his hand under Gabe's dick, letting it rest in his palm as he stroked it with his thumb. It immediately started to lengthen and fill, similar to dripping liquid on a crumpled straw wrapper. He didn't love giving handjobs as much as fucking or giving blowjobs, but the advantage was that he could watch himself play with Gabe's cock, and see how it—and the guy attached to it—reacted to different motions.

God, sex hadn't been this fun in *forever*.

He buried his nose in Gabe's neck, breathing in the scent of him. It was especially sexy right now, because Gabe had gotten up hours ago to deal with the horses, then come back to bed smelling like a working man.

"Mmm." Gabe shifted, rolling onto his back and widening his legs, giving Lucas room to work. Which of course Lucas took advantage of, settling between Gabe's legs, holding Gabe's cock between his palms and rolling it gently. He played forever, watching Gabe's expression as he grimaced in pleasure and gasped occasionally, and the way his hips lifted and his thighs tightened. Rubbing his own dick against the mattress but not touching himself until Gabe said, "Finish it," and started pumping himself through Lucas's fist rather than letting Lucas set the rhythm. For that last minute, Lucas put his lips over Gabe's head, letting it thrust in and out of his mouth a lot like Gabe's tongue did when they were deep into kissing. He came before Gabe, moaning, and then the warm, salty rush of Gabe's cum filled his mouth.

"Can't believe your ex was stupid enough to let you do that to other guys," Gabe said a while afterward, while Lucas still had his head resting on his thigh.

"Are you saying if I was your boyfriend, you wouldn't let me touch anyone else?" Lucas teased.

"Fuck no," rumbled out of Gabe's chest, then he chuckled. "I'm starting to suspect your ex wasn't the sharpest tool in the shed."

Talking about Drew with Gabe was beginning to seem normal. Even when he had to admit embarrassing details. Stuff he hadn't even told Audrey. "We sort of had to open up the relationship after the first year if we were going to stay together." He riffled Gabe's leg hairs with his fingers, waiting for his response.

First, though, Gabe had to yawn. "Why's that?"

"He's a total bottom too."

Gabe huffed, but Lucas couldn't tell if he was amused or disdainful. Either way, he didn't sound particularly interested in discussing it further. Instead he changed the subject. "You got a plan for this afternoon?"

"Oh, yeah." He army-crawled up the bed and rested his head on the pillow next to Gabe's. "I want to get started on my basic design for the wedding favors." Normally, he couldn't have kept himself out of the studio once he had the idea, but for once he'd found something more compelling to interest him. "I've barely got four weeks to finish them."

Rolling onto his side to face Lucas, Gabe kissed him on the forehead, then rolled the other way, pushing up on his elbow at the edge of the bed. "I gotta get moving too. I don't have much time to get Bruce trained up to pull a carriage."

"The one Zach is restoring?"

Glancing over his shoulder, Gabe frowned. "How'd you know about that?"

Mostly because he'd overheard Gabe and Zach talking about keeping something from him, so he went looking. "I'm not *totally* unobservant."

"Huh." Gabe sat on the edge of the mattress. "Well, you aren't telling Audrey, are you?"

"Why would she care that he's restoring a carriage?" Leaning over, he found his pack on the floor next to his side of the bed, and pulled some briefs out of them.

"It's a surprise for the wedding. To take them from the chapel around to the reception area."

"Ooooh, that's sweet."

"It is, kinda." Caressing Lucas's head as he went by, Gabe walked toward the bathroom, and Lucas paused in getting dressed to watch him go. Maybe it was the freckles, or the curve of his lower spine, but something about his back was really sexy. And masculine. It could have been the faint delineation of the muscles under his shoulder blades, or the slight love handles just above his hips that recalled Renaissance nudes. Lucas pondered it long after he couldn't see it anymore, then shook his head at himself and finished putting on his clothes.

A few minutes later he was in the kitchen, scrounging up a couple of quick sandwiches for them, when a fully dressed Gabe walked in and continued the conversation about his to-do list as if they hadn't been interrupted. "I also gotta go up to the main house and check on Momma and Gramma. Looks like they didn't even go to church this morning."

So cute how he called his mother that. "Okay." Little shivers of awareness worked down his neck as Gabe came up right behind him, brushing against his bare arm.

"Momma's gonna want me to come to dinner there tonight since it's Sunday." His fingers landed on Lucas's lower back, the touch much lighter than usual. "She's also gonna want you to come."

Lucas froze and stared at the mayonnaise-laden knife he was pressing into a slice of bread.

"You don't have to. I mean, if you were planning on going back to Audrey's . . ."

Shit. More sticky issues to navigate around. "Sunday is still the weekend. You said I could stay the weekend." But did he really want to have dinner with Gabe's mother and grandmother? It wasn't as if he'd be meeting them for the first time or anything, just the first time as an adult. And the guy who was sleeping with their son/grandson.

"'Course you can stay." Gabe's fingertips moved an inch or so in a quickly aborted caress. "So you do wanna have dinner with them?"

He bit his lip and finally started spreading mayo again. What exactly was Gabe asking him? Was this just the family of an old friend who wanted to see how he'd turned out? Or was it a "meet the boyfriend's parents" kind of thing? "Ummm . . ."

Gabe pressed his scratchy chin against Lucas's neck and circled his waist. "You don't have to. Not a big deal."

Oh, but it was. He could hear the reluctance in Gabe's voice, and he even knew what it was about—the guy wasn't looking forward to telling his mom that Lucas wouldn't be coming for Sunday dinner, even though he was only about three hundred yards away. In this part of the world, rejecting his (sort of) hosts' hospitality was borderline rude. Lucas's own mother would be ashamed of his behavior. So, it wasn't really a meet the boyfriend thing, it was a being neighborly thing. He finished with the food and turned, resting his hands on Gabe's shoulders. "It's fine, I'll go."

Gabe didn't respond for a few seconds while he searched Lucas's face with concerned eyes. "Sure?"

Lucas assured him with a squeeze. "Positive."

He might have been nervous about it, but the kiss Gabe gave him before snatching up a sandwich and leaving made it okay.

Hours later, after a productive afternoon in the studio, he was back to being nervous. Enough so that Gabe had to pat his knee under his mother's dinner table to keep it from jogging up and down.

"Thank you for inviting me to dinner, Mrs. Savage." *Dammit.* Everyone in town knew she'd never married Gabe's father. Mostly because he'd died in a drunk-driving accident while she was still pregnant.

She only smiled at him, though. "I think we both know I was no missus, and you're old enough to call me Jane."

He couldn't do much but chuckle at his gaffe, and his nerves. Slowly, after that, he loosened up. Eventually relaxing to the point where he laughed out loud at hearing stories about Gabe as a kid, and gossip about who was sleeping with whom at the retirement home. Gramma Savage told those anecdotes with a twinkle in her eye, and lots of winking.

It was like having dinner with family he liked, but hadn't been reunited with in years.

Once they'd finished eating and he and Gabe had loaded the dishwasher, Lucas didn't feel the sense of relief he'd expected. He couldn't say for sure what he felt, but he gave Jane and Gramma each a hug as he left.

Walking back across the pasture in the moonlight, he mused, "Once I leave and find a place to settle, I'm going to have to visit more often."

Gabe didn't say anything. Instead, he took Lucas's hand and held it right up until they got back in his bed.

Monday morning after feeding the horses and letting them out into the pasture, Gabe went back up to his place to crawl in next to Lucas. Screw all the chores he should be doing but wasn't right now. They could wait.

A split-second attack of nausea knocked him off-kilter when he found the bedroom empty. The clock told him it was only about eight thirty, which was early for Lucas to drag his ass out of bed.

Unless the guy got hit by a bolt of inspiration. The studio, that's where Lucas must be.

Coming out onto the landing, he was about to head down to the first floor when he noticed the door to the unused part of the barn was ajar. Through the gap, he could see a silhouetted figure standing in front of the windows, staring out, those familiar lips slightly parted. Even with so few clues, Gabe could easily tell Lucas had gone into his own little world again.

The apartment took up about a third of the east end of the barn's second floor, and the hayloft took up about another third of the west end. All the space between them was empty, and Lucas was smack-dab in the middle of it, entranced by the view of the Olympic mountain range disappearing up into the low, gray clouds.

This vacant area was wired with electricity, and light fixtures were attached to the gigantic rafters in the gloom above it, but Gabe didn't bother flipping the switch. It was too peaceful this way to ruin it with the buzz of fluorescent bulbs.

His footsteps echoed around the space as he followed the dusty prints Lucas had left, walking softly so as to not startle him.

"Hey," Lucas mumbled when Gabe came to a halt behind him, sounding as vacant as he'd looked. He was wrapped up in a blanket from the bed, one side of his hair still mashed from sleep. When Gabe took him into his arms, Lucas's body was warm, and relaxed against his immediately. "If I lived here," he whispered. "This is where I'd build my studio."

"Too bad it's not possible."

Lucas had no call to stay, same as when he was a teenager, and Gabe would do well to remember that.

"You're right."

"What's wrong with the one downstairs?"

"Nothing." Lucas shrugged. "I just like it here better." He continued to speak in a hushed voice, as if they were in church. Sighing, he turned so he was sideways to the windows and could kiss Gabe's neck. Then he rested his head on Gabe's shoulder, angled so he could still look out at the mountains.

"It's a beautiful view." The same as from the living room. It had dictated the whole layout of his apartment.

"I have to go back into town soon," Lucas said after a few minutes of peaceful silence. "Audrey called. She has something she wants me to do with her for the wedding."

Gabe forced the unexpected tension that rose inside him to heel. "Yeah?" Hair tickled the underside of his jaw as Lucas nodded. "Well, it was a nice weekend, while it lasted." Damn, he sounded hoarse. Probably from holding back the part of him that wanted to ask for this not to end. It wouldn't have worked last time, and this time was the same.

Lucas shifted, and Gabe thought he heard him swallow. "Is it over?"

Halfway between relief at Lucas bringing it up and fear over where this was going, Gabe closed his eyes and said, "It doesn't have to be." He didn't know if he wanted forever, but he knew he wanted more.

"Even though I just got out of a relationship, and I can't stay beyond the wedding?" Lucas's voice and muscles vibrated with sudden tension.

Eyes popping open, he shook his head. "Doesn't matter." He tightened his hold, and had to consciously take a breath to say what needed saying. "I told you this wasn't a one-time thing the other night, but that doesn't mean I'm expecting you to move in with me, or call yourself my boyfriend."

In his arms, Lucas relaxed.

"I'm not ready to be done with you, though," he said easily, in contrast to the way his chest constricted around his lungs.

"Me neither." The response was immediate. "I think this is a little more than friends with benefits."

"We're on the same page." He'd planned on a do-over, after screwing things up when they were younger and he'd been near cross-eyed with wanting Lucas. 'Course it would be more than just sex. "So, this is kind of . . . what?"

After a second, Lucas nodded. "It's a vacation thing. A fling."

A fling. That sounded a hell of a lot better than friends with benefits. He could have an emotional attachment to a fling, and it wouldn't be weird. "Well, feel free to come stay whenever you want. You're welcome to." More than welcome.

"I'll be here tomorrow night, then." Turning and stretching up, Lucas lifted his chin in a clear request for a kiss. It was exactly what Gabe wanted.

CHAPTER TWELVE

"*I*'ve hardly seen you in the last two weeks."

Lucas looked up from the grapefruit Audrey had halved and sectioned for him. It was a very different breakfast than he'd become used to at Gabe's. Healthier but less yummy. For Gabe it was usually a second breakfast, since he'd been up for hours already. "I still live here."

"One night in four."

"I stayed here last night." Grapefruit juice squirted into his eye when he dug the spoon in. The food might be healthier here, but it had a mean streak.

"Because I made you interview DJs with me."

He squinted at her. "What are you getting at?"

"It's time for you to accept that you've moved out to the farm." She tilted her head in that cutesy way she had and smiled.

Oh, please. "I have not." He couldn't be *living* there—he and Gabe hadn't talked about it. Or rather they had talked about it, obliquely. He could stay all he wanted, until he left. Simple. And finite. Finally getting a bite of fruit from his spoon to his mouth, he nearly spit it back out because it was so sour. He gave up on the grapefruit, taking it over to the sink. He'd find something at Gabe's.

Back in his room, he looked for some more clean clothes, since he was running out. *See, I totally still live here—my clothes are here.*

Except he couldn't find any. The huge suitcase he'd never unpacked was nearly empty when he opened it. A couple of toiletries he rarely used and some of his socks lay scattered on the bottom of it. Didn't he have more than this?

Yes, he did. In the storage cube. At Gabe's.

Maybe he should have done some laundry in the last couple of weeks . . . Gabe had offered to throw some of Lucas's clothes in with his a few times, but Lucas had assured him it wasn't necessary.

But apparently he'd been hiding his head in the sand. *Maybe I do sort of live there.*

Oh God, did that mean they had to talk about it? Gabe had only invited him to "stay," not move in. As soon as he realized Lucas kind of had, how would he react? Two weeks was hardly long enough to make an informed, mature, adult decision about living with someone.

I want to, though. He knew Gabe was really into him, for now, but the guy hadn't extended an invitation for it to last longer than the short time Lucas would be in Bluewater Bay.

Did he even want an invitation?

Mulling it over, he picked up his mostly empty pack, then went down the stairs and out to his car on autopilot. He finally came to standing next to the driver's side, when something unusual caught his eye. A bright-orange envelope had been left under his windshield wiper.

Any place else, he'd have assumed it was a parking ticket, but that didn't seem possible, here.

Except it was. *Not* on autopilot, he jogged back across the street and through the side entrance to find Audrey on the staircase, halfway to the first floor. "Since when does Bluewater Bay give tickets?"

She stopped and blinked at him. "I don't know, but they've been doing it as long as I've been back. You didn't get a downtown residents' parking permit?" she asked, like he should have just known, without her telling him.

"I'm only here for another few weeks. Bluewater Bay has a downtown?"

"Yes. And you need a permit to park in it all night long." She pursed her lips at him, then came the rest of the way down.

He followed her to the shop's interior entry. "Why didn't you tell me that?"

"I did." Rounding on him, she planted her hands on her hips.

Which was unnecessary, because he wasn't going to argue. If she said she had, she probably had and he probably hadn't really been listening. "Sorry."

She tilted her chin in acceptance and turned back to unlock the store. "Now go get yourself a permit."

He nodded, but didn't really intend to. He'd get around to it, sometime. For now, he'd keep his car at Gabe's. Where he'd mostly been keeping it for the last two weeks, which was probably how he'd avoided a ticket until today.

As he was leaving for a second time, halfway out the door, Audrey called over to him across the little lobby. "Are you coming back to town tonight?"

Was there some MOH thing he'd forgotten about? Dammit. He'd just have to admit it. "I didn't think I needed to."

"You don't, it's just that Zach and I are having dinner with your parents at the brew pub. You're invited."

He grimaced, toying with the old-fashioned doorknob on the entry. He'd only seen his parents a few times since returning to Bluewater Bay, so he really *should* go to dinner. "Can I bring Gabe?" They liked him, plus he *was* the best man.

"I assumed you would."

"We'll be there." Probably. Although he was pretty sure Gabe didn't have other plans, because he'd asked if Lucas was coming back today.

Lucas hadn't been to the new microbrewery in town, partly because it was called Ma Cougar's, which scared him even as it piqued his interest. That night, as Gabe parked the truck, Lucas craned his head and studied the place through the window. It was a new building, he was pretty sure, but located in what some might call the historical part of town. In other words, almost his parents' neighborhood.

"Audrey says Dad spends a lot of time here."

"Yep," Gabe agreed, cranking the steering wheel and then putting his arm across the bench seat so he could see out the rear window while he backed into a spot.

"I thought he was drinking less." Ma Cougar's electric bill must be huge every month. They had spotlights illuminating all the landscaping, and every architectural detail had rows of lights skirting it, picking out the interesting parts.

"He is." Gabe shut off the ignition. "By the way, Seth Larson is a waiter here."

His shoulders tensed at the name of that guy. "Why are you telling me?" He refused to look at Gabe.

"'Cause sometimes you seem like you don't like him."

"I don't." He shrugged airily and pretended to still be fascinated by the conspicuous energy consumption of the brewery.

"He's a nice guy, Lu. Wasn't he in your class at school?"

Sighing, Lucas gave up on being a brat. "My problem with him is that he was out in high school, and I didn't want to get outed by association, so I avoided him when I could, and I was a dick to him when I couldn't." He had to let his head rest on the cool glass of the window before he could admit it all. "And I'm ashamed of that, so I pretend I have another reason to dislike him, but I don't. I barely know him."

"'S'okay, babe." Gabe's fingers brushed across his shoulder.

That endearment was still new enough that Lucas's heart fluttered every time Gabe used it, and it had the power to distract him from even the most self-absorbed trains of thought. He got out of the truck and waited for Gabe to come around to his side, wondering if they'd hold hands walking in. He'd never been big on public displays, but Gabe was incredibly tactile.

They didn't hold hands, although Gabe settled his fingers on the small of Lucas's back as they went through the entryway. A young teenage girl was standing at the hostess station. Just as they approached, Seth Larson walked up from the restaurant side.

"Hey guys." He smiled, then caught Lucas's eye, but Lucas couldn't quite maintain the contact. "The rest of your family is already here, let me show you the way."

"I should probably get to know him better, shouldn't I?" he asked Gabe in a whisper as they followed the guy.

"Probably." Gabe brushed Lucas's back with his fingers again, in a touch that reassured him, whether it was meant to or not.

Trailing behind Seth, he checked out the crowded, noisy restaurant. It was huge, and not very well lit. The decor leaned toward "industrial," with unfinished wood paneling and concrete floors.

It could have been a brewpub anywhere on the West Coast, or the East, and probably points in between.

Seth led them to a large booth against a wall. Audrey, Dad, and Zach were seated on one side, and Mom was all by herself on the other. As they approached, she jumped up and beamed, kissing Lucas on the cheek when he was within range. "I'm so glad you're here, honey."

Yeah, he really should have made more of an effort to see his parents. He hugged her tightly. "It's nice to see you, Mom."

"Well, siddown," Dad called, beaming. Somehow, Lucas ended up on the interior of the booth, with Gabe next to him and his mother on the outside. The noise of the place was partially blocked by the height of the booth walls, but he could barely make out the menu that Zach shoved into his hands. He had to hold it next to the little candle on the table. "Do you need to see it?" he asked Gabe.

"Nah, that's just the beer menu. I know what I'm having."

"They make a beer with coffee in it. It's a real time-saver for some of the barflies," Dad interjected.

Seth hung around long enough to take their drink orders—the others already had pints—then left them to their family gathering.

Lucas was unaccountably tense, but it wasn't until he heard his father asking Gabe about the farm that he realized why. It was because he was here with a guy he was seeing. The last (and only) time he'd brought a guy home to meet his parents, it had been a disaster.

"Things're all right, Carl," Gabe responded to Dad's question, and all the tension eased out of Lucas's shoulders. His family *knew* Gabe, nearly as well (and maybe better) than they knew him. He didn't have a thing to worry about. Under the table, he squeezed Gabe's thigh, and in return Gabe rubbed against his.

The talk quickly turned to forestry. Gabe and Zach still worked in the industry, and Dad had for years. Mom was cut off from him and Audrey, but she was actually joining in the men's conversation, so that left Lucas able to lean across the table and speak to Audrey.

"This is a little weird," he said.

"Because you're here with your boyfriend?"

He widened his eyes at her, trying to communicate that she should shut up and not use that word.

She smirked, which he took to mean he'd gotten the message across. "I had to change the wine tasting to next Thursday at eleven," she said, pulling out her phone and opening her calendar app. "Becca can't get there any earlier to watch the shop for me."

Lucas dug out his own cell, and they conferred on that and other wedding things until Gabe was poking him in the side, handing him the beer Seth had brought him, and telling him he needed to decide what to order.

It was fun, in the end. His dad was drinking, yes, but not at the rate Lucas was used to. He seemed animated, taking part in the conversation and even directing it at times, laughing a lot. Lucas relaxed into the unexpected pleasure of actually enjoying his family, twining his fingers with Gabe's under the table and contributing the occasional comment. Mostly he watched them, though. Audrey caught his eye a few times, smiling over things his dad had said. Not in a mocking way, but more of an *isn't he cute?* way.

Once they did order, it took forever for the food to arrive. "It's normal for this place," Audrey said when he commented on it. Lucas had finished his first beer when Seth finally came back with their meals.

Really, Seth *was* a good-looking guy. Lucas couldn't make out his eyes very well in this lighting, but he had an attractive face, with strong bone structure. It was enhanced by the close-trimmed beard and mustache that most guys their age were sporting now. Plus his body was pretty toned.

Alarm tightened his stomach muscles when he realized Seth was probably more attractive than he was, but then Gabe wrapped his arm around Lucas's shoulders in a semihug and it didn't seem to matter anymore. Even, a minute later, after he removed his arm so he could eat his dinner.

Before starting on the pasta he'd ordered, a passing waiter caught his attention. This guy had nearly the same beard as Seth, but he was much older. Looking at the guys in his family—and Gabe—for the first time it struck him as odd that none of them had one.

"How come you guys don't have beards?"

He got a couple of muttered "Dunno's" but was mostly ignored in favor of eating.

"I mean," Lucas persisted. "*Everyone* has some kind of facial hair lately, haven't you noticed?"

This caused more of a reaction—snorts and smirking among the men, and a thoughtful look from Audrey. Mom was still simply eating, unconcerned.

"It's the whole lumbersexual thing, you know?" he addressed his best friend, since she was the only one who cared about it enough to listen.

"Oooooh." Her eyes sparkled. "That's a *great* word. Can I use it?"

Waving his permission, he confessed, "I didn't make it up. Some guy in a magazine did. Or maybe online, I don't know."

"What in *hell* is a lumbersexual?" Zach demanded.

Oh, sure, *now* he had their attention. "It's like the next iteration of metrosexual."

Blank looks from everyone.

"He means," Audrey explained, turning to her fiancé and placing a hand on his arm, "it's popular culture's idealized version of manly men who do manly labor. Like loggers. It's *flattering*."

Strange. None of the guys seemed flattered. They mostly wore screwed-up expressions of disgusted disbelief.

"*Beards*?" Dad asked. "That don't make a logger."

"And mustaches," Lucas offered. "I don't think it's necessarily lumberjacks they're aping. I'm pretty sure 'oil rigger-sexual' and 'cowsexual' just didn't sound as catchy."

"*Cowsexual*?" Dad nearly spit out his beer, rearing forward to plant his hands on the table and gawk at Lucas.

"Like from *cowboys*."

"Gotta admit," Gabe said, "'cowsexual' has other possible definitions that don't really recommend it." He alone looked amused, along with the disgust and disbelief.

"It's strange," Audrey said, getting at the point Lucas hadn't quite been able to. "You guys are all loggers, or were, but none of you have beards."

"*Most* actual loggers don't wear beards," Zach told her before taking a bite of his burger. "And if they do, they're damn small ones."

"That's true." Lucas jumped on what his brother said. "I can't think of anyone, the whole time I was growing up around here, who regularly had a beard. What's that about?"

The men in his family—and Gabe—all looked at him like he was crazy.

"What?"

That was when Mom finally weighed in. "Of course loggers don't have beards, not unless they like combing wood chips out of it every day."

Ooooh.

"Well," Zach mused. "I suppose if they wore one of those chin nets over 'em, like they make guys do down at the bakery."

That brought down the house. Even Audrey was giggle-snorting uncontrollably.

See? Totally fun time with his family.

Lucas's good evening was partially destroyed as they left, though.

"Carl!" someone shouted from the bar as they were making their way out.

"Huh?" Dad peered around, then saw whoever had yelled his name. "Hang on, gotta go talk to Denny Schultz. Promised him I'd make a delivery tonight. Meet ya outside," he said to Mom.

Delivery?

A few minutes later, they were standing out front still saying their farewells when Dad showed up. "Well, got that all squared away." He clapped his hands together and rubbed them, beaming.

"What?" Lucas asked.

"Oh, Denny's one a' my regular customers, but he lives damn near a half hour away. When he's in town, I like ta make sure and connect with him."

"Customers?" Sharing a look with Audrey didn't clear up anything, but it did make him warier. "You have customers?"

"'Course I do. You don't think I grow all that cannabis for myself, do you?"

"I thought you grew it for the guys who needed it medicinally?"

"Oh, I sell to them fellers too. I'm no discriminator." Dad winked and grinned, then pulled something out of his pocket and held it in his palm, showing it to Lucas.

A small ziplock baggie full of bud.

Oh. My. God. His father was a drug kingpin. "Is that actually *legal*?"

"'Course it's legal, didn't you hear?" his father scoffed. "Passed the medical marijuana law way back in '98, and the recreational use one just a coupla years ago."

"No, I mean, can you just sell it like this? To anybody at any time? At the bar?" It smacked way too much of dealing drugs on the street corner. Wasn't it supposed to be more official than that?

"Why the hell not?"

"Aren't there regulations? Don't you have to pay taxes or something? I mean, you're just taking money and handing over pot. In baggies." It was *exactly* like high school.

"I label 'em!" Dad objected, flipping the package in his hand over to reveal what looked a lot like one of Mom's canning jar stickers. Scrawled across it in his father's barely legible handwriting was a "net weight" and a phone number. "I don't want my consumers to be misled about the content or nothing."

"Uhhh, Dad? I don't think—"

"Babe." At the same time he was speaking into Lucas's ear, Gabe took his hand. "Maybe you better try and have this conversation later, when he hasn't had four pints of beer and plenty of smoke."

He was probably right. Lucas bit his lip, looking at his parents, who were in the process of hugging Audrey and Zach. "They're not driving, right?"

"Don't worry, they walked over. Your mom's not stupid."

He noticed Gabe didn't pass any judgments on his father's intelligence.

Suddenly Mom was in front of him, reaching for a hug. "Now, you don't be a stranger. We don't see near enough of you." Squeezing him tightly, she whispered, "Told you that boy's always been sweet on you."

Momma had fed the horses that night since he and Lucas were going out, but Gabe still went down and checked on them when they got home. Truth was, he didn't need to, but the last week or so not having much to do had really started to weigh on him. Bruce's training was almost too damn easy, and while he'd been busy looking for downed snags and limbs after the big storm, that was nearly taken care of. He only had a few dangerous hangers-on to get to, which would take a dry couple of days, considering the slopes they were on.

Once or twice, he'd found himself with hours' worth of not much to do while Lucas was busy making wedding favors. Ever since Gabe had hitched up July to his potter's wheel and dragged it into the studio for him, the guy spent most days in there, either throwing pots or carefully cutting them apart once they were what Lucas called "leather hard." The most perplexing thing had been the entire afternoons he spent just rubbing them, over and over, sometimes with a polished up bit of plastic, and sometimes with various cloths. It wasn't until he'd fired off the first set of wedding favors earlier in the week, then cleaned them up, that Gabe saw the point of that. Every place Lucas had burnished before firing came out lustrous. Even shinier than the spots on the sculpture of Bruce. He'd made a whole series of small bowls shaped like peonies, each with multiple, removable petals. Glossy inside and rougher on the exterior.

The simple beauty of them blew Gabe away. His boy was talented as shit, and twice as sexy.

Thinking about it, Gabe took the stairs two at a time going back up to the apartment. Lucas would be waiting in bed for him. He made a pit stop in the bathroom, then shed most of his clothes on his way into the room, finding Lucas all tucked in and . . . staring at his phone.

It was kinda disappointing, but he'd give it a few minutes. It probably wouldn't last, just he'd half-expected Lucas to put it down once he'd arrived. Gabe shucked his sweats and climbed under the blankets, waiting for Lucas to notice he had a naked man next to him.

Didn't happen.

Instead, Lucas kept muttering things to himself, then stabbing at the screen. "Oh no," he whispered, then bit his lip as he furiously poked at the cell.

After about five minutes of activities in that vein, Gabe'd had enough. "What's so interesting on that thing you can ignore a horny guy waiting on you?"

"Sorry." But Lucas's eyes were dazed and unfocused. "My dad is totally breaking the law."

"Well, what are the chances he'll get caught?" Best thing for this was distraction. He found Lucas's naked thigh under the covers, and ran his palm up the inside. Lucas shivered.

But he didn't put down the damn phone. "I don't know, but growing *and* selling is illegal. He can grow and process, but he can't sell unless he's not growing *or* processing."

"Well, you'll talk to him about it." Working his fingers under the leg of Lucas's briefs, Gabe found the sensitive spot where his thigh met his groin.

"I will?" Lucas wiggled closer and bent one knee. Gabe took advantage of his increasing interest, working Lucas's underwear down until Lucas kicked them off under the covers.

Then he scooted up until he was nosing under Lucas's jaw. "Someone's got to talk to him, and you've done all the research." Finding a tender spot, he nipped it.

Lucas took a shuddery breath and finally set the phone on the nightstand. "Guess I will. Later."

Turning until he faced Gabe, he took his newly free hand and searched under the blankets, finding Gabe's naked chest and belly. Settling in, sinking down into the bed, and mashing their bodies together.

Gabe rolled, pulling him on top. "C'mon, baby. Ride me." He grabbed the lube off his nightstand, slicked up Lucas's dick and then his, then held both in his fist while Lucas straddled his hips and worked in and out of his grip. For a guy with a couple of kinks, Lucas could be strangely shy sometimes. It had taken lots of coaxing to get him to be on top, but it was Gabe's favorite way to watch him as he got more excited and lost in the sex. With his free hand, he stroked Lucas's body, hitting all his most sensitive spots. Following the changes in his tempo and listening for the building desire in his breath.

When Lucas was gasping and thrusting fast, face screwed up in exertion, Gabe levered himself up until he could reach around and slide his fingers between Lucas's cheeks, finding his hole and pushing inside. Lucas's rhythm stuttered between Gabe's finger and the slide of their cocks in his hand. Eyes flying open, he stared into Gabe's as he came, his testicles jerking and his dick pumping against him.

Then Gabe eased him down until Lucas was resting on top, breathing heavily. After a moment or two he rolled off, plastering himself against Gabe's side and kissing his neck over and over while he stroked Gabe in his hand.

Lucas could make it last forever like this. Working Gabe's cock fast with a tight grip, then suddenly slowing down, changing things up to counter the movements of Gabe's hips. The guy liked to tease, but deep down Gabe knew Lucas would never leave him hanging, so he let him. When he finally did come, with Lucas half on top of him again, tonguing his nipples and fondling his balls in his free hand, he had a split second where he knew he was the luckiest man in the world, to be here with this guy, and he very nearly babbled out all kinds of things he didn't know if he meant. Instead he groaned and spilled cum on his belly while Lucas squirmed against him and whispered encouragement.

As he recovered, Lucas kissed him slowly. Deep, sensual forays of his tongue into Gabe's mouth. The sex might be over, but the togetherness wasn't. Moments like this, he was pretty sure they were making love.

It was about the best way to fall asleep in the world.

He woke up a little after three, thinking about marijuana. Carl had said he was making a ton of money. "Between retirement and my pharmaceutical sales, I'm making more now than when I was working."

Lucas's old room couldn't be more than 100 square feet.

Gabe had a whole damned field waiting for a crop.

Untangling himself from Lucas's hold, he crept out into the living room and fired up his computer, planning on doing a little research of his own.

It took him hours of trolling confusing state websites and overly enthusiastic pothead ones, but by daybreak Gabe was convinced this was a possibility. What had him most excited was the chance to try something different with the farm. He'd never thought about raising anything but timber before, but if he could make enough to keep it going while using only a small part of the land, he could let the whole forest ecosystem regenerate. Even let it reseed naturally. It didn't have to be forever, and as long as he kept it from getting dangerously overgrown, it might be good.

Hell, it might be great. Whistling softly to himself, he went down to feed the horses before crawling back into bed and snuggling up to his boy.

Waking up a while later, Gabe found the bed next to him empty. Made sense, it was after ten. Lucas would already be downstairs working.

He wasn't though. Wandering into the kitchen so he could poke his head in the fridge to find some breakfast, Gabe found his boy instead. He was standing in front of the window in nothing but a pair of briefs, eating peanut butter from a spoon and spacing off in that way he did. Gabe watched him for a minute, getting a hell of a lot of enjoyment from the way Lucas stuck out his tongue and burrowed it into the peanut butter, prodding and licking and twisting sinuously. Then he'd take his payload back into his mouth, swallowing. In between each bite, he'd space out for long seconds, occasionally swaying, eyes glazed over.

Damn, he was a unique one, wasn't he? Sauntering up behind him, Gabe pressed his groin into Lucas's cheeks, smiling as the guy jolted in surprise and then pushed back into him.

"Sure do like to watch you sucking on that." He skimmed his lips up the back of Lucas's neck, imagining he could feel the shivers coursing down Lucas's body. His boy was so sensitive to touch. "Almost as much as I like watching you suck me."

Lucas turned around and dropped to his knees, taking Gabe's words as an invitation. Having his sweats yanked off and peanut butter caked all over his balls and dick wasn't what he'd been intending to offer, but he wasn't about to stop the action, not when it made Lucas cross-eyed with excitement. "You better lick every speck of that off of me," he said, twisting his fingers in Lucas's hair. Just like every time he got commanding, Lucas made happy moaning noises in his throat. Then he proceeded to make more noises as he sucked all the mess off while jerking himself, coming before Gabe did.

It wasn't until later, when they were showering the peanut butter off, that Gabe explained what he'd figured out in the middle of the night about legal marijuana production, and how he and Carl could work it to both their advantages. "See, your dad already has a grower's license."

"God, I hope so," Lucas said, pouring more shampoo into his palm. He'd already lathered, rinsed, and repeated once, but his hair still wasn't clean.

"He does," Gabe assured him, lathering up his own pubes for the third time.

"Dammit, this stuff is hard to get out, isn't it?" Lucas grinned at him.

"Yeah, you're gonna have to use more shampoo." He was even having to work it into his belly hair again.

Frowning, Lucas asked. "How do you know that?"

What, he thought Gabe had done that before? "I use peanut butter to get pitch off." Shortening worked better for sap, but he wasn't much of a baker so he didn't keep it around. Lucas was still squinting at him questioningly, so Gabe swatted him lightly on his butt, making him flush from the chest up and bite his lip. *Huh.* He'd have to remember that reaction. Matter of fact, more investigation now might be in order. Cupping the cheek he'd just swatted, he rubbed it, then swatted it again, watching Lucas's face when his eyes went wide and his lips parted as he gasped softly.

"Um." Flushing more, Lucas ducked his head. "So you were saying about Dad?"

His kinky boy was going shy again. Definitely promising, but better to leave it for later. "Yeah. That's one thing Zach made sure of, that your dad had a license to grow. I guess he didn't worry too much about the details of distribution."

Lucas rolled his eyes and stepped under the spray of water to wash out his hair again.

"Anyway, thing is, in order to grow someplace else, all your dad has to do is file more paperwork. He doesn't have to get a whole new license, which is a good thing, 'cause they aren't issuing them right now." He had to wait while Lucas finished up, then wiped the water out of his eyes, moving so Gabe could rinse off.

Lucas didn't actually respond to that until they were out of the shower, drying themselves.

"Okaaay . . ." His brow was furrowed up. "Are you saying you'd let him grow here? In that hay field?"

"'S'what I'm saying." Knotting the towel around his waist, Gabe dug out his shaving cream and razor from the top drawer.

Lucas got between him and the mirror and took the things out of his hands. He set them down and twined their fingers together, as if he needed to make sure he had Gabe's full attention. "I don't understand— Do you mean you'll lease the field to him?"

"I'm thinking," Gabe responded, gazing into his clear blue eyes, "of going into business with him."

Lucas's jaw dropped. "With my *dad*?"

Smiling, Gabe kissed his nose. "He's a handful, all right." Kind of like his son. "But I think it's worth a one-year trial, especially since I won't be working the farm much otherwise. And I can handle Carl Wilder. Savage and Wilder. What do you think?"

Lucas's brow wasn't quite so furrowed, but his concern was clear. "Well, I guess I think . . . if anyone can keep him from doing something really stupid, it would be you."

Damn, knowing someone he cared about had faith in him was like getting a shot of steroids in the arm. "There's a ton of advantages to him doing it here, too. I never pursued getting organic certification, 'cause who the hell cares if their trees are organic? I mean, if I was milling it myself I might try, but I'm not. Anyway, I've kept all the records, and I know Savage Tree Farm can get certified within a few years. I bet those weed smokers will pay a premium for organic marijuana."

Lucas snorted. "Probably." He finally moved, pressing his lips to the ball of Gabe's shoulder before he pulled away.

As Gabe shaved, he alternately watched Lucas get dressed and followed the razor's slide up his neck in the mirror. "You know, I think there might even be some eco-pot-tourism opportunities. I mean, I got a farm that's in a beautiful spot—"

"Yes, you do."

"—and better than that, it's a *horse-powered* farm. I know we can't sell the weed, but we can give tours and shit, right? Convince consumers to ask for our product by name."

Glancing at Lucas again, as he swished the razor in the sink water, he nearly lost his breath. The way his boy was looking at him was enough to make Gabe's chest squeeze tight. His eyes had gone soft and glowing, and the small smile on his face was downright affectionate. Holding Gabe's gaze in the mirror, Lucas came up behind him and hugged him tightly around the waist, kissing along the back of his shoulder, then up his neck.

"You're amazing," he whispered in Gabe's ear, smile growing until he just looked so damned content. Like everything he needed in the world was right here, in this bathroom.

"So are you, baby," he rasped.

Lucas just shook his head, still smiling, then pressed one more kiss to the nape of his neck before letting go and leaving the room.

CHAPTER THIRTEEN

*L*ucas didn't spend very long dwelling on it after Gabe dropped his bomb. While the idea of his dad and his boyfriend working together to grow pot, of all things, was a mind-bender, it was secondary to Lucas's inexplicable anxiety over what this meant for them. Him and Gabe.

If Gabe was in business with his father, that increased the connections between them. And as the connections increased, so did Lucas's uncertainty over what exactly was happening. Or rather, his certainty over his feelings for Gabe, but the unavoidable end to this nonrelationship of a relationship.

Earlier, in the bathroom, he'd kind of let it all hang out. He'd been unable to keep the warmth inside to himself, but at least had managed to limit the display of it to just a few kisses and some simple words. *"You're amazing."*

Gabe's strangled response had seemed perfect at the time, but as soon as Lucas left the room, he started to wonder if the guy's difficulty in speaking was from discomfort rather than shared sentiment. Was he worried Lucas would try to make this temporary interlude more permanent? Gabe had never even hinted that he'd be open to more, and God knew, he'd nearly shoved Lucas out of town last time they got together.

He'd drive himself crazy thinking about this all day, and there was only one sure distraction.

As soon as he had settled into his studio, but before he got his hands dirty, his phone rang. He could have ignored the call if he was already working, and he almost did anyway because he didn't recognize the number. On the other hand, there might be a lot of locals who had his number, while he didn't necessarily have theirs.

It turned out to be Kitty, Audrey's sister.

"Oh, hey," he said when she'd identified herself. He'd never been really close to her, since she was about five years older than Audrey, but they'd always gotten along. Besides, he'd been starting to wonder about the bachelorette thingy. The wedding was only two weeks away, shouldn't he have heard something by now? "Are you calling about the party?"

"I am." Her voice was bright and cheerful, which he thought boded well. "It's this coming weekend, do you think you'll make it? Saturday."

"Um, sure." Could he bring Gabe? Maybe he needed to feel this out before asking. "Where is it?"

Kitty didn't immediately answer his question. "It's going to be *awesome*," she gushed instead. "Check it out: we're going to Seattle and staying in the presidential suite at the Four Seasons—"

Overnight? "How many of us?"

He didn't care what kind of suite it was, if there were too many people, he'd have to share a bed if this was a sleepover thing. Plus it reduced his chances of persuading Gabe to come along. Dammit. If necessary, he'd call dibs on bunking with Audrey. Being her main wedding attendant had to have some perks, right?

"Um, six, with you."

Not good. "How many beds does this suite have?"

"Does it matter? *Listen*."

He was pretty sure he had no choice.

"I rented a limo, and just guess where it's taking us."

"The Chihuly Garden?" That'd be cool, because he hadn't seen it yet. Although he had zero hope that was her plan.

"*No*." She made that scoffing noise in the back of her throat, like maybe she was trying to cough up a hairball. "We're going to hit every. Gay. Strip Bar. In town!"

It took Lucas the entire twenty seconds of her squealing to process that. "*What*?"

"Oh my God, you do like gay strippers, right? I mean, you know, you're gay and all—"

"Are you sure this is the right kind of, um, event for Audrey? Your sister?" Picturing the swank, old-school-style wedding she had planned and contrasting it to a night of drunken debauchery . . . Just, no.

"Well, yes, I mean, it's a once-in-a-lifetime event, so she should do something wild and crazy that she's never done before."

Lucas took the phone away from his ear and stared at it a second. Then he yanked it back. "What makes you think she's never been to a gay strip bar? You do know she was my roommate in Los Angeles after we finished school. We were in our *twenties.*"

"So?"

"So what do you think we *did* on weekends?"

Her stunned silence didn't last as long as her excited squealing had. "Okaaay, so it's a new thing for her friends. Just not her or her *man of honor.*"

"I'm not totally au courant on straight-people nuptials," he snarked, knowing he was failing at diplomacy but unable to believe this woman. "But since it's her bachelorette party, shouldn't it be something she'd *like?*"

"And just how do you know she won't like it?"

"Because she's over it. She's done it to death. I lived with her for two years, trust me."

"I lived with her for fourteen."

Dammit, she'd trumped him. He might have to backtrack and take a stab at diplomacy. "Kitty, hon, I know you're only trying to make her happy on her wedding day."

"I am." She sniffed. Tearing up or feeling superior? He couldn't tell.

"I simply think that, when you take into account the *type* of ceremony she's having, doing the gay club circuit is a little . . ." *Trashy.* "Down-market."

"*Everyone* does this at their bachelorette party," she bit out. "It's *expected.*"

How did that make it a once-in-a-lifetime experience?

"Except me," she added after a moment. "My bachelorette party was more subdued."

"Oh." *Ooooh.* "So, you don't want her to miss out on the experience?" More like she wanted to make up for a blank space on her bingo card of life.

"Exactly."

He drew breath to take another stab at dissuading her, but she cut him off.

"Listen, sweetie." *Uh-oh.* Hopefully his voice hadn't been that syrupy when he'd tried diplomacy. "I'm in charge, and I'm telling you, I know my sister—"

Yeah . . . no.

"And this will make her very, very happy."

He'd be a *horrible* MOH if he didn't make one more attempt to right this impending wrong. "You *are* planning on running it by her first, aren't you?"

"No! Oh my God, no. It's a surprise. And you better not tell her either, Lucas Wilder." She was probably wagging her index finger right this second. "Promise me."

"Kitty, I'm not sure—"

"I will call you back 24-7 until you swear."

The potential horror was too overwhelming. "I won't say a word to Audrey about the party." It was all he could do not to add in an evil hiss, *And just so you know, some of those dancers are* straight.

"Good." All the satisfaction of having won laced her voice.

After hanging up, it took Lucas a few moments of pressing the corner of his phone to his lips before he came up with a solution. Well, not actually—more like he came up with a solution for finding a solution.

He called Audrey.

"What if there's something I swore not to tell you, but I feel you really should know?" he asked as soon as she answered.

Audrey sighed. "Does this have something to do with my sister?"

Kitty'd never made him promise not to say that. "Yes."

"Is it about my bachelorette party?"

"Eeeehhh . . ." That might be a violation of his oath.

She sighed. "Do you see why I didn't want her to be my matron of honor?"

"*Matron* of honor? Really?"

"Because she's married. She's only a maid if she's single."

"Wow, that's way less sexy than maid of honor."

"*And* man of honor."

"Word."

"Anyway, if you swore not to tell me, you shouldn't."

"But I really feel you should *know*."

"Okay." Good, that decisive note in her voice boded well. "You can hint around until I figure—"

"Mmm, that kinda feels like telling."

"Did you swear not to tell *anybody*?"

Oh, he might see her direction, here. "No, just you." He could always rely on her for ways around social conundrums.

"So you *could* tell Gabe . . ."

"Who'll tell Zach—"

"And since it would involve *me*, he'd never keep it a secret."

"You are *so* good at this." He could only strive to be half the devious machinator she was.

"Thank you. You may kiss my ring."

"That dirty old thing?" They hadn't bantered like this in forever. He'd forgotten how fun it could be.

"You're just jealous *my* fiancé has such amazing taste."

Wait! His heart called a time-out, fluttering up into his throat. "Why did you say it that way?"

"Say what?"

"*My* fiancé, with the emphasis on 'my.'" Gabe hadn't— He and Gabe weren't— Oh, God, he couldn't go there.

"Well, same-sex marriage is legal in Washington."

In reaction, Lucas made the *ick* face, with extended tongue and everything. Thank God she'd managed to sidetrack him. "I hate that word. *Same-sex*. It's just marriage."

"Is same-sex really just one word? It might be two."

"Depends on whether you spell it with a hyphen." And they were off again, bantering, because Audrey knew when to make it light. He appreciated that about her.

Once they were finally off the phone, he threw himself into his work because now he had a few things to avoid thinking about.

Gabe had gone into town after lunch for something, then showed up around dinnertime, when Lucas told him about Kitty's bachelorette party plan. "Um, she made me swear not to tell Audrey when I told her I didn't think it was a good idea, so maybe you could tell Zach?"

Glancing up from his chili, Gabe smirked. "S'pose I ought to do that." An hour later, when Zach showed up to work on his carriage, Gabe went out to the machine shed to talk to him. It was like a very elaborate game of "telephone."

Mission accomplished.

Then, of course, Gabe came back and they watched TV and made out lazily before heading to bed and getting naked. So Lucas's little gaffe in the bathroom that morning must not have been noticeable. Relieved, he settled back into his happy, sated world, and focused on his sculptures, his sex life, and his best friend's wedding for the next few days.

Thursday he went into town early to pay his fine and ask about getting a parking permit before he met Audrey for the wine tasting. It seemed wise to do that first, rather than wandering into city hall with alcohol on his breath, even though he was pretty sure they wouldn't be having enough wine to get more than a mild buzz.

Paying the ticket was easy. Getting a permit was impossible.

"We don't give temporary resident permits," the woman at the "Parking" window insisted for the tenth time. "You have to pay for a whole year."

"I can't be the only person who's here for an extended period of time and needs to park downtown overnight."

"First one I've met."

He stared at her. "But what about the television show? It doesn't film year round. You must have people who need permits for short periods all the time."

"They pay for the year." Her mouth was set in a hard line by then, and Lucas had just enough presence of mind to stop arguing. It wouldn't do him any good, and besides, he didn't really need the permit. His MOH duties were almost over, and then he'd have no reason to stay in town overnight.

Probably. If he wanted to spend a lot of time reflecting on it, he might discover that not knowing what was going to happen with Gabe had a lot to do with his irritation over the parking permit. He didn't have time for reflection, thank God, because he had to meet Audrey at Ma Cougar's. Apparently the wine distributor had a deal with the microbrewery, and held tastings there.

He was a few minutes late, so he didn't have a chance to complain to Audrey or find out what she'd said to Kitty before they were sipping tiny amounts of wine. While his favorite MOH duty thus far, it was also the one he was least qualified for. No matter how much Drew tried, or how much he'd faked it, Lucas had never really enjoyed wine. As far as he could tell, there were really only two kinds: red and white.

In wine's favor, it was amazing how a dozen small sips over a half hour could improve his mood. When Audrey had made her selection, assisted by approving yet meaningless murmurs from him, he was ready to go back to the farm and forget his worries about parking permits and the questions about where his car might spend its nondriving time in the future. He could probably find Gabe—he just had to follow the sound of the chainsaw. This morning the guy had been headed out to cut up the last of the windfall from the storm for firewood. The thought of jumping him (once the saw was safely shut down) while he was drenched in manly sweat, smelling strongly of wood chips and faintly of two-stroke engine oil, was enough to make Lucas Homer Simpson–drool.

"Can you stay for lunch?" Audrey asked as he stood and grabbed his coat.

"Uh . . ." *Shit.* He knew that expression. She was upset about something, and wanted to talk. Probably about Kitty. "Sure, I can stay." Audrey didn't often ask for support, and considering the amount she gave Lucas, he always gave it if she asked.

The microbrewery was only about half-full, so they were able to move to a small booth near the windows. As soon as their waitress came by, Audrey ordered a glass of wine.

"What are you having?" she asked Lucas, and his head swam a tiny bit. He wasn't used to drinking in the middle of the day. On the other hand, he was already mildly buzzed from the wine tasting.

"I'll have a pint of your lager," he said to the waitress. Then, as soon as she was out of earshot, he hunched over the table to be nearer Audrey. "What's wrong?"

She sighed and rolled her eyes. "It's just this crap with Kitty."

He made his most sympathetic noise, combining it with a grimace of empathy.

"I don't really need to talk about it so much as I'd like to forget about it." But she was fidgeting with her water glass, head lowered and eyes focused on her fingers.

"Are you going to have to go to the party?"

"No." She waved her hand in the air dismissively. "I told them to go on their own and think about me."

Thank God, because if she'd felt she had to go, then he really couldn't have gotten out of it. It took him a few seconds of studying her as she unrolled the silverware from its napkin and arranged it into a pleasing pattern before he thought he might understand exactly what was getting her down. "But now you won't have a bachelorette party."

Her shoulders drooped, and she nodded.

Reaching out, Lucas snagged her hand. "We could have one, just the two of us."

The preoccupied frown lines eased off Audrey's forehead. "We could . . . What would we do?"

He shrugged. "What would be your ideal party?"

"Um, well, we'd reminisce, probably. About when we were single."

He wasn't sure he qualified as no longer single, but he wasn't about to argue. "Okay. Anything else?"

"We'd have to get tipsy." Pulling her hand out of his, she held up a stern palm. "Not drunk, just tipsy. It's much more sophisticated."

Very true. He dipped his chin.

"I think that's about it."

"We can do that right now," he said, and was rewarded by Audrey's face lighting up. "We'll call it your anti-bachelorette party."

To cap off the moment, their drinks arrived then. "Are you going to be having any food?" the waitress asked after serving them. "My shift is about to end, but your new server can take your order if you aren't ready."

For expediency Lucas asked for the same dish he'd had the other night, since he hadn't bothered to look at the menu. He was pretty sure Audrey did the same. Once alone again, he let her direct the conversation—because it was her anti-party—knowing full well she'd choose to discuss Gabe.

"He's so different from Drew or any other guys you've been with." Pausing to squint thoughtfully out the window, she corrected herself. "Well, he's a little like that professor of yours you were seeing in college."

"Shhhh!"

"What? That was, like, ten years ago. They can't fire him for sleeping with a student now, can they?"

"I don't know." It had nothing to do with why he'd not wanted her to say more, anyway. That had all been about him not wanting to remember how much Professor Ledbetter had reminded him of Gabe, and how much that had had to do with why Lucas ended up with his drawing instructor.

Plus, it felt uncomfortably close to cheating, which made no sense because he and Gabe had never spoken about exclusivity, at least not in regard to them. They didn't even plan on trying for anything long-term. "How is Gabe different from those other guys?" He prodded her back onto the slightly more comfortable topic.

"Physically. I mean, you were always with people who were so image-conscious."

"I was?" But even as he tried to deny it, numerous, very serious conversations with Drew about things like which gyms had the most attractive men came to mind. Conversations he found himself completely scornful of now. "God, I guess I kind of was."

"Do you remember how many times you had workout dates? They all had those perfect bodies."

"They weren't perfect," he refuted.

"You seemed to think so at the time."

He made a face, trying to stall until he figured out exactly why he'd objected. "It's more like they were perfect if you spent all your time exercising, but . . . it's not like any of those guys had muscles that were achieved through actual labor. They were decorative. It would be like if I made a pot that looks like it can function usefully, but it doesn't actually do a job. Sometimes I make pots that look only okay, but function really well, and that makes them *graceful*." Which was so much more elegant than being decorative for the sake of being decorative.

She stared at him.

"Sorta," he added lamely.

"Okay, so you're saying a beer gut is fine, as long as the biceps that go along with it are capable of functionally wielding a chainsaw?"

"That's not what I meant at *all*." Other than being exactly what he meant.

"Okaaaay," she said, nodding.

Well, yes, Gabe had a bit of a gut, but Lucas had been thinking of it as barrel-abdomened. Like barrel-chested, but a little further south. Just as firm, and just as masculine, but just not as . . . culturally idealized. An imperfectly perfect body achieved through work. By manhandling beasts five times his strength and *mastering* them. And all of it was sprinkled with wiry reddish hairs and dusted with a few freckles, like a perfectly decorated truffle.

Ungh.

"Fine. It's exactly what I meant."

She tilted her chin in smug acknowledgment of her point.

Their food appeared just then, much faster than the other evening. "Oh, look." Head swaying as if being blown by a gentle breeze, Audrey squinted up at their waiter. "There's Seth Larson."

"How are you guys doing? Can I get you anything else?"

Dammit. Lucas downed the rest of his beer. Of course Seth would be their replacement for the waitress. "I think we might need another round of drinks." Lucas offered up his friendliest smile. He got an eyebrow quirk in return before Seth moved on.

Hmmm. "You think Seth still hates me for being a dick in school?"

"I would," Audrey said. "D'you remember that girl a year behind us, Melody Jenkins?"

Squinting didn't jog his memory. "No."

"She sewed too, and she was always copying my clothes."

"Oh." He snapped his fingers, although the sound wasn't as crisp as he'd expected. "I remember her. She had *really* bad hair."

"She's dead," Audrey announced.

He winced. "Her hair wasn't *that* bad."

"I was a *bitch* to her." Poking the table with her index finger, Audrey leaned forward. "And it was because I felt threatened by her. Never got a chance to apologize, though. Not before she was hit by a bus in Seattle." All the intensity bled out of her, and she drifted back to lean against the booth cushion, vacantly staring at her glass.

"That's sad."

"'Tis." Picking her wine up, she drank down the rest. "What I'm sayin' is, you should learn from my pain. And I have to pee." Scooting out of the booth, she stood, steadying herself with a hand on the table for a second before swanning off to the ladies'. She tended to get more elegant as she got drunker.

Tipsy. Tipsier.

"Here you go." Like a sign from God, Seth appeared just then, setting their drinks on the table.

This is my chance. "I want you to know, when I avoided you and stuff in high school? That was all me, man. That wasn't about you."

"Yeah." Seth straightened and held his empty serving tray vertically in front of him like a shield. "I figured that out a while ago." His eyebrows flew up then, as if he expected something more from Lucas.

Apologize. "Okay, well. Just wanted you to know I'm sorry. I was a dick."

His smirk wasn't exactly unkind, but definitely condescending. "I forgive you."

Whew, that was over. Lucas slumped against the vinyl cushion at his back. "Thank you. I don't know if I'd forgive me."

"Well, I think that's one of the differences between you and me."

"You—" he pointed his finger at Seth, but it kept wavering off to the side. "Are wise beyond your years. And mine. My years too."

"What about your ears?" Audrey plopped back into her side of the booth. "Hey, Seth, I think we need another round— We need another, right?" She nodded wide eyes at Lucas. "Yeah. Another round."

"He just *brought* us another round," Lucas objected.

"Oh." She blinked at her fresh glass of wine. "Well, in about a half hour, then?"

Seth hesitated a moment first, but then nodded. "Coming up."

Audrey squinted after him as he walked away. "Do they place their orders by phone?" she asked. "'Cause he just took his outta his apron and he's texting it in. That's cool, huh? *Technology*."

"Technology." Lucas toasted to it. Audrey raised her glass as well.

"I wonder if Seth is going to the bachelor party," she mused, sipping at her new drink. Well, swallowing, more.

"Bachelor party?" There was a bachelor party? "I didn't get invited."

She jerked her head around to stare at him. "What do you mean you didn't get invited? You're the brother of the groom, you *have* to be invited."

He shrugged. "Well, who's organizing this thing?"

"I dunno. It should be Gabe because he's the best man."

It couldn't be. "He definitely would have said something to me." Wouldn't he?

"Agreed." She set her glass down with a clink. "So. Kitty, huh?"

"Can you *believe* that?" Lucas slapped the table. "She thought you'd never seen boys take off their clothes for money before." Now that was *funny*. He chuckled, until a snort slipped out, then he realized it was actually giggling.

"I know, right? She hates you again, by the way."

"Me?" He rested offended fingertips on his breastbone. "What'd *I* do?"

"She thinks you told me about her plan."

"I *didn't*." They'd made sure of it.

"I told her that, but she doesn't trust me. What's the world coming to when my sister can't trust her own sister? Huh?"

"Dunno. Except maybe if you'd made her the MOH, she'd trust you more."

"Whatever."

"You don't think they need a guide or something? I mean, bad things sometimes happen to thirty- and forty-something women with credit cards in gay bars." Twinks were often short on cash, and always long on charm.

"Well . . ." She raised her brows and bobbed her head back and forth. "True."

"Who could we possibly get to babysit them?"

Seth broke in, setting their new drinks in front of them. Had it been a half hour already? Lucas peered at his old pint glass, which was, in fact, nearly empty.

Then Audrey kicked him under the table.

"*Excuse* me?" Rearing back in offense, he found her gazing almost raptly at Seth.

Oooooh. Lucas beamed at him.

"What?" Seth asked. "I got the order right, I know I did. I'm the *sober* one."

Pressing his lips together—it wouldn't do to get too excited just yet—Lucas whipped his head around to look at Audrey. Judging by her wide-eyed excitement and her widemouthed smile, she was thinking along the same lines: the perfect babysitter for a gaggle of women playing bachelorettes. In tandem, they both turned back to Seth.

"Um, I think I'm going to have to cut you off now." Seth tilted his head at the table. "That was your last round, sorry, but." He shrugged exaggeratedly.

"Seth." Audrey reached out and laid her fingers on his arm. "Seth, Seth, Seth. Honey." She smiled engagingly. "We have this very important job we need to assign, and we can't trust just *anyone* to do it."

"Were you like this in high school? I can see why we weren't friends," he said, shaking off her ministrations.

"Wouldn't you be willing to do a little something for me? You're the *only* man in Bluewater Bay who is qualified."

"You've had too much to drink." Lucas pointed at her. "Your manipill—manipla—man-ip-u-la-tor-y instinct is malfunctioning." He leaned across the table, holding his palm up between them and Seth so the guy couldn't hear him. "He's gay. Imperverse to your feminine wiles."

She held up her own hand shield and hissed back, "Do you mean 'impervious'?"

"Show-off," he muttered, then chugged a third of his beer.

Seth rested his splayed fingertips on the table's edge. "Whatever you two are trying to talk me into? It's not happening."

If he was really imperverse, wouldn't he just leave? "What'd you get Audrey and Zach as a wedding gift?" Lucas asked the guy. Oh, look at *him*, manipulating people. Apparently it only took a few beers.

Seth's eyes went wild as he glanced around the room. Like he'd hidden it here, or (more likely) was hoping something suitable would present itself. "Uuuuum . . ."

"It's *fine*." Lucas did a little arm petting of his own, but only briefly. "I un'erstand. You don't have a lot of time to shop"—or much of a budget—"and you wanna give 'em something *personal*."

"Sure." Seth nodded for long seconds.

"And this is your oppor'unity to do that." *Bring it home.* "By performing a small service—" he held up his forefinger and thumb, pinching a teeny-tiny amount of air between them to demonstrate "—that'll be greatly appreciated."

"Definitely." Audrey nodded, getting back into the swing of things. "Plus." She leaned forward, employing her hand shield against the curious ears of the room. "Naked men're involved."

"That might have worked in high school," Seth snarked.

Lucas sallied forth bravely. "All we're asking is that you go to a bunch of gay bars in Seattle with Audrey's bridesmaids." He held up generous palms. "We'll pay for the hotel room, and they'll cover drinks. They think it's the—" he finger-quoted "—'experience of a lifetime.'"

Seth squinted suspiciously, and Lucas held his breath. If he recalled correctly, Seth had a ton of female cousins. He might have been the token gay for countless women in bars, and if so, why would he ever want to repeat the experience?

"I'm sure I'll regret it . . ." Seth said, holding his gaze.

He made his countenance as trustworthy as his state of inebriation would allow.

Heaving a sigh, Seth gave in. "I guess I'll do it." He pointed at Audrey. "But this is your wedding present."

"Yay!" she burst out. "Um, but how about I call you later with details? Y'know, when I'm sober."

"That'd probably be best."

"I think we blew past tipsy a while ago," she said after Seth left.

Yeah. "I might have to sleep this off at your house before I go back home. To Gabe's."

"You might."

"Hey."

He knew that voice. Craning his head around and closing one eye to see clearly, Lucas confirmed it was Gabe. "What're you doing here in the middle of the day? Sit down. What're you doing? Thought you were busy all afternoon. Si'down."

Gabe snorted, chuckling as he settled next to Lucas. "I heard you might need assistance getting home." Then he looked over at Audrey. "And I'm under orders from your fiancé to make sure you make it back to your place."

"Oh," Audrey sighed. "Tha's so romantic, you coming to pick up your drunk boyfrien'—"

"He's my *man*," Lucas clarified.

"—'n make sure he doesn' get a DUI. Why didn't Zach come too? Woulda been sweet thing to do."

"Out of the two of us, I'm the only one that can leave my job in the middle of the day to fetch our partners out of the bar."

"Partner." Lucas petted Gabe's chest. "I like that word."

Smiling at him, Gabe draped his arm across Lucas's shoulders. "Now, let's get your bill paid and get you two moving."

"Okay." Sighing happily, he melted all over his man's side, until Gabe prodded him and made him stand up, then helped him walk in a relatively straight line to the pickup.

CHAPTER FOURTEEN

*L*ucas and Audrey were a cute coupla drunks, but a handful—pretty much the same as they were sober. Since Gabe didn't have a crew cab, Lucas sat right next to him as they drove Audrey to her store. He was half-turned toward him, resting his head on Gabe's shoulder and petting his leg repeatedly.

"He's your man," Audrey announced. "'M so glad. Wish my man was here."

"We'd have to squeeze in to fit," Lucas objected.

"I'd sit on his lap."

"Not sure you can do that. Think it's illegal."

They continued their pointless conversation right up until Audrey was trying to figure out which key worked in the exterior entrance. "I don't wanna go through the store in my 'nebriated state." Finally she found the right one, and let herself in. Gabe left Lucas in a chair at the bottom of the stairs while he made sure Audrey made it to the second floor and into her apartment safely.

Then he guided Lucas back to the pickup, helping him in and putting his seat belt on for him, as Lucas insisted earnestly, "I can' leave my car there; I'll get another ticket." Grabbing Gabe's shoulder, he shook it, trying to get into Gabe's face.

"I thought you were gonna get a resident's permit."

He snorted and dropped his hand. "They wouldn' give me one. Douchebonnets."

Gabe shut his door and went around to the driver's side since he had the chance. Once he had the truck on the road, he continued the conversation. "What the hell's a douchebonnet?"

Lucas flailed his hand in the air. "'S just something my ex and I used to say."

"Huh." Most of the time, he thought Drew sounded like a waste of space, but occasionally, when Lucas brought up little inside jokes like this or other things that were only between him and his ex, it sort of got Gabe's underwear in a bind. He tried to shake it off. *Doesn't matter, he's with me now.*

"It's from when you stay in those hotels that give you tons'f toiletries. Not just shampoo, conditioner, and lotion, but, like, face soap an' bath oil an' a shower cap."

"A shower cap, huh?" He didn't remember ever staying in a place that had shower caps for his use. 'Course, he mostly stayed in motels, not hotels. And didn't *that* make him feel a whole lot better about comparing himself to Lucas's ex?

"The package always says 'shower cap' 'n English, then 'n French: *bonnet de douche.*"

French. Fuck. "What the hell kinda hotels you been staying in?"

"Um, douchebonnet ones?" Lucas slurred.

Chill out, man, he's drunk. Trying to bring it back to a humorous level, Gabe said, "Can't say I've ever been to a douchebonnet hotel."

"'S not a big deal." Lucas flailed again.

Okay, screw this. Time for a subject change. "So, why wouldn't they give you a parking permit?"

The guy crossed his arms over his chest and stuck out his lower lip. "They won't give me a temporary one, they wan'ed me to buy one for the whole year, but I'm leaving right after the wedding, y'know?"

All the blood drained out of Gabe's head so fast he damn near drove off the road, but he got away with just hitting the rumble strip, then yanking the truck back into his lane. His fingers had gone numb on the steering wheel, so he'd have to rely on experience and familiarity to steer them down this stretch of the highway.

God*damm*it. He'd let himself forget that there had always been an expiration date on this relationship. Over the last couple of weeks, he'd gotten too comfortable with having Lucas around, and he'd ignored the future looming over them. The one that wouldn't have Lucas in it every day.

Well, wasn't he just a damn fool?

"You're still planning on leaving?" His anger made his words sharp, but he didn't care about softening them right now. He kind of wanted to inflict a little pain.

"You knew that." When he glanced over, Lucas's eyes were huge, and his mouth was hanging open.

"That you were leaving *right after* the wedding?" He was grasping at straws, but he needed a few more minutes or days or something. Some time to get his head around the fact that he might want a bigger piece of pie than was allowed. Shifting in his seat, trying to get rid of the irritation inside him, he admitted, "I thought maybe things had changed."

"Like what?" Lucas scrunched up his face.

"You can't think of anything that might make you stay a little longer?" Long enough for Gabe to get used to the idea of not having him around?

Lucas's frown grew more confused. He let his head flop back on the seat, hitting it hard and rebounding once, then blinking repeatedly.

Arguing with a drunk guy was pointless. He had to bite his tongue on the urge to continue anyway. "Forget it," he finally said.

Then he ignored the way Lucas worried his lip for the next few miles. Eventually, though, Lucas spoke up again. "Um, what d'you know about the bachelor party?"

"Everything," he said shortly. "I'm organizing it."

"You never said anything t'me."

Truth was, it had slipped his mind. "I haven't thought about it since I reserved a room at the golf club." That had been weeks ago, before Lucas was even back in town. "Other'n that, I just had to send out invitations."

"You didn't send *me* an invitation."

Dammit, he sounded like Gabe had run over his dog. Clearing his throat, he tried to explain. "I didn't think I needed to. I thought you were going with me." He'd thought they were a unit, hadn't he? Let himself view this as something other than a fling, when that's what they'd agreed on. Then let himself get angry when he had no call or right to.

"Go with you? Like, as your date?"

"I guess." Damn that sounded good, but also painful. But what was a little more pain at this point? "Yeah, sure. You'll be my date."

Lucas screwed up his face, inspecting Gabe out of one eye while closing the other. "Can y'bring dates to bachelor parties?"

"*I* can." He tightened his grip on the steering wheel.

"Oh."

Neither of them spoke the rest of the way to the farm, but Gabe did a hell of a lot of thinking. About how, when Lucas was eighteen, he'd known in his viscera that it was the right thing for the guy to leave, and he'd done what he could to make sure it happened.

Now was a different time, though, and he didn't know anything, because he felt like he'd been gut-shot. All the parts of his instinct he usually relied on were bloody and wounded, and nothing made sense. One thing he did know, though—nothing about Lucas had fundamentally changed. He was still a talented artist meant to travel the world and make amazing things. And Gabe was still a fifth-generation logger who'd never give up his roots or his heritage.

Well, this is getting damn depressing.

Lucas didn't know what time he fell asleep, but when he woke up hours later, it was dark outside. The bedroom lights were off, but the glow and the noise of the television seeped in through a crack in the door.

Concentrating, trying to place himself in time and space, he finally put it all together. *Got drunk with Audrey.* Then Gabe had come to pick him up. He had hazy memories of the conversation on the way home, although he couldn't put his finger on what, exactly, was filling him with guilt-laced dread. He only knew it hadn't gone well.

Bachelor party. Something about that. Gabe was organizing it, but hadn't invited Lucas for some reason. *Why?* He wanted to believe it was an oversight, but doubts that had been lurking in the back of his mind refused to keep silent anymore. How come it was so easy for Gabe to forget him? Because Lucas wasn't a real part of his life? *Just a fling.*

That's all they'd said they wanted. Both of them. But now his feelings were all mixed up about it, and he didn't know what he wanted. Except to be *more*. Not the kind of more he'd wanted in high school or college, but a very personal kind that had nothing to do with how the world saw him and everything to do with how the man he was sleeping with did.

Apprehension throbbed under his ribs at the thought, reminding him that something wasn't right between them. That he might have fucked up somehow during his drunken binge.

How, though?

He lay there a long time before he worked up the courage to go find Gabe. Sitting up, he realized he had on sweats and a T-shirt. He didn't remember changing, but he had a hazy recollection of Gabe force-feeding him water, ibuprofen, and toast, then shoving him in the shower. His head wasn't aching now, probably because of those ministrations.

Maybe Gabe *wasn't* angry with him?

Gotta go find him. He had a whole lot of *I don't want to* balled up in the pit of his stomach, but he forced himself to stand and walk out of the room, into the living area.

Gabe was sitting on the couch, watching some hunting show. Lucas crept closer, not sure why he was being so stealthy. A floorboard creaked under his feet, and Gabe looked around at him, then shut off the television. Only the lamp on the far side of the room illuminated him now.

Swallowing, Lucas held still, waiting for something to happen.

Gabe held out his hand. A silent request for Lucas to come be with him. Relieved, Lucas rushed over, letting Gabe pull him down into his lap, then drape his hand casually over Lucas's groin. Almost as if he didn't realize his fingers were curling under Lucas's balls, or the heel of his hand was sliding along Lucas's dick. Except the way he pressed his own hardening cock against Lucas's tailbone proved that false. "Why'nt you sit down with me a bit?" he murmured, raising goose bumps on the skin of Lucas's neck.

Oh thank God. Everything seemed all right. Relief sharpened his sudden desire. "'Kay." Lucas closed his eyes and rested his head on Gabe's shoulder, languidly working his hips in time with Gabe's soft strokes and raising his arms up to wrap them around Gabe's neck. "Mmmmmm."

"Mmmmm?" Gabe kissed his ear, then nibbled along the upper curve of it.

"Mm-*hmmm*." His fears of Gabe's anger or annoyance faded further away as Gabe caressed him. "I'm sorry you had to come pick me up at the bar." Craning his neck, he managed to kiss Gabe on the temple.

"No harm done," Gabe murmured. "How's your head?"

"Surprisingly okay. I should be more hungover." He ground his ass against Gabe's dick, trying to signal him to use more pressure. "You make me all melty inside. Like a grilled cheese sandwich."

"'Zat right." Shifting their weight, Gabe slumped further on the couch, then with his free hand he palmed the inside of Lucas's thigh, pulling it wider. Automatically, Lucas moved the other one, until his legs bracketed Gabe's knees. In this position, his feet couldn't touch the floor, so he had less leverage. And Gabe had more control.

He wasn't doing anything with that control, though, other than what he had been already—a too-gentle, too-slow fondling of Lucas's dick. Barely perceptible through the layers of clothes Lucas had on. "You aren't fully taking advantage of me."

"Don't you worry." Gabe nipped his neck, causing him to suck in a breath and squirm. "That'll happen."

"When— *Oh*." Unerringly, Gabe had found Lucas's nipple through his T-shirt and pinched it. "Lemme blow you." Then he could stroke himself while sucking on Gabe's cock.

"Huh-uh." Finally, Gabe was touching his bare skin, working his fingers under Lucas's shirt. But they traveled up to his chest, not down to his dick. "I'm not done playing yet." He followed the contour of Lucas's sternum with his thumb.

"I'm never gonna come like this," Lucas panted.

"Maybe I don't plan on letting you."

Oh God. His pulse pounded in his eardrums, and desire tightened his ass muscles. Bowing his spine and planting his hands on the couch, he ground down harder on Gabe, swiveling his hips. Trying to work the hard line of Gabe's cock between his cheeks. It was no good. With the sweats and briefs and jeans between them, he couldn't do more than tease himself with the idea of riding Gabe's erection. "Tell me what I have to do so you'll let me come."

"Gonna *make* you come, boy." Finally, Gabe's fingers tightened over Lucas's dick, and he squeezed it before he went right back to that light rubbing.

Lucas whimpered.

Gabe stopped moving, clamping his hand on Lucas's hip to keep him still. "You like to beg me for it, don't you, baby?"

"Yes," he admitted in a whisper, pure lust swirling through him. "Please make me come. Any way you want." He held his breath, waiting for Gabe's permission to move, sure he wasn't supposed to until signaled.

"Asking for it isn't enough this time. You have to earn it." Gabe's voice was liquid sin. Lucas had never thought that much about sin, other than as something to avoid. *This* kind of sin, though . . . he wanted to get naked and roll around in it until it coated him like a viscous film and seeped into all his orifices.

"Anything," he choked out, losing the fight to hold still, rocking his hips to caress Gabe's hard-on with his ass.

"Suck my dick."

He jumped up and turned, but Gabe grabbed him before he could kneel. "Take off your clothes first."

There wasn't a lot of room between the couch and the coffee table for a striptease, plus he was bounded by Gabe's spread legs. And he couldn't dance. So, instead, he just got naked as Gabe watched—lounging on the couch, hands behind his head, the hard line of his cock visible under the denim, and a smile on his face. Following Lucas's every move with his eyes, then inspecting each newly exposed stretch of skin, until Lucas was completely bare and his dick was pointing out as stiff as it could be. Embarrassingly desperate for touch.

Gabe left him hanging there for long seconds, until he pushed up from the couch too, standing within inches of him. He undid his fly and pulled his jeans down to his thighs, letting his big red fatty free. When he ran the knuckles of his hand up the underside of Lucas's dick, Lucas's ass clenched in anticipation.

Then Gabe sat back down, fully clothed except for that small slice of himself he'd exposed. From just above his hip bones to the tops of his hairy thighs. "On your knees, then. And I want your hands where I can see them the whole time."

Lucas had already dropped to the floor and was halfway to fisting himself when Gabe issued the order. "Really? *Please* let me—"

"No." Sitting forward, Gabe reached for Lucas's wrists and placed them on his legs, just above the knees, where they were still covered in denim. "You don't touch yourself unless I say it's okay." Then he slouched, positioning his butt on the edge of the sofa, and his cock right under Lucas's chin. "Get to work, boy."

The demanding way he stared at Lucas was making him light-headed. Bending to his job, he caught sight of his own dick—a single drop of pre-cum oozing out, and so hard it trembled with his heartbeat. *Be patient. If I'm very, very good, he'll reward you.*

Then he slid his lips over the head of Gabe's prick, and threw himself into giving an exemplary blowjob. Gabe made it as difficult as he could, skipping his usual hold on Lucas's hair and instead reaching past it to play with Lucas's nipples. The more of him Lucas took in, the rougher Gabe got, until he was pinching and twisting while Lucas was forcing Gabe's head into his throat, gagging on it.

He nearly came just from that. If he'd had a plug up his ass, or—better—some of Gabe's fingers, he would have. He was starting to think he would blow anyway, but suddenly Gabe let go to clamp his hands over Lucas's ears and held him immobile, shoving his cock farther into him and dumping his load. As soon as he could, Lucas groaned with the frustration of having been jerked back from the edge of orgasm, but his whole body also pounded with the knowledge that they weren't done. Gabe *had* to have other plans for him.

It took Gabe a while to unveil those plans. First he seemed intent on enjoying his postcoital state, *hmmm*ing and letting Lucas suck and lick him until he was completely soft. Then he pushed Lucas out of his lap, eyelids half-closed, watching himself stroke Lucas's cheek. Completely languid, in direct contrast to Lucas's quivering anticipation.

He was already on his knees, but if he kissed Gabe's feet, would that—

"Go get a condom and some lube."

Wait. That meant . . . Lucas swallowed. "You're going to fuck me?"

"Eventually."

Oh no. Gabe fucked like a god, but his recovery time was about double Lucas's. "Do I get to come before then?"

"You ask me one more time, and you won't come until tomorrow."

Lucas bowed his head and stood, going to the bedroom and grabbing the supplies out of the drawer, returning as fast as he could. After setting the stuff on the coffee table, he knelt again for good measure.

Which was apparently the wrong thing to do. "Stand up." Gabe straightened, sitting forward so that as Lucas stood, his dick was within inches of Gabe's mouth. He clenched his hands by his sides and squeezed his eye shut, chanting *please please please* inside his head.

"Now we're gonna do something I've been meaning to for a while." The mild threat in his tone sent prickles along Lucas's skin, and he bit his lip, waiting for more orders. "Turn around and bend over."

Chills ran down his spine as he did it, and for a brief second he considered going so far as to grab his ankles, but he honestly didn't know if he was that limber, so instead he planted his hands on the coffee table, because whatever Gabe was about to do to him? He'd need to brace himself.

Oh God, what if he's going to spank me? It had never sounded exciting before, but something about Gabe's big logger's hands reddening his ass was so thrilling his legs trembled uncontrollably.

Instead, Gabe's big logger's thumbs ran along each side of the crevice between Lucas's cheeks, then pulled them open.

"Oh God," Lucas breathed, tensing so much he pushed up on tiptoes.

"Settle down." Gabe's rough lips scraped across his ass, toward the center. "This is gonna take a while." Then he licked around Lucas's hole, and Lucas shuddered. Both from the way Gabe's tongue slithered over his entrance again and again, and from the scrape of his beard on delicate skin. It took far too long before Gabe prodded his sphincter, then pushed inside.

Gabe rimmed him forever, until Lucas wanted to cry with desperation and was sure he was about to expire from orgasm denial. No matter how deeply Gabe tongue-fucked him, it wasn't quite enough. Not big enough or hard enough, but definitely more than enough to keep his whole body throbbing with lust, so close to exploding, but it was like chasing a light down a dark tunnel that had no end. Always ten feet ahead of him.

Finally Gabe drew back, but only to move down to Lucas's balls and start sucking them. Relief came when Gabe shoved his lubed-up thumb into Lucas's ass and slid across his prostate. Lucas's moan was nearly a shout, and he pushed back, trying to get it deeper. The pulse pounding in his ears was so loud he couldn't hear anything else, and the base of his dick was hammering at him. *Just a little more.*

Gabe stopped.

Lucas nearly sobbed when Gabe pulled his thumb completely out, then let go of his balls with a sucking slurp.

"Oh God, please don't, please, I need to come, Gabe," he managed to babble and pant at the same time. As Gabe stood behind him, he tilted his hips up, hoping to make a more tempting target. "I *need* you. I need it. Fuck me. Please, please *pleeease*—"

"Shush," he grated, grabbing the condom off the table. The sound of the package ripping open was almost enough to make Lucas collapse with relief, except then his ass wouldn't be primed and ready, exposed to Gabe, with Gabe's saliva drying on it and the skin around it tingling from his whiskers.

Kneeing Lucas's legs wider, Gabe finally, *finally* pushed his cock insistently against Lucas's hole, forcing him open. In spite of being so willing he'd been literally begging, it felt like surrendering when his muscles gave way and let Gabe's head inside. Acknowledgment of Gabe's mastery over him. His arms failed him, and he had to bend over further, resting his elbows on the coffee table as Gabe entered him to the hilt in one long, slow stroke, until his balls were brushing against Lucas's taint. Waves of heat and then chills washed over Lucas's body at the intensity of the pressure, and everything in the room started to go blurry as Gabe pulled back out and shoved in again, working into a hard and fast rhythm.

Gabe fucked the orgasm out of him. Lucas was barely in control of his body, held up mostly by Gabe's fingers digging into his hips and the cock reaming his ass, thrusting in and out even when Lucas's muscles were convulsing around him. Lucas came so hard his cum hit his chin with the first volley, then his abdomen, then jetted out onto the coffee table. Still reeling from aftershocks, his legs went to jelly, but before he collapsed Gabe grabbed him around the middle and guided them both back onto the couch, slipping out of him. They landed in a messy tangle, breathing so loudly it echoed, or seemed to. Lucas was only half on the cushions, one butt cheek and the companion leg hanging off, but his head was on Gabe's shoulder and he was too weak to move.

He drifted a while, until his weird position began to cause him discomfort, so he rearranged himself, kissing Gabe's neck on the way. When he opened his eyes, Gabe's still-hard dick was directly below them.

"You didn't come?"

"'S'okay," Gabe murmured. "I did before."

It wasn't okay, not with Lucas, so he slid back down to the floor, sitting on his haunches between Gabe's legs yet again, and stripped off the condom, then started helping Gabe out of his jeans.

"You don't have to." Gabe stroked fingers through his hair. "I was kinda hard on you."

Lucas ignored him, and grabbed the bottle of lube from where it had ended up on the floor next to him. Squirting some onto his fingers, he let it warm for a few seconds before wrapping his hand around Gabe's shaft and beginning to stroke.

"Baby," Gabe whispered.

"I want to." He needed to. They'd crossed some kind of boundary Lucas didn't understand and couldn't explain, so he just went by instinct, knowing devoting himself to Gabe's orgasm was part of it. Like a ritual.

"Wasn't arguing."

"Good." He placed a very chaste kiss on the head of Gabe's cock, because: latex. *Ew.* Then he took the whole thing between both of his palms, and formed it. Sculpted it like clay, putting movement and rhythm into his work until Gabe groaned, lifted his hips up, and the cum flowed out of him.

Then Lucas cleaned him off with his sweats and crawled back onto the couch, curling up next to his man.

That had been crazy. Gabe couldn't believe he'd pushed things so far, but Lucas had gone with it. Even enjoyed it, if the way he'd gasped out Gabe's name at the end was any indication.

Then, that handjob . . . Gabe knew he was spoiled by being with a guy who lavished so much attention on his dick, but that had been more along the lines of worship. He wasn't sure he deserved it, not after what he'd done.

What he'd done was to try to show Lucas what he'd be missing when he left. Worse, he'd done so while also taking his frustration over the situation out on the guy. It probably shouldn't have turned into the most profound sex of his life, but there you had it.

Pulling Lucas into his arms and murmuring instructions, he shifted them until they were lying on the couch facing each other, then arranged the afghan Gramma had made over them. Lucas wasn't really conscious, never even opening his eyes. Once he'd wiggled himself into place between Gabe and the cushions, he settled his head on Gabe's arm and curled his hand under his chin, sighing softly, then breathing heavily though his parted lips.

So beautiful. Gabe had never thought it about a guy before, but he'd never been in love with one before, at least not like this. He'd been out here the whole time Lucas had been sleeping it off—nearly five hours—thinking things over, and that was one unavoidable truth.

That, and he suspected Lucas didn't feel the same way, not if he was still planning on leaving.

He'd always known that Lucas's life couldn't be here, but this evening he'd started to question why not, exactly. The guy didn't actually have to be present in these galleries he showed in, except for the openings, right? And he seemed to be producing lots of work just fine on the farm.

So. It came down to one thing: Lucas didn't have a strong enough incentive to stay.

Gabe would pretty much give up anything to be that incentive. If Lucas wanted him that much, though, he wouldn't be casually mentioning leaving.

Lucas snuffled. For a brief few seconds he seemed to be conscious as he shifted closer to Gabe, then pressed his lips against Gabe's chest, right over his heart. Tucking his head in the bend of

Gabe's neck, Lucas went limp and vulnerable as he fell further into sleep. Like his unconscious mind knew this was where he was safest and most loved.

Well, then. Gabe didn't have it in him to push the guy away, either literally or figuratively. Instead, he kissed Lucas's forehead, and tried to mentally prepare himself for the five steps to mangling a heart: pound flat, dip in sorrow, coat in pain, cook in a cast-iron skillet, turning regularly until done to death. Chicken-fried heartbreak.

CHAPTER FIFTEEN

*F*riday morning, when Lucas woke up, there was no Gabe in the bed, but there was a small envelope on the pillow next to him.

An invitation to the bachelor party. It turned out it was that Saturday afternoon. Which it would have to be, because they were having the rehearsal Sunday (instead of the traditional night before—Lucas suspected it was to spare his parents the expense of paying for it by making it "nontraditional"), and the wedding was the following Saturday. Tomorrow was the only opportunity they had left for a party, if not tonight.

The bachelorette party was also tomorrow. What if he'd *had* to go to that, would Gabe have invited him to this party anyway? He wasn't sure he wanted to know the answer.

Instead, he wrote a small RSVP note on the envelope. *Thank you for thinking of me. I'd love to go with you.* He signed it with his name and a small heart.

Oh God, that looked like a girl had done it. It was so . . . sentimental. Sitting at the kitchen table with the occasionally running refrigerator to keep him company, he chewed on the end of his graphic pen for a half hour, trying to decide what to do. Should he trash it and just tell Gabe in person he was going? Or try to make the heart into something else? A horse's head, maybe?

He couldn't do either of those things, in the end. It was true that he didn't know what was going to happen, and Gabe hadn't said anything about extending their fling, but Lucas had drawn that heart unthinkingly, not censoring himself. It held a tiny bit of the feeling he had for Gabe in it, and he just couldn't crush that crumb of his love.

So he left it there, totally exposed for Gabe to find and interpret how he would, and went down to his studio.

He'd fired all the pots he'd made for Audrey's wedding at this point, and ended up with twenty-seven that had all their pieces and had come out of the pit kiln without mishap. It was a good survival rate, considering how often the smaller parts went missing. He'd started setting them in a steel mesh box Gabe had found for him, but he still lost a fair number.

Today, though, he didn't want to work on the wedding favors. He only had cleanup and packing left to do, so it wasn't absolutely necessary, was it? It didn't really matter, anyway, because he recognized this mood. A strangely peaceful mix of melancholia and acceptance that had led him to make some of his best works in the past. Not every time, but often enough for him to now follow the urge to pull a ten-pound block of clay out of its plastic storage bag.

Spring in the Pacific Northwest was the most unpredictable season. The weather was sometimes impossible to forecast, or seemed so, with high winds, thunderstorms, hail, sunshine, and temperatures in the lower seventies occasionally all happening within a twelve-hour period. He'd never confirmed it through any sort of meteorological means, but Lucas had always believed their spring sunshine was unique. Rare and beautiful, as if it had an extra color mixed up with the usual seven suspects on the spectrum. An impish, mercurial wavelength that could—if it felt like it—illuminate details regular light couldn't even detect. It wasn't always present, either, only on those most special of days, when the clouds were sparse but also heavy with rain, and the wind played tricks on people, whipping their hair into their eyes no matter which direction they faced. When the sun broke through on those days, that was when it was at its most magical.

Today was exactly that kind of day. So Lucas took his huge lump of clay and dumped it onto the workbench built under the windows, then pulled up a stool, watching and waiting for the weather and his mood to show him what to make.

It could take a while, but his mind was used to this, going into this zone. He had endless patience once he'd lulled himself into a self-induced creative trance. Time tended not to mean much then, so he had no idea how long he sat there, watching the wind and the sunshine and the leaves make wildly shifting patterns on his block of clay. At the right moment, Lucas began to work it, letting everything happening around him inform his hands, but not really taking in any of it.

It was nearly dark before he started coming back to the land of the living. If the sun could shine all night, he might have just kept working, but the decreasing visibility made it impossible. As he became more aware of his body and his surroundings two things made themselves clear: his back hurt like hell, and his feet were so cold he couldn't feel his toes. Groaning, he reached around and dug his fingers into his sore muscles, standing after a moment and trying to shake some heat back into his extremities.

The lights came on and then Gabe was behind him. "Hey, baby." His warm hands landed on Lucas's, moving them and kneading in the same places Lucas had been. He was so much better at it. Bending forward, Lucas folded his arms on the workbench, letting Gabe massage him.

"Thank you." He rested his forehead on his hands and sighed.

"Mmm." Gabe moved closer, so he was just behind Lucas, bumping his thighs against Lucas's butt, although in a nonsexual way. "You've been in here for hours."

"Have I? What time is it?"

"Nearly eight thirty."

"Whoa." It wasn't that unusual. This was, though—having a caring man who would help him transition back to real life. This was *heaven*.

"What are you working on?"

Shifting just enough to rest his cheek on his wrist, Lucas looked at the clay. "I don't know yet." It seemed to be sort of humanoid. He thought that indentation down the center of the side he'd been smoothing and shaping looked a little like a spine.

"You work this way a lot, not knowing what you're making for sure?" Gabe didn't sound mystified or confused or anything, simply curious.

"Sometimes. It hasn't happened for a long time." Staring at the piece, he realized what he'd done—he'd started working on the upcoming show. Whatever this turned into would be the conceptual basis for *all* his works. *Oh thank God.* Coming up with a theme had never been this easy before.

Pulling him up to standing gently, Gabe circled an arm around Lucas's waist, using it to move him along toward the door. "C'mon up and have dinner, then I'll draw you a bath."

"Did you already eat?"

"Yup. Saved some homemade mac and cheese for you, though. Momma sent it out." He prodded Lucas up the stairs.

"Will you get in the tub with me?" The old-fashioned clawfoot Gabe had put in was easily big enough for both of them.

"If you want." Holding Lucas against his side on the landing, Gabe opened the door to the apartment. He had a fire going in the stove, Lucas could smell it. What was more welcoming than home fires burning?

"I do want."

Much later, as Lucas lounged half-asleep in the warm water against Gabe's chest, Gabe leaned close to his ear. "I got your note." His lips skimmed Lucas's hair. "I'm glad you're gonna go with me."

"Me too." Lucas reached back and cupped his man's cheek.

Lucas had left him a heart on that invite to the bachelor party. Maybe it wasn't any kind of promise or clue, but it told Gabe something that got him through the next few days: Lucas cared about him.

He'd *miss* Gabe when he left. At least some.

Damn sight better than the last time Lucas had fled town. It didn't shore up any hope Gabe had for him staying this go-round, though. He might feel that his heart was big enough to contain the guy, but he knew damn well this backwater town wasn't. Better to get the most out of the time they had left.

Thinking that way, once or twice he went by the studio while Lucas was working and peeked in the door, hoping it was a good time and he might say hi. It wasn't a good time, ever. Lucas was under the spell of that sculpture he'd started the other day.

The better Gabe knew him, the easier it was for him to see when the guy had gone into his own universe. Now, he could simply stand in the doorway and tell by the paleness of his skin whether Lucas had gotten lost in his head. If his cheeks were flushed at the same time his nose and chin were near white? Forget it.

Worse, though, were the times his lips were raw and reddened from chewing on them over and over. It was torture, wanting to soothe them but knowing he'd only be interrupting Lucas's process. He was unreachable in a way Gabe hadn't understood before. Simply watching him now brought on guilt for all the times he'd disturbed him in the past and shouldn't have.

Piece by piece, Gabe's heart got on board and accepted that, while Lucas cared in his way, this relationship wasn't meant to be anything more than the fling they'd originally agreed on. Lucas was meant to live large and make his mark on the world, and Gabe was meant to detach and go on with his own life. Best plan he could come up with was to start rationing himself, soaking up enough Lucas time to keep from going into withdrawal, but forcing himself not to gorge or become more dependent. Like managing an addiction, or an eating disorder. That way, when Lucas left . . . Well, then, he'd be prepared for it.

On Saturday, when he and Lucas went to the bachelor party, it brought a few things he'd been ignorant of to his attention. Things like: he hadn't actually announced to the universe that he liked dick. He'd assumed word would just get around.

Apparently it hadn't.

They got to the Salt Creek Golf Club early. After checking to make sure the food and drinks were as he'd ordered, Gabe snagged a beer and hung out near the door with Lucas, relaxing and saying "hey," as guys arrived. He kept having to introduce Lucas, mostly as a way to remind him what people's names were, rather than because no one recognized *him*. It made sense. Most of these dudes were older than he was, plus a few of them hadn't been around when Lucas lived here.

After about the fifth introduction, Lucas leaned over and asked him quietly, "Um, why are we getting those weird looks?"

"What d'you mean?"

"Like just now, when you introduced me to those guys you went to school with, Ray and Sunny?"

"Yeah?"

"As soon as they walked off, they started talking to each other really quietly, and glancing back at us." Lucas was biting his lip, obviously worried about it.

Gabe rubbed his back a few times. "They're probably just wondering where you've been the last few years."

Lucas was frowning after the guys. "Are you sure that's it? Because just now, when you touched me, they both did double takes." Turning back to Gabe, Lucas lifted his brows and tilted his head, giving him a meaningful look.

Huh. He took a thoughtful sip of his beer, studying the room and its occupants. A whole lot of eyes slid away from his.

Stretching up to whisper in his ear, Lucas asked the obvious. "They don't know you're gay, do they?"

Hell. "Guess not." Years before, when they'd first hooked up, Gabe had made that stupid-ass comment to Lucas about not being gay, only *"appreciating the male form."* Even at the time he'd known it wasn't really true, but back then he still hadn't figured out a guy like him could really own up to lusting after dudes.

Someone should give out awards for that kind of denial. Although he'd met other guys who were worse.

Since then, he'd pretty much figured out his shit, though. He'd told all the people who mattered, like his closest friends and his parents. Even Lucas's parents knew.

"I thought you were out." Now there was a note of uncertainty in Lucas's voice, and Gabe couldn't ignore that—he had to reassure him. This time, though, he let his touch linger while making another visual sweep of the room. About half the guys jolted back or made it painfully clear they weren't looking at him and Lucas.

Well, that was damn annoying. "I *am* out. Only I forgot to buy that full-page spread in the paper."

A quick snort of laughter burst out of Lucas. "Yeah, hon? If you thought people were going to figure it out on their own, you were wrong. *No one* would ever peg you as gay."

Hon. He liked that. So much he forgot all about their audience and instead moved closer to Lucas, smiling down at him.

Then the man of the hour walked in and that stopped him from doing something like kissing Lucas. He shoulda. That'd end all speculation right there.

"Hey!" Zach pulled Gabe into a bro-hug, slapping him on the back.

"Think I just came out to all our straight friends, dude," Gabe muttered quickly.

"'Bout time." When Zach let go of Gabe and turned to greet his brother, he was smirking. Then he started dragging them around the room, saying hi to everyone, and normalizing shit. Or maybe that was the beer. Gabe had set this party up for the afternoon because Zach had asked him specifically to not let it turn into some kind of stag night. There were no strippers, or ex-girlfriends, or anything questionable like that. Sure, there was drinking going on, but no one did it in excess.

Only enough to eventually loosen up and start asking him questions.

The first brave soul was someone Lucas knew, but he barely did: Guy Parker. After responding to Lucas's greeting, he turned to Gabe. "Seriously dude, *you're* gay? Never would've thought."

"I see your social skills haven't improved," Lucas snapped, baring his teeth in a smile.

Gabe got him out of there and dragged him to a corner while Guy was still looking confused. "It's not that big a deal," he said softly. "Chill, okay?"

Lucas was practically snorting fire out of his nose, but he made an effort to calm himself, breathing deeply for a few seconds. "I'm sorry, it's just . . ." He shook his head. "Seriously, *none* of these people knew you're gay?"

"Your brother."

"Yeah, but the others?"

"Nope, didn't know." Really, it was kinda funny. The gossip was probably already doing the rounds. He'd seen some guys texting.

Lucas planted his fists on his hips. "How could I have missed the fact that you weren't out?"

Gabe laughed softly. "Baby, there's a lot of stuff you miss, but that's okay."

Finally Lucas gave up his annoyance, lips quirking at the corners. "This is nothing at all like I expected a straight-guy bachelor party to be like."

Gabe huffed and took a sip of his beer. "Yeah, it's not like any I've ever been to."

"Don't they usually feature female strippers?"

He shrugged one shoulder. "Zach didn't want one, and I wasn't about to argue."

"Doesn't matter; it's still a party no one will ever forget." Lucas smirked at him.

"Yeah, that's unlikely now." He began leaning toward Lucas without thinking, but caught himself halfway. "If I wanna make certain of that, I'd kiss you right now." He couldn't just do it, because if he kissed Lucas, everyone would assume not only that he was gay, but that Lucas was his boyfriend. Partner. He ignored the pang of regret in his heart, just like he had the last two days. Better to ask Lucas's permission if they were going to be starring in that kinda gossip.

"What are you waiting for, then?" Lucas tilted his head, appearing coquettish and at the perfect angle for a serious kiss, rising up to meet Gabe's lips.

"Nothing," Gabe said, then he made damn sure no one could ever again think he was straight.

They took it easy after the party, picking up burgers on the way back to Gabe's, then lazing around once they were home. Lying on the couch, naked in Gabe's arms while watching yet another hunting show, Lucas drifted somewhere between awake and asleep.

I could stay here forever.

All the contentment he'd been experiencing bled out of him, sinking into the couch, then the floor, and then dispersing into the atmosphere.

Giving Gabe a quick kiss on the biceps, he shoved up from the sofa and wandered into the kitchen. Not trying to outrun the sudden uncertainty, rather . . . getting a drink of water. The window over the sink showed him the lights of Bluewater Bay, although only as a small part of the expansive view. The sight flooded his chest with nostalgia.

Familiar.

Life had a way of playing tricks, didn't it? He'd been so desperate to leave twelve years before, yet now he'd seriously consider staying if the right man asked him to. He could *be* a local without acting like one, after all.

The right man didn't seem that interested, though.

While he thought Gabe was really into him, the guy had refused to ask him to stay last time, and he might not do it this time, either. Gabe had only come out at the party because Lucas was *there*. He'd even felt he had to ask first. It wasn't like coming out *for* him. He shouldn't read too much into it. If Gabe was serious about him, wouldn't he have said something by now?

Lightning coursed through his neurons: *he* could ask Gabe for more than these last few weeks.

Except . . . he didn't know what he would ask for, precisely. Plus he was terrified. Gabe had more or less pushed him out of the nest last time, and while *that* had been painful and insulting, if it happened *this* time it could destroy him.

Maybe he could casually mention settling in Seattle and visiting on weekends? Find out what Gabe's reaction to that was. He might like the occasional hookup.

At this point, though, he'd have to wait until after the wedding, because if Gabe didn't want him to visit on weekends? Well, he wasn't sure he could go through all the forced closeness of a marriage ceremony and reception knowing the guy didn't really care for more than a fling.

CHAPTER SIXTEEN

*L*ucas was done with his mystery sculpture by Monday afternoon. He'd figured out what it was a while ago, and that had pushed him to finish even faster.

It was beautiful, and not because he'd formed it. It was beautiful because he'd made a faithful rendition of the subject, realistically capturing it instead of wandering into abstraction. Well on one side, the side that depicted Gabe's back from his neck to his buttocks. The other side was totally abstract. Reminiscent of the innards of a human, or Lucas's idea of them, having never seen someone without skin.

Except he didn't have an actual theme, yet. He still had stuff to do—burnish it for example, then carefully apply dots of slip on the shoulders, letting them fade out as he reached the sway of Gabe's back, just like those real-life freckles did. The problem was, it looked incomplete, and he knew from experience that finishing the details wouldn't satisfy him, or help him figure out the concept.

Gabe's back. *Needs a front.*

I can do that. Shrouding the sculpture in plastic, he got up and found the bag with all the scraps from that original block of clay. There had to be almost seven pounds remaining, since he'd hollowed out most of the center of the piece, working from the base up. The leftovers from modeling Gabe's body would be more than enough for the image slowly forming in his mind.

Judging from the view outside the studio windows, Gabe had successfully trained Bruce.

More than successfully. Beautifully. The stallion literally took Lucas's breath away as he pranced around the barn, pulling the carriage Zach had restored. The very long whip Gabe held while he drove the horse from the box was ridiculously sexy, as a bonus.

Before the pair could get too far down the gravel road, Lucas ran out the door and stuck out his thumb. They were a bit past him, but Gabe tipped his chin, then circled around. As he halted in front of Lucas, he leered, waggling his brows. "You looking for a ride, boy?"

Laughing, Lucas walked around the carriage to the other side. The step—sort of like a running board on a pickup—was nearly two feet off the ground, he'd guess. "How's Audrey supposed to get in this thing in her wedding dress?"

"Dunno." Gabe held out his hand and helped Lucas up when he grabbed his forearm. "S'pose I'll have to make sure Zach thought about that."

"Should I really be riding in it before she does? It's like opening someone else's birthday present, then wrapping it back up."

Winking, Gabe glanced over at him. "I won't tell if you won't."

"Okay." He settled onto the black leather cushion. The carriage was mostly blond wood, but there were some bronze fittings, and two seats. Lucas's was a small horizontal square, but the driver's seat was a little larger, and set at a slant so that Gabe was semistanding, bracing the toes of his boots against the dash. Or whatever that front part was called.

Bruce walked on when Gabe made a clucking sound with his tongue, down the driveway that led to the outbuildings. On a long stretch, Gabe clucked twice and the stallion began to trot.

Lucas *ooh*ed admiringly. It was an incredibly graceful thing to watch, and the arch of Bruce's neck seemed so proud as he pulled the carriage. If he were Audrey, he'd be giving the pageant wave on a parade float. "He's so good-looking."

Gabe's grunt was noncommittal. Hopefully Bruce hadn't picked up on that.

"You are," Lucas crooned to him, trying to make up for the lack of praise. "You're a very attractive horse."

Gabe snorted a laugh, so Lucas squinted some side-eye at him, then laughed himself. It was nice—a moment where they were both on the same wavelength. Gabe had been subdued since the day he'd had to come get Lucas and Audrey at the brewery. Like he was preoccupied most of the time. He seemed to be all here now, though largely focused on Bruce. Taking a huge breath, Lucas exhaled and let himself enjoy the ride.

It was another one of those quintessential Pacific Northwest spring days, where the weather couldn't decide what it wanted to be, so it tried a little bit of everything. At the moment, it was mostly sunny, but clouds large enough to be threatening floated in the blue sky. They were like mullets: business up front, party in the rear. Except it was more along the lines of fluffy up top, soak-your-ass on the bottom.

So, yeah, not the best analogy. But he liked it.

As they came to the junction with the lane that led to the big house, Gabe clucked once and Bruce slowed to a brisk walk. Lucas hoped they'd hang a right and head toward the main road. It'd take them through what Gabe called "the woodlot," which, as far as Lucas had figured, meant he didn't replant it with Douglas firs for eventual logging, but let all conifers and deciduous trees grow naturally. Most of the hardwoods had leafed out, but still had that new-green color of spring.

Gabe made some motion Lucas couldn't discern, and they turned left, toward the house. "Are you going to show him off?"

"Thought I might." Gabe smiled. "Momma's gotta hitch him up on Saturday since I'll be in the wedding."

"Oh." Presumably someone had to, because they couldn't just leave the horse standing on his own, could they? "So she'll miss the ceremony?"

"Nah, she's gonna harness him just before it starts, then one of the Paulson kids'll walk him a bit. Conrad, you know him?"

Lucas snorted.

"Forgot who I was asking," Gabe said while chuckling. "He's about sixteen. Becca Lundgren's youngest cousin. 'Parently, he doesn't see any need to be at the official, mushy part."

Not surprising. Lucas made a humming noise to show he'd heard, and let Gabe concentrate on his task. He was leaning sideways, peering intently at Bruce's front hooves as they lifted off the ground.

Frowning, he shook his head and brought the horse to a halt in front of the garage with a low, "Ho."

Jane came out of the house just as Gabe was somehow making Bruce pivot around. "Looking good," she called, walking toward them.

"S'pose," Gabe grunted, still wrapped up in directing Bruce.

"I think he's amazing." Lucas meant both the man and the beast, and from the way Gabe's mom glanced at her son, then smiled at Lucas, he figured she'd picked up on that. But then she narrowed her eyes and focused on the stallion, who was now standing in front of her. She made that same noncommittal noise Gabe had earlier.

"Apparently," Lucas said after putting up with a good ten seconds of their critical—yet silent—inspection of Bruce, "I'm unaware of some of the finer points of how a horse should pull a carriage."

They both laughed. "He's still kinda rough around the edges," Gabe explained. "No one'll complain this weekend, but he won't win any ribbons without some more training. His action isn't crisp enough."

Whatever that meant. And, *ribbons*? Lucas's expression must have made his confusion clear because he didn't even have to ask Gabe to explain.

"Remember when I said his foals had to outperform him in order for his stud services to be valuable?"

"Yeah?"

"Well, they gotta have a performance yardstick. I'm going to take him to some events this summer, see how he places."

Jane beamed at her son. "Well, it's good to see you found something."

Something what? Glancing at Gabe, Lucas was surprised to see him tucking his chin to his chest. And were his cheeks flushed, or was that the spring breeze?

"You thinking about the Washington Classic?" Jane continued, placing her hands on her hips and cocking her head in a gesture so like Gabe that Lucas had to turn away to hide his smile. As Gabe and his mother spoke about the various shows they might take Bruce to, his fond feelings drained away, and his heart slowly sank. Like a waterlogged stick spiraling to the bottom of the pond.

He'd like to see Bruce prancing in front of a crowd. Be proud of him along with Jane and Gabe.

The jerking of the carriage yanked him from his melancholy wishes, and reminded him that he didn't know what the future held. Maybe, after moving to Seattle, he could come back and see Bruce frequently.

And Gabe, of course. *Plenty of opportunities.* "Are you going to tell your mom about planting marijuana?" They were moving at a fast clip again, so Gabe must have started Bruce at a trot.

"I figured I'd talk to Carl first, make sure we can come to some terms before telling her." Shooting Lucas a sideways smile, he added, "She won't object, don't worry."

"Are you waiting until after the wedding to talk to him?"

"Nope, we're having lunch Friday afternoon." Clucking again, he slowed the stallion just before the turn back to the barn.

It was starting to make sense—one cluck must mean walk, and two must mean trot. Lucas thought about asking if they could take a ride out to the road, but the clouds were thickening and the wind was picking up. The carriage was open to the elements, and he didn't want to ride through the rain. *Mental note: next time, bring an umbrella. Or two.*

If there was a next time.

"I have to go into town this afternoon and show Audrey the wedding favors. It's too bad you aren't meeting Dad today, then we could go together."

Gabe made another of those noncommittal grunts and leaned back, pulling on the reins and calling out "Ho" in a low tone. As slick and natural as a real mountain man.

Longing and loss filled Lucas's chest. An ache that wanted things to stay the same, and a gaping void because he could feel Gabe separating from him. What could he do to stop it? Was this like that first time they got together next to the kiln, where he had to ask for what he wanted? *I want to be with you as much as possible.*

The question was, did Gabe feel the same? Lucas *thought* they were simpatico, but Gabe seemed to be looking forward to a life that went on without him in it. Driving Bruce and growing pot with Carl.

"Climb on down," Gabe instructed, looking at him with eyebrows raised. How long had they been stopped in front of the studio while Lucas thought?

"Um, okay." He dug his fingernails under the bench seat, gripping it tightly.

"I gotta unharness Bruce, then clean all the tack." Gabe's voice was gentle. As if he was afraid Lucas was some kind of weirdo. A loose cannon.

For a split second, Lucas felt completely hollow, but then Gabe leaned forward and cupped his chin, kissing him.

"Go show the peonies to Audrey. She'll love 'em." Another kiss, this one a little longer. "I'll be waiting for you to come home."

Oh thank God. He closed his eyes for a moment, letting his spine relax. "Okay. I should be back by dinnertime?"

"I'll have something warmed up and ready for you to eat."

Lucas clapped his hand over his mouth, trying to prevent the snerking snort that wanted to escape, only not succeeding. Relief made his amusement too strong to contain. Gabe's gaze went vacant, then sharpened again as he started laughing. "That's not what I meant."

"Yeah, but—"

"But I'll have *that* ready for you too." Gabe kissed him once more, then, when Lucas stood, patted his butt in a *get a move on* gesture. Once Lucas had climbed down, Gabe clucked once, and he and Bruce headed around the barn to the stable entrance.

The peony bowls were beautiful, even Lucas thought so.

Audrey really, really agreed, if her *ooohs* as Lucas unpacked the four he'd brought to show her were any guide. He set them carefully on the antique glass and oak display case next to her register, arranged equidistantly. When he started disassembling one—pulling out the puzzle-like upper pieces and the inner petals, to reveal the shallow dish that comprised the main structure—she squealed so loudly a customer came over to see what the fuss was.

"That's *beautiful.*" The woman dug her fingers into Lucas's upper arm for a split second, then dropped her hand and composed herself, veiling open admiration behind a cooler, eyebrow-peaked facade. "I'm very impressed."

"Thanks." She seemed familiar. Was it just because she was so obviously Hollywood? Had she bought something from him in the past? He leaned closer and cocked his head, as if that might make her more recognizable.

"Lucas Wilder, this is Anna Maxwell," Audrey announced.

"Nice to meet you." The woman offered her hand, but Lucas was so caught up in trying to place her that he didn't offer his own in return. Not until he remembered that shaking was a basic gesture of etiquette—then he flung his arm out, knocking his knuckles against her fingernails.

Very nice.

Audrey's giggle seemed rude for a second, then she said, "Lucas is an *artist*."

Clearly, the woman *was* Hollywood, because her wary frown was immediately replaced by a smile. "This is some of your work?"

Being eccentric was *always* acceptable among "creative types" in Southern California. "Um, it is. Audrey and Zach's wedding favors. Zach's my brother." He peered at her, trying to exude Warhol-ism from his pores.

"Relax, sweetie," Audrey murmured, only loud enough for him to hear. Hopefully. "Lucas has been doing some 'outsider' work since he returned to town. You know." Audrey waved her hand in an explanatory gesture. "Wood-firing techniques and stuff."

Oh, *really*? "It's a little more complicated than *that*." And please, "outsider art" was so nineties.

She shot him an apologetic grimace, but didn't have a chance to say more before Anna interjected, "This isn't Los Angeles. We're all allowed to admire each other for our work, not because of how popular it is."

Oh. His staring at her was considerably less Warhol and more confused this time, at least until he got it. *She's like us.* Then he laughed. "Sorry. I mean, for being a dork, but for a second . . ."

Audrey was giggle-snorting behind her palm. "I know, right? Anyway, Lu, Anna is one of the producer-directors of *Wolf's Landing*."

"Oooooh. I remember." Pointing at Anna, he grinned at Audrey like a proud child. Because his occasional social awkwardness wasn't restricted to interactions with *poseurs*.

Both ladies ignored his stupidity, though, and they began discussing the pieces, pulling the parts of the peonies out with increasing confidence, then fitting things back together.

"Um, I did this, too." Lucas brought out his phone and called up the pictures of the horse sculpture. Test or not, he loved that work. Thank God it lived with someone who'd never let go of it. "Scroll forward." He handed it to Audrey, and Anna hustled around the display case to look over her shoulder.

"Do you do other animals?" she asked, glancing up at him with a sharp glint in her eye. "Like wolves?"

"Wolves? I mean, I never thought about it, but if I was inspired . . ." Did he *want* to do something because someone asked him to? He'd been enjoying his freedom from commissions and market pressures for the last month.

But if he wanted to continue not to starve, how long could he keep following his whims? Reality for an artist was that he had to be sellable.

Swallowing down the acidic taste of resistance in his throat, he gave in to the inevitable. "We could talk about it. Do you have a card?"

CHAPTER SEVENTEEN

*G*abe had a lot of shit to take care of before Zach and Audrey got hitched. Friday morning, first thing on his to-do list was to clean out his pickup. He had to meet with Carl at noon, so he'd need to get that done first. Audrey had decreed he had to wear a tux with a gleaming white shirt, cummerbund, and tie, and he was afraid just being in the vicinity of dirt would make it look dingy, even swaddled in the plastic rental bag. So, after he'd finished his barn chores, he dragged the shop vac into the parking area.

As he was sucking the layer of dust off the dashboard he found the boutonniere. Well, refound it. He'd never lost it, but he'd had it forever—twelve years, longer than he'd owned this vehicle—and he mostly ignored it. Not because it was ignorable, but because he was used to it being around.

Kind of like he was used to Lucas being around.

Gabe shut off the damn vacuum cleaner and picked up the dried-out carnation, leaning against the seat in the open doorway to study it. Twelve years ago, the night Gabe had found Lucas on the side of the road—and yes, he *had* been looking for him—walking home from a high school dance, the kid had accepted a ride in his truck, then taken this very boutonniere off and forgotten about it lying on the seat next to him. It was right after Lucas had finally told his family he was gay. That hadn't been a surprise to Gabe, but what had been was the news that Lucas was leaving after he graduated that spring. He'd never expected the guy to stay in Bluewater Bay after high school, but the fact of his actually having a plan, and a college that wanted him, had made it more real and present.

So that night Gabe had taken a chance on the kid he'd been fixated on for years. Then he'd left him alone, intending to never look back.

Well, he'd kinda fucked that up, hadn't he?

When Lucas left this time, what mementoes of him would remain?

Tucking the boutonniere into his shirt pocket, he switched on the vacuum cleaner and finished the job. Then, when he was done with the pickup, he took the faded old carnation inside and set it on the table beside the front door. Right next to the horse sculpture Lucas had given him.

Might as well keep all his favorite—and most painful—memories in one place.

Things had gone all right at Gabe's meeting with Carl Friday afternoon. The guy was excited as hell to "expand the operation," and they had a rough agreement of a plan for growing cannabis—as Carl insisted on calling it—to start on once the wedding was over. It was after they'd settled that, when the conversation had wandered on to Lucas, that Gabe found himself itchy all over inside, with no way to scratch.

"That boy's always been a free spirit. No one'll ever pin him down," Carl had opined. The way the guy had looked at him right then . . . Gabe couldn't decipher what that expression meant. Was it Carl daring him to try? Or Carl telling him to give up? Or Carl so goddamned high he was talking out his ass?

He didn't know, and he hadn't asked, but he sure as hell let it bother him the whole way home.

When he made it back to the farm, he was ready for some Lucas time. He needed his next fix. He parked next to the barn and went in through the studio, but Lucas wasn't in there, only that sculpture he'd been working on. Gabe'd been curious about it, but at the moment he was too intent on finding his boy to take a gander. The creak of boards above his head, then footsteps, told him where to look, and he took the stairs two at a time.

He caught Lucas packing when he walked into the apartment. Frozen in the act of stuffing a shirt from the laundry basket on the kitchen table into his bag, lips parted and eyes wide as he stared.

Leaving. With no warning. Gabe's heart flipped over, then started racing, spreading anger through his veins.

"I'm glad you're here." Lucas dropped everything and came his way. "I'm getting ready to go, but I wanted to say good-bye." Reaching him, he slid his arms over Gabe's shoulders and pressed against him, chin tilted up like it always did when he wanted to be kissed.

As if he was doing nothing wrong.

For fuck's sake, it came down to this? *This* was the good-bye Gabe would get? Showed how much he meant to the guy, didn't it? The urge to grab Lucas by the scruff of his neck and escort him out forcibly made his fingers twitch, but he didn't move them, keeping them fisted at his sides. Well, he couldn't stop the rage trembling through his arms.

Lucas's mouth turned down at the corners, and he pulled back slightly. "What's wrong?"

"Nothing," he answered on autopilot. A muscle in his cheek twitched, over and over, and his pulse boomed hollowly under his ribs, echoing around in all the sudden nothingness. "Just didn't know you were packing up *today*," he bit out, trying to hang on to the anger. It was no good. Seeing Lucas leaving him had ripped a hole in his gut, and he could feel himself draining into it, losing the fight. Losing everything.

Drawing away more, Lucas slid his hands down to Gabe's chest, his touch light and insubstantial. Was he shaking too, or was that all Gabe? "Did you expect me to take everything? I thought . . ." His gaze slid away from Gabe's. "I mean, I planned on coming back."

Coming back? Sudden relief weakened him, and he swayed, grabbing on to Lucas, digging his fingers into the guy's sides. Trying to make sense of what he'd seen and thought. "Why were you . . .?" He bobbed his head toward the table.

Lucas rolled his eyes. "Audrey called, and of course, now that it's the eleventh hour, she wants to try that abstinence thing." Lifting up on tiptoe, he gave Gabe a quick kiss, then pulled out of his arms, heading back toward his bag. "She said I have to come over and stay the night or she might not be able to resist temptation.'"

"What?" Suddenly everything seemed normal. Except for the dizziness left over from his anger and fear, and his inability to figure out what the actual fuck was going on. Like he was only getting part of the picture.

"I know, right?" Lucas huffed and balled up some briefs he'd gotten out from the clean clothes.

Know what?

"Who cares if she and Zach get it on the night before the wedding? I mean, they have been all along." Waving his hand in the air, he added, "But she was irrational. So I kind of *had* to agree to stay with her tonight." He grimaced. "Sorry."

"Oh." It took a few seconds before Gabe could relax enough to bend his knees, then walk over to fall onto his ass on the couch. Lucas wasn't leaving. *Yet.* Was he? "When're you coming back?"

"Tomorrow night." He glanced away, the curve of his cheek so youthful. "Depending on you."

Got it. The whole image revealed itself in that single gesture of uncertainty. It was gonna be just like last time, wasn't it? Lucas didn't want to stay, but he didn't want to give up Gabe, not completely. He couldn't see the writing on the wall, so he'd try to keep them on life support, never committing to the full treatment or pulling the plug. Gabe had seen it in his eyes twelve years ago, and he could detect the same thing now in the way Lucas bit his lip.

Which meant he had to force the issue. "I wouldn't want to make you do something you aren't into," he said flatly, digging his fingernails into his knees for the sharpness and sting of pain. Keeping himself thinking straight, listening to Lucas's tone and watching his body language rather than relying on what came out of his mouth. His nerves were strung so tight they vibrated waiting for Lucas to make a move, give him a response he could read. Hesitantly, Lucas went back to packing, picking things up much more slowly and inspecting them before putting them in his bag.

So this *was* the way it was going to go. Nausea attacked, but he fought it off and closed his eyes a second, preparing himself for what he had to do next. "Lu." He kept his voice as level as he could. "I need you to tell me what you're going to do."

"I don't understand what you're asking me." When Gabe looked at him, the guy was still again, one hand on his bag but the other just hanging there as he stared at the ground.

No, he didn't understand, and he couldn't see he was making this harder, could he? Because he was content to float along in life. Like that ex he had, who he'd stayed with for years but hadn't loved anymore. This was the same, wasn't it? The tiny bit of hope harboring in Gabe's heart, that Lucas *would* commit, snuffed itself out.

Fuck. "I'm asking—" An involuntary breath of air shuddered into him as he rose from the couch. Because he had to be standing to make this last, brutal cut. Soonest done, soonest over. "I'm asking if you're *really* interested in continuing this."

Jerking his head up, Lucas finally met his eyes. His mouth was hanging open and his skin had gone pale. "I don't . . . I—" He coughed, like trying to dislodge something stuck in his craw. "I'd been thinking I could settle in Seattle, and we could see each other on weekends, and . . . stuff."

"*Stuff?*" Gabe repeated back to him, voice rising. But dammit, why couldn't Lucas have taken the out he'd handed him? Did he think *he* would find it easier to just let things dwindle down to nothing? That a lingering death would be less painful?

Lucas bobbed his head. "What do you think?"

Don't do me any favors. Throwing his arm up, Gabe nearly shouted, "I think I run a farm. I don't *have* weekends. You know what? I see what's going on even if you can't—you're meant for bigger things, and this town and this farm and everything that goes along with it are all too damn small for you. You wouldn't even be here if it wasn't for Audrey. But me?" He slapped his hand over his chest. "This is where I'm supposed to be. It's where I *wanna* be. You leave tomorrow anyway, so let's just end it now, okay? Neat and clean. None of this shit where you waffle on making a fucking decision." He sliced his hand through the air and a line of pain sliced his soul. "I don't *need* it." What he needed was for Lucas to just fucking be gone, so he could get drunk and forget this ever happened.

As if that'd work.

"So . . ." Blinking rapidly, Lucas swallowed once more and turned his head away, showing Gabe only his ear and the angle of his jaw. "You're dumping me?"

"Hell yes," Gabe spit out, hoping the words hurt Lucas as much as Lucas was forcing him to hurt. "Why wouldn't I?" So it could hurt even worse when Lucas finally did slip away? Everyone knew a lingering death was more painful than the unexpected heart attack, didn't they? Gabe sure the fuck knew; he'd lived it with Grampa. He was about to rush across the living room and grab the guy's arm to hustle him out of there, because the dude wasn't leaving fast enough and Gabe needed him gone.

"But—"

Riiiiing.

As Lucas swung around to look at his phone, Gabe caught a glimpse of stark pain on his face, but he hardened his heart and jerked toward the noise. Spying the cell on the end table next to him, he snatched it up. "It's Audrey." He charged toward Lucas, thumb hovering over the Okay button.

"Don't answer it." Lucas met him halfway, reaching for his cell, but Gabe lifted it out of his range.

"You better talk to her." He knew his voice had gone nasty and probably his expression, too. "I mean, she's the reason you're here in the first place, right?" He wasn't a big enough man to avoid the dig, and he wasn't gonna feel sorry about it, no matter how lost Lucas seemed right now. Dude could just choke on his guilt. Maybe he'd learn something from the experience. Like a clean cut healed fastest. All at once, he lowered the phone, answered the call, and shoved it into Lucas's chest, then walked out while the guy was still fumbling with it.

Ending it.

"Um, hi—"

He slammed the door on Lucas's voice and ran down the stairs, digging his keys out of his pocket on the way.

When he got back from wherever he was going, Lucas better damn well have finished moving his shit out, because Gabe couldn't take a single reminder of him around.

In spite of telling Audrey he'd be over as soon as possible, Lucas couldn't make himself leave. He wandered around Gabe's apartment, finding things that were his, yet unable to pick them up. Like it might make his skin blacken and shrink away if he packed anything else up. Even now, doubt and loss were licking at him like flames, although he could barely feel the burn. His brain was nothing but static, incapable of tuning in to the reality of what had happened.

Gabe told me to leave. He ended us.

Oh, yeah. That.

When he'd asked if Lucas was interested in continuing *this*, Lucas had been unable to say anything. It was everything he'd been waiting for from Gabe, but he'd stood there mute, probably with his mouth hanging open. Not capable of even a simple yes. A lot like he stood now, dazed.

Which was a good thing, because he'd misread the whole situation. Hadn't he? He was still too stunned to remember the exact events. It was all a blur of words and the anger in Gabe's eyes.

Through the numbing blanket of confusion, the first arrow pricked his heart. A dull ache for now. Later, it would be sharp and piercing.

He'd never expected things to end this way. And the *wedding*. Tomorrow, he'd have to stand up beside his best friend and his brother and try to get through it . . .

Oh God.

Finding himself in front of the door, next to where he'd set his bag, Lucas stared absently at the statue of Bruce when the small thing snuggled up to the side of the figure suddenly made sense—resolved from nameless blob into something he recognized. And it was the most gut-wrenching thing possible. *Heart*-wrenching. That dried-out boutonniere from Gabe's dashboard was *his*, or had been twelve years before when he'd forgotten it in Gabe's truck that night. He remembered it instantly this time, because today was his day for facing reality. His mother had given it to him to wear to the Valentine's dance, and for reasons he couldn't remember, he'd taken it off and set it on the seat next to him after Gabe had picked him up on the side of the road.

Gabe had kept it all these years. He didn't even have the same truck anymore, yet it meant enough to him that he'd saved it, and transferred it to the new vehicle.

Lucas broke out in a cold sweat. *Oh my God, I left him behind.* Abandoned him, like that flower. And he'd been about to do it again, because Seattle *was* too damned far away.

When his phone rang he answered it and told Audrey, "I'm leaving in a few minutes," in a monotone. She'd probably know he was lying.

"Uh . . ." a man's voice said.

Gabe. Even as his heart leapt, Lucas knew it wasn't him, because the tone was too high, a lot like Drew's voice.

Oh. "Drew?" Why would he be calling? They hadn't actually spoken since before Lucas had left Los Angeles. Everything he had to say to the guy since then was best handled by lawyers.

Actually, he hadn't felt the urge to talk to his ex about anything in a long time.

"Hi," Drew responded after a second. "Um, not who you expected?"

"I thought you were Audrey."

"I see."

The awkward pause that followed was . . . strange. Similar to the kind of uncertainty he'd feel if he'd reached out to an old high school classmate. *Just somebody that I used to know.*

"I called to tell you we have a buyer for the house," Drew finally said.

"We do?" The house? He'd kind of forgotten about that. "I don't need to do anything, right? I mean, you can handle it?" Because he really couldn't care less at the moment.

"Oh, yeah, I just thought you'd want to know . . ."

Under other circumstances, when a guy he was in love with hadn't kicked him out? He probably would have. "Well, thanks for telling me."

"You aren't interested in how much they're offering?" The dryness and slight disdain in Drew's voice brought to mind everything Lucas might have forgotten about why their relationship had ended.

When he didn't respond within a half minute, a soft breath escaped Drew, and that was also easy to interpret. He was frustrated, annoyed Lucas wasn't having the conversation *he'd* planned for them to have.

Yeah, he didn't need to do this anymore. He was no longer with this guy, for all the right reasons, and he had a heart that was about to break as soon as it wasn't quite so numb. So he said his expected line. "How much is the offer?"

"Nearly sixty thousand above our asking price."

"*What?*"

"There was a bidding war. Three couples wanted it. Our neighborhood is *hot*, but isn't that always the way? The gays move in, make it hip, and then the—"

He stopped listening when it hit him that, with the money, he could afford to stay in Bluewater Bay for longer. How long, though? Damn it, if he could work with another gallery, it wouldn't be that big a deal to ship his work from here, would it? Profits would be lower, but so would his cost of living.

But would Gabe take him back? He glimpsed the boutonniere out of the corner of his eye.

"You know we never would have made it, don't you? Not long term." *Not twelve years.* "Did you even keep any mementos of us?" He certainly hadn't, not even when they were still a couple. Nothing stupidly romantic like the ticket stub from their first movie together.

And he'd *never* made a statue of his ex. Never felt the urge.

"Uh." Drew half coughed. Then, to Lucas's shock, he answered. The first question, at least. "We wouldn't have, you're right. I'm kinda—" A nervous laugh erupted from him. "I don't know how we made it as long as we did."

Lucas's laugh wasn't nervous. "Open relationship."

Drew said the exact same thing, a half beat behind him. Then he added, "Maybe when you find the guy you could never imagine sharing with anyone else, that's when you know he's the one."

How did he get that strange reverb effect on his voice? It wasn't on Drew's end, though, it was the way "he's the one" echoed in Lucas's ears. *Oh my God.*

"—you ever find a guy like that?" Drew was saying when Lucas tuned back in. "Hang on to him."

If he'll let me. "I will. I'm going to do whatever it takes," he vowed, in spite of the terror knotting up his insides. Fear over having lost Gabe forever, and over staying in town and what that said about him. A local. *I could be a local.* Had he really cared so much about it? The guy still yammering in his ear certainly had, and Lucas had rejected not only him, but the lifestyle he aspired to.

What if Gabe's scared too? Could the guy's fear of being left again have made him say those things? Lucas ran through the bits he remembered, and it both comforted him and made him want to puke. Because it *could* be that—Gabe might have been asking if Lucas wanted more because *he* did, and then when Lucas's stupid, socially-backward-self had taken over, Gabe might have lashed out, thinking he was being rejected.

Again. And just like last time, Gabe had said hurtful things to *make* him leave, assuming it was inevitable. In Lucas's best interest, even. Pushing him away before Lucas could hurt him first.

Well, fuck that. He wasn't going to make it that easy for the guy this time.

"Drew," he cut his ex off in the middle of whatever the guy had been saying. "I'm sorry, I really don't have time to talk right now. There are things I need to do."

"Oh." Drew's voice went dry again. "Audrey's *wedding.*" *Prick.* He'd never gotten along with her.

"Sure," Lucas agreed. "I'll definitely be calling you in a couple of days. I think I might have a way to work out the gallery contracts. Bye." He hung up on his ex's cautiously pleased murmurs, then flipped the mute switch on the side and chucked it in the direction of his bag.

He'd left this town twelve years ago thinking there was a better life for him elsewhere, but in doing so he'd abandoned the one guy who made him the happiest. It didn't matter if doing it then was the right thing or the wrong one. What mattered was the choice he made *this* time. Repeating the good parts of their history was one thing, but no way was he repeating a mistake like that.

Setting his chin, he stood, grabbed his bag—forget packing up all the rest of his shit, because he was coming back regardless of what Gabe had said—and walked out onto the landing.

Oh, but wait. He'd forgotten something very important. Cracking the door behind him, he snaked his arm in and grabbed the boutonniere off the table.

He was going to need it.

CHAPTER EIGHTEEN

When Zach's phone rang, Gabe knew it was Lucas. The dude had already called his cell a dozen times. "Answer it."

"You sure?"

"Yeah."

He closed his eyes and let his head fall back on the armchair he was occupying in the Wilders' living room, listening to the conversation.

Lucas spoke first, but Gabe caught only his own name.

"Nope, haven't seen him," Zach said.

A very low murmur was all the response he could make out from five feet away.

Zach sighed. "Is Audrey okay with you talking to the best man, night before the wedding?"

"I don't care." This time Lucas came across loud and clear. "This has nothing to do with her. I'm not *here* for her. Tell him that."

Zach looked at him.

Gabe nodded.

"I'll be sure and tell him. If I see him."

Once Zach hung up, he tossed the phone onto a pile of his mother's magazines on the coffee table, then he subsided back into the couch, his expression going all pensive, same as it had been since Gabe had gotten here an hour before and found the dude alone in the house, sitting in a darkened living room.

"Your brother's dense."

"Yup." Zach took a long pull off his beer. "Not the only one, though."

He didn't even try to pretend not to know Zach was talking about him, because the guy was probably right. *Whatever.* He needed to think about something else, if only for a minute or two. "'S the night before you get married, shouldn't we be partying?"

"Nope."

"Usually I'm the man of few words."

"Sometimes a guy has to think. Conversation messes that up."

"Where are your parents?" Seemed weird they'd leave their son on his own the night before the wedding, especially when he was mopey.

"I sent them to the Resort at Juan de Fuca a day early, on my dime. Needed to be alone."

Hell. "You want me to leave?"

"Nope." He blasted some air out of his nose, then chugged the rest of his beer.

"What's wrong?"

"I don't wanna have a big wedding," he snapped.

"Bit late for second thoughts."

"I wanna marry her." He threw out a hand, showing Gabe his palm as if it would retroactively stop him from suggesting that. "You know how much I do, man."

He nodded, the knowledge weighing down his chest. He and Zach were quite a pair. Two idjits who'd never gotten over their high school crushes. Least one of them had gotten a happily ever after.

"It's just . . ." Launching himself off the couch, he started pacing. "*Everyone's* gonna be there, you know?"

"Yep." He still didn't get where the guy was going with this, but that didn't mean he couldn't be supportive.

"We already gotta promise to love and honor each other in front of everybody—seriously, dude, if a guy means it as much as I will when I say it to her? That shit should be private. I don't really want the whole world to see me . . . you know."

Now he got it. "Cry?"

Zach kicked the coffee table leg. "Probably."

Gabe understood that better than he ever would have imagined. He'd fought a few tears since he'd slammed out of his place, leaving Lucas behind. Choosing maximum pain now. No malingering. No chance for false hope or recovery.

"Anyway, then I gotta spend my wedding night around those same jackasses we grew up with. Remember when Billy Martin got married and someone hid a goat in the bathtub of their honeymoon suite?"

"Yep." They'd turned the shower on, so the soaking-wet goat had run around the room, climbing onto the bed, even.

"Shi-it," Zach muttered. "I'll string up anyone who dishonors my bride that way." Pointing at Gabe as if he were considering the merits of bathing livestock, he added, "Or any other way."

"So don't stay there. Get in your truck afterward and drive her to Port Angeles, or Sequim, or the Victoria ferry. You got choices, man." At least one of them did. *You* made *a choice.*

"Got the honeymoon suite reserved," Zach responded gloomily. "It's got a Jacuzzi tub and a king-size waterbed, plus one of those Kama Sutra love kits and a bottle of champagne comes with. Seems a shame for all of that to go to waste."

Not so much, but Gabe just shrugged. Probably it had douchebonnets too. "Maybe you should ask Audrey what she wants to do."

"Maybe," he sighed, flopping back onto the couch. "So what happened with you and my brother?"

"Bunch of shit." Things that made him uncomfortable to think about. Things he'd said that he maybe shouldn't have. Lucas sometimes needed time to process things, and it made him seem a little slow. Gabe hadn't given him much time for that.

I forced the issue.

"You get mad?"

"Yep."

Zach didn't need to be told that Gabe sometimes spoke before he thought when angry. The dude had lived it more than once. Some people might even say he got irrational.

"What triggered it?"

He peeled the label off of his beer bottle before he answered. He'd been nursing the same one so long, it was warm. "I came home and found him packing to leave."

"To leave *you?*" Zach squinted across the room at him, like he was inspecting Gabe for signs of insanity.

He snorted. "That's what I thought when I walked in. I mean, you know he's been going on about how he's only here for the wedding..."

"I'm pretty sure he's here for you too. Least, he is now. Matter of fact, I'm pretty sure he just told me to tell you that when I see you."

"Yeah, well." Damn, he was a dumbass. He'd let his fear out as anger, hadn't he?

"You got scared, didn't you?" Zach shoved up from the couch, pointing at him.

"No." He slouched further in the chair, as if it could shield him from too much truth.

"'Cause you were afraid of him leaving you again."

Coming to stand right in front of his chair, Zach gave him the hairy eyeball until he had to admit it. "Think so, yeah. Not like I calculated that all out, though. 'Sides, he wasn't about to stick around last time."

"Last time was different. He was a kid, and you were too. You know, it's like you told me when I was trying to decide whether to ask Audrey out. You said the only guaranteed outcome was, if I never asked her out, then I'd never have a chance with her. At least if I tried, I had a chance. It's the same principle."

A swig of his room-temperature beer didn't help him swallow down that little nugget. "Things were easier for you, because you weren't stupid when Audrey left the first time, and then when she came back you had longer to sweet-talk her into being with you."

"Gabe." Zach's voice had gone so gentle it made him squirm. "I'm pretty sure he'd stay if you asked him. Or at least settle nearby."

"Fuck." He hid his eyes—and his embarrassment—behind his fingers. "He told me he'd been thinking about moving to Seattle and we could see each other on weekends. But I shut him down." Didn't even give it the consideration it deserved, and he should've. Because he knew damn well Momma could handle his weekend chores, and if not, Zach'd help.

"And that's worse than the shit you're in now how, exactly?" The scorn in his tone was a big improvement over earlier.

Made the next part easier to admit. "It'd be a damn sight better than going back to the nonrelationship we had the last twelve years."

Zach's footsteps were quiet as he walked away, and Gabe could tell from the cadence—and long experience—that the guy was doing his thinking walk. "Looks like you got some groveling to do."

"If I get a chance." His stomach roiled, the beer—or something—not sitting right with him. "Might've already fucked that up."

"You'll have tomorrow to fix it. At the wedding."

Gabe grunted, because the thing writhing in his chest wouldn't let him say more. A mix of pain and fear and shame over having done this to himself. And Lucas.

I'm an asshole. Maybe even a douchebonnet.

"Hell." He sat forward and rested his beer bottle on the floor next to the chair, then steepled his fingers in his lap, watching as he flexed, then relaxed them against each other for a while.

He'd never gotten over Lucas leaving the first time, had he? He'd just carried that pain around, thinking he could stifle it. Never realizing it'd come spilling out as soon as he got into a similar situation. *Looks like pop psychology got that one right.*

"You don't talk to him, he'll skedaddle, I guarantee it," Zach broke into his ruminations. "You gotta tell him how you feel, man."

Hell yes. If he didn't, even knowing there was a chance Lucas could shoot him down, he'd live with this pain the rest of his life, and that was worse than any other option. Plus, he'd never have a chance to get what he really wanted most, now or in the future. "Tell you what: if he ever agrees to marry me? I'm not having a big ol' wedding like you are."

Zach snorted. "Now you're thinking, dude."

"'Bout damned time," he muttered.

Gabe made it home about six thirty in the morning, after a restless night on the Wilders' couch. He needed to start getting ready for Zach and Audrey's wedding. Even though it was an evening thing, he still had to be at the resort by three. Before that, he had to have Bruce ready to go, not to mention get the carriage ready for Charley Sykes to trailer over. It was too big for Gabe's horse trailer, and he didn't want to put it unprotected on the flatbed. Once the wedding was finished, Zach could leave it out in the elements all he wanted. For now, Gabe wasn't going to let it get ruined on his watch.

Maybe he could get a nap in after feeding the horses and putting them out.

Walking into the barn, he found Momma forking a couple of flakes of hay into June's stall. "I can do that." He stopped reaching for the wheelbarrow when she gave him a scathing look and then carried on as if he hadn't spoken. Her mouth was set in a tight, annoyed line.

Aw, hell. He shoved his hands in his pockets and hung his head. "Guess you noticed Lucas left?" She somehow always managed to cotton on to shit in his life.

She huffed. "Saw you tear out of here in an awful damn hurry first."

Stepping carefully—because of his mother, not because he was afraid of any horse manure—Gabe went to the tack room to see if she'd started the grain soaking for May. The old mare still had the majority of her teeth, and they softened her food in an effort to help her keep them.

As he was filling the feed bucket with water, Momma passed by with the empty wheelbarrow. "Guess you didn't see the sculpture he's been working on?" she called as she tilted it up against the wall, where it lived when it wasn't hauling hay.

Huh? "Uh, no."

She came to stand in the doorway, hands on her hips. "Best go look when you're done with the grain. Then I expect you got a few apologies to make for whatever you said to him."

He swallowed down the retort that first tried to spring out, and simply said, "Yes, Momma."

Once the horses were all set and happily munching away, he found himself standing in front of the studio's half-open door, peeking inside. It swung open the rest of the way when he grazed it with his fingertips. The sculpture was on the workbench farthest from the windows, uncovered. Every other time he'd seen it—besides that first glimpse when Lucas had just started it—it had been wrapped in plastic. He hadn't dared to disturb it, even though his curiosity was killing him. Lucas had been so absorbed in that thing, missing dinner a few times to work on it.

He wasn't sure he should actually go in, now. It felt a little like a violation, at least until he'd worked things out with Lucas.

But damn, he wanted to see what his boy had been making.

And he *was* gonna work things out with him, come hell or high water.

Plus, Momma had more or less ordered him to look.

Just go, dammit. His inner voice propelled him into the room, until he got close enough to really make out the shapes he was seeing, expecting it to be as abstract as most of Lucas's "conceptual" stuff. The clay was grayish-orange, just like all the pots the guy had made were before they were fired. It was a tall piece, and burnished on the sides, so the surface had that sort of blurry glow of reflected light. From what he could see, it had a jagged, rough crevice running down the center that looked like it split the whole thing in half.

Probably it did split it in half, and the two sides fit together to make a whole. Assemblages, Lucas had called those types of sculptures.

It wasn't until he was standing in front of it that he realized what it was. The torsos of two people—men—huddled together so that their backs created a sort of shell while their chests were protected against each other.

The larger one on the left had small, rough spots scattered across his shoulders. *Freckles.* Inspecting the one on the right closer, he could see things about it that made him sure it was Lucas. The specific curve of his lower back, and the skinniness of the muscles—stringier than Lucas actually was, but very much how he saw himself.

Us. He'd made *them*. As a unit.

He stroked the spine of the Lucas half, letting his fingers rest where the vertebral bumps ended, right above the swell of his butt. Then, carefully, he pried the two sides apart, just enough to see into the shadowed interior.

That was where all the abstraction had gone. Raw, and rough, but still beautiful in its way. He didn't find anything obvious, like a heart, but it was clear the two sides were built to fit snugly together. Like puzzle pieces. No one would see it, though. Those parts of the figures were hidden when they were together, sheltering against each other, and the smooth, strong whole was the only thing visible to the world in general. When he gently pushed the pieces into place again, he realized that like this, the sculpture was sort of heart shaped.

Dammit, he was getting choked up. He didn't know if it was from unshed tears, or the need to set things right with Lucas immediately. Find out if Lucas would forgive him.

He just couldn't before the wedding, though. It was Audrey and Zach's day, plus Lucas wouldn't thank him for waking him up before nine, so he'd have to live with the anxiety a bit longer.

And yeah, the guy could refuse to forgive him. Who needed to go through a wedding with that on their shoulders?

After he'd put the horses out and gone up to his place, he found it still full of Lucas's things. His sweatshirt on the back of the sofa, and his laundry on the table, and the toiletries he didn't need daily in the bathroom.

He's doesn't want *to leave me.* Gabe knew it as certainly as he knew his name. Even if they had to live in separate towns (well, one town, one city), Lucas would still spread his stuff around Gabe's place. They could make this work if Gabe stopped letting his fear get in the way.

CHAPTER NINETEEN

*M*ost of Lucas's conviction that he and Gabe would stay together had gone into hiding by the time the wedding rolled around Saturday. He could hear the words in his mind—his voice asking if Gabe was dumping, and Gabe's answering "Hell yes"—and each replay stung like a whip.

But still, he pinned the twelve-year-old boutonniere next to the one Audrey'd had made for him. The dried-out carnation was dwarfed by the half-open peony bud, but when he checked in the mirror, he liked the effect. As if the carnation was sheltering in the strength of the other flower.

Like the statue he'd made of them. No matter what happened, Lucas had his theme: security. Even if he and Gabe couldn't work things out, he'd always know Gabe had his best interests at heart.

"It looks good," Audrey said, and he started, but she was used to that so didn't react herself. He studied her reflection, right beside his. She hadn't put on her dress yet, having just returned to the bride's dressing room from the hotel's spa. Her dark hair had been put up in a sleek French roll—he thought that's what it was called—and her makeup was perfect. The deep red of her lips and nails would match the dress closely, if not exactly.

"You look beautiful." *My best friend's about to become a wife.* Thank God he didn't have to worry about mascara running, like the other bridesmaids.

"You think?" she asked softly, a niggle of doubt on her face. "I mean, we stayed up most of the night talking, and my eyes are puffy—"

"They aren't. You look amazing, honey." Turning, Lucas kissed her on the cheek, trying to avoid smearing any beauty products, then he hugged her. "I can't believe you're going to be my sister-in-law."

"Believe it." She smiled, then went off to get dressed. When Lucas turned back to the mirror, the lipstick she'd left on his cheek marked him like a brand. One he could wipe off, but still, he could feel it long after that.

He thought he'd be anxious. That the impending meeting between him and Gabe would gnaw at him. Because of everything going on, they wouldn't get a chance to see each other before the wedding, and he didn't know what to expect. Would he have a lot of resistance and anger to try to deal with before he could get through to the guy? He and Audrey had talked over approaches for the half of the night they weren't talking about her impending marriage. He hadn't exactly formed a plan, but he had a goal.

But the time flew by, what with getting Audrey ready, and dealing with stupid details and having a few "before" pictures taken by the photographer.

Next thing he knew, it was happening. He was seeing Gabe across the chapel's narthex. As soon as the groom's party started walking in, their eyes locked, but this far away he couldn't read anything. Couldn't even make out the color, although his memory supplied him with images.

Gabe dipped his chin in acknowledgment.

What did that *mean*?

He was still trying to decide when they were lining up for the procession. One of Audrey's cousins—designated as keeper of the schedule—hustled him along to stand beside Gabe, and their moment was there. He felt light-headed, and nothing he'd been planning to say came to mind, and the heat of the body next to his was disorienting and beguiling and—

Gabe took Lucas's hand and tucked it into the crook of his arm.

Lucas jerked, then stared at him. "What are you doing?"

"Well, the rest of the couples are doing it." The barest of smiles teased Gabe's lips as he nodded his head toward the flower girl and ring bearer—Audrey's niece and nephew—paired up in front of them, then the other attendants behind them.

Lucas would just have to trust him, because he could only watch Gabe. His smile was shaky, but there, and there was no anger in his eyes, but something much more vulnerable. "Uh . . ." Trying to get something that made sense to pop up, his tongue seized on the stupidest thing. "How come my arm is going through yours?"

"It just seemed natural."

"I'm not a girl." As if Gabe needed to be told, but his faculties of logic had run away with this conversation train.

"Oh, I know." Gabe leaned closer, right in Lucas's face, and leered in a way that made hair all over Lucas's body stand on end. In a not-totally-unpleasant way. "If it makes you feel better, I can put my arm through yours. But I'm telling you, people looking at us will find it more natural if I have the dominant arm."

"I don't—" Shaking his head violently, trying to reset it, he then asked, "Why are we discussing this? I have stuff to talk to you about—"

The music started.

"We can talk after," Gabe whispered, leaning close enough for his breath to send shivers up Lucas's neck. "I got stuff that needs to be said too. I gotta apologize."

"Gabe, you don't—" Someone on his other side hissed, prodding them into moving. "When you said everything here was too small for me, you didn't mean *you*, did you?" He dug his fingernails into Gabe's tuxedo jacket, then forced his muscles to relax. "Because I can't imagine anything *bigger* for me than you. Us."

"Lu." Gabe cleared his throat, then swallowed and looked straight ahead, pacing slowly the way they'd been instructed. "I acted like an ass yesterday, and I'm sorry," he said quietly just before they passed through the doors into the main aisle. "I guess I kinda did think I wasn't enough for you, but I'm not gonna argue with you if you wanna keep seeing me."

Out of the side of his mouth, trying to maintain a smile, Lucas whispered, "I need to apologize too. I *realized* things, about us and about my work. I don't *have* to—"

"Babe, I know we need to talk, but maybe there's a better time?"

He had one thing that had to be said *now*. Tipping his head closer to Gabe's, he got it out. "I *want* to continue this relationship with you." *There.* He could devote his attention to the wedding, at least for now.

Why were so many people smiling at them?

"Baby," Gabe's voice was laced with amusement. "I think you need to keep your voice down, unless you want to invite everyone in on this convo?"

His face flamed up hot and probably as bright as a beacon. Folding his lips together, he dug his fingers into Gabe's arm and just held on until they got to the front of the chapel. When he tried to let go and retreat to the bride's side, though, Gabe's hand landed on his.

"I get that boutonniere when you're done with it," Gabe whispered.

How could so few words make his eyes prickle with tears and his skin pebble up in anticipation at the same time?

Not surprisingly, Lucas spent most of the wedding in a daze. The ceremony was performed by a Unitarian minister, which he knew was the one thing his mother was upset about, but personally, he thought it was beautiful. The parts where he was paying attention.

Besides, it was short, and how could that not be beautiful?

When he was tuned in to the wedding, his eyes leaked the whole time, brought on by that strange mixture of pride, nostalgia, and longing. Every time he looked, he thought Gabe must be feeling many of the same things, based on his expression.

Although he didn't have tears creeping down his cheeks.

The most emotional time was when Zach read the vows he wrote. No one could understand a word the guy said, because he kept choking up. His hands shook until the paper he held rattled audibly. It was ridiculously touching. Lucas wasn't sure what his brother had promised Audrey if she'd only become his wife, but he was sure Zach meant it with every scrap of his being.

The best part was when Zach kissed his bride, bending her back over his arm in keeping with the silver-screen atmosphere of the wedding. Lucas glanced at Gabe at that moment, and was trapped in his gaze. As the audience cheered, Gabe smiled at him. When the bride and groom had made their way out and Lucas met him at the head of the aisle, he tried to take Gabe's arm again, but Gabe wouldn't let him.

Instead, he twined their fingers together, and led Lucas down the walkway.

CHAPTER TWENTY

*A*s much as they'd settled with just a few words, there was so much more to say, and Lucas was eager to talk now that he knew they would work out. The reassurance of Gabe holding his hand told him it really was going to. Every time Gabe tightened his grip, squeezing Lucas's fingers in his, it felt like a whole-body hug.

I love him. He needed to tell him, as soon as they were out of this church and could be alone.

Except right outside the chapel there was a kid holding Bruce's reins, waiting with the carriage.

Oh yeah. Audrey and Zach's wedding. He still had a whole list of duties to fulfill, literally. She'd presented it to him last night.

And so did Gabe. The boy seemed to be eyeing the horse warily, and Bruce kept trying to yank his head up. He had blinders on, but Lucas was certain the stallion was giving that Paulson kid some evil looks.

"I'll be back as soon as I can," Gabe said in his ear, lips brushing his skin. "Don't go anywhere."

"I'll be waiting for you."

A quick kiss on his cheek, and his man was walking over to the carriage.

And wait he did. All the people had to file out of the chapel, then Zach and Audrey appeared on the steps (where had they been hiding? Had this been part of the plan?), and she squealed before rushing down to the carriage and petting the horse and blah-blah-blah.

Zach pulled a small, ornate step stool out from somewhere and helped his bride alight before climbing up himself. Lucas thought he'd have a moment with Gabe after that, but his mother grabbed his arm, delighted and glowing. He couldn't help but get wrapped up in her joy as the carriage circled the drive of the Resort at Juan de Fuca a few times.

He was less wrapped up the fourth and fifth times it went around.

It was forever before he and Gabe got to be alone again. First the whole wedding party had to take pictures, which always seemed to require them to stand on opposite sides, so they barely got to touch, let alone speak. Once or twice, he managed to grab Gabe's hand and squeeze it, getting a squeeze in return.

Immediately after that, the Keeper of the Schedule forced them all into the reception hall, and to dinner—that period where everyone got some free time after the ceremony was apparently only available to guests not in the wedding party. Even though Gabe stayed by his side whenever possible, circumstances mostly didn't allow it. They were seated at the same table, but Gabe was next to Zach, and Lucas was next to Audrey.

Finally, after the cutting of the cake and the beginning of the dancing, they were left with no duties for a while. People kept trying to talk to them as they made their way across the reception hall in search of privacy, including old Mrs. Larson. She was towing Seth along with her, apparently trolling for a husband for her grandson. "It's lovely to see you two worked things out." She beamed at them, then at their clasped hands, the large feathered butterfly on her yellow hat trembling with her every head bob.

Wait, she'd known they'd had a fight? How did these things become public knowledge so easily?

"Why, thank you, Mrs. L.," Gabe said. Thank God, because Lucas wasn't sure what the proper response was.

"Tell me, are there any *single* homosexual gentlemen here tonight?" She blinked up at them earnestly. "Someone without a history of philandering, yet with a steady income?"

"*Grandma*," Seth hissed. "Stop it. I don't *want* a husband."

She gave him a sour look, but didn't say any more about it, although she did imbibe in some weather-related chitchat before moving on.

Seth didn't go with her. Instead, he fixed Lucas with a look, lips pursed and eyebrows at half-mast. "Meant to tell you and Audrey,

I *really* owe you for making me go on that bachelorette-weekend thing."

Oh, that tone was cringe-making. So was Gabe's snort of amusement. "I don't suppose you 'owe us' in a good way?"

"No." If he'd been an emoticon, it would have been that flat-eyed, flat-mouthed *I'm annoyed* one. "I'm going to pay you back someday."

What could he say? "That's fair," Lucas agreed, and then they shared a strangely macho, strangely impromptu fist bump. Seth looked as startled as he felt.

"'Scuse me," Gabe broke in to their bro-mo. "I'm needing to take my boyfriend out for a spin around the dance floor."

Oooh, boyfriend. Gabe had led him to the edge of the parquet floor before he got over the heart fluttering caused by that word.

Except wait. "You can dance?"

"'Course I can dance." Gabe wrapped one arm around Lucas's waist, palm flat on his lower back (but not quite low enough, in Lucas's opinion), then took his hand in the other, holding it at shoulder height. "Are you saying you can't?"

"Um, yeah. I am." He nodded his head and resisted Gabe's gentle nudges to start moving.

"We learned it in PE in eighth grade." Jockeying into a different position, Gabe worked one leg between Lucas's.

"I don't remember that." He couldn't believe Gabe could.

"Just follow my lead," Gabe instructed, then used his increased leverage to make Lucas start spinning around the floor.

It wasn't that hard. Maybe because he knew all of Gabe's moves intimately. Waltzing (or whatever they were doing), it turned out, was much more sexual than Lucas had expected. Back in eighth grade, he'd been dancing with girls. No wonder he'd never noticed the eroticism of it before—he couldn't even *recall* it.

This he'd never forget. Being held by the sexiest logger in the world and having all his attention and care and the friction of his body as they worked out a rhythm together. What would this look like as a sculpture?

"So." Gabe blew out a heavy breath, signaling they were about to begin the real talking. "If you're gonna live in Seattle, we can make that work. I won't have that much time—"

"*Seattle*?" He had said that, hadn't he? "I don't want to live in Seattle anymore."

Gabe's face went blank. "You don't? I thought you said you couldn't stay in Bluewater Bay, 'cause it wasn't a good career move."

Damn, another thing he'd said that had no bearing on his real desires. He shook his head, stumbling slightly, but Gabe escorted him firmly into the next steps of the dance. "Drew called to tell me the house sold for a lot more than we asked, so there's that, and as I was talking to him it felt more like a business relationship than anything, you know? So I thought, why *can't* I keep my stuff in his gallery? I might ask for some concessions, but it's not like I have to be *there* to make stuff. I can work here as well as anywhere else, and ship my pieces. I think I work *better* here."

Gabe glanced away, over his head. "Is that what you wanna do, then? Stay in Bluewater Bay?"

Wait. He curled his fingers, gripping Gabe tightly on the shoulder, and that was enough to bring Gabe's eyes back to his. "You've never once told me what *you* want."

"I know." They danced silently for a minute, gazing at each other. Then he stepped on Gabe's foot. "Ow!"

"Sorry." After that he thought they were done and stopped, but Gabe yanked him back into the rhythm of it, curling Lucas's hand in his and holding it against his chest, wrapping Lucas's fingers around his thumb.

Tilting his chin down, he said softly into Lucas's ear, "I want you to not step on my feet when I dance."

He grimaced. "I'll do my best."

They kept revolving, Gabe's cheek bumping Lucas's temple, getting intimate with it. Gabe's breath hitched a couple of times, convincing Lucas he had more to say, but hadn't decided how to put it into words.

Or he was afraid.

Lucas slid his arm along Gabe's shoulder until he could hold the back of his neck, and now they were so close he could follow Gabe's steps through the movements of his thighs. Gabe's fingers flexed on the small of his back, then he whispered, "Don't leave me again. Stay with me? At the farm."

The quaver in Gabe's voice nearly broke his heart, but he had to know something before he could answer. He tucked his head into Gabe's neck, blinking away the emotions that welled up. "For how long?" He couldn't live here without some assurances. Well, one.

"Forever." The answer was immediate, no hesitation. But his heart pounded next to Lucas's breastbone.

"Yes." He clung to Gabe so tightly it brought their dance to a stop. "I'll stay. I *want* to stay with you."

"I love you," Gabe said, hand slipping lower, then his other joining it. "I do. I'm in love with you."

"Oh thank God," Lucas breathed, then threw his arms around Gabe's neck and pulled himself up, stretching until their bodies were perfectly aligned and he could say, "I love you," in Gabe's ear.

Gabe's hands slid down to cup his ass and lift him, until Lucas's legs wrapped around his hips, even though they were in public and he shouldn't be so obvious—but Gabe had that figured out. Without Lucas realizing it, they'd ended their dance near the patio door, and as soon as Gabe had a nice, tight, finger-searching hold on him, they were out the door into the privacy of the night.

Gabe pulled Lucas out onto the patio. It was dark and deserted, although the lights from the reception exposed them until he found a spot between two windows that was shadowy and private where he could press Lucas up against. Making it easier to kiss him as deep as Gabe needed to get, and for one of his hands to go wandering, working under the tuxedo jacket to find one of his nipples.

"I can't—" Lucas jerked his head back, hitting the wall with the back of it. "I can't do an open relationship, not with you. I mean, yes, I know it may get boring, but you fuck like a steam engine, and how boring could *that* possibly get? Not v—"

"You worship my cock—that sure the hell ain't boring." Grinding his pelvis into Lucas's groin, Gabe got as intimate as he could with clothes on.

"I do." Lucas nodded fervently. "I *love* your cock. But mostly because you're attached to it. Although, I mean, it is totally beautiful. I'm thinking about sculpting it, actually—"

"I saw the one you just finished." Like he had in the studio with that piece, Gabe traced the path of Lucas's spine, although this time his knuckles had to scrape the siding of the reception hall. "Of us."

Lucas immediately dropped his gaze from Gabe's eyes to his neck. "Did you like it?"

His boy would always be like this, uncertain about some things. The parts of his inner self he exposed to the world. And he'd need someone to shore him up. Tell him how talented and beautiful and lovable he was. *I'm going to be that man.* Gabe's throat was closing up on him, thickening with emotion. "Love it." He gripped Lucas's head, thumb under his chin. Positioning him for a short but explicit kiss. "I love *you.*"

"*Ahem.*"

"Jesus Christ, *seriously*?" Lucas tore his mouth away and whipped his head around to glare at Audrey.

Gabe couldn't swear he wouldn't have met her with a similar welcome if he'd even had a clue she was there.

"I just wanted to let you know you're officially excused from any more MOH duties." She beamed at him, then at Gabe, then back at Lucas.

"Oh. Um." Lucas wiped his mouth with the back of his hand, but it didn't help how huge his lips looked. "I can't abandon you. You gave me that list, and I promised—"

"Kitty is delighted to take over. I already asked her. Now . . ." She fisted her hands on her hips and fake-glared at them. "Go get a room, you two." With that, she threw something she'd been holding their way, but it sorted of fluttered along, rather than arrowing straight toward them. Gabe managed to snatch it out of the air, juggling Lucas to keep him from falling, squeezing his ass hard enough to make him gasp.

Staring at what he'd caught, he tried to figure it out. It *looked* like—

"A key card?" Lucas asked, squinting at Audrey. "It's got the Juan de Fuca logo on it."

She smirked and tilted her head. "It's your room. The honeymoon suite. Number one hundred, first floor at the west end."

He got it instantly, based on his conversation with Zach last night, but Lucas didn't.

"That's *your* room! We can't take it, where will—"

"Oh, honey, you need it more than we do. Besides, we're escaping this place as soon as we can for our *real* honeymoon." Still looking like the cat that ate the canary, she glided off, back into her reception.

"Well." Gabe tucked the card into his pocket, having to juggle Lucas some more and getting a few more interesting noises out of him. Not to mention a few nudges from his definitely hard dick. "Guess this little soiree is over for us. Now we can get on with our life." His other hand free again, he secured it under Lucas's ass, pulling him away from the wall and stumbling toward the main hotel.

"*Our* life," Lucas breathed, eyes shining in the dimness. "Singular."

"You bet, baby. Just you and me. Way it always shoulda been. Oh, but hey, remind me to look for farm animals in the bathroom."

Explore more of *Bluewater Bay*:

riptidepublishing.com/titles/universe/bluewater-bay

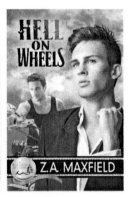

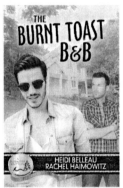

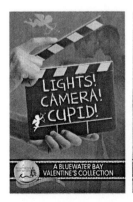

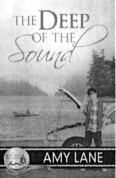

Dear Reader,

Thank you for reading Anne Tenino's *Wedding Favors*!

We know your time is precious and you have many, many entertainment options, so it means a lot that you've chosen to spend your time reading. We really hope you enjoyed it.

We'd be honored if you'd consider posting a review—good or bad—on sites like **Amazon, Barnes & Noble, Kobo, Goodreads, Twitter, Facebook, Tumblr,** and your blog or website. We'd also be honored if you told your friends and family about this book. Word of mouth is a book's lifeblood!

For more information on upcoming releases, author interviews, blog tours, contests, giveaways, and more, please sign up for our weekly, spam-free newsletter and visit us around the web:

Newsletter: tinyurl.com/RiptideSignup
Twitter: twitter.com/RiptideBooks
Facebook: facebook.com/RiptidePublishing
Goodreads: tinyurl.com/RiptideOnGoodreads
Tumblr: riptidepublishing.tumblr.com

Thank you so much for Reading the Rainbow!

RiptidePublishing.com

As usual, there are a million people to thank, and I'm probably going to forget someone. Please forgive me in advance. First I'd like to thank Audra Gilpatrick of Country Girl Farms (countrygirlfarm.com) for not only being an awesome riding instructor, but for all the training and breeding information. Second, my main beta reader this time around was Alec Edge, and, like always, he provided insightful, useful, and greatly appreciated feedback. MC, Thorny, Andrea, Ellen, LC, and Edmond, thank you for your support, and I hope you know how much I value you. I'd also like to thank my editors, Sarah Frantz, Delphine Dryden, and Alex Whitehall for catching all the glitches and talking me down from ledges.

Most importantly, though, I'd like to thank my family. Especially the 13-year-old, for being a nitpicky stickler about equinology. I always knew your natural inclination to argue would result in some positive benefits, someday. Please ignore all the times I told you otherwise, past, present, and future.

Theta Alpha Gamma series
Frat Boy and Toppy
Love, Hypothetically
Sweet Young Thang
Good Boy
Poster Boy

Romancelandia series
Too Stupid to Live
Billonaire with Benefits

Horny (in the *My Haunted Blender's Gay Love Affair,
and Other Twisted Tales* collection)

Task Force Iota series
18% Gray
Turning Tricks
Happy Birthday to Me

Whitetail Rock
The Fix (Whitetail Rock, #2)

Raised on a steady media diet of Monty Python, classical music, and the visual arts, Anne Tenino rocked the mental health world when she was the first patient diagnosed with Compulsive Romantic Disorder. Since that day, with her trusty psychiatrist by her side, Anne has taken on conquering the M/M world through therapeutic writing. Finding out who those guys having sex in her head are and what to do with them has been extremely liberating.

Anne's husband finds it liberating as well, although in a somewhat different way. He has accepted her need for "research," and looks forward to the benefits said research affords him. He thinks it's kind of cool she manages to write, as well. Her two daughters are mildly confused by Anne's need to twist Ken dolls into odd positions. They were raised to be open-minded children, however, and other than occasionally stealing Ken1's strap-on, they let Mom do her thing without interference.

Anne's thing is writing gay romance and erotica.

Wondering what Anne does in her spare time? Mostly she lies on the couch, eats bonbons and shirks housework.

Check out what Anne's up to now by visiting her site at AnneTenino.com.

Riptide: riptidepublishing.com/authors/anne-tenino
Chicks & Dicks Blog: chicksanddicksrainbow.com
Twitter: twitter.com/AnneTenino
Goodreads: goodreads.com/author/show/4831235.Anne_Tenino
Facebook: facebook.com/anne.tenino
Amazon: amazon.com/Anne-Tenino/e/B005FQZOHS

Enjoy more stories like *Wedding Favors* at RiptidePublishing.com!

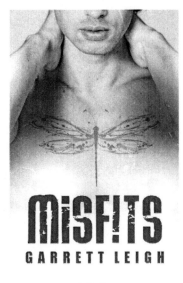

Misfits
ISBN: 978-1-62649-247-9

Illumination
ISBN: 978-1-62649-051-2

Earn Bonus Bucks!

Earn 1 Bonus Buck for each dollar you spend. Find out how at
RiptidePublishing.com/news/bonus-bucks.

Win Free Ebooks for a Year!

Pre-order coming soon titles directly through our site and you'll
receive one entry into a drawing to win free books for a year! Get
the details at RiptidePublishing.com/contests.

CPSIA information can be obtained at www.ICGtesting.com
Printed in the USA
LVOW08s2208031115

461022LV00003B/188/P

9 781626 492936